1

The Willoughby Captains

by Talbot Baines Reed

Copyright © 9/18/2015
Jefferson Publication

ISBN-13: 978-1517415129

Printed in the United States of America

Table of Contents

Chapter One.

The last of the old Captain.

Something unusual is happening at Willoughby. The Union Jack floats proudly over the old ivy-covered tower of the school, the schoolrooms are deserted, there is a band playing somewhere, a double row of carriages is drawn up round the large meadow (familiarly called "The Big"), old Mrs Gallop, the orange and sherbert woman, is almost beside herself with business flurry, and boys are going hither and thither, some of them in white ducks with favours on their sleeves, and others in their Sunday "tiles," with sisters and cousins and aunts in tow, whose presence adds greatly to the brightness of the scene.

Among these last-named holiday-making young Willoughbites no one parades more triumphantly to-day than Master Cusack, of Welch's House, by the side of his father, Captain Cusack, R.N. Cusack, ever since he came to Willoughby, has bored friend and foe with endless references to "the gov., captain in the R.N., you know," and now that he really has a chance of showing off his parent in the flesh his small head is nearly turned. He puffs along like a small steam-tug with a glorious man-of-war in tow, and is too anxious to exhibit his prize in "The Big" to do even the ordinary honours of the place to his relative.

Captain Cusack, R.N., the meekest and most amiable of men, resigns himself pleasantly to the will of his dutiful conductor, only too pleased to see the boy so happy, and pardonably gratified to know that he himself is the special object of that young gentleman's jubilation. He had come down, hoping for a quiet hour or two to see his boy and inspect Willoughby, but he finds that, instead, he is to be inspected himself, and, though he wouldn't thwart the lad for the world, he would just as soon have dropped in at Willoughby on a rather less public occasion.

Young Cusack, as is the manner of small tugs, assumes complete control of his parent and rattles away incessantly as he conducts him through the grounds, past the school, towards the all-attracting "Big."

"That's Welch's," he says, pointing to the right wing of the long Tudor building before them—"that's Welch's on the right, and Parrett's in the middle, and the schoolhouse on the left. Jolly rooks' nests in the schoolhouse elms, only Paddy won't let us go after them."

"Who is Paddy?" inquires the father.

"Oh, the doctor, you know—Dr Patrick. You'll see him down in 'The Big,' and his dame, and—"

"And what's written up over the door there?" inquires Captain Cusack, pointing up to the coat-of-arms above the great doorway.

"Oh, some Latin bosh! I don't know. I say, we'd better look sharp, father, or they'll have started the open hurdles."

"What are the open hurdles?" mildly inquires the somewhat perplexed captain, who has been at sea so long that he is really not up to all the modern phrases.

"Why, you know, it's the sports, and there are two open events, the hurdles and the mile, and we've got Rawson, of the London Athletic, down against us in both; but I rather back Wyndham. He made stunning time in the March gallops, and he's in prime form now."

"Is Wyndham a Willoughby boy?"

"Rather. He's our cock, you know, and this will be his last show-up. Hullo! you fellows," he cries, as two other small boys approach at a trot; "what's on? Have the hurdles started? By the way, this is my father, you know; he came down."

The two small boys, who are arrayed in ducks and running-shoes, shake hands rather sheepishly with the imposing visitor and look shyly up and down.

"And are you running in any of the races, my men?" says Captain Cusack, kindly.

He couldn't have hit on a happier topic. The two are at their ease at once.

"Yes, sir, the junior hundred yards. I say, Cusack, your gov—your father's just in time for the final heat. In the first I had a dead heat with Watkins, you know," continues he, addressing the captain. "Watkins was scratch, and I had five yards, and the ruck got ten. It was a beastly shame giving Filbert ten, though—wasn't it, Telson?—after his running second to me in the March gallops; they ought to have stuck him where I was. But I ran him down all the same, and dead-heated it with Watkins, and Telson here was a good second in his heat."

"I was sure of a first, but that young ass Wace fouled me," puts in Telson.

"And now it's dead-even which of us two wins. We both get five yards on Watkins, and he'll be pumped with the long jump, and none of the others are hot men, so it's pretty well between us two, isn't it, Telson?"

"Rather, and I think I back you to do it, Parson, old man," rejoins the generous Telson.

"Oh, I don't know," says Parson, dubiously; "you're a better man on the finish, I fancy."

"All depends on how I take off. Gully's such a boshy starter, you know; always puts me out. Why can't they let Parrett do it?"

And off they rattle, forgetting all about Cusack and his gallant father, and evidently convinced in their own minds that the flags and the carriages and the rosettes and all the festivities are solely in honour of the final heat of the junior hundred yards, in which they two are to take part.

Captain Cusack, with a smile on his face, watches them trot off, and asks his son, "Who are those two nice young fellows?"

"Oh, a couple of kids—not in our house," replies Master Cusack, by no means cordially. "Jolly cheek of them talking to you like that, though!"

"Not at all," says the captain. "I'd like to see their race, Harry."

But Harry has no notion of throwing his father away upon the "junior hundred yards," and as they are now in "The Big," in the midst of the festive assembly there congregated, he is easily able to shirk the question.

An important event is evidently just over. The company has crowded into the enclosure, and boys, ladies, gentlemen, masters are all mixed up in one great throng through which it is almost impossible for even so dexterous a tug as young Cusack to pilot his worthy relative.

The band is playing in the pavilion, distant cheers are audible in the direction of the tents, a shrill uproar is going on in the corner where the junior hundred yards is about to begin, and all around them is such a buzz of talking and laughing that Captain Cusack is fairly bewildered.

He would like to be allowed to pay his respects to the Doctor and Mrs Patrick, and to his boy's master, and would very much like to witness the exploits of those two redoubtable chums Telson and Parson; but he is not his own master, and has to do what he is told. Young Cusack is shouting every minute to acquaintances in the crowd that he has got his father here. But every one is so wedged up that the introductions chiefly consist of a friendly nodding and waving of the hand at the crowd indefinitely from the gallant father, who would not for the world be anything but gracious to his son's friends, but who cannot for the life of him tell which of the score of youthful faces darting sidelong glances in their direction is the particular one he is meant to be saluting. At last in the press they stumble upon one boy at close quarters, whom Cusack the younger captures forthwith.

"Ah, Pil, I was looking for you. Here's the—my father, I mean—R.N., you know."

"How are you, captain?" says the newcomer. He had heard Captain Cusack was coming over, and had mentally rehearsed several times what it seemed to him would be the most appropriate salutation under the circumstances.

The captain says he is very well, and likes the look of Mr "Pil" (whose real name is Pilbury), and looks forward to a little pleasant chat with his son's friend. But this hope is doomed to be a disappointment, for Pil is in a hurry.

"Just going to get the house tubs ready," he says; "I'll be back in time for the mile."

"Then is the hurdles over?"

"Rather!" exclaims Pil, in astonishment. "Why, where have you been? Of course you know who won?"

"No," says Cusack, eagerly—"who?"

"Why, Wyndham! You never saw such a race! At the fourth hurdle from home Wyndham, Bloomfield, Game, Tipper, and Rawson were the only ones left in. Game and Tipper muffed the jump, and it was left to the other three. Bloomfield had cut out grandly. He was a yard or two ahead, then Wyndham, and the London man lying out, ten yards behind. He had been going pretty easily, but he lammed it on for the next hurdle, and pulled up close. The three went over almost even, and then Bloomfield was out of it. My eye, Cusack! you should have seen the finish after that! The London fellow fancied he was going to win in a canter, but old Wyndham stuck to him like a leech, and after the last fence ran him clean down—the finest thing you ever saw—and won by a yard. Wasn't it prime? Ta, ta! I'm off now; see you again at the mile;" and off he goes.

The glorious victory of Willoughby at the hurdles has evidently been as much of a surprise as it has been a triumph, and everyone is full of hope now that the result of the "mile" may be equally satisfactory. In the midst of all the excitement and enthusiasm it suddenly occurs to the business-like Master Cusack that he had better secure a good position for the great race without delay, and accordingly he pilots his father out of the crush, and makes for a spot near the winning-post, where the crowd at the cords has a few gaps; and here, by a little unscrupulous shoving, he contrives to wedge himself in, with his father close behind, at about the very best spot on the course, with a full view of the last two hundred yards, and only a few feet from the finish.

It is half an hour before the race is due, and, by way of beguiling the time, Cusack shouts to one and another of his acquaintances opposite, and introduces his father to the crowd generally. The course has not yet been cleared, so there is plenty of variety as the stream of passers-by drifts along. Among the last, looking about anxiously for a place to stand and watch the big race, are Telson and Parson, arm-in-arm.

5

Captain Cusack hails them cheerily.

"Well, who won, my boys? who won?"

The dejected countenances of the two heroes is answer enough.

"Watkins won," says Parson, speaking in a subdued voice. "The fact is, my shoe-lace came undone just when I was putting it on at the end."

"And the swindle is," puts in Telson, "that just as I was spurting for the last twenty yards Watkins took my water. I could have fouled him, you know, but I didn't care to."

"Fact is," says Parson, insinuating himself under the cords, greatly to the indignation of some other small boys near, "it's a chowse letting Watkins enter for the juniors. I'm certain he's not under thirteen—is he, Telson?"

"Not a bit of him!" says Telson, who has also artfully squeezed himself into the front rank hard by; "besides, he's a Limpet, and Limpets have no right to run as juniors."

"What is a Limpet?" asks Captain Cusack of his son.

"I don't know what else you call him," says young Cusack, rather surlily, for he is very wroth at the way Telson has sneaked himself into a rather better position than his own; "he's—he's a Limpet, you know."

"Limpets," says a gentleman near, "are the boys in the middle school."

"Rather a peculiar name," suggests the captain.

"Yes; it means an inhabitant of Limbo, the Willoughby name for the middle school, because the boys there are supposed to be too old to have to fag, and too young to be allowed to have fags."

"Ha, ha!" laughs Captain Cusack, "a capital name;" and he and the gentleman get up a conversation about their own school days which beguiles the time till the bell sounds for the great race of the day.

The starting-point is a little below where our friends are standing, and the race is just three times round the course and a few yards at the end up to the winning-post. Only four runners are starting, three of whom have already distinguished themselves in the hurdle-race. Wyndham, the school captain, is that tall, handsome fellow with the red stripe in front of his jersey, who occupies the inside "berth" on the starting-line. Next to him is Ashley; also wearing the school stripe; and between Ashley and the other schoolboy, Bloomfield, is Rawson, the dreaded Londoner, a practised athlete, whose whiskered face contrasts strangely with the smooth, youthful countenances of his competitors.

"Ashley's to cut out the running for Willoughby this time," says Telson, "and he'll do it too; he's fresh."

So he is. At the signal to start he rushes off as if the race was a quarter of a mile instead of a mile, and the Londoner, perplexed by his tactics, starts hard also, intending to keep him in hand. Bloomfield and Wyndham, one on each side of the track, began rather more easily, and during the first lap allow themselves to drop twelve or fifteen yards behind. The Londoner quickly takes in the situation, but evidently doesn't quite know whether to keep up to Ashley or lie up like the others. If he does the latter, the chances are the fresh man may get ahead beyond catching, and possibly win the race; and if he does the former—well, has he the wind to hold out when the other two begin to "put it on"? He thinks he has, so he keeps close up to Ashley.

The cheers, of course, all round the field are tremendous, and nowhere more exciting than where Telson and Parson are located. As the runners pass them at the end of the first lap the excitement of these youths breaks forth into terrific shouts.

"Well run, Ashley; keep it up! He's blowing! Put it on there, Wyndham; now's your time, Bloomfield!" And before the cries have left their lips the procession has passed, and the second lap has begun.

Towards the end of the second lap Ashley shows signs of flagging, and Bloomfield is quickening his pace.

"Huzza!" yells Parson; "Bloomfield's going to take it up now. Jolly well-planned cut-out, eh, Telson?"

"Rather!" shrieks Telson. "Here they come! Whiskers is ahead. Now, Willoughby—well run indeed! Lam it on, Bloomfield, you're gaining. Keep it up, Ashley. Now, Wyndham; now!"

Ashley drops gradually to the rear, and before the final lap is half over has retired from the race, covered with glory for his useful piece of work. But anxious eyes are turned to the other three. The Londoner holds his own, and Bloomfield's rush up seems to have come to nothing. About a quarter of a mile from home an ominous silence drops upon the crowd, and for a few moments Willoughby is too disheartened to cheer. Then at last there rises a single wild cheer somewhere. What is it? The positions are still the same, and— No! *Both* Wyndham and Bloomfield are gaining; and as the discovery is made there goes up such a shout that the rooks in the elms start away from their nests in a panic.

Never was seen such a gallant spurt in that old meadow. Foot by foot the two Willoughby boys pull up and lessen the hateful distance which divides them from the leader. He of course sees his danger, and answers spurt for spurt. For a few yards he neither gains nor loses, then, joyful sight, he loses!

"Look at them now!" cries Telson, as they approach—"look at them both. They're both going to win! Ah, well run, Willoughby—splendidly run; you're going like mad—keep it up! Huzzah! level. Keep it up! Wyndham's ahead; so's Bloomfield. Both ahead! Well run both. Keep it up now. Hurrah!"

Amid such shouts the race ends. Wyndham first, Bloomfield a yard behind, and the Londoner, dead beat, a yard behind Bloomfield.

What wonder if the old school goes mad as it swarms over the cords and dashes towards the winner? Telson actually forgets Parson, Cusack deserts even his own father in the jubilation of the moment, each striving to get within cheering distance of the heroes of the day as they are carried shoulder-high round the ground amid the shouts and applause of the whole multitude.

So ended, in a victory unparalleled in its glorious annals, the May Day races of 19— at Willoughby; and there was not a fellow in the school, whether athlete or not, whose bosom did not glow with pride at the result. That the school would not disgrace herself everyone had been perfectly certain, for was not Willoughby one of the crack athletic schools of the country, boasting of an endless succession of fine runners, and rowers, and cricketers? But to score thus off a picked London athlete, beating him in two events, and in one of them doubly beating him, was a triumph only a very few had dared to anticipate, and even they were considerably astonished to find their prophecy come true.

Perhaps the person least excited by the entire day's events was the hero of the day himself. Wyndham, the old captain, as he now was—for this was his last appearance at the old school—was not the sort of fellow to get his head turned by anything if he could help it. He hated scenes of any sort, and therefore took a specially long time over his bath, which his fag had prepared for him with the most lavish care. Boys waylaid his door and the schoolhouse gate for a full hour ready to cheer him when he came out; but he knew better than to gratify them and finally they went off and lionised Bloomfield instead, who bore his laurels with rather less indifference.

The old captain, however, could not wholly elude the honours destined for him. Dinner in the big hall that afternoon was crowded to overflowing. And when at its close the doctor stood up and, in accordance with immemorial custom, proposed the health of the old captain, who, he said, was not only head classic, but *facile princeps* in all the manly sports for which Willoughby was famed, you would have thought the old roof was coming down with the applause. Poor Wyndham would fain have shirked his duty, had he been allowed to do it. But Willoughby would as soon have given up a week of the summer holiday as have gone without the captain's speech.

As he rose to his feet deafening cries of "Well run, sir; well run!" drowned any effort he could have made at speaking; and he had to stand till, by dint of sheer threats of violence, the monitors had reduced the company to order. Then he said, cheers interrupting him at every third word, "I'm much obliged to the doctor for speaking so kindly about me. You fellows know the old school will get on very well after I've gone. (No! no!) Willoughby always does get on, and any one who says, 'No! no!' ought to know better."

The applause at this point was overpowering; and the few guilty ones tried hard, by joining in it, to cover their shame.

"I've had a jolly time here, and am proud of being a Willoughby captain. I shouldn't be a bit proud if I didn't think it was the finest school going. And the reason it's the finest school is because the fellows think first of the school and next of themselves. As long as they do that Willoughby will be what she is now. Thank you, doctor, and you, fellows."

These were the last words of the old captain. He left Willoughby next day, and few of the boys knew what they had lost till he had gone.

How he was missed, and how these parting words of his came often to ring in the ears of the old school during the months that were to follow, this story will show.

Chapter Two.

Four Hours in a Fag's Life.

Willoughby wore its ordinary work-a-day look on the morning following the eventful May races. And yet any one who had seen the old school just then would have admitted that a more picturesque place could hardly have been found. It was one of those lovely early summer days when everything looks beautiful, and when only schoolboys can have the heart to lie in bed. The fresh scent of the sea came up with the morning air across the cliff-bound uplands; and far away, from headland to headland of Craydle Bay, the waters glowed and sparkled in the sunlight. Inland, too, along by the river, the woods were musical with newly-awakened birds, and the downs waved softly with early hay. And towering above all, amid its stately elms, and clad from end to end with ivy, stood the old school itself, glowing in morning brightness, as it had stood for two centuries past, and as those who know and love it hope it may yet stand for centuries to come.

But though any one else could hardly have failed to be impressed with the loveliness of such a morning in such a spot, on Master Frederick Parson, head monitor's fag of Parrett's House, as he kicked the bedclothes pensively off his person, and looked at the watch under his pillow, the beauties of nature were completely lost. Parson was in a bad frame of mind that morning. Everything seemed against him. He'd been beaten in the junior hundred yards yesterday, so had Telson. Just their luck. They'd run in every race for the last two years, and never won so much as a shilling penknife yet. More than that; just because he had walked across the quadrangle to see Telson home after supper last night (Telson belonged to the SchoolHouse) he had been caught by a monitor and given eight French verbs to write out for being out-of-doors, after lock-up. What harm, Parson would like to know, was there in seeing a friend across the quad? Coates, the monitor, probably had no friend—he didn't deserve to have one—or he wouldn't have been down on Parson for a thing like that.

Then, further than that, he (Parson) had not looked at his Caesar, and Warton had promised to report him to the doctor next time he showed up without preparation. Bother Warton! bother the doctor! bother Caesar! what did they all want to conspire together for against a wretched junior's peace? He'd have to cram up the Caesar from Telson's crib somehow, only the nuisance was Bloomfield had fixed on this particular morning for a turn on the river with Game, and Parson would of course have to steer for them. Just his luck again! He didn't mind steering for Bloomfield, of course, and if he must fag he'd as soon fag for him as anybody, especially now that he would be captain of the eleven and of the boats; but how, Parson wanted to know, was he to do his Caesar and his French verbs, and steer Bloomfield and Game up the river at one and the same time? He couldn't take the books in the boat.

Well, he supposed he'd have to get reported; and probably "Paddy" would give it him on the hands. He was always getting it on the hands, far oftener than Telson, who was Riddell's fag, and never had to go and steer boats up the river. In fact, Riddell, he knew, looked over Telson's lessons for him—catch Bloomfield doing as much for Parson!

All these considerations tended greatly to impair the temper of Master Parson this beautiful morning. But the worst grievance of all was that he had to get up that moment and call Bloomfield, or else he'd get a licking. That would be worse any day than getting it on the hands from the doctor.

So he kicked off the clothes surlily, and put one foot out of bed. But the other was a long time following. For Parson was fagged. He'd dreamt all night of that wretched hundred yards, and wasn't a bit refreshed; and if he had been refreshed, he'd got those eight French verbs and the Caesar on his mind, and he could have done them comfortably in bed. But—

A sudden glance at the watch in his hand cut short all further meditation. Parson is out of his bed and into his flannels in the twinkling of an eye, and scuttling down the passage to his senior's room as if the avenger of blood was at his heels.

Bloomfield, if truth must be told, is as disinclined to get up as his fag has been; and Parson has almost to use personal violence before he can create an impression on his lord and master.

"What's the time?" demands the senior.

"Six—that is, a second or two past," replies Parson.

"Why didn't you call me punctually?" asks Bloomfield, digging his nose comfortably into the pillow. "What do you mean by a second or two?"

"It's only seven past," says Parson, in an injured tone.

"Very well; go and see if Game's up."

Parson skulks off to rouse Game, knowing perfectly well that Bloomfield will be sound asleep again before he is out of the door, which turns out to be the case. After super-human efforts to extract from Game an assurance that he's getting up that moment, and Parson needn't wait, the luckless fag returns to find his master snoring like one of the seven sleepers. The same process has to be repeated. Shouts and shakes, and an occasional sly pinch, have no effect. Parson is tempted to leave his graceless lord to his fate, and betake himself to his French verbs; but a dim surmise as to the consequences prevents him. At last he braces himself up for one desperate effort. With a mighty tug he snatches the clothes off the bed, and, dragging with all his might at the arm of the obstinate hero, yells out, "I say, Bloomfield, it's half-past six, and you wanted to be up at six. Get up!"

The effect of these combined efforts is that Bloomfield sits up in bed, rubbing his eyes, and demands, "Half-past six! Why didn't you call me at six, you young cad, eh?"

"So I did."

"Don't tell crams. If you'd called me at six I should have been up, shouldn't I?" exclaimed Bloomfield. "I tell you I did call you," retorts the fag.

"Look here," says Bloomfield, becoming alarmingly wide-awake, "I don't want any of your cheek. Go and see if Game's up, and then see if the boat's ready. The tub-pair, mind; look sharp!"

"Please, Bloomfield," says Parson, meekly, "do you mind if I get Parks to cox you? I've not looked at my Caesar yet, and I've got eight French verbs to do besides for Coates."

8

"Do you hear me? Go and see if Game's up," replies Bloomfield. "If you choose not to do your work overnight, and get impositions for breaking rules into the bargain, it's not my lookout, is it?"

"But I only went—" begins the unfortunate Parson.

"I'll went you with the flat of a bat if you don't cut," shouts Bloomfield. Whereat his fag vanishes.

Game, of course, is fast asleep, but on him Parson has no notion of bestowing the pains he had devoted to Bloomfield. Finding the sleeper deaf to all his calls, he adopts the simple expedient of dipping the end of a towel in water and laying it neatly across the victim's face, shouting in his ear at the same time, "Game, I say, Bloomfield's waiting for you down at the boats." Having delivered himself of which, he retreats rather hastily, and only just in time.

The row up the river that morning was rather pleasant than otherwise. When once they were awake the morning had its effect on the spirits of all three boys. Even Parson, sitting lazily in the stern, listening to the Sixth Form gossip of the two rowers, forgot about his Caesar and French verbs, and felt rather glad he had turned out after all.

The chief object of the present expedition was not pleasure by any means as far as Bloomfield and Game were concerned. It was one of a series of training practices in anticipation of the school regatta, which was to come off on the second of June, in which the rival four-oars of the three houses were to compete for the championship of the river. The second of June was far enough ahead at present, but an old hand like Bloomfield knew well that the time was all too short to lick his crew into shape. Parrett's boat, by all ordinary calculation, ought to win, for they had a specially good lot of men this year; and now Wyndham had left, the schoolhouse boat would be quite an orphan. Bloomfield himself was far away the best oar left in Willoughby, and if he could only get Game to work off a little of his extra fat, and bully Tipper into reaching better forward, and break Ashley of his trick of feathering under water, he had a crew at his back which it would be hard indeed to beat. This morning he was taking Game in hand, and that substantial athlete was beginning to find out that "working off one's extra fat" in a tub-pair on a warm summer morning is not all sport.

"I wonder if Tipper and Ashley will show, up," said Bloomfield, who was rowing bow for the sake of keeping a better watch on his pupil. "They promised they would. Ashley, you know—(do keep it up, Game, you're surely not blowed yet)—Ashley's about as much too light as you are too fat—(try a little burst round the corner now; keep us well out, young 'un)—but if he'll only keep his blade square till he's out of the water—(there you go again! Of course you're hot; that's what I brought you out for. How do you suppose you're to boil down to the proper weight unless you do perspire a bit?)—he'll make a very decent bow. Ah, there are Porter and Fairbairn in the schoolhouse tub—(you needn't stop rowing, Game; keep it up, man; show them how you can spurt). I never thought they'd try Porter in their boat. They might as well try Riddell. Just shows how hard-up they must be for men. How are you?" he cried, as the schoolhouse tub went clumsily past, both rowers looking decidedly nervous under the critical eye of the captain of Parrett's.

Poor Game, who had been kept hard at it for nearly a mile, now fairly struck, and declared he couldn't keep it up any longer, and as he had really done a very good spell of work, Bloomfield consented to land at the Willows and bathe; after which he and Game would run back, and young Parson might scull home the tub.

Which delightful plan Master Parson by no means jumped at. He had calculated on getting at least a quarter of an hour for his Caesar before morning chapel if they returned as they had come. But now, if he was expected to lug that great heavy boat back by himself, not only would he not get that, but the chances were he would get locked out for chapel altogether, and it would be no excuse that he had had to act as galley-slave for Bloomfield or anybody else.

"Look alive!" cries Bloomfield from the bank, where he is already stripped for his header. "And, by the way, on your way up go round to Chalker's and tell him only to stick up one set of cricket nets in our court; don't forget, now. Be quick; you've not too much time before chapel."

Saying which, he takes a running dive from the bank and leaves the luckless Parson to boil over inwardly as he digs his sculls spitefully into the water and begins his homeward journey.

Was life worth living at this rate? If he didn't tell Chalker about the nets that imbecile old groundsman would be certain to stick up half a dozen sets, and there'd be no end of a row. That was 7:30 striking now, and he had to be in the chapel at five minutes to eight, and Chalker's hut was a long five minutes from the boat-house. And then those eight French verbs and that Caesar—

It was no use thinking about them, and Parson lashed out with his sculls, caring little if that hulking tub went to the bottom. He'd rather like it, in fact, for he wanted a swim. He hadn't even had time to tub that morning, and it was certain there'd be no time now till goodness knew when—not till after second school, and then probably he'd be spending a pleasant half-hour in the doctor's study.

At this point he became aware of another boat making down on him, manned by three juniors, who were making up in noise and splashing what they lacked in style and oarsmanship.

Parson knew them yards away. They were rowdies of Welch's house, and he groaned inwardly at the prospect before him. The boy steering was our old acquaintance Pilbury, and as his boat approached he shouted out cheerily, "Hullo, there, Parson! mind your eye! We'll race you in—give you ten yards and bump you in twenty! Pull away, you fellows! One, two,

9

three, gun! Off you go! Oh, well rowed, my boat! Now you've got him! Wire in, now! Smash him up! scrunch him into the bank! Hooroo! two to one on us! Lay on to it, you fellows; he can't go straight! Six more strokes and you're into him! One, two, three—ha, ha! he's funking it!—four, five—now a good one for the last—six! Hooroo! bump to us! Welch's for ever!"

So saying, the hostile boat came full tilt on to the stern of the Parrett's tub, and the outraged Parson found himself next moment sprawling on his back, with the nose of his boat firmly wedged into the clay bank of the river, while his insulting adversaries sped gaily away down stream, making the morning hideous with their shouts and laughter.

This little incident, as may be supposed, did not tend to compose the fluttered spirits of the unhappy Frederick. To say nothing of the indignity of being deliberately run down and screwed into the bank by a crew of young "Welchers," the loss of time involved in extricating his boat from the muddy obstacle which held her by the nose, put all chance of getting in in time to go round to Chalker's before chapel out of the question. Indeed, it looked very like a shut-out from chapel too, and that meant no end of a row.

By a super-human effort he got his boat clear, and sculled down hard all, reaching the boat-house at seven minutes to eight. He had just presence of mind enough to shout the message for Chalker to the boat-boy, with a promise of twopence if he delivered it at once; and then with a desperate rush he just succeeded in reaching the chapel and squeezing himself in at the door as the bell ceased ringing.

Chapel was not, under the circumstances, a very edifying service to Parson that morning. His frame of mind was not devotional, and his feelings of bottled-up wrath at what was past, and dejected anticipation of what was to come, left between them no room for interest in or meaning for the words in which his schoolfellows were joining. The only satisfaction morning prayers brought to him was that, for ten minutes at least, no one could harry him; and that at least was something to be grateful for.

Morning chapel at Willoughby was supposed to be at 7:15, and was at 7:15 all the months of the year except May, June, and July, when, in consideration of the early-morning rowing and bathing, it was postponed for three-quarters of an hour—a concession made up for by the sacrifice of the usual half-hour's interval between breakfast and first lesson.

This arrangement was all against Parson, who, if the half-hour had been still available, could at least have skimmed through his Caesar, and perhaps have begged a friend to help him with the French verbs, and possibly even have had it out with Pilbury for his morning's diversion. As it was, there was no opportunity for the performance of any one of these duties, and at the sound of the pitiless bell he slunk into first lesson, feeling himself a doomed man.

His one hope was Telson. Telson sat next him in class, and, he knew well, would help him if he could.

"Telson," he groaned, directly he found himself beside his faithful ally, "I've not looked at it!"

Telson whistled. "There'll be a row," he muttered, consolingly; "it's a jolly hard bit."

"Haven't you got the crib?"

Telson looked uncomfortable. "Riddell caught me with it and made me give it up."

"What on earth business has Riddell with your cribs, I'd like to know?" exclaimed Parson, indignant, not at all on the question of morality, but because the last straw on which he had relied for scrambling through his Caesar had failed him.

"He didn't take it, but he advised me to give it up."

"And you were fool enough to give in to him?"

"Well, he made out it wasn't honourable to use cribs," said Telson.

"Grandmother!" snarled Parson. "Why, Telson, I didn't think you'd have been such a soft!"

"No more did I, but somehow—oh! I'm awfully sorry, old man; I'll try and get it back."

"Doesn't much matter," said Parson, resignedly. "I'm in for it hot to-day."

"I'll prompt you all I can," said the repentant Telson.

"Thanks; I'd do the same to you if I could," replied Parson.

"It is a long lane that has no turning," as the proverb says, and Parson, after all, was destined to enjoy one brief glimpse of the smiles of fortune that day. The first boy put up to translate stumbled over a somewhat intricate point of syntax. Now Mr Warton, the master—as the manner of many masters is—was writing a little book on Latin Syntax, and this particular passage happened to be a superb example of a certain style of construction which till this moment had escaped his notice. Delighted with the discovery, he launched out into a short lecture on the subject generally, citing all the examples he had already got in his book, and comparing them with other forms of construction to be found scattered through the entire range of Latin classical literature.

How Parson and Telson enjoyed that lecture! They listened to it with rapt attention with hearts full of gratitude and faces full of sympathy. They did not understand a word of it, but a chapter out of "Midshipman Easy" could not have delighted them more; and when they saw that the clock had slowly worked round from nine to ten they would not have interrupted it for the world.

"Ah!" said Mr Warton, taking out his watch, "I see time's up. We've had more Syntax than Caesar to-day. Never mind, it's a point worth remarking, and sure to be useful as you get on in Latin. The class is dismissed."

Little he knew the joy his words carried to two small hearts in his audience.

"Jolly good luck that!" said Parson, as he strolled out into the passage arm-in-arm with his friend. "Now if I can only get those beastly verbs done before Coates asks for them! I say, Telson, do you know the dodge for sticking three nibs on one pen and writing three lines all at one time?"

"Tried it once," said Telson, "but it didn't pay. It took longer to keep sticking them in when they fell out, and measuring them to write on the lines, than to write the thing twice over the ordinary way. I'll write out part, old man."

"Thanks, Telson, you're an awful brick. I suppose Riddell wouldn't think it wicked of you to write another fellow's impot, would he?"

"I half fancy he would; but I won't tell him. Hullo! though, here comes Coates."

A monitor wearing his "mortar-board" approached.

"Where's your imposition, Parson?" he asked.

"I'm awfully sorry," said Parson, "but it's not quite done yet, Coates."

"How much is done?" demanded Coates.

"Not any yet," said Parson, with some confusion. "I was just going to begin. Wasn't I, Telson?"

"Won't do," said Coates; "you were up the river this morning, I saw you. If you can go up the river you can do your impositions. Better come with me to the captain."

Coming with a monitor to the captain meant something unpleasant. The discipline of Willoughby, particularly in outside matters, was left almost entirely in the hands of the monitors, who with the captain, their head, were responsible as a body to the head master for the order of the school. It was very rarely that a case had to go beyond the monitors, whose authority was usually sufficient to enable them to deal summarily with all ordinary offenders.

It was by no means the first time that Parson, who was reputed by almost every one but himself and Telson to be an incorrigible scamp, had been haled away to this awful tribunal, and he was half regretting that he had not met his fate over the Caesar after all, and so escaped his present position, when another monitor appeared down the passage and met them. It was Ashley.

"Hullo! Coates," said he, "I wish you'd come to my study and help me choose half a dozen trout-flies, there's a good fellow. I've had a book up from the town, and I don't know which are the best to use."

"All serene," said Coates, "I'll be there directly. I'm just going to take this youngster to the captain."

"Who is the captain?" said Ashley. "Wyndham's gone, and no one's been named yet that I know of. I suppose it's Bloomfield."

"Eh? I never thought of that. No, I expect it'll be a schoolhouse fellow. Always is, isn't it. Parson, you can go. Bring me twelve French verbs written out to my study before chapel to-morrow. Come on, Ashley."

And Parson departed, consoled in spirit, to announce to Telson and the lower school generally that Willoughby was at present without a captain.

Chapter Three.

The Vacant Captaincy.

Who was to be the new captain of Willoughby? This was a question it had occurred to only a very few to ask until Wyndham had finally quitted the school. Fellows had grown so used to the old order of things, which had continued now for two years, that the possibility of their bowing to any other chief than "Old Wynd" had scarcely crossed their minds. But the question being once asked, it became very interesting indeed.

The captains of Willoughby had been by long tradition what is known as "all-round men." There was something in the air of the place that seemed specially favourable to the development of muscle and classical proficiency at the same time, and the consequence was that the last three heads of the school had combined in one person the senior classic and the captains of the clubs. Wyndham had been the best of these; indeed he was as much ahead of his fellows in the classical school as he was in the cricket-field and on the river, which was saying not a little. His predecessors had both also been head boys in classics; and although neither of them actually the best men of their time in athletics, they had been sufficiently near the best to entitle them to the place of honour, which made the Willoughby captain supreme, not only in school, but out of it. So that in the memory of the present "generation"—a school generation being reckoned as five years—the Willoughby captain had always been cock of the school in every sense in which such a distinction was possible.

But now all of a sudden the school woke up to the fact that this delightful state of things was not everlasting. Wyndham had left and his mantle had fallen from him in two pieces.

The new head classic was Riddell, a comparatively unknown boy in the school, who had come there a couple of years ago from a private school, and about whom the most that was known was that he was physically weak and timid, rarely taking part in any athletic exercises, having very few chums, interfering very little with anybody else, and reputed "pi."—as the more irreverent among the Willoughbites were wont to stigmatise any fellow who made a profession of goodness. Such was the boy on whom, according to strict rule, the captaincy of Willoughby would devolve, and it need hardly be said that the discovery spread consternation wherever it travelled.

Among the seniors the idea was hardly taken seriously.

"The doctor would never be so ridiculous," said Ashley to Coates, as they talked the matter over in the study of the former. "We might as well shut up the school."

"The worst of it is, I don't see how he can help it," replied Coates.

"Help it! Of course he can help it if he likes. There's no written law that head classics are to be captains, if they can't hold a bat or run a hundred yards, is there?"

"I don't suppose there is. But who else is there?"

"Why, Bloomfield, of course. He's just the fellow for it, and the fellows all look up to him."

"But Bloomfield's low down in the sixth," said Coates.

"What's that to do with it? Felton was a muff at rowing, but he was made captain of the boats all the same while he was cock of the school."

At this point another monitor entered.

"Ah, Tipper," said Ashley, "what do you think Coates here is saying? He says Riddell is to be the new captain."

Tipper burst into a loud laugh.

"That would be a joke! Think of Riddell stroking the school eight at Henley, eh! or kicking off for us against Rockshire! I suppose Coates thinks because Riddell's a schoolhouse boy he's bound to be the man. Never fear. You'll see Parrett's come to the front at last, my boy!"

"Why, are *you* to be the new captain?" asked Coates, with a slight sneer.

Tipper was not pleased with this little piece of sarcasm. He was a good cricketer and a fine runner, but in school everybody knew him to be as poor a scholar as a fellow could be to be in the sixth at all.

"I dare say even I would be as good as any schoolhouse fellow you could pick out," said he. "But if you want to know, Bloomfield's the man."

"Just what I was saying," said Ashley. "But Coates says he's not far enough up in the school."

"All bosh," said Tipper. "What difference does it make if a fellow's first or twentieth in the school, as long as he's cock of everything outside! I don't see how the doctor can hesitate a moment between the two."

This was the conclusion come to at almost all the conclaves which met together during the day to discuss the burning question. It was the conclusion moreover to which Bloomfield himself came as he talked the matter over with a few of his friends after third school.

"You see," said he, "it's not that I care about the thing for its own sake. It would be a precious grind, I know, to have to be responsible for everything that goes on, and to have to lick all the kids that want a hiding. But for all that, I'd sooner do it than let the school run down."

"What I hope," said some one, "is that even if Paddy doesn't see it himself, Riddell will, and will have the sense to back out of it. I fancy he wouldn't be sorry."

"Not he," said Bloomfield. "I heard him say once he pitied Wyndham all the bother he had, especially when he was wanting to stew for the exams."

"Has any one seen Riddell lately?" asked Game. "It wouldn't be a bad thing for some of us to see him, and put it to him, that the school would go to the dogs to a dead certainty if he was captain."

"Rather a blunt way of putting it," said Porter, laughing. "I'd break it to him rather more gently than that."

"Well, you know what I mean," replied Game, who was of the downright order.

"You see," said Bloomfield, who, despite his protestations, was evidently not displeased at the notion of his possible honours, "I don't profess to be much of a swell in school; but—I don't know—I fancy I could keep order rather better than he could. The fellows know me."

"They ought to, if they don't," said Wibberly, who was a toady.

"Fancy Riddell having to lick a junior," said Game. "Why he'd faint at the very idea."

"Probably take him off to his study and have a prayer-meeting with Fairbairn and a few more of that lot upon the top of him," said Gilks, a schoolhouse monitor, and not a nice-looking fellow.

"I guess I'd sooner get a hiding from old Bloomfield than that," laughed Wibberly.

"I hope," said Game, "snivelling's not going to be the order of the day. I can't stand it."

"I don't think you've any right to call Riddell a sniveller," said Porter. "He may be a muff at sports, but I don't fancy he's a sneak. And I don't see that it's against him, either, if he does go in for being what he professes to be."

"Hear! hear!—quite a sermon from Porter," cried Wibberly.

"Porter's right," said Bloomfield. "No one says it was against him. All I say is that I don't expect the fellows will mind him as much as they would a fellow who—well, who's better known, you know."

"Rather," said Game, "I know it would seem precious rum being a monitor under him."

"Well," said Bloomfield, "I suppose it will be settled soon. Meanwhile, Game, what do you say to another grind in the tub? You didn't half work this morning, you beggar."

Game groaned resignedly, and said "All right;" and hue and cry was forthwith made for Master Parson's services at the helm.

But Master Parson, as it happened, was not to be found. He was neither in the school nor in his house, and a search through the grounds failed to unearth him. He had not been seen since his escape from the monitorial fangs after morning school. The natural thing, of course, on not finding him at home in his own quarters, was to look for him in Telson's. But he was not there, nor, strange to say, was Telson himself. And, what was still more odd, when search came to be made, Bosher, another fag of Parrett's house, was missing, and so was Lawkins, and Pringle, and King, and Wakefield, and one or two others of the same glorious company. After a fruitless search, the oarsmen had finally to go down to the river without a fag at all, and impound the boat-boy to steer for them.

The fact was, Parson's miraculous release from the hands of the law that morning, and the reason which led to it, had suggested both to himself and the faithful Telson that the present was rather a rare opportunity for them in the annals of Willoughby. If there was no captain, there was no one to give them a licking (for the worst an ordinary monitor could do was to give an imposition), and that being so, it would surely be a waste of precious opportunity if they failed to signalise the event by some little celebration. And, as it happened, there was a little celebration which badly wanted celebrating, and for which only a chance like the present could have been considered favourable. In other words, there was a rather long score which the juniors of Parrett's were anxious to settle up with the juniors of Welch's. The debt was of long standing, having begun as far back as the middle of the Lent term, when the Welchers had played upon some of Parrett's with a hose from behind their own door, and culminating in the unprovoked outrage upon the luckless Parson on the river that very morning.

Now if there was one thing more than another the young Parretts prided themselves in, it was their punctuality in matters of business; and it had troubled them sorely that circumstances over which they had no control (in other words, the fear of Wyndham) should have prevented their settling scores with the Welchers at an earlier date.

Now, however, an opportunity was come, and, like all honest men, they determined at once to avail themselves of it.

So the reason why Bloomfield and Game could find no fags in Parrett's house to steer for them was because all the fags of Parrett's house, aided by Telson of the schoolhouse, were at that moment paying a business call at Welch's, and having on the whole rather a lively time of it.

The juniors of Welch's were, take them altogether, a rather more rowdy lot than the juniors of either of the two other houses, or, indeed, than those of both the other houses put together. Somehow Welch's was always the rowdy house of Willoughby. The honours of the school, whether in class or in field, always seemed to go in any direction but their own, and as, for five or six years at any rate, they had been unable to claim any one distinguished Willoughbite as a member of their house, they had come to regard themselves somewhat in the light of Ishmaelites. Everybody's hand seemed to be against them, and they therefore didn't see why their hand shouldn't be against every one.

It was this feeling which had prompted the assaults of which the youthful Parretts had come to complain, and which the Welchers distributed as impartially as possible among all their fellow Willoughbites.

The fact was, Welch's was a bad house. The fellows there rarely made common cause for any lawful purpose, certainly never for the credit of the school. They were split up into cliques and sets of all sorts, and the rising generation among them were left to grow up pretty much as they liked.

On the afternoon in question an entertainment on a small scale was going on in the study jointly occupied by Cusack and Pilbury. Captain Cusack, R.N., when he had parted from his dutiful son the night before, had put five shillings into his hand as a pleasant memento of his visit; and Master Cusack, directly after second school that morning, had skulked down into Shellport with his hat-box, and returned in due time with the same receptacle packed almost to bursting with dough-nuts, herrings, peppermint-rock, and sherbet. With these dainties to recommend him (and his possession of them soon got wind) it need hardly be said he became all of a sudden the most popular youth in Welch's. Fellows who would have liked to kick him yesterday now found themselves loving him like their own brother, and the enthusiasm felt for him grew to such a pitch that it really seemed as if not only his hat-box, but he himself, was in danger. However, by a little judicious manoeuvring he got safe into his study, and, after a hasty consultation with Pil, decided to ask Curtis, Philpot, Morrison, and Morgan, their four most intimate friends, to do them the pleasure of joining in a small "blow-out" after third school. These four worthies, who, by a most curious coincidence, happened to be loafing outside Cusack's study-door at the very moment when Pilbury started off to find them, had much pleasure in accepting their friend's kind invitation; and the rest, finding themselves out of it, yapped off disconsolately, agreeing inwardly that Cusack was the stingiest beast in all Willoughby.

If punctuality is a test of politeness, Curtis, Morgan, Philpot, and Morrison were that afternoon four of the politest young gentlemen in the land; for they were all inside Cusack's study almost before the bell dismissing third school had ceased to sound.

"Jolly brickish of you, old man," said Morrison, complacently regarding the unpacking of the magic hat-box. "I've not seen a dough-nut for years."

"I got these at a new shop," said Cusack, trying to rescue some of the sherbet which had fallen in among the herrings. "Gormon never has anything but red-currant jam in his. These are greengage."

"How jolly prime!" was the delighted exclamation.

"Three-halfpence each, though," said Cusack, laying the herrings out in a row on the table. "I say, I wish we'd got some forks or something to toast these with."

"Wouldn't the slate do to stick them on?" suggested Curtis.

"Might do, only Grange wrote out a lot of Euclid questions on it, and I've got to show them to him answered to-morrow, and I'd get in an awful row if it was rubbed out."

"Rather a bore. I tell you what, though," exclaimed Philpot, struck with the brilliant idea, "there's the pan in the chemistry-room they mix up the sulphur and phosphorus and that sort of thing in. I'll cut and get that. It's just the thing."

"All serene," said Cusack; "better give it a rub over in case it blows up, you know."

Philpot said "All right," and went, leaving the others to poke up the fire and get all ready for the reception of the pan.

He was a long while about it, certainly, considering that the chemistry-room was only just at the end of the passage.

"I wonder what he's up to?" said Pilbury, when after about three minutes he did not return.

"I wish he'd hurry up," said Curtis, whose special attraction was towards the dough-nuts, which of course could not come on till after the herrings.

"I wonder if he's larking about with some of the chemicals. I never knew such a fellow as he is for smells and blow-ups—"

"I'll blow him up if he's not sharp," said Cusack, losing patience and looking mournfully at the row of herrings on the table.

"Let's begin without him," said Pilbury.

"So we would if we had anything to do them on."

"I'll go and see if I can get a fork or two," said Morrison.

"Thanks, and wake up Philpot while you're out."

Morrison went, and the others kicked their heels impatiently and eyed the good things hungrily as they waited.

Cusack tried toasting a herring on one of the small forks, but the heat of the fire was too great for him to hold his hand at such close quarters, and he gave it up in disgust.

What was the matter with everybody this afternoon? Morrison was away ages and did not return.

"Oh, bother it all!" exclaimed Cusack, whose patience was now fairly exhausted, "if they don't choose to come I'm hung if they'll get anything now. I'll go and get the pan myself."

And off he went in high dudgeon, leaving his guests in charge of the feast.

"If he can't get the pan or a toasting-fork," said Curtis, disinterestedly, "wouldn't it be as well to have the dough-nuts now, and leave the herrings till supper, eh, Pil? Pity for them to get stale."

Pilbury said nothing, but broke off a little piece of the peppermint-rock in a meditative manner, and drummed his feet on the floor.

"Upon my word," he broke out after a good three minutes' waiting, "that blessed pan must be jolly heavy. There's three of them sticking to it now!"

"Wait a bit, I hear him coming," said Curtis, going to the door. He stepped out into the passage, Morgan following him.

Pilbury heard a sudden scuffling outside, and a sound of what did not seem like Welchers' voices. He hurried to the door to ascertain the cause, and as he did so he found himself caught roughly by the arm and slung violently against the opposite wall, while at the same moment Telson, Parson, Bosher, and half a dozen Parrett juniors rushed past him into the empty study, slamming and locking and barricading the door behind them!

It was all so quickly done that the luckless Welchers could hardly believe their own senses. But when they heard the distant voice of Philpot shouting that he was locked up in the chemistry-room, and of Morrison complaining that he couldn't get out of his own study, and of Cusack demanding to be released from the lavatory; and when their combined assault on the door produced nothing but defiant laughter mingled with the merry frizzing of the herrings before the fire, they knew it was no dream but a hideous fact. They had presence of mind enough to release their incarcerated comrades and attempt another assault in force on the door. But it came to nothing. In vain they shouted, threatened, entreated, kicked. They only received facetious answers from inside, which aggravated their misery.

"Go it, you fellows," shouted one voice, very like Parson's, only the mouth was so full that it was hard to say for certain. "Jolly good dough-nuts these; have another, Bosher, you've only had four. I say, Cusack, where did you catch these prime herrings? Best I've tasted since I came here. Afraid your slate's a little damaged; awfully sorry, you ought to keep a toasting-fork—ha! ha!" and a chorus of laughter greeted the sally. Cusack groaned and fumed.

"You pack of young cads," he howled through the key-hole. "Come out of there, do you hear? you thieves you. I'll warm you, Parson, when I get hold of you."

"Just what we're doing to the bloaters," cried Telson. There was a pause. Then Pilbury cried in tones of feigned warning, "Here comes the doctor! We'll see what he says."

"Won't do," shouted Parson from within. "Won't wash, my boy. Paddy's down at Shellport. Any more sherbet left, King?"

"I'll go and tell the captain, that's what I'll do," said Pilbury.

"Won't wash again," cried Parson. "There's no captain to tell; I say, we're leaving something for you, aren't we, you fellows? There'll be all the heads of the herrings and the greengage stones— jolly blow-out for you."

It was no use attempting further parley, and the irate Welchers were compelled to lurk furiously outside the door while the feast proceeded, and console themselves with the prospect of paying the enemy out when it was all over.

But the skill which had accompanied the execution of the raid so far was not likely to omit all precautions possible to make good a retreat. While most of the party were making all the noise they could, and succeeding with jest and gibe in keeping the attention of those outside, the barricade against the door had been quietly removed, and decks cleared for the sortie.

"Now then, you fellows," cried Parson to his men, in a voice which those outside were intended to hear, "make yourselves comfortable. Here's a stunning lot of peppermint-rock here, pass it round. Needn't go home for half an hour at least!"

The watchers outside groaned. There was no help at hand; and for one of them to go and seek it was only to increase the odds against them. The only thing was to wait patiently till the enemy did come out. *Then* it would be their turn. So they leaned up against the door and waited. The revelry within became more and more boisterous, and the chances of a speedy retreat more and more remote, when all of a sudden there was a sharp click and the door swung back hard on its hinges, precipitating Cusack, Pilbury, and Curtis backwards into the room in among the very feet of the besieged as, in a compact body, they rushed out. Morrison, Philpot, and Morgan did what little they could to oppose them but they were simply run over and swept aside by the wily troop of Parretts, who with shouts of derisive triumph gained the staircase with unbroken ranks, and gave their pursuers the parting gratification of watching them slide down the banisters one by one, and then lounge off arm-in-arm, sated and jubilant, to their own quarters.

Chapter Four.

The New Captain's Introduction.

Of course a row was made, or attempted to be made, about the daring exploit of the fags of Parrett's House narrated in the last chapter. The matter was duly reported to the head monitor of Welch's by the injured parties. But the result only proved how very cunning the offenders had been in choosing this particular time for the execution of their raid.

The head of Welch's reported the matter to Bloomfield, as the head of Parrett's. But Bloomfield, who had plenty to do to punish offences committed in his own House, replied that the head of Welch's had better mention it to the captain of the school. *He* couldn't do anything. The head of Welch's pointed out that there was no captain of the school at present. What was he to do?

Bloomfield suggested that he had better "find out," and there the matter ended. Wherever the head Welcher took his complaint he got the same answer; and it became perfectly clear that as long as Willoughby was without a captain, law and order was at a discount.

However, such a state of things was not destined long to last. A notice went round from the doctor to the monitors the next day asking them to assemble directly after chapel the following morning in the library. Every one knew what this meant; and when later on it was rumoured that Riddell had gone to the doctor's that evening to tea, it became pretty evident in which direction things were going.

"Tea at the doctor's" was always regarded as rather a terrible ordeal by those who occasionally came in for the honour. Some would infinitely have preferred a licking in the library, and others would have felt decidedly more comfortable in the dock of a police-court. Even the oldest boys, whose conduct was exemplary, and whose conscience had as little to make it uneasy in the head master's presence as in the presence of the youngest fag in Willoughby, were always glad when the ceremony was over.

The reason of all this was not in the doctor. Dr Patrick was one of the kindest and pleasantest of men. He could not, perhaps, throw off the Dominie altogether on such occasions, but he always tried hard, and if there had been no one more formidable than "Paddy" to deal with the meal would have been comparatively pleasant and unalarming.

But there was a Mrs Patrick and a Mrs Patrick's sister, and before these awful personages the boldest Willoughbite quailed and trembled. From the moment the unhappy guest entered the parlour these two (who were always there) fastened their eyes on him and withered him. They spoke ceremoniously in the language in which the grand old ladies used to speak in the old story-books. If he chanced to speak, they sat erect in their chairs listening to him with all their ears, looking at him with all their eyes, freezing him with all their faintest of smiles. No one could sit there under their inspection without feeling that every word and look and gesture was being observed, probably with a view to recording it in a letter home; and the idea of being at one's ease with them in the room was about as preposterous as the idea of sleeping comfortably on a wasp's nest!

And yet, if truth were known, these good females meant well. They had their own ideas of what boys should be (neither having any of their own), and fondly imagined that during these occasional ceremonies in the doctor's parlour they were rendering valuable assistance in the "dear boy's" education by giving him some idea of the manners and charms of polite society!

It was in such genial company that Riddell, the head classic of Willoughby, was invited to bask for a short time on the evening of the day before the appointment of the new captain. He had been there once before when his father and mother had come over to visit him. And even with their presence as a set-off, the evening had been one of the most awful experiences of his life. But now that he was to go all alone to partake of state tea with those two, this shy awkward boy felt about as cheerful as if he had been walking helplessly into a lion's den.

"Well, Riddell," said the doctor, pleasantly, as after long hesitation the guest at last ventured to arrive, "how are you? My dear, this is Riddell, whom I believe you have seen before. Miss Stringer too I think you met."

Riddell coloured deeply and shivered inwardly as he advanced first to one lady then to the other and solemnly shook hands.

"I trust your parents are in good health, Mr Riddell," said Mrs Patrick in her most precise tones.

"Very well indeed, thank you," replied Riddell; "that is," he added, correcting himself suddenly, "my mother is very poorly, thank you."

"I regret to hear you say so," said Mrs Patrick, transfixing the unhappy youth with her eyes. "I trust her indisposition is not of a serious character."

"I hope she will, thank you, ma'am," replied Riddell, who somehow fancied his hostess had said, or had been going to say, she hoped his mother would soon recover.

"Er, I beg your pardon?" said Mrs Patrick, leaning slightly forward and inclining her head a little on one side.

"I mean, I beg your pardon," said Riddell, suddenly perceiving his mistake and losing his head at the same time, "I mean, quite so, thank you."

"You mean," interposed Miss Stringer at this point, in a voice a note deeper than her sister's, "that your mother's indisposition *is* of a serious character?"

"Oh no, not at all, I'm sure," ejaculated the hapless Riddell.

"I am glad to hear you say so, very," said Miss Stringer.

"Very," said Mrs Patrick.

At this point Riddell had serious thoughts of bolting altogether, and might have done so had not the servant just then created a diversion by bringing in the kettle.

"Sit down, Riddell," said the doctor, "and make yourself at home. What are the prospects for the regatta this year? Is the schoolhouse boat to win?"

"I'm sorry I can't say," replied Riddell. "I believe Parrett's is the favourite."

"Mr Riddell means Mr Parrett's, I presume?" asked Mrs Patrick in her sweetest tones, looking hard at the speaker, and emphasising the "Mr"

"I beg your pardon," he said, "I'm sorry."

"We shall miss Wyndham," said the doctor.

"Yes, thank you," replied Riddell, who at that moment was dodging vaguely in front of Miss Stringer as she stood solemnly waiting to get past him to the tea-table.

It was a relief when tea was at last ready, and when some other occupation was possible than that of looking at and being looked at by these two ladies.

"You're not very fond of athletics, Riddell?" asked the doctor.

"No, sir," answered Riddell, steadily avoiding the eyes of the females.

"I often think you'd be better if you took more exercise," said the doctor.

"Judging by Mr Riddell's looks," said Mrs Patrick, "it would certainly seem as if he hardly did himself justice physically."

This enigmatical sentence, which might have been a compliment or might have been a rebuke or might have meant neither, Riddell found himself quite unable to reply to appropriately, and therefore, like a sensible man, took a drink of tea instead. It was the first dawn of reviving presence of mind.

"Apart from your own health altogether," continued the doctor, "I fancy your position with the other boys would be better if you entered rather more into their sports."

"I often feel that, sir," said Riddell, with a touch of seriousness in his tones, "and I wish I could do it."

"I hope that there is no consideration as to health which debars you from this very desirable exercise, Mr Riddell," said Mrs Patrick. "I beg your pardon," said Riddell, who did not quite take it in. Mrs Patrick never liked being asked to repeat her speeches. She flattered herself they were lucid enough to need no second delivery. She therefore repeated her remark slowly and in precisely the same words and tone—

"I hope that there is no consideration as to health which debars you from this very desirable exercise, Mr Riddell?"

Riddell took half a moment to consider, and then replied, triumphantly, "I'm quite well, thank you, ma'am."

"I am pleased to hear that," said Mrs Patrick, rather icily, for this last observation had seemed to her a little rude. "Very," chimed in Miss Stringer.

After this there was a silence, which Riddell devoutly hoped might last till it was time to go. Had the ladies not been there he would have liked very much to speak to the doctor about school matters, and the doctor, but for the same cause, would have wished to talk to his head boy. But it was evident this tea-table was not the place for such conversation.

"I hear," said the doctor, after the pause had continued some time, addressing his sister-in-law, "there is likely to be an election in Shellport before long; Sir Abraham is retiring."

"Indeed, you surprise me," said Miss Stringer. "It is unexpected," said the doctor, "but it is thought there will be a sharp contest for the seat."

"And are you a Liberal or a Conservative, Mr Riddell?" asked Mrs Patrick, thinking it time that unfortunate youth was again tempted into the conversation.

"A Liberal, ma'am," replied Riddell. "Oh! boys are generally Conservatives, are they not?" She asked this question in a tone as if she expected him to try to deceive her in his answer. However, he evaded it by replying bashfully, "I hope not."

"And pray," said Miss Stringer, putting down her cup, and turning full on her victim, "will you favour us with your reasons for such a hope, Mr Riddell?"

Poor Riddell! he little thought what he had let himself in for. If there was one subject the two ladies were rabid on it was politics. They proceeded to pounce upon, devour, and annihilate the unlucky head classic without mercy. They made him contradict himself twice or thrice in every sentence; they proved to him clearly that he knew nothing at all of what he was talking about, and generally gave him to understand that he was an impertinent, conceited puppy for presuming to have an opinion of his own on such matters!

Riddell came out of the ordeal very much as a duck comes out of the hands of the poulterer. Luckily, by the time the discussion was over it was time for him to go. He certainly could not have held out much longer. As it was, he was good for nothing after it, and went to bed early that night with a very bad headache.

Before he left, however, the doctor had accompanied him into the hall, and said, "There are a few things, Riddell, I want to speak to you about. Will you come to my study a quarter of an hour before morning chapel to-morrow?"

Had the invitation been to breakfast in that horrible parlour Riddell would flatly have declined it. As it was he cheerfully accepted it, and only wished the doctor had thought of it before, and spared him the misery of that evening with the two Willoughby griffins!

He could hardly help guessing what it was the doctor had to say to him, or why it was he had been asked to tea that evening. And he felt very dejected as he thought about it. Like most of the other Willoughbites, the idea of a new captain having to be appointed had never occurred to him till Wyndham had finally left the school. And when it did occur, and when moreover it began to dawn upon him that he himself was the probable successor, horror filled his mind. He couldn't do it. He was not cut out for it. He would sooner leave Willoughby altogether. The boys either knew nothing about him, or they laughed at him for his clumsiness, or they suspected him as a coward, or they despised him as a prig. He had wit enough to know what Willoughby thought of him, and that being so, how could he ever be its captain?

"I would much rather you named some one else," said he to the doctor at their interview next morning. "I know quite well I couldn't get on."

"You have not tried yet," said the doctor.

"But I've not the strength, and the boys don't like me," pleaded Riddell.

"You must make them like you, Riddell," said the doctor.

"How can I? They will dislike me all the more if I am made captain. I have no influence with them, indeed I have not."

"How do you know?" said the doctor again. "Have you tried yet?"

"I could never do what Wyndham did. He was such a splendid captain."

"Why?" asked the doctor.

"I suppose because he was a splendid athlete, and threw himself into all their pursuits, and—and set a good example himself."

"I think you are partly right and partly wrong," said the doctor. "There are several fine athletes in Willoughby who would make poor captains; and as for throwing oneself into school pursuits and setting a good example, I don't think either is beyond your reach."

Riddell felt very uncomfortable. He began to feel that after all he might be shirking a duty he ought to undertake. But he made one more effort.

"There are so many others would do it better, sir, whom the boys look up to already," he said. "Bloomfield, for instance, or—"

The doctor held up his hand.

"We will not go into that, Riddell," he said. "You must not suppose I and others have not considered the good of Willoughby in this matter. It remains for you to consider it also. As you grow older you will constantly find duties confronting you which may be sorely against your inclination, but which as an honest man you will know are not to be shirked. You have a chance of beginning now. I don't pretend to say you will find it easy or pleasant work, or that you are likely to succeed, at first at any rate, as well as others have done. But unless I am mistaken you will not give in on that account. Of course you will need to exert yourself. You know what boys look for in a captain; it's not mere muscle, or agility. Get them by all means if you can; but what will be worth far more than these will be sympathy. If they discover you are one with them, and that in your efforts to keep order you have the welfare of the school chiefly at heart, they will come out, depend upon it, and meet you half-way. It's worth trying, Riddell."

Riddell said nothing, but his face was rather more hopeful as he looked up at the doctor.

"Come," said the latter, "there's the bell for chapel. It's time we went in."

Riddell entered chapel that morning in a strangely conflicting frame of mind. The hope was still in his face, but the misgivings were still in his heart, and the whole prospect before him seemed to be a dream.

As the slight shy boy walked slowly up the floor to his place among the Sixth, the boys on either side eyed him curiously and eagerly, and a half-titter, half-sneer greeted his appearance.

Some regarded him with a disfavour which amounted to positive dislike, others with disdain and even contempt, and others thought of Wyndham and wondered what Willoughby was coming to. Even among the Sixth many an unfriendly glance was darted at him as he took his seat, and many a whispered foreboding passed from boy to boy. Only a few watched him with looks of sympathy, and of these scarcely one was hopeful.

Happily for Riddell, he could not see half of all this; and when in a moment the doctor entered and prayers began, he saw none of it. For he was one of a few at Willoughby to whom this early-morning service was something more than a mere routine, and who felt, especially at times like this, that in those beautiful familiar words was to be found the best of all preparations for the day's duties.

Telson, as he stood down by the door, with his hands in his pockets, beside his friend Parson, was void of all such reflections. What was chiefly occupying his lordly mind at that moment was the discovery suddenly made, that if Riddell was the new captain, he of course would be captain's fag. And he was not quite sure whether to be pleased or the reverse at his new dignity.

"You see," said he to his ally, in a whisper, "it's good larks marking the fellows off every morning as they come into chapel, but then, don't you twig that means I've got to be here the moment the bell begins ringing? and that's no joke."

"No, unless you got leave to ring the bell, too," said Parson. "Then of course they couldn't troop in till you were there. I'd come down and help with the bell, you know."

"Wouldn't do, I fancy," said Telson. "Then, of course, it's swell enough work to have to go about and tell the monitors what they've got to do, but I'm not so sure if it's a good thing to mix altogether with monitors—likely to spoil a chap, eh?"

"Rather," said Parson. "Look out, Porter's looking."

18

Whereupon this brief but edifying dialogue broke off for the present.

The monitors duly assembled in the doctor's library after chapel. They all of them knew what was coming, and their general attitude did not seem promising for the new *régime*. Each one possibly fancied he had the interests of Willoughby at heart, and all but one or two felt convinced that in putting Riddell into the position of captain the doctor was committing a serious mistake. Every one could have given good reasons for thinking so, and would have asserted that they had no personal ill-feeling towards the new captain, but for the sake of the school they were sure he was not the fit person. Whether each one felt equally sure that he himself would have filled the post better is a question it is not necessary to ask here.

The doctor was brief and to the point.

"I dare say you know why I have called you together," he said. "Wyndham—whom every one here liked and respected, and who did a great deal for the school"—("Hear, hear," from one or two voices)—"has left, and we shall all miss him. The captain of the school has always for a long time past been the head classical boy. It is not a law of the Medes and Persians that it should be so, and if there seemed any special reason why the rule should be broken through there is nothing to prevent that being done."

At this point one or two breathed rather more freely and the attention generally was intensified. After all, this seemed like the preface to a more favourable announcement. But those who thought so found their mistake when the doctor proceeded.

"In the present case there is no such reason, and Riddell here is fully aware of the duties expected of him, and is prepared to perform them. I look to you to support him, and am confident if all work heartily together no one need be afraid for the continued success of Willoughby."

The doctor ended his speech amid the silence of his audience, which was not broken as he turned and left the room. At the same moment, to the relief of no one more than of Riddell, the bell sounded for breakfast and the assembly forthwith broke up.

Chapter Five.

The New Captain is discussed on Land and Water.

The doctor's announcement was not long in taking effect. As soon as third school was over that afternoon the monitors assembled in the Sixth Form room to discuss the situation. Fortunately for Riddell's peace of mind, he was not present; but nearly all the others, whether friendly or otherwise, were there.

Game, with his usual downrightness, opened the ball.

"Well, you fellows," said he, "what are you going to do?"

"Let's have a game of leapfrog while the fags aren't looking," said Crossfield, a schoolhouse monitor and a wag in a small way.

"It's all very well for you to fool about," said Game, ill-temperedly. "You schoolhouse fellows think, as long as you get well looked after, Willoughby may go to the dogs."

"What do you mean?" said Fairbairn. "I don't think so."

"I suppose you'd like to make out that Riddell is made captain because he's the best man for the place, and not because the doctor always favours the schoolhouse," snarled Wibberly.

"He's made captain because he's head classic," replied Fairbairn; "it has nothing to do with his being a schoolhouse fellow."

"All very well," said Tucker, of Welch's, "but it's a precious odd thing, all the same, that the captain is always picked out of the schoolhouse."

"And it's a precious odd thing too," chimed in Crossfield, "that a head classic was never to be got out of Welch's for love or money!"

This turned the laugh against the unlucky Tucker, who was notoriously a long way off being head classic.

"What I say is," said Game, "we want an all-round man for captain—a fellow like Bloomfield here, who's well up in the Sixth, and far away the best fellow in the eleven and the boats. Besides, he doesn't shut himself up like Riddell, and give himself airs. I can't see why the doctor didn't name him. The only thing against him seems to be that he's not a schoolhouse gentleman."

"That's the best thing about him in my opinion," said Ashley.

If Game and his friends had determined to do their best to gain friends for the new captain, this constant bringing-up of the rivalry between Parrett's house and the schoolhouse was the very way to do it. Many of the schoolhouse monitors had felt as sore as anybody about the appointments, but this sort of talk inclined not a few of them to take Riddell's side.

"I don't want any row made on my account," said Bloomfield. "If Paddy thinks Riddell's the best man, we have no choice in the matter."

"Haven't we, though!" said Wibberly. "We aren't going to have a fellow put over our heads against our will—at any rate, not without having a word in the matter."

"What can you do?" asked Coates.

"We can resign, I suppose?" said Tucker.

"Oh, yes!" said Crossfield. "And suppose Paddy took you at your word, my boy? Sad thing for Welch's that would be!"

"I don't know why you choose to make a beast of yourself whenever I speak," said Tucker, angrily; "I've as much right—"

"Shut up, Tucker, for goodness' sake!" said Bloomfield; "don't begin by quarrelling."

"Well, then, what does he want to cheek me for?" demanded Tucker. "He's a stuck-up schoolhouse prig, that's what he is!"

"And if I only had the flow of costermonger's talk which some people possess—" began Crossfield.

"Are you going to shut up or not?" demanded Bloomfield.

"Hullo! you aren't captain yet, old man!" replied the irrepressible Crossfield; "but if you want to know, I am going to shut up now till I want to speak again."

"We might get up a petition to the doctor, anyhow," suggested Game, returning to the subject; "he'd have to take notice of that."

"What will you say in the petition?" asked Porter.

"Oh! easy enough that. Say we don't consider Riddell fit to be captain, and we'd sooner have some one else."

"Better say we'd sooner have Bloomfield at once," said Wibberly.

"No; please don't mention my name," said Bloomfield.

"Wouldn't the best thing be to send Riddell back with a label, 'Declined, with thanks,' pinned on his coat-tail?" suggested Crossfield.

"Yes; and add, 'Try again, Paddy,'" said Coates, laughing.

"And just mention no schoolhouse snobs are wanted," said Tucker.

"And suggest, mildly, that a nice, clever, amiable, high-principled Welcher like Tom Tucker would be acceptable," added Crossfield.

"Look here," said Tucker, very red in the face, advancing towards his tormentor, "I've stood your impudence long enough, you cad, and I won't stand any more."

"Sit down, then," replied Crossfield, cheerfully, "plenty of forms."

"Look here, you fellows," said Bloomfield again, "for goodness' sake shut up. Have it out afterwards if you like, but don't fight here."

"I don't mind where I have it out," growled Tucker, "but I'll teach him to cheek me, see if I don't."

So saying, much to the relief of every one, he turned on his heel and left the room.

After this the discussion again got round to Riddell, and the question of a petition was revived.

"It would be quite easy to draw something up that would say what we want to say and not give offence to any one," said Ashley.

"But what do you want to say?" asked Fairbairn. "If you want to tell the doctor he's wrong, and that we are the people to set him right, I don't see how you can help offending him."

"That's not what we want to say at all," said Game. "We want to say that the captain of Willoughby has always been a fellow who was good all round, and we think the new captain ought to be of the same sort for the sake of the school."

"Hear, hear," said one or two of Parrett's house; "what could be better than that?"

"Well," said Porter, "I don't see much difference between saying that and telling the doctor he doesn't know what he's about."

"Of course *you* say so—that's your schoolhouse prejudice," replied Wibberly.

"It's nothing of the sort," said Fairbairn, warmly; "you know that as well as I do, Wibberly."

"I know it is," retorted Wibberly; "you'd put up with anybody as long as he wasn't a Parrett fellow."

And so the wrangle went on; and at the end of it the company was as near agreeing as they had been at the beginning.

Finally one or two of the schoolhouse fellows, such as Fairbairn, Coates, and Porter, withdrew, and the Parrett faction, having it then pretty much their own way, drew up the following petition:

"We the undersigned monitors respectfully hope you will reconsider your decision as to the New Captain. The captain has hitherto always been an 'all-round man,' and we think it would be best for the discipline of the school to have a fellow of the same sort now. We wish to say nothing against Riddell except that we do not think he is the best fellow for the position. We hope you will excuse us for stating our opinion."

To this extraordinary document all the monitors of Parrett's and Welch's houses present put their names, as well as Gilks and one or two others of the schoolhouse, and after deciding not to present it till next day, by which time it was hoped other signatures might be procured, the august assembly broke up.

The reign of Riddell had not, to say the least of it, opened auspiciously as far as his fellow-monitors were concerned. And outside that body, in Willoughby at large, things did not look much more promising.

The feeling in Parrett's house was of course one of unmingled wrath and mutiny. When once the heads of the house were known to have declared so unmistakably against the new captain, it was not much to be wondered at that the rank and file followed their lead in a still more demonstrative manner.

It happened that Parson and his friends, Telson (who, though a schoolhouse boy, seemed to live most of his life in Parrett's), King, Wakefield, and Lawkins, had planned a little expedition up the river between third school and "call-over" that afternoon, and the present state of affairs in the school formed a rather lively topic of discussion for these worthies as they pulled the Parrett's "Noah's Ark"—by which complimentary title the capacious boat devoted to the use of the juniors of the house was known—lazily up on the tide towards Balsham.

The river was pretty full, as usual at that time of day, and as one form which the wrath of the youthful Parretts took was to insult, and if opportunity arose, to run down the craft of either of the other houses, the discussion on the condition of Willoughby was relieved by more than one lively incident.

"Think of that chap being captain," said Parson, standing up on the back seat, with the rudder-lines in his hands so as to command a good view of the stream ahead. "He couldn't row as well as old Bosher there."

As "old Bosher" was at that moment engaged in super-human efforts to keep his balance with one hand, and extricate his oar, which had feathered two feet under the surface of the water, with the other, this illustration was particularly effective and picturesque.

"Oh, he's an awful cad," said Wakefield, who was rowing bow. "He reported me to Wyndham last term for letting off crackers in bed."

"What a beastly shame!" was the sympathising chorus.

"And you know—" added King.

But as Bosher fell rather violently backward into his lap at this instant, and let his oar go altogether, what King was going to say did not come out.

After a vast amount of manoeuvring, back-watering, shouting, and reaching to recover the lost oar, the voyage proceeded.

They had not proceeded far when the racing-boat of their house, manned by Bloomfield, Game, Tipper, and Ashley, and coached from the bank by Mr Parrett himself, spun past them in fine style and at a great rate. As became loyal Parretts, the juniors pulled into the bank to let the four-oar pass, and, not content with this act of homage, they volunteered a round of vehement applause into the bargain.

"Bravo! Well rowed, our house! Two to one on Parrett's! Three cheers for Bloomfield! Three cheers for the captain! Hooroo!"

With this gratifying salute the boat darted out of sight round the bend, leaving the juniors once more to continue on their festive way.

"Isn't old Bloomfield a stunner?" said Lawkins. "He's the sort of fellow for captain! Not that schoolhouse idiot, Riddell."

"Easy all there about the schoolhouse," shouted down Telson from his place at stroke. "I'll fight you if you say it again."

"Hurrah! let's land and have a mill!" cried King. "I back you, Telson, old man."

"Oh, I didn't mean to cheek you, Telson," said Lawkins, humbly. "I'll apologise, you know."

"Jolly good job," said Telson, grandly, "or I'd have licked you."

"All the same," said Lawkins, "old Bloomfield's—"

"Look out now!" suddenly broke in Parson, who had been gradually getting excited where he stood; "there's the Welchers coming! Pull hard, you fellows, or they'll cut us out. Now then! Row, Bosher, can't you, you old cow? Yah! hoo! Welchers ahoy!" he cried, raising his voice in tones of derisive defiance. "Yah! boo! herrings and dough-nuts, jolly cowards, daren't wait for us! Booh, funk-its!"

With such taunts the Hector of Parrett's endeavoured to incite the enemy to battle. And the enemy, if truth must be told, needed very little persuasion, especially as the crew in question consisted of Cusack, Pilbury, and the three other ill-starred victim of the raid of two days ago.

21

They lay on their oars and waited for the foe to come up, Cusack shouting meanwhile, "Who'd be afraid of a pack of thieves like you! *I* wouldn't! I dare you to land and fight us! Dare you to run into us! Dare you to stand still till we lick you! Dare you to do anything but steal other fellows' grub! Ye-ow!"

"Now, you fellows," cried Parson, "put it on."

A few strokes brought the two boats level, and then, as they lay side by side at oar's distance, ensued a notable and tremendous splashing match, which was kept up with terrific vigour on both sides, until not only was every combatant splashed through, but the two boats themselves were nearly swamped.

Then, after either side had insultingly claimed the victory, the boats separated, and the dripping warriors parted with a final broadside.

"There you are, take that, and go and tell the captain!" shouted Parson.

"You wouldn't dare do it if Bloomfield was captain," retorted the Welchers. "We'll have him captain, then see how you'll smile! Yah! bah!"

And, amid terrific cat-calling on either side, the crews parted.

This last taunt was a sore one for the young Parretts. It had never occurred to them that Bloomfield, if he were captain, might perhaps spoil their sport more than Riddell. But it was only a passing annoyance. After all they were Parretts, and Bloomfield was their man, whether he spoiled their sport or not. Telson had no objection to this sentiment as long as no one presumed "to cheek the schoolhouse" in uttering it. Whenever that was done he insisted on his unalterable determination to fight the offender unless he swallowed his words, which the offender usually did.

The tide was getting slack, and it was time for them to turn if they were to be in for "call-over." Just, however, as they were about to do so, a shout behind attracted them, and they became aware of another four-oared boat approaching with the schoolhouse flag in the prow. It came along at a fair pace, but with nothing like the style which had marked the Parretts' boat.

The crew consisted of Fairbairn, Porter, Coates, and Gilks, with Crossfield steering: the first time a complete schoolhouse crew had appeared on the river this year.

The blood of the young Parretts was up, and the credit of their house was in question.

"Put it on now," said Parson to his men, as the schoolhouse boat came up. "Show 'em what you can do! Now then, slide into it! Race 'em!"

And the young heroes laid into their work and made Noah's Ark forge along at an unwonted pace. Parson busily encouraged them, varying his exhortations by occasional taunts addressed to the other boat.

"Now then," he shouted, "two to one on us. Come on, you there, jolly schoolhouse louts—"

"Parson, I'll fight you if you say it again," interposed Telson by way of parenthesis.

"Oh, beg pardon, old man. Pull away, you fellows! Parretts for ever! No Riddell for us! Three cheers for Bloomfield! You're gaining, you fellows. Oh, well pulled indeed our boat!"

The schoolhouse boat had slackened speed, and paddling gently alongside, was taking careful note of these audacious youngsters, who, puffing and plunging along, fully believed they were beating the picked four of the rival house by their own prowess.

The big boys seemed amused on the whole, and good-humouredly kept up the semblance of a race for about half a mile, taking care to give the challenging crew a wide berth.

At last, after about ten minutes had been spent in this way, and when the young champions were all, except Parson, fairly exhausted, Crossfield took out his watch and said to his crew, winking as he did so, "Time we turned, you fellows; it's five o'clock. Easy all, pull bow side! back water, stroke!"

And so saying, the schoolhouse boat suddenly turned round and started off at a smart pace down stream, where it was soon out of reach of the parting taunts and opprobrious noises which Parson, for the credit of his house, continued to hurl at its crew till they were beyond earshot.

Then it suddenly began to occur to these elated young navigators that if it had been time for the four-oar to turn three minutes ago it was possibly time for them to turn also.

"What did he say the time was?" asked King.

"Five o'clock!" said Lawkins.

"Five o'clock! and call-over is at 5:20! We can't do it in the time!" exclaimed Parson, aghast.

"My eye, what a row there'll be," groaned Telson. "I've been late for call-over twice this week already, and I'm certain to get reported now!"

"So shall I be," said Bosher.

"It's all a vile dodge of those schoolhouse cads," exclaimed King. "I mean," said he (perceiving that Telson was about to make a remark), "of those cads. They did it on purpose to make us late. I see it all now. And then they'll report us. Ugh! did you ever know such blackguards?"

The discovery was too late to be any good—that is, as far as the hope of reaching Willoughby before call-over was concerned. However, it warned them the sooner they turned now the sooner they would get back at all. So they turned viciously and started homewards.

The rowers were all too tired and enraged to talk much, and the journey down stream was silent and gloomy. They heard, about a mile from home, the school bell ringing for call-over, and groaned inwardly when presently it ceased, and they knew their names were being called over and not one of them there to answer. Parson alone made any attempt to keep up the drooping spirits of his crew.

"Never fear. We'll pay them out, you see. And if they do report us we'll only get impots. The beasts! I wish we'd run into them and drowned them all! so I do."

At this point the speaker became aware of an outrigger skiff rapidly approaching them. The rower of course had his back turned, and evidently not expecting anything ahead, was steering himself "over his toes," as the term is—that is by some landmark behind the boat. Who he was Parson could not make out, but he wore a light-blue ribbon on his straw, and that was enough. Light-blue was the schoolhouse colour. Here was a chance of paying out of the enemy, anyhow!

So he ordered his men to "easy all" and allow the unconscious sculler to come close up. Then when he was within a few yards he started up, and with a wild shout of, "Yah booh, cad!" gave the signal to his crew to pull on, and brought his boat close alongside the skiff. The rower, startled by the sudden shout, turned quickly round.

Horror of horrors! It was Mr Parrett himself!

There was no time to do anything. At the instant he turned, his left scull came into violent contact with the oars of the Noah's Ark, and was jerked from his hand, and at the same time the light boat gave a violent lurch over and capsized, sending her occupant headlong into the river!

The small boys, pale with fright and dazed by the suddenness of the accident, sat for a moment unable to move or cry out. Then by a sudden wild impulse Parson sprang boldly into the water, followed in a second or two first by Telson, then by Lawkins. The other three held to the oars and waited where they were.

The tide was running down at a good pace, and the river was fairly wide, but there was not much danger to any of the immersed ones. All Willoughby boys could swim, and as Mr Parrett had taught most of them to do so himself, he hardly stood in need of the help of his three pupils. A few strokes brought them all to the bank in safety.

An uncomfortable moment ensued. Mr Parrett said nothing to the three dripping boys who stood before him, but called to the boys in the boat to row in, bringing the skiff with them.

All the while this was being done, Telson and Parson looked despairingly at one another, and darted scared looks at Mr Parrett. He appeared not to notice them, but stood impatiently waiting for the boats.

"Is the scull broken?" he called out as they approached.

"No, sir," said Wakefield.

The skiff was put in close to the bank, and a brief examination showed that it was not damaged. Mr Parrett got into it, and without saying a word began to push off.

"Please, sir," cried Parson at this point, feeling that his last chance was going, "I'm so sorry. We didn't know it was you, sir. It was all my fault."

"No, sir," shouted Telson, "it was all my fault. We're awfully sorry, sir."

Mr Parrett took no notice of these protestations, but said, quietly, "You'd better get home quickly and change your things."

So saying he sculled off, with a face hardly less puzzled than the small scared faces which, after watching him go, turned dismally to their own unlucky Noah's Ark.

On their arrival at the school some half-hour later, Parson, Telson, Bosher, King, and Lawkins were informed that, having been reported for being absent at call-over, the captain wished to see them in his study after breakfast the next morning.

Later on that same evening another notice reached them that they were wanted in Mr Parrett's room at once.

Chapter Six.

Breakers ahead.

Mr Parrett was a popular master at Willoughby. He was an old Cambridge "blue," and it was to his influence and example that the school in general, and Parrett's house in particular, were chiefly indebted for their excellence in all manly sports. He was the most patient of trainers, and the most long-suffering of "coaches." Nearly all his spare time was given up to the public service. Every afternoon you would be sure to find him in his flannels running along the bank beside some boat, or standing to be bowled at by aspiring young cricketers in the meadow, or superintending a swimming party up at the Willows.

Boys didn't give Mr Parrett credit for all the self-denial he really underwent; for he had a way of seeming to enjoy even the drudgery of his self-imposed work, and it rarely occurred even to the most hopeless of "duffers" to imagine that all the trouble spent over him was anything but a pleasure to the master who spent it.

Mr Parrett had his reward, however, in the good will of the boys generally, which he prized highly, and nowhere was he more popular than among the juniors of his own house.

What was their dismay, therefore, at the accident of that unlucky afternoon, and with what doleful faces did they present themselves in a melancholy procession at the door of his room at the appointed hour!

"Come in," said Mr Parrett, who was still in his flannels, and had not quite done tea. "Oh, you are the boys that I met on the river this afternoon. All except one belonging to my house, I see."

"Yes, sir," exclaimed Telson, who was the distinguished exception, "they're all Parretts except me, and it was all my fault, sir, and I'm—"

"No," interrupted Parson, "it was all my fault; I was steering."

"It was all our faults," said Lawkins.

"Oh," said Mr Parrett, who could not help looking a little amused at the eager faces of the young culprits. "Perhaps it was my fault for not looking where I was coming to."

"Oh, sir," said Parson, "that wouldn't have been any good. We ran you down on purpose."

"Eh?" said Mr Parrett, not quite sure whether he had heard correctly.

"That is, we didn't know it was you, sir; we thought it was a schoolhouse—" (here Telson looked threatening)—"I mean we thought it was some one else. We wouldn't have done it if we thought it was you, sir—indeed we wouldn't."

"No, sir, that we wouldn't," chimed in the chorus.

"And who did you think it was, pray?" inquired Mr Parrett.

"A schoolhouse fellow," replied Parson, avoiding Telson's glances.

"Which schoolhouse boy?" asked the master.

"Any one, sir. It didn't matter much which."

"Indeed. And what has the schoolhouse done to you?" said Mr Parrett, leaning back in his chair and pushing his plate away.

It wasn't an easy question, but Parson felt something ought to be said.

"Some of them are rather cads, sir," he said.

("Parson," whispered Telson. "I'll fight you when you get outside.")

"I mean, sir," said Parson, hurriedly, "that is—(I beg pardon, Telson, old man, I didn't mean)—they don't like us, and—"

"And we don't like them," said Lawkins.

"And you think they ought to like you?" asked Mr Parrett, severely.

This was a poser. The Parrett juniors had never asked themselves the question before.

"Now listen to me," said Mr Parrett. "I'm angry with you, and I'm going to punish you. I am not angry with you for capsizing me this afternoon. You did it by mistake, you say, and no harm was done. And I'm not going to punish you for being out late, for that the captain will do. But boys who make nuisances of themselves and then complain that other boys don't like them are not to be put up with in Willoughby. You five have had a lesson already. You might have caused a much worse accident than you did by your folly. You may be thankful you did not. For a week neither of you is to go on to the river at all, and after that till the end of the term you will only be allowed to go with the captain's permission, or in the company of a senior. You can go."

The party turned to obey, when Mr Parrett added, "Three of you, Telson, Parson, and Lawkins, remain a moment."

The other two went off, leaving their three comrades standing at the end of the table, wondering what on earth was coming next.

Mr Parrett's manner changed as he turned to them. He became embarrassed, and spoke almost nervously.

"You three," he said, "jumped in after me this afternoon, did you not?"

"Yes, please, sir," said Telson; "Parson was first, sir."

Mr Parrett rose from his seat, and, without saying a word, shook hands with each one of them, greatly to their astonishment and confusion.

"You can go now," said the master, when the ceremony was concluded; "good-night, boys."

"Good-night, sir," said they, and filed out of the room.

It was some time before Parson and Telson, as they walked slowly back along the passage, could find words suitable to the occasion. Then Telson said, "Well, that was a rum thing of him to do!"

"What did he mean?" asked Parson.

"Goodness knows. But, I say, it's a jolly soak being stopped the river, though."

"Yes, and having to get a 'permit' when the time is up. I'd sooner not go on than beg a 'permit' of the captain."

"I wonder what he'll say to us to-morrow," said Telson. "He won't lick us, eh?"

"He'd better not," said Parson. "You and I could lick him easy."

"I suppose he'll give us a howling impot. I say I'm getting fagged of impots. I've had four this week."

"I've had three," sighed Telson. "Heigho! Willoughby's going to the dogs. I've a good mind to cut the whole concern."

And so in rather desponding mood the two friends separated, and Telson had an exciting chase across the quadrangle to avoid two monitors who were prowling about there (as he concluded) for the express purpose of "potting" him.

In this, however, he was mistaken. The two monitors were Gilks of the schoolhouse and Silk of Welch's, who were taking the air this hot summer evening, and thinking and talking of anything but Master Telson.

"I tell you," said Gilks, "I detest the fellow."

"You detest such a lot of fellows, Gilks," said Silk.

"I know I do," said Gilks, "but I hate Riddell more than the lot put together."

"I should have thought he was rather an inoffensive duffer," suggested Silk.

"That's just the worst of it. I'd give anything to catch him out in anything that wasn't quite square, just to pay him out for his sickening priggishness. Why," he exclaimed, with increasing anger in his tone, "what do you think he did the other day, long before he was captain, or had any pretence to give himself airs? He pulled me up before all the fellows for—well, for using—"

"For swearing?" said Silk.

"Yes, if you like. For swearing. What business is it of his what I say? I should like to know."

"Usen't Wyndham to be down on fellows for swearing too?" asked Silk.

"Yes, he was," said Gilks (who had good reason to know); "but he had a right to do it. This cub hasn't."

"What did Riddell say?"

"What did he say? He said it didn't make what I said any better worth hearing for sticking in an oath, and that— Oh, I don't know what precious impudence he didn't give me."

"Ha, ha," said Silk, "it wasn't bad. But I agree with you, the fellow is a prig—"

"I know I mean to make a stand now," said Gilks. "He shan't stick up his sanctimonious nose over us all, now he's captain, if I can help it."

"Why, what will you do?" asked Silk.

"Do! I'll punch his head the first time he dare lecture me."

"My dear fellow," said Silk, "don't be such a fool. You won't do a bit of good by that. If you do want to pay him out, pay him out in his own coin."

"How do you mean?" inquired Gilks.

"I mean, keep a sharp lookout till you catch his holiness tripping."

"But the beggar never does trip. He's so vilely careful, he never gives a chance," growled Gilks.

"Awfully uncivil of him, when he knows how grateful we should be to him," said Silk, laughing. "Never mind, old man, keep in with him if you can. Something's sure to turn up. He won't suspect you, as you're in the schoolhouse; and we ought to be able to manage to put a spoke in his wheel somehow."

"Wish you may do it," said Gilks. "Anyhow, I dare say you are right; it's no use flaring up too soon, if there is a chance of doing him. By the way, Fairbairn's pretty nearly as bad as Riddell; they're a pair, you know."

"Yes, but Fairbairn's in the boat," said Silk.

"So he is; and what's more, he's got a spite against me, and wants to turn me out of it."

"Why?"

"He says I don't do enough work. I should like to know how a fellow is to work behind a sanctimonious ass like him?"

"I hear the schoolhouse boat isn't a bad one, even without Wyndham," said Silk.

"Pretty fair. But if I'm in it I'll see it doesn't win," said Gilks.

"What a nice boy you are, to be sure! I suppose you've a bet on Parrett's, like me?"

"No, I haven't," said Gilks, "but I want it to win all the same, because of Bloomfield. If Parrett's gets to the head of the river, there's all the better chance of getting Bloomfield for captain next term; and things would be far pleasanter then."

"Yes. I don't suppose Bloomfield's very particular," said Silk.

"Not he. You can make him do what you like. He's not all the notions of his own that the Reverend Riddell has, hang him!"

"Well, old man," said Silk, "as I said before, you're a nice boy, and a sweet companion for a tender youth like me. Ha, ha! Good-night. Are you one of the deputation that's going to present the petition in the morning?"

"Yes, I am," said Gilks.

"Take my advice and back out of it. It won't come to anything, and if you're not mixed up in it our pious friends will think you are one of them, and that'll pay. Do you twig? Good-night. You *are* a nice boy!"

So saying these two worthies separated.

Gilks acted on his friend's advice, and contrived to be absent after chapel next morning, when it was proposed to present the petition to the doctor. He managed to invent some excuse for his desertion which made it appear it was unavoidable. Nevertheless it was a good deal complained of, because he had been the only representative of the schoolhouse who had promised to go with the others to the doctor.

However it was decided not to postpone the ceremony any further. As it was, one or two were beginning to have their doubts as to its wisdom, and Game and those like him, who were the prime movers in the matter, began to fear the whole thing might fall through.

So, directly after morning chapel, the deputation, consisting of three, marched boldly to the doctor's library and knocked at the door.

"Come in," said Dr Patrick.

He was surprised to see three monitors obey the invitation. It was very rarely that a petition was presented from the school to the head master at Willoughby. Once, some years ago, a petition signed by the entire school, from the captain down to the junior fag, praying for a holiday in honour of an old Willoughbite having led the British troops to victory in a great battle, had been presented and granted. And once since then, a petition from the monitors of each house requesting that the head of each house might be allowed to use the cane when necessary, instead of the captain of the school only, had been presented and declined.

Now came a third petition, signed by certain monitors of two houses, asking the doctor to withdraw one captain and substitute another.

"What is it?" asked the head master.

"A petition, sir," said Game, handing the momentous document in.

The doctor opened it and glanced at it with a puzzled look, which soon darkened into a frown.

"What is all this?" he asked, looking up.

His aspect was not promising. Nevertheless it was necessary for some one to speak, and Game therefore blurted out, "We don't think Riddell will make a good captain, sir, and—" and here stopped.

"And what, sir?" demanded the doctor.

"And," said Game, in rather a faltering voice, "we thought you would not be angry if we petitioned you about it."

"Do you speak for yourself, Game," said the doctor, "or for others?"

"For the monitors, sir; that is, for those who have signed that paper."

The doctor folded up the petition and handed it back to Game without reading it.

"I am glad you have told me what it is all about," said he, sternly, "in time to prevent my reading either the petition or the names attached. It does not do you credit as monitors, and I hope you will soon see the matter in the same light. I did not expect it of you, but I regret it less on your account than on account of the school, to whom you have set a bad example. You may go."

The doctor spoke in tones of unwonted anger, not unmixed with scorn. He rarely "flared up," but when he did it was always uncomfortable for those against whom his wrath was roused.

The deputation slunk off sheepishly, carrying their petition with them, and too glad to get out of the angry presence of the head master to think of anything else.

The doctor may have been right, and probably was right in thus summarily extinguishing the petition and the petitioners. But he had done it in a manner which was hardly calculated to smooth matters.

Indeed, when the deputation reported their bad success to the monitors who awaited them, the general feeling was far more one of anger at being snubbed than of repentance for having done a foolish thing.

"If Paddy had only taken the trouble to read the thing through," said Ashley, "and honour us with one or two reasons for not doing what we asked, it wouldn't have been so bad."

"As it is he's as good as told us to mind our own business and he'll mind his," said Tipper, little thinking how exactly he had described the case.

"If we're not to be allowed to say a word about the management of the school," said Game, "I don't see what right he has to expect us to do his work for him, and keep order."

"Oh, it won't do to resign or anything of that sort," said Ashley. "That would be like funking it altogether."

"He'll soon find his mistake out, never fear," said another. "He won't listen to us, but he can't help believing his own eyes."

"Yes, it can't go on for long," said Tipper. "Riddell's bound to show that he's not up to his work sooner or later, and I won't interfere to prevent it."

"Meanwhile," said Game, who of all the malcontents was the most honest, "what's to become of Willoughby? We must keep some sort of order, whoever is captain."

"Why, whatever authority can we have when the most we can do is to report fellows to that milksop?" said Tipper.

"I'll tell you what," said Ashley, "if we're compelled to *call* Riddell captain, there's nothing to prevent us considering another fellow so."

"What do you mean?" asked some one.

"He means," said Game, "and it's not half a bad idea, that if Bloomfield will help us to keep order, we can consider him captain whether he's called so or not. If once the fellows know they'll get reported to him, we shall have some sort of authority."

"Of course," said Bloomfield, who had not yet spoken, "I'll do my best to keep order and all that; but as I'm not captain, it's no use to pretend being it."

"Oh, we'll see about that," said Ashley. "If you choose to work for the school after what has happened, all I can say is you deserve to be backed up, and I'll back you up for one."

"So will I," said Wibberly.

Bloomfield could not resist flattery. As soon as it was represented to him that the hope of Willoughby centred in him, and that he was acting a beautiful and Christian part in still taking an interest in its welfare after the way he had been treated, he felt as if he really ought to meet his admirers half-way.

"Already a lot of the kids consider you as captain," said Game. "Didn't you hear a boatful of them cheering you yesterday?"

"Yes," said Bloomfield, "I heard that."

"Very well, they're much more likely to keep order for you than for that other fellow. We'll try it anyhow."

"I know a lot of the schoolhouse monitors think just the same as we do," said Tipper, "but they're so precious jealous for their house. They'd sooner stick to Riddell than allow a Parrett's fellow to be cock of the school."

"A Parrett's fellow is cock of the school all the same," said Wibberly. "I wish the regatta was over. That will put things right."

"Yes; when once Parrett's boat is at the head of the river the schoolhouse won't have much to crow for," said Ashley.

"For all that," replied Bloomfield, "they seem to be grinding a bit with the crew they have got."

"Let them grind," said Game, laughing. "I'd as soon back Welch's boat as theirs. Fairbairn's the only man that does any work, and he's no form at all. Why don't they put the new captain in the boat, I wonder?"

The bare idea was sufficient to set the company laughing, in the midst of which the assembly-dispersed.

"By the way," said Game to Ashley, as they went into the "Big," "to-night is the opening meeting of the School Parliament. I mean to propose Bloomfield for president; will you second it?"

"Rather," said Ashley.

Chapter Seven.

The New Captain enters on his Duties.

The morning that witnessed the collapse of the famous Monitors' Petition had not been idly spent by the new captain. He had made the worst possible preparation for his new duties by lying awake half the night, brooding over his difficulties and working himself into a state of nervous misery very unlike what one would expect of the captain of a great public school.

What worried him was not so much that he felt himself unpopular, or that he knew all Willoughby was in arms against him. That wasn't cheerful, certainly, or precisely solacing to a fellow's self-esteem; but it was not nearly so disheartening as the feeling that he himself was unequal to cope with the difficulties he would have to face. How could he cope with them? He had never succeeded yet in keeping Telson, his own fag, in order. How was he to expect to administer discipline to all the scapegraces of Willoughby? It would be bad enough, even if the monitors as a body were working with him, but when he was left almost single-handed, as seemed probable, what chance was there? Whatever would he do supposing a boy was reported to him for some offence, such as going out of bounds or—

By the way! And here a horrible thought flashed across his mind. He had been so flurried last night with one thing and another that he had hardly noticed a message sent him after call-over by the Register Clerk. But it occurred to him now that it was about some boys who had not answered to their names.

He got out of bed with a groan and searched the mantelpiece for the note. Ah! here it was:

"Co. Fr. p.m., Telson (S.H.), Bosher, King, Lawkins, Parson (P), Abs. Go Capt. 8½ Sa. (Telson 2, Bosher 1, Parson 2.)"

After a great deal of puzzling and cogitation Riddell managed to translate this lucid document into ordinary English as follows:

"Call-Over, Friday evening, Telson (schoolhouse), Bosher, King, Lawkins, Parson (Parrett's), absent. To go to the captain at half-past eight on Saturday. (Telson has already been absent twice this week, Bosher once, Parson twice.)" And with the discovery the unhappy captain found his worst fears realised.

Whatever would he do? It was now half-past five. In three hours they would be here. What would Wyndham have done? Caned them, no doubt. Riddell had no cane. Ruler? He might break one of their ringers, or they might resist; or worse still baffle him with some ingenious excuse which he would not know how to deal with.

He sat by his bed staring hopelessly at the paper and wishing himself anywhere but head of the school—and then as no new light appeared to dawn on the question, and as going back to bed would be a farce, he proceeded to dress.

He had just completed his toilet when he heard some one moving in the next study.

"There's Fairbairn getting up," he said to himself. "I wonder if he could help me?"

He thought he could. And yet, under the nervous exterior of this boy there lurked a certain pride which held him back from acting on the impulse. After all, if he was to do the work, why should he try to shunt part of his responsibility on to another?

So, though he went to his friend's study, he said nothing about the batch of juniors from whom he expected a morning call.

Fairbairn was arraying himself in his boating things, and greeted his friend cheerily.

"Hullo, Riddell, here's an early start for you!"

"Yes," said Riddell; "I couldn't sleep very well, so I thought I might as well get up."

"Best thing for you. But why haven't you your flannels on?"

"I'm not going out," said Riddell. "Besides, I don't believe I have flannels," added he.

"What, a Willoughby captain and no flannels! You'll have to get a suit at once, do you hear? But, I say, why don't you come down to the river with Porter and me? We're going to have a little practice spin, and you could steer us. It would do you more good than sticking indoors. Come along."

Riddell protested he would rather not, and that he couldn't steer; but Fairbairn pooh-poohed both objections, and finally carried off his man to the river, where his unwonted appearance in the stern of the schoolhouse pair-oar caused no little astonishment and merriment among the various early visitors who usually frequented the waters of the Craydle.

Despite these unflattering remarks, and despite the constant terror he was in of piloting his boat into the bank, or running foul of other boats, Riddell decidedly enjoyed his little outing, the more so as the exercise and occupation drove away entirely for a time all thoughts of the coming visit of the ill-behaved juniors.

But as soon as he returned to the school the prospect of this ordeal began again to haunt him, and spoilt morning chapel for him completely.

As he stood during the service in his captain's place he could not prevent his eye wandering hurriedly down the ranks of boys opposite and wondering how many of them he would be called upon to interview in his study before the term was over. As he reached the end of the array his eye rested on Telson close to the door, talking and laughing behind his hand with Parson, who listened in an unconcerned way, and looked about him as if he felt himself to be the monarch of all he surveyed. These were two of the boys who would wait upon him in his study immediately after prayers! Riddell turned quite miserable at the idea.

Prayers ended at last, and while the other monitors repaired to the Sixth Form room to discuss the presentation of the petition as narrated in our last chapter, Riddell walked dejectedly to his study and prepared to receive company.

No one came for a long time, and Riddell was beginning to hope that, after all, the dreaded interview was not to come off, or that there was a mistake somewhere, and some one else was to deal with the culprits instead of himself, when a scuttling of footsteps down the passage made his blood run cold and his heart sink into his boots.

"I *must* be cool," he said to himself, fiercely, as a knock sounded at the door, "or I shall make a fool of myself. Come in."

In response to this somewhat tremulous invitation, Telson, Parson, Bosher, Lawkins, King, trooped into his study, the picture of satisfaction and assurance, and stood lounging about the room with their hands in their pockets as though curiosity was the sole motive of their visit.

Riddell, while waiting for them, had hastily considered what he ought to say or do. But now, any ideas he ever had darted from his mind, and he gazed nervously at the small company.

"Oh!" said he at length, breaking silence by a tremendous effort, and conscious that he was looking as confused as he felt, "I suppose you are the boy—"

"Yes," said Bosher, leaning complacently against the table and staring at a picture over the mantelpiece.

"The boys who were late," said Riddell, stammering. "Let me see." Here he took up the paper and began to read it over: "'Co. Pri. Telson (S.H.).' Ah, yes! Telson. You were late, weren't you? Why were you late?"

A question like this was decidedly a novelty; Wyndham's formula had invariably been, "Telson, hold out your hand," and then if Telson had anything to remark he was at liberty to do so. But to be thus invited to make excuses was an unexpected treat which these cunning juniors were quite sharp enough to jump at.

"Oh, you know," began Telson, "it wasn't our fault. We were up-stream in the Ark, and meant to be back all right, only the schoolhouse boat overhauled us, and we had to race them a bit—didn't we, you fellows?"

"Rather," said Parson; "and a spanking race it was. We held up to them all down the Willow Reach, and were just collaring them for the finish up to Balsham Weir, when the beasts pulled in and funked it."

"And then, of course, we couldn't get back in time," said Lawkins. "We were jolly fagged—weren't we, you fellows?—and it was all a plant of those schoolhouse cads."

"Fight you!" said Telson, menacingly.

"Oh, beg pardon, old man, didn't mean. They ran us up on purpose to make us late. You ask them. It was a beastly low trick!"

"And then coming back," continued Telson, "we ran down old Parrett in his skiff and spilt him, and we had to fish him out—didn't we, you chaps?—and that made us late. You ask Parrett; he's potted us for it, last night."

Riddell listened to all this in a bewildered way, not knowing what to make of it. If the boys' story was correct, there certainly might be some force in their excuse. It would hardly be fair to punish them if they were decoyed out of their way by some seniors. And then, of course, this story about Mr Parrett; they would never make up a story like that. And if it was true—well, he did not see how they could have done otherwise than stay and help him out of the water after capsizing him into it. It really seemed to him as if these boys did not deserve to be punished. True, Telson and Parson had been twice late this week, but that was not what they were reported for now. The question was, were they to be chastised for this third offence or not?

"What did Mr Parrett do to you?" he asked presently. "Oh," said Parson, gaily, fully taking in the situation so far, "he was down on us hot. He's stopped our going on the river a week, and then we've got to get a permit till the end of the term. Jolly hard lines it is, especially race term. I shan't be able to cox. Parrett's boat at the regatta. No more will young Telson cox the schoolhouse boat. You ask Parrett," said he, in tones of manly appeal.

"Then you mean Mr Parrett has already punished you?" asked Riddell.

"Rather," said Telson. "I'd sooner have had a licking any day than get stopped river-play. Wouldn't you, Parson?"

"I should think I would," said Parson.

"Well," said Riddell, dubiously, "of course if Mr Parrett has already punished you—"

"You ask him!" again said Parson. "You ask him if he's not stopped our river-play. Ah five of us! Mayn't go on at all for a week, and then we've got to get your permit. Isn't that what he said, you chaps?"

"Yes," chimed in the "chaps," in injured voices.

"Well, then," said Riddell, "as that is so, I think you can—that is, I wish just to tell you—you—it mustn't occur again."

"Oh, all right," said Parson, making for the door.

"And I hope," began Riddell—

But what it was he hoped, his youthful audience did not remain to hear. They had vanished with amazing celerity, and the captain, as he walked pensively up to the door and shut it, could hear them marching jauntily down the passage shouting and laughing over their morning's adventures.

A moment's reflection satisfied Riddell that he had been "done" by these unscrupulous youngsters. He had let them off on their own representations, and without taking due care to verify their story. And now it would go out to all Willoughby that the new captain was a fool, and that any one who liked could be late for call-over if only he had the ingenuity to concoct a plausible story when he was reported. A nice beginning this to his new reign! Riddell saw it all clearly now, when it was too late. Why ever had he not seen it as clearly at the time?

Was it too late? Riddell went to the door again and looked down the passage. The young malefactors were out of sight, but their footsteps and voices were still audible. Hadn't he better summon them back? Had not he better, at any cost to his own pride, own that he had made a mistake, rather than let the discipline of Willoughby run down?

He took a few hurried steps in the direction of the voices, and was even making up his mind to run, when it suddenly occurred to him, "What if, after all, their story *had* been true, and the calling of them back should be a greater mistake even than the letting of them off?"

This awkward doubt drove him back once more to his study, where, shutting the door, he flung himself into his chair in a state of abject despondency and shame.

Twenty times he determined to go to the doctor at once, and refuse for an hour longer to play the farce of being captain of Willoughby. And as often another spirit kept him back, and whispered to him that it was only the cowards who gave in at a single failure.

From these unpleasant reflections the summons to first school was a welcome diversion, and he gladly shook off the captain for an hour, and figured in his more congenial part of a scholar. But even here he was not allowed wholly to forget his new responsibilities. Nearly all those around him were fellow-monitors, who had just come smarting from the doctor's summary rejection of their petition; and Riddell could tell by their angry looks and ill-tempered words that he, however innocent, was the object of their irritation. He had never been a favourite before, but it certainly was not pleasant to have to learn now by the most unmistakable signs that he was downrightly unpopular and disliked by those from whom he should have had his warmest backing up.

And yet, strange to say, it was this sense of his own unpopularity which more than anything nerved him to a resolution to stick to his post, and, come what would of it, do his best to discharge his new unwelcome tasks. If only he could feel a little more sure of himself! But how was it likely he could feel sure of himself after his lamentable failure of the morning?

But the lamentable failure of the morning, as it happened, was nothing to other failures speedily to follow on this same unlucky day.

Scarcely was Riddell back in his study after first school, hoping for a little breathing space in which to recover his fluttered spirits, when Gilks entered and said, "I say, there's a row going on in the Fourth. You'd better stop it, or the doctor will be down on us."

And so saying he vanished, leaving the captain about as comfortable with this piece of intelligence as he would have been with a bombshell suddenly pitched into his study.

A row in the Fourth! the headquarters of the Limpets, each one of whom was a stronger man than he, and whom Wyndham himself had often been put to it to keep within bounds!

With an ominous shiver Riddell put on his cap and sallied out in the direction of the Fourth. A man about to throw himself over a precipice could hardly have looked less cheerful!

Gilks's report had certainly been well founded, for long before the captain reached his destination the roar of battle sounded up the passage. It may have been an ordinary Limpet row, or it may have been a special diversion got up (with the connivance of one or two unfriendly monitors) for the special benefit of the new captain. Be that as it may, it was a disturbance calling for instant suppression, and the idea of Riddell going to suppress it was ridiculous even to himself.

He opened the door, unnoticed by the combatants within both on account of the noise and the dust. It was impossible to tell what the fight was about; the blood on both sides was evidently up, and the battle, it was clear, was anything but a mock one. Riddell stood there for some time a bewildered and unrecognised spectator. It would be useless for him to attempt to make himself heard above all the din, and worse than useless to attempt single-handed to interpose between the combatants. The only thing to do seemed to be to wait till the battle was over. But then, thought Riddell, what would be the use of interfering when it was all over? His duty was to stop it, and stop it he must!

With which resolve, and taking advantage of a momentary lull in the conflict, he advanced with a desperate effort towards a boy who appeared to be the leader of one of the two parties, and who was gesticulating and shouting at the top of his voice to encourage his followers. This champion did not notice the captain as he approached, and when he did, he mistook him for one of the enemy, and sprang at him like a young tiger, knocking him over just as the ranks once more closed, and the battle began again.

What might have been Riddell's fate it would be hard to say had not a loud shout of, "Man down there! Hold hard!" suddenly suspended hostilities.

Such a cry was never disregarded at Willoughby, even by the most desperate of combatants, and every one stood now impatiently where he was, waiting for the obstruction to regain his feet.

The spectacle which the new captain of Willoughby presented, as with scared face and dust-covered garment he rose slowly from the floor, was strange indeed. It was a second or two before any one recognised him, and then the boys seemed not to be sure whether it was not his ghost, so mysteriously had he appeared in their midst, coming from no one knew where.

As, however, the true state of affairs gradually dawned on them, a loud shout of laughter rose on every hand, and the quarrel was at once forgotten in the merriment occasioned by this wonderful apparition.

Riddell, pale and agitated, stood where he was as one in a dream, from which he was only aroused by voices shouting out amid the laughter, "Hullo! where did you come from? What's the row? Look at him!"

At the same time fellows crowded round him and offered to brush him down, accompanying their violent services with bursts of equally violent merriment.

With a hard effort Riddell shook himself free and stepped out of the crowd.

"Please let me go," he said. "I just came to say there was too much noise, and—"

But the laughter of the Limpets drowned the rest, in the midst of which he retired miserably to the door and escaped.

In the passage outside he met Bloomfield, with Wibberly and Game, hurrying to the scene of the riot. They scarcely deigned to recognise him with anything more than a half-curious, half-contemptuous glance.

"Some one must stop this row!" said Bloomfield to his companions as they passed. "The doctor will be down on us."

"You stop it, Bloomfield!" said Wibberly; "they'll shut up for *you*."

This was all the unfortunate Riddell heard, except that in a few moments the uproar from the Fourth Form room suddenly ceased, and was not renewed.

"What did Bloomfield do this morning when he came into your room?" asked Riddell that evening of Wyndham junior, a Limpet in whom, for his brother's sake, the new captain felt a special interest, and whom he invited as often as he liked to come and prepare his lessons with him.

"Oh!" said Wyndham, who had been one of the combatants, "he gave Watkins and Cattermole a hiding, and swore he'd allow no removes from the Limpets' eleven to the school second this term if there was any more row."

This reply by no means added to Riddell's comfort.

"Gave Cattermole and Watkins a hiding." Fancy *his* attempting to give Cattermole and Watkins a hiding! And not only that, he had held out some awful threat about Limpets' cricket, which appeared to have a magical effect.

Fancy the effect of *his* threatening to exclude a Limpet from the second-eleven—when it was all he knew that the school had a second-eleven!

The difficulties and perplexities which had loomed before him in the morning were closing around him now in grim earnest! The worst he had feared had happened, and more than the worst. It was now proved beyond all doubt that he was utterly incompetent. Would it not be sheer madness in him to attempt this impossible task a day longer?

The reader has no doubt asked the same question long ago. Of *course* it's madness of him to attempt it. A muff like Riddell never *could* be captain of a school, and it's all bosh to suppose he could be. But, my dear reader, a muff like Riddell *was* the captain of a school; and what's more he didn't give it up even after the day's adventures just described.

Riddell was not perfect. I know it is an unheard-of thing for a good boy in a story-book not to be perfect, and that is one reason which convinces me this story of mine must be an impossible one. Riddell was not perfect. He had a fault. Can you believe it—he had many faults? He even had a besetting sin, and that besetting sin was pride. Not the sort of pride that makes you consider yourself better than your neighbours. Riddell really couldn't think that even had he wished it. But his pride was of that kind which won't admit of anybody to help it, which would sooner knock its head to bits against a stone wall than own it can't get through it, and which can never bring itself to say "I am beaten," even when it is clear to all the world it is beaten.

Pride had had a fall this day at any rate; but it had risen again more stubborn than ever; and if Riddell went to bed that night the most unhappy boy in Willoughby, he went there also resolving more than ever to remain its captain.

Other events had happened that day which, one might suppose, should have convinced him he was attempting an impossibility. But these must be reserved for the next chapter.

Chapter Eight.

The Willoughby Parliament in Session.

The "Parliament" at Willoughby was one of the very old institutions of the school. Old, white-headed Willoughbites, when talking of their remote schooldays, would often recall their exploits "on the floor of the house," when Pilligrew (now a Cabinet Minister) brought in his famous bill to abolish morning chapel in winter, and was opposed by Jilson (now Ambassador to the Court at Whereisit) in a speech two hours long; or when old Coates (a grandfather, by the way, of the present bearer of that name in the school) divided the house fifteen times in one afternoon on the question of presenting a requisition to the head master to put more treacle into the suet puddings! They were exciting days, and the custom had gone on flourishing up to the present.

The Willoughby Parliament was an institution which the masters of the school wisely connived at, while holding aloof themselves from its proceedings. There was no restraint as to the questions to be discussed or the manner and time of the discussion, provided the rules of the school were not infringed. The management was entirely in the hands of the boys, who elected their own officers, and paid sixpence a term for the privilege of a seat in the august assembly.

The proceedings were regulated by certain rules handed down by long tradition according to which the business of the House was modelled as closely as possible on the procedure of the House of Commons itself. Every boy was supposed to represent some place or other, and marvellous was the scouring of atlases and geography books to discover constituencies for the young members. There was a Government and an Opposition, of course, only in the case of the former the "Ministers" were elected by the votes of the whole assembly, at the beginning of each session. They were designated by the titles of their office. There was a Premier and a Home Secretary, and a First Lord of the Admiralty, and so on, and great was the pride of a Willoughbite when he first heard himself referred to as the Right Honourable!

Everything that came before the house had to come in the form of a bill or a resolution. Any one anxious to bring up a subject (and there was nothing to prevent the junior fag bringing in a bill if he liked) usually handed in his motion early in the session, so as to stand a good chance of getting a date for his discussion. Later on, when more subjects were handed in than there were evenings to debate them, the order was decided by ballot, and due notice given every Friday of the business for the next evening.

Another feature of these meetings was, of course, the questions. Any one was entitled to question the "Government" on matters affecting the school, and the putting and answering of these questions was usually the most entertaining part of an evening's business. Naturally enough, it was not always easy to decide to whose department many of the questions asked belonged, but tradition had settled this to some extent. The Home Secretary had to answer questions about the monitors, the First Lord of the Admiralty about the boats, the Secretary of State for War about fights, and so on, while more doubtful questions were usually first asked of the Premier, who, if he didn't find it convenient to answer them, was entitled to refer the inquirer to some other member of the Government.

It need hardly be said that the meetings of the Willoughby Parliament were occasionally more noisy than dignified, and yet there existed a certain sense of order and respect for the "authority of the House" which held the members in check, and prevented the meetings from degenerating into riots. Another reason for the same result existed in the doctor, who sanctioned the Parliament only as long as it was conducted in an orderly manner, and did not offend against the rules of the school. And a final and more terrible reason still was in the fact that the House had the power of expelling a member who was generally obnoxious.

The session at Willoughby always opened on the Saturday after the May sports, and notice had been duly given that Parliament would assemble this year on the usual date, and that the first business would be the election of a Speaker and a Government.

The reader will easily understand that, under present circumstances, an unusual amount of interest and curiosity centred in the opening meeting of the school senate, and at the hour of meeting the big dining-hall, arranged after the model of the great House of Commons, was, in spite of the fact that it was a summer evening, densely packed by an excited assembly of members.

Most of the boys as they entered had stopped a moment to read the "order paper," which was displayed in a prominent place beside the door. It was crowned with notices, the first three of which gave a good idea of the prospect of a lively evening.

1. "That the captain of the school be elected Speaker of this House." Proposed by T. Fairbairn; seconded by E. Coates.

2. "That Mr Bloomfield be elected Speaker of this House." Proposed by G. Game; seconded by R. Ashley.

3. "That Francis Cusack, Esquire, member for the Isle of Wight, be elected Speaker of this House." Proposed, A. Pilbury, Esquire; seconded, L. Philpot, Esq.

The humour of the last notice was eclipsed by the seriousness of the other two. It had always been taken for granted that the captain of Willoughby was also the Speaker of the House, and a contested election for that office was without precedent. Now, however, the old rule was to be challenged; and as the members waited for the clock to strike six they discussed the coming contest among themselves with a solemnity which could hardly have been surpassed in Westminster itself.

The clock sounded at last; every one was in his place. The seniors sat ranged on the front benches on either side of the table, and the others crowded the benches behind them, impatiently waiting for the proceedings to commence.

According to custom, Riddell, as captain of the school, rose, and briefly proposed, "That Mr Isaacs, Senior Limpet, be requested to preside until after the election of a Speaker."

The appearance of the captain to move this resolution had always been the signal for a loud ovation from the House. But this year the cheers were confined to a very small cluster of schoolhouse boys, and died away languidly in the general silence which prevailed elsewhere. Riddell's motion being seconded and carried, Mr Isaacs, a pallid unintelligent-looking Limpet, rose and advanced to the chair at the end of the table usually occupied by the Chairman of Committees, and, knocking with a hammer once or twice, demanded silence. This being secured, he called out, "Mr Fairbairn!" and sat down.

Fairbairn's speech was brief and to the point.

"I beg to move that the captain of the school be elected Speaker of this House. I don't know that I need say anything in support of this." ("Oh, oh!" from a voice opposite.) "The captain always has been Speaker, and Mr Riddell has already taken an active part in the business of the house and knows what the Speaker's duties are. We all miss old Wyndham,"—(loud cheers)—"but I'm sure Riddell will be a worthy successor to him in the chair of this House."

Coates having said, "I beg to second the motion," Mr Isaacs put it to the meeting, and asked if there was any amendment. Whereupon Game rose, amid loud cheers from all quarters.

Game, as has already been said, was an honest fellow. He meant what he said, and generally said what he meant. He was fully convinced in his own mind that Willoughby would go to the dogs under the new captain, and therefore if Riddell had been his own twin-brother he would have protested against him all the same.

"I beg to move an amendment," he said, "and it is this: That Mr Bloomfield be appointed Speaker of this House instead of Mr Riddell." (It will be noticed by the way that when Willoughby sat in Parliament everybody was "Mr") "And the reason I do so is because I consider Mr Bloomfield ought to be captain of the school instead of Mr Riddell. (Loud Parrett cheers.) I've nothing to say against Mr Riddell—(cheers from the schoolhouse)—except that I don't consider he's the right man in the right place. (Great applause.) He's been made captain against our wishes,"—("Hear, hear," and "Oh, oh!")—"and we can't help it. But we're not obliged to have him captain here, and what's more, we don't mean to! (Terrific cheers, especially from the juniors.) Mr Bloomfield's our man. Only to-day he stopped a row in the Fourth in two minutes which Mr Riddell couldn't have stopped if he'd stayed till now." (Laughter, and cries of "Give him a clothes-brush!") "The fellows all look up to Mr Bloomfield. He ran grandly for the school at the sports the other day, and licked the London fellow. (Here the enthusiasm became positively deafening.) What's Mr Riddell done for the school? I should like to know. We want a fellow who has done something for the school, and, I repeat, Mr Bloomfield's our man, and I hope you'll elect him Speaker."

Game sat down amidst a tempest of applause, which brought a flush of pleasure even to his serious face.

Many curious eyes were turned to Riddell to see the effect of this uncomplimentary oration upon him.

At first he had looked nervous and uncomfortable, and had even whispered to Fairbairn, who sat next him, "Don't you think I'd better go?"

"For goodness' sake, no!" exclaimed Fairbairn. "Don't be a fool, Riddell."

The caution had its weight. Riddell saw he must brave it out; and that being settled, he felt more comfortable, and listened to all the unpleasant things that were said in a composed manner which greatly perplexed his adversaries.

Ashley, who seconded Game's motion, was hardly so fortunate in his remarks as his predecessor.

"I second the motion, gentlemen," he said. "It's time we made a stand against this sort of thing." ("What sort of thing?" from voices on the schoolhouse side.) "Why, schoolhouse tyranny. (Frantic Parrett cheers.) Why is the whole credit of Willoughby to be sacrificed for the sake of your precious schoolhouse?" ("Question!" "Order!" drowned by renewed cheers.) "Why, just because he's a schoolhouse fellow, is a muff to be stuck over us? and just because he's a Parrett's fellow, is a splendid fellow like Mr Bloomfield to be snubbed in the face of the whole school? (Loud cheers.) It's time Willoughby found out that Parrett is the cock house of the school." ("Oh! oh!" from the Welchers.) "It's got the best men in it. (Parrett cheers.) It's head of the river." ("Oh no, not yet," from Fairbairn.) "Well, it will be very soon. It's ahead in everything." ("Except intelligence," from Crossfield.) "No, I don't even except intelligence. (Loud cheers from Bosher, and laughter.) And, as a sign of its intelligence, I beg to second the motion."

This abrupt and somewhat vague termination to Ashley's spirited address did not detract from the applause with which it was greeted by his own partisans, or from the wrath with which it was received by the schoolhouse boys.

The moment he sat down Crossfield sprang to his feet. This was the signal for loud schoolhouse cheers, and for general attention from all quarters, for Crossfield usually had something to say worth listening to.

"Mr Limpet, sir,"—(loud laughter; Isaacs, who had been drawing niggers on the paper before him, started, and blushed very much to find himself thus appealed to)—"I am sure we are all much obliged to the honourable member who has just sat down for the 'sign of intelligence' he has just favoured us with. (Laughter.) We've been looking for it for a long time—(laughter)—and it's come at last! (Cheers and laughter.) Sir, it would be a great pity to let such an occasion pass without notice. I'm not sure that the doctor might not think it worth a half-holiday. A sign of intelligence from the hon. gentleman! And what is the sign, sir? (Laughter.) The hon. member seconds the motion." ("Hear, hear!" from Parrett's.) "Gentlemen of the same party say 'Hear, hear!' as much as to say, 'We, too, show signs of intelligence!' Do you really, gentlemen? I could not have believed it. (Loud laughter.) Why does he second the motion? Because he's a Parrett's boy, and Mr Bloomfield is a Parrett's boy, and all Parrett's boys say a Parrett's boy ought to be the head of the school! Gentlemen, parrots aren't always to be trusted, even when they show signs of intelligence! (Cheers and laughter.) Don't you believe all a parrot tells you about parrots. (Laughter.) I prefer the arguments of the gentleman who moved the amendment. He says he doesn't think Mr Riddell is fit to be captain. (Cheers.) I agree with him—(tremendous Parrett's cheers, and consternation of schoolhouse)—I don't think Mr Riddell is fit to be captain. He doesn't think so himself." ("Hear, hear!" from Riddell, and laughter.) "But the gentleman says Mr Bloomfield is the man. (Loud cheers.) I don't agree with that at all. Mr Riddell knows very little about sports, though I do hear he was seen coxing a schoolhouse boat this morning. (Derisive cheers.) Mr Bloomfield knows almost as little about classics! (Loud laughter from the schoolhouse.) Why, gentlemen, do you mean to say you think a fellow who couldn't translate 'Balbus hopped over a wall' without looking up three words in a lexicon is fit to be a Willoughby captain?" (Laughter from the juniors, and cries of "Time!" from Parretts.) "I say not. Even though he's a Parrett's boy, and therefore can show a sign of intelligence! (Laughter.) No; what I say is, whether we believe in him or not, Mr Riddell is captain; and until you can show me a less bad one, I'll vote for him."

This oration, delivered with great animation and amidst constant laughter, helped to put the meeting in rather better humour, all except the Parrett's fellows, who did not enjoy it at all.

However, before any of them could make up his mind to reply, a shrill voice was heard from the other end of the hall, "Sir! It is time the Welchers had a word!"

This innocent announcement caused a loud burst of laughter, in which every one joined, especially when it was discovered that the orator was none other than the youthful Mr Pilbury himself!

He stood surrounded by a small cluster of admiring juniors, who glared defiantly out on the assembly generally, and "backed up their man" till he could hardly breathe.

"It's all very well," screamed Pilbury. (Loud cheers from Cusack and Philpot.) But here the chairman's hammer sounded and cries of "Order" checked the orator's progress.

"The hon. member," said Isaacs, "cannot propose his motion till the motion before the House is disposed of."

Pilbury scowled fiercely at the speaker.

"I *shall* propose it," he cried, "and you'd better shut up, old Ikey!"

Game, amid much laughter, rose to order, and asked if these expressions were parliamentary?

Isaacs said, "Certainly not, and Mr Pilbury must withdraw them."

Mr Pilbury said "he'd withdraw his grandmother," and attempted to continue his speech, when Fairbairn rose and suggested to the hon. member that if he would only wait a bit the House would be delighted to hear him. After this conciliatory advice Pilbury let himself be pulled down into his seat by his admirers, and the debate on Game's amendment continued.

It was hot and exciting. The arguments were mostly on the side of the schoolhouse, and the vehemence on the side of Parrett's. Once or twice a Welcher dropped in a speech, attacking both parties and once or twice a schoolhouse boy spoke in favour of Bloomfield, or a Parrett's boy spoke in favour of Riddell. At last, after about an hour's angry debate, the House divided. That is, all those in favour of Game's amendment moved over to one side of the room, and those against it to the other, and those who did not want to vote at all kept their seats in the middle.

There was no need to count the numbers of the rival parties as they stood. Only about twenty-five stood beside Fairbairn and the schoolhouse, while nearly two hundred and fifty boys crowded the side of the room along which Game and his followers took their stand. The triumph of the opponents to the new captain was complete, and the school had given him and the head master a most emphatic reply to the late appointment.

Riddell would have much preferred to be allowed to withdraw of his own accord rather than remain to be beaten. But his friends had all opposed the idea as cowardly, and he had given in to them. He now took his defeat very placidly, and even joined in the laughter which greeted Mr Isaac's call.

"Now, Mr Pilbury!"

Mr Pilbury was "off his speech." If he had been allowed to proceed when he first rose, he had the steam up and could have let out, as he told his friends; but now the spirit had been taken out of him. However, he was compelled to make an effort, and began as before, "Sir, it is time the Welchers had a word."

He didn't mean anything funny, he was certain, but everybody laughed.

"Why shouldn't old Cusack here—" ("Order, order")—"What's the row?"

Isaacs informed the hon. gentleman that members of that House were always called "Mr"

"Mr Cusack, then," said Pilbury, "it's just a dodge of Ikey to floor me in my speech. Why shouldn't old Mr Cusack— Eh, what say?"

This was addressed to Philpot, who was eagerly trying to prompt his ally.

"Go it, let out at them," he whispered.

"Why shouldn't old Mr Cusack go it and let out—that is—all right, Philpot, you pig, I'll pay you out, see if I don't. Why shouldn't old Mr Cusack, gentlemen—er—"

"Do," suggested Cusack himself.

"Do," shouted Pilbury, "do, gentlemen—do? Why shouldn't—(all right, Gus Telson, I see you chucking darts)—why shouldn't old Mr Cusack—"

"Does any gentleman second the amendment?" asked Mr Isaacs, evidently getting hungry and anxious to be released from his post.

"Yes," shouted Philpot, "Mr Gentlemen, yes, I do—and—"

"Wait a bit, you howling cad," exclaimed Pilbury, in excitement. "I've not done yet!"

"Mr Philpot!" said Mr Isaacs.

"Philpot be blowed," cried the irate Pilbury, "wait till I'm done."

"Order, order," shouted members on all sides.

"Moved by Mr Pilbury, seconded by Mr Philpot," began Isaacs.

"Easy all," cried Philpot, "I've not spoken yet."

"Order, order," cried Isaacs.

"Order yourself," retorted Philpot, "I've got a right to speak."

"So have I," said Pilbury, "and I was up first."

"Forge away," said Philpot, "you'll be all right."

"Nothing to do with you if I *am* all right," snarled Pilbury.

"You seem to think you're the only fellow can talk."

"Ays to the right, noes to the left," said Isaacs, in a loud voice.

The House instantly divided, and before either Pilbury or Philpot could make up their minds about proceeding, the motion had been declared lost by a majority of three hundred odd to one.

In a great state of wrath the injured Welchers left the hall, making as much noise as they possibly could in doing so.

As soon as they were gone, Isaacs put the question that Bloomfield be elected Speaker, and this was carried without a division, the schoolhouse fellows not caring to demand one.

Amid loud and long-continued cheers the new Speaker took his seat, and as soon as silence could be restored, said, "I'm much obliged to you all for your vote. I hope Willoughby won't go down. I'll try to prevent it for one. (Loud cheers.) I'm very proud to be elected your Speaker, and feel it quite as much honour as if I was captain of the school." (Loud cries of "So you are!"—from Parrett's.) "In reference to what one gentleman said about me, I hope you won't believe it. I'm twelfth in classics. (Laughter from the schoolhouse and terrific applause from Parrett's.) That's all I have to say."

The remaining business of the afternoon was dull compared with what had gone before. The elections for the various posts in the Government did not excite very much enthusiasm, especially among the juniors, who deserted the meeting soon after they began. After what had occurred it is hardly to be wondered at that the partisans of Bloomfield and the Parretts had the matter pretty much in their own hands, and used it to their own advantage. When the list was finally declared, it was found that only one schoolhouse fellow, Porter, had a place in the "Cabinet." He was appointed Chancellor of the Exchequer. Game was First Lord of the Admiralty, Wibberly, War Secretary, Ashley, Home Secretary, and Strutter, a comparatively obscure boy, Premier. All these, as well as the other officers appointed, were Parrett's fellows, who may have flattered themselves their election was a simple recognition of merit in each case, but who, taken altogether, were a long way off being the most distinguished boys of Willoughby.

Parliament did not adjourn till a late hour that evening, and no one was particularly sorry when it did.

Chapter Nine.

A Scientific Afternoon in Welch's.

"Pil," said Cusack, a few days after the unfortunate end to that gentleman's "motion" in Parliament—"Pil, it strikes me we can do pretty much as we like these times. What do you think?"

"Well, I don't know," said Pil, meditatively; "I got a pot from Coates to-day for playing fives against the schoolhouse door."

"Oh yes; of course, if you fool about out of doors you'll get potted. What I mean is, indoors here there's no one to pull us up that I can see."

"Oh! I see what you mean," said Pil. "Yes, you're about right there."

"Gully, you know," continued Cusack—"Gully's no good as master of a house; he's always grubbing over his books. Bless his heart! it doesn't matter to him whether we cut one another's throats!"

"Not it! I dare say he'd be rather glad if we did," replied Pilbury.

"Then there's Tucker. No fear of his reporting us, eh!"

"Rather not! when he's always breaking rules himself, and slinking down to Shellport, and kicking up rows with the other chaps. What do you think I found in his brush-and-comb bag the other day? Thirteen cigar-ends! He goes about collecting them in Shellport, I suppose, and finishes them up on the quiet."

"Oh, he's a beast!" said Cusack. "And old Silk's about as bad. He doesn't care a bit what we do as long as he enjoys himself. Don't suppose he'd be down on us, do you?"

"No fear! He might pot us now and then for appearances' sake, but he wouldn't report us, I guess."

"And suppose he did," said Cusack; "the new captain's as big a muff as all the lot of them put together. He's afraid to look at a chap. Didn't you hear what he did to the Parrett's kids the other day?"

"Yes; didn't I!" exclaimed Pilbury. "He let them all off, and begged their pardons or something. But I'm jolly glad Parrett was down on them. He's stopped their river-play, and they won't be able to show up at the regatta."

"I'm jolly glad!" said Cusack; "chaps like them deserve to catch it, don't they, Pil?"

"Rather!" replied Pilbury.

A silence ensued, during which both heroes were doubtless meditating upon the unexampled iniquities of the Parrett juniors.

Presently Pilbury observed somewhat dolefully, "Beastly slow, isn't it, Cusack?"

"What's beastly slow?"

"Oh, everything! No fun kicking up a row if there's no one to pull you up. I'm getting sick of rows."

Cusack stared at his friend with rather concerned looks. He could not be well, surely, or he would never come out with sentiments like those.

"Fact is," continued Pilbury, contemplatively balancing himself on one foot on the corner of the fender, "I've half a notion to go in for being steady this term, old man, just for a change."

As if to suit the action to the word, the fender suddenly capsized under him, and shot him head first into the waistcoat of his friend.

Cusack solemnly restored him to his feet and replied, "Rather a rum start, isn't it?"

"Well," said Pilbury, examining his shin to see if it had been grazed by the treacherous fender, "I don't see what else there is to do. Any chap can fool about. I'm fagged of fooling about; ain't you?"

"I don't know," said Cusack, doubtfully. "It's not such a lark as it used to be, certainly."

"What do you say to going it steady this term?" asked Pilbury.

"Depends on what you mean by 'steady.' If you mean never going out of bounds or using cribs, I'm not game."

"Oh, I don't mean that, you know," said Pilbury. "What I mean is, shutting up rows, and that sort of thing."

"What can a fellow do?" asked Cusack, dubiously.

"Oh, lots to do, you know," said Pilbury—"dominoes, you know, or spellicans. I've got a box at home."

"Jolly slow always playing dominoes," said Cusack, "or spellicans."

"Well, then, there's—"

"Hold hard!" broke in Cusack, struck with a sudden idea. "What's the name of the thing old Philpot's always at?"

"What, chemistry? Jolly good idea, old man! Let's go in for that."

"Not a bad lark," said Cusack—"lots of explosions and things. Philpot told me he could make Pharaoh's serpents, and smells like rotten eggs. We'll get him to coach us, eh, Pil?"

"I'm game," said Pil, no less delighted than his friend at this happy thought.

And, full of their new idea of "going it steady," the two worthies forthwith sallied out and made hue and cry for Philpot.

Unless Philpot in his leisure moments was engaged in some predatory expedition, or happened to be serving a term of imprisonment in the detention room, it was a pretty safe guess to look for him in the laboratory, where as an ardent student of science he was permitted to resort, and within certain limits practise for himself. Philpot himself bore the office of "second under bottle-washer" in Willoughby; that is, he assisted the boy who assisted the chemistry fag who assisted the assistant master to the science master; and *on* the strength of this distinction he was allowed some special privileges in the way of improving himself in his favourite branch of study. He was on the whole rather a promising pupil, and had a very fair idea of the properties of the several substances he was allowed to experiment with. Indeed he had had to pass an examination and perform some experiments in the presence of the master before he was allowed to enter the laboratory as a private student at all. No one knew exactly how he distinguished himself on that occasion, or how he succeeded with his experiments, but it was well-known that, if he had succeeded then, he had never done so since; that is, according to anybody's idea but his own.

Cusack and Pilbury found him busy blowing through a tube into a bottle of water, looking very like a purple cherub bursting at the cheeks. He was so engrossed with his task that he did not even notice their entry, indeed it was not till Pilbury had stepped behind him and clapped him suddenly on either side of the face, making his cheeks explode like a small balloon, and spilling the contents of his bottle all over the table, that he became aware that he had visitors. "What a frightful idiot you are, Pilbury!" he exclaimed; "you've spoilt that whole experiment. I wish you'd shut up fooling and get out."

"Awfully sorry, old man," said Pilbury, "but you did look so jolly puffed out, you know; didn't he, Cusack?"

"Now you've done, you'd better hook it," said Philpot, "you've not got leave to come here."

"Oh, don't be riled," said Cusack; "the fact is, Pil and I came to see if you'd put us up to a thing or two in this sort of business."

"We've gone on the steady, Phil, you know," explained Pilbury, in conciliatory tones, "and thought it would be rather jolly if we three worked up a little chemistry together."

"We'd watch you do the things at first, of course," said Cusack, "till we twigged all the dodges."

"And it would be jolly good practice for you, you know, in case ever old Mix-'em-up is laid up, and you have to lecture instead."

Philpot regarded his two would-be pupils doubtfully, but softened considerably as they went on.

"You'll have to promise not to fool," said he, presently, "or there'll be a row."

"Oh, rather; we won't touch anything without asking, will we, Pil?" replied Cusack. "Awfully brickish of you, Philpot."

Philpot took the compliment very complacently, and the two students settled themselves one on either side of the table and waited for operations to begin.

"Wire in, old man," said Pilbury, encouragingly; "cut all the jaw, you know, and start with the experiments. Can't you give us a jolly flare-up to begin with?"

"All serene," said Philpot, who had now quite recovered his humour, and was pleased to find himself in the position of an instructor of youth, "wait a bit, then."

He reached down from a shelf a large saucer containing water, in which lay a round substance rather like the end of a stick of peppermint-rock. On this Philpot began to operate with a pair of scissors, greatly to the amusement of his spectators, for try all he would he couldn't get hold of it.

"What are you trying to do?" said Cusack.

"Cut a bit off," said Philpot, trying to stick the substance with a long bodkin, in order to hold it steady.

"Why, that's not the way to cut it, you old dolt," said Pilbury. "Here, I'll do it," and he advanced to the saucer.

"What'll you do?"

"Why, fish it out, of course, and cut it then."

"You'd better not try. It's phosphorus."

"Is it, though—and what does it do?"

"Burn you, rather, unless you keep it in water. Ah, got him at last."

So saying Philpot triumphantly spiked the obstinate piece of phosphorus, and succeeded in cutting off a small piece.

"Is that what makes the flare-up?" asked Cusack.

"Yes, wait a bit, till I get the jar."

"What jar?" asked Pilbury. "Here's one; will this do?"

"Look out, I say!" exclaimed Philpot, in great excitement; "let it go, will you?"

"What's the row?" asked Pilbury and Cusack, both in alarm.

"Why, that's got my oxygen in it," cried Philpot, securing the bottle and gently lifting it on to the table, taking care to hold the glass plate that covered the mouth in its place.

"Got his what in it?" asked Cusack.

"Oxygen. It took me an hour to get."

"There's nothing in that empty jar," said Pilbury, laughing. "Isn't there, though?" said Philpot; "it's full."

"You mean to say that jar's full of something," said Cusack. "Look here, don't you try to stuff us up. What's the use of saying it's full when it's empty?"

"It's full of gas, I tell you," said Philpot. "Don't you talk till you know."

This rebuke somewhat silenced the two devotees of science, who, however, continued to regard the jar sceptically and rather contemptuously.

Philpot next dived into a drawer and drew from it a large cork, through which passed a long wire having a small cup at the lower end.

"Now look out," he said.

He proceeded to shovel the small piece of phosphorus into the little cup under the cork, and drawing it out of the water, applied a light. The phosphorus lit up immediately, and at the same instant he slipped the glass plate off the mouth of the oxygen jar, and clapped the cork, with the wire and cup hanging down from it, in its place. The effect was magical. The moment the phosphorus was introduced into the oxygen it flared up with a brilliancy that perfectly dazzled the spectators, and made the entire jar look like one mass of light.

The two pupils were delighted; Philpot was complacently triumphant; when all of a sudden there was a loud report, the illumination suddenly ceased, and the jar, broken to pieces, collapsed.

Pilbury and Cusack, who at the first alarm had retreated somewhat suddenly to the door, returned as soon as they perceived there was no danger, and were profuse in their praises of the experiment and the experimenter.

"Awfully prime, that was!" cried Cusack; "wasn't it, Pil?"

"Stunning!" said Pilbury.

"Jolly grind that jar bursting up, though," said Philpot, with a troubled countenance.

"Why, wasn't that part of the show-off?" asked Pilbury. "Part of the show-off! No!" exclaimed Philpot. "I thought it was the best part of it all," said Cusack. "So did I. No end of a bust up it was."

"You see," said Philpot, solemnly, "what I ought to have done was to dilute the oxygen with a little air first, but you fellows flurried me so I forgot all about it."

"Jolly glad you did, or we'd have missed the bust up," said Cusack. "I say, can't we try now? I know the way to do it quite well."

But this proposal Philpot flatly declined to accede to, and could only appease their disappointment by promising to perform one other experiment for their benefit.

This was of rather an elaborate nature. The operator first placed in a saucer some stuff which he explained was iodine. On to this he poured from a small bottle which smelt uncommonly like smelling-salts a small quantity of liquid, and then proceeded to stir the concoction up.

The two students were not to be restrained from offering their services at this point, and Philpot yielded. After they had stirred to their hearts' content, Philpot ordered them to desist and let it stand a bit.

This they consented to do, and occupied the interval in taking down and smelling all the bottles within reach, with a hardihood that frightened the wits out of poor Philpot.

"Look here," he said, when presently Pilbury suddenly dropped one bottle with a crash to the floor, and began violently spitting and choking, "you promised you wouldn't touch anything, and I'll shut up if you go on fooling any more. Serves you right, Pil, so it does."

It was some time before the unfortunate Pil recovered from the results of his unlucky experiment, and even when he did, the odours from the broken bottle were so offensive that the windows had to be opened wide before the atmosphere of the room became tolerable. It wouldn't have taken so long, only it was deemed advisable to shut the door at the same time to prevent the smell getting outside and telling tales to the school at large.

By the time this pleasant diversion was disposed of the concoction in the saucer had recovered from its stirring, and Philpot declared it was ready to go ahead with.

He therefore placed another saucer upside down upon this one, and carefully strained off between the two all the liquid, leaving only a black powder in the saucer, which he announced was iodide of nitrogen.

"Jolly rum name," said Cusack, "what does it do?"

"You wait a bit," said Philpot, scooping the wet powder up with the end of a knife and spreading it out on small separate pieces of paper.

"Fellow's born a chemist," said Pilbury, watching him admiringly; "that's just what old Joram does at the dispensary. What's all the spread out for?"

"To dry it," said Philpot.

"Why don't you stick it on the shovel and hold it over the gas?" suggested Cusack. "Jolly fag waiting till it dries itself."

"Oh, it won't be long," said Philpot.

"And what's it going to do when it's done?" asked Cusack.

"Hope it'll flare-up like the other," said Pilbury.

"It ought to," said Philpot.

"Ought it? Hurrah! I say, Cusack, what a jolly clever beggar old Phil is, isn't he?"

"Rather," said the admiring Cusack, perching himself on the side of the table and swinging his legs to pass the time.

"Oh," said Philpot, condescendingly, "it only wants a little practice."

"Rather; I mean to practise hard, don't you, Cusack?"

Cusack said, Yes he did, and proceeded to prowl round the laboratory in a manner that made Philpot very uncomfortable.

It was a relief to all parties when the powders were at last pronounced to be dry.

"Now," said Philpot, taking up one of the small papers gently on the flat of his hand, "we shall have to be careful."

"That little lot won't make half a flare," suggested Pilbury; "let's have two or three at once."

So saying he lifted up one of the other papers and emptied its contents into the paper on Philpot's hand.

"Look out," said Philpot, "it'll blow up."

"Eh, what?" cried Cusack, jumping off the table in his excitement at the glorious news.

As he did so Philpot uttered a cry, which was accompanied by a loud crackling explosion, and a dense volume of blue smoke, which made the boys turn pale with terror. For a moment neither of them could move or utter a sound except Philpot, who danced round and round the room in the smoke howling and wringing his hand.

When at last they did recover presence of mind enough to inquire of their preceptor if he was injured, it was in tones of terrible alarm.

"Oh, Phil, old man, are you hurt? What was it? We're so awfully sorry. Is your hand blown off?"

"No," said Philpot, continuing to wring his injured hand, but otherwise considerably recovered, "it was your fault jumping off the table. The beastly stuff goes off almost if you look at it. It's lucky it wasn't all dry, or I might have had my eyes out!"

It was a great relief to find matters were no worse, and that in a very few minutes Philpot's hand had recovered from the smart of the explosion. This accident, however, decided the young enthusiasts that for the present they had perhaps had enough chemistry for one lesson.

In a few days, however, they had all sufficiently got over the shock of the last afternoon's experiments to decide on a fresh venture, and these lessons continued, on and off, during the rest of the term. It can hardly be said that by the end of the term Pilbury or Cusack knew any more about chemistry than they had known this first day. They persistently refused to listen to any of Philpot's "jaw," as they rudely termed his attempts at explanation, and confined themselves to the experiments. However, though in many respects they wasted their time over their new pursuit, these volatile youths might have been a good deal worse employed.

In fact, if every Welcher had been no worse employed that house would not have brought all the discredit on Willoughby which it did. As it was, everybody there seemed to follow his own sweet will without a single thought for the good of the school or the welfare of his fellows. The heads of the house, Tucker and Silk, did not even attempt to set a good example, and that being so, it was hardly to be expected those below them would be much interested to supply the deficiencies.

On the very afternoon when Pilbury and Cusack had been sitting at the feet of the learned Philpot in the laboratory, Silk, a monitor, had, along with Gilks, of the schoolhouse, a monitor too, gone down to Shellport, against all rules, taking Wyndham junior, one of their special *protégés*, with them.

They appeared to be pretty familiar with the ins and outs of the big town, and though on this occasion they occupied their time in no more disgraceful a way than waiting on the harbour pier to see the mail steamer come in, they yet felt, all three of them, as if they would by no means like to be seen by any one who knew them.

And it appeared as if they were going to be spared this embarrassment, for they encountered no one they knew till they were actually on their way home.

Then, just as they were passing the station door, they met, to their horror, a boy in a college cap just coming out with a parcel under his arm. To their astonishment, it proved to be no other than Riddell himself.

Riddell, who had come down by a special "permit" from the doctor to get a parcel—containing, by the way, his new boating flannels—at first looked as astonished and uncomfortable as the three truants themselves. He would sooner have had anything happen to him than such a meeting. However, as usual, his sense of duty came to his rescue.

He advanced to the group in a nervous manner, and, addressing Wyndham, said, hurriedly, "Please come to my room this evening, Wyndham," and then, without waiting for a reply, or staying to notice the ominous looks of the two monitors, he departed, and proceeded as fast as he could back to Willoughby.

Chapter Ten.

Wyndham Junior and his Friends.

Wyndham, the old captain, just before leaving Willoughby, had done his best to interest Riddell in the welfare of his young brother, a Limpet in the Fourth.

"I wish you'd look after him now and then, Riddell," he said; "he's not a bad fellow, I fancy, but he's not got quite enough ballast on board, and unless there's some one to look after him he's very likely to get into bad hands."

Riddell promised he would do his best, and the elder brother was most grateful.

"I shall be ever so much easier *now*," he said, "and it's awfully good of you, Riddell. I wouldn't care for the young 'un to go wrong, you know. Thanks very much, old man."

And so it came to pass that among the legacies which the old captain left behind him at Willoughby, the one which fell to Riddell was a young brother, slightly rickety in character and short of ballast.

A parting request like Wyndham's would have been very hard for any friend to refuse; but to Riddell the promise "to look after young Wyndham" meant a great deal more than it would have done to many other fellows. It was not enough for him to make occasional inquiries as to his young *protégé*, or even to try to shield him when he fell into scrapes. Riddell's idea of looking after a rickety youngster included a good deal more than this, and from the moment the old captain had left, amid all his *own* tribulations and adversities, the thought of young Wyndham had saddled itself on Riddell's conscience with an uncomfortable weight.

This was the reason why he made the boy free of his study, and gave up a good deal of his own time in helping him with his work. And it was the same reason which prompted him on the afternoon spoken of in the last chapter, much against his inclination, to accost the three truants in Shellport, and request Wyndham to come to his study.

"You're in for a nice sermon, my boy," said Gilks, as the three walked home.

"I wish he hadn't seen us," said Wyndham, feeling uncomfortable.

"Why, you don't suppose he'll lick you?" said Silk, laughing.

"No, but he'll be awfully vexed."

"Vexed!" cried Gilks. "Poor fellow! How I'd like to comfort him! Take my advice and forget all about going to his study. He'll not be sorry, I can tell you."

"Oh, I must go," said Wyndham. "I don't want to offend him."

"Kind of you," said Silk, laughing. "Funny thing how considerate a fellow can be to another fellow who does his lessons for him."

Wyndham blushed, but said nothing. He knew these two companions were not the sort of boys his brother would have cared to have him associate with, nor did he particularly like them himself. But when two senior boys take the trouble to patronise a junior and make fun of his "peculiarities," as they called his scruples, it is hardly surprising that the youngster comes out a good way to meet his patrons.

Wyndham, by the way, was rather more than a youngster. He was a Limpet, and looked back on the days of fagging as a long-closed chapter of his history. Had he been a junior like Telson or Pilbury, it would have been less likely either that Game and Silk would take such trouble to cultivate his acquaintance, or that he would submit himself so easily to their patronage. As it was, he was his own master. Nobody had a right to demand his services, neither had he yet attained to the responsibilities of a monitor. He could please himself, and therefore yielded himself unquestioningly to the somewhat flattering attentions of the two seniors.

No, not quite unquestioningly. Short as was the time since his brother had left, it had been long enough for Riddell to let the boy see that he wished to be his friend. He had never told him so in words, but Wyndham could guess what all the kind interest which the new captain evinced in him meant. And it was the thought of this that kept alive the one or two scruples he still retained in joining himself to the society of Gilks and Silk.

And so he declined the invitation of these two friends to defy the captain's summons.

"Well," said Gilks, "if you must put your head into the lion's mouth, you must, mustn't he, Silk? But I say, as you *are* to get pulled up, I don't see why you shouldn't have all the fun you can for your money. What do you say to a game of skittles at Beamish's?"

"*What* a nice boy you are!" said Silk, laughing; "the young 'un doesn't know Beamish's."

"Not know Beamish's!—at the Aquarium!" said Gilks.

"No. What is he?" inquired Wyndham.

"He's the Aquarium!" said Gilks, laughing.

"And do they play skittles in the Aquarium?" asked the boy.

"Rather!" said Silk; "it amuses the fishes, you know." Beamish's was, as Gilks had said, another name for the Shellport Aquarium—a disreputable place of resort, whose only title to the name of Aquarium was that it had in it, in an obscure corner which nobody ever explored, a small tank, which might have contained fishes if there had been any put into it. As it was, the last thing any one went to Beamish's for was to study fishes, the other attractions of the place—the skittles, bowls, and refreshment bars—being far more popular. These things in themselves, of course, were not enough to make Beamish's a bad place. That character was supplied by the company that were mostly in the habit of frequenting it, of which it is enough to say it was the very reverse of select.

At this time of day, however, the place was almost empty, and when, after a good deal of chaff and persuasion, Wyndham was induced to take a little turn round the place, he was surprised to find it so quiet and unobjectionable. The boys had a short game at skittles and a short game at bowls, and bought a few buns and an ice at the refreshment stall, and then departed schoolwards.

They reached Willoughby in good time for call-over, no one except Riddell being aware of their pleasant expedition. Still Wyndham, when it was all *over*, did not feel altogether comfortable. Not that he thought what he had done was very bad, or that he had sinned in deceiving the masters and breaking the rules of the school. What troubled him was that he knew Riddell would be vexed.

He repaired to the captain's study with his books as usual after evening chapel and found him busy over his work.

But as soon as the boy entered, Riddell pushed the papers away rather nervously.

"Well, Wyndham," said he, "I'm glad you've come."

Wyndham deposited his books and looked rather uncomfortable.

Riddell had rather hoped the boy would refer to the subject first, but he did not. Riddell therefore said, "I was sorry to see you down in Shellport this afternoon, Wyndham. You hadn't a permit, had you?"

"No," said Wyndham.

"It's hardly the thing, is it?" said the captain, quietly, after a pause.

His voice, devoid of all anger or self-importance, made Wyndham still more uncomfortable.

"I'm awfully sorry," said he. "I suppose I oughtn't to have gone. I beg your pardon, Riddell."

"Oh!" said Riddell, "don't do that, please."

"You know," said Wyndham, "as those two took me, it didn't seem to be much harm. We only went to see the steamer come in."

"The thing is," said Riddell, "it was against the rules."

"But Gilks and Silk are both monitors, aren't they?"

"They are," said the captain, with a touch of bitterness in his tone.

There was another pause, this time a long one. Neither boy seemed inclined to return to the subject. Wyndham opened his books and made a pretence of beginning his work, and Riddell fidgeted with the papers before him. In the mind of the latter a hurried debate was going on.

"What had I better do? I might send him up to the doctor and perhaps get him expelled. It might be the best thing for him too, for if those two have got hold of him he's sure to go wrong. I can't do anything to keep him from them. And yet, I promised old Wynd—I must try; I might help to keep him straight. God help me!"

Is the reader astonished that the captain of a great public school should so far forget himself as to utter a secret prayer in his own study about such a matter as the correction of a young scapegrace? It *was* an unusual thing to do, certainly; and probably if Wyndham had known what was passing in the captain's mind he would have thought more poorly of his brother's friend than he did. But I am not quite sure, reader, whether Riddell was committing such an absurdity as some persons might think; or whether you or I, or any other fellow in a similar position, would be any the worse for forgetting ourselves in the same way. What do you think? It is worth thinking over, when you have time.

"God help me," said Riddell to himself, and he felt his mind wonderfully cleared already as he said it.

Clearer, that is, as to what he ought to do, but still rather embarrassed as to how to do it. But he meant to try.

"I say, Wyndham," he said, in his quiet way. "I want to ask your advice."

"What about?" asked Wyndham, looking up in surprise. "About those fellows?"

"Not exactly. It's more about myself," said the captain.

"What about you?" asked Wyndham.

"Why, there's a fellow in the school I'm awfully anxious to do some good to," began Riddell.

"Rather a common failing of yours," said Wyndham.

"Wanting to do it is more common than doing it," said Riddell; "but I don't know how to tackle this fellow, Wyndham."

"Who is he? Do I know him?" asked the boy.

"I'm not sure that you know him particularly well," said the captain. "He's not a bad fellow; in fact he has a lot of good in him."

"Is he a Limpet?" asked Wyndham.

"But," continued Riddell, not noticing the question, "he's got a horrid fault. He won't stand up for himself, Wyndham."

"Oh," observed Wyndham, "there's a lot of them like that—regular cowards they are."

"Exactly, this fellow's one of them. He's always funking it."

Wyndham laughed.

"I know who you mean—Tedbury, isn't it?"

"No, that's not his name," said Riddell. "He's a nicer sort of fellow than Tedbury. There are one or two fellows that are always down on him, too. They see he's no pluck, and so they think they can do what they like with him."

"Meekins gets a good deal mauled about by some of the others," said Wyndham.

"This fellow gets a good deal more damaged than Meekins," said the captain. "In fact he gets so mauled his friends will soon hardly be able to recognise him."

Wyndham looked sharply at the speaker. Riddell was quite grave and serious, and proceeded quietly, "The worst of it is, this fellow's quite well able to stick up for himself if he likes, and could easily hold his own. Only he's lazy, or else he likes getting damaged."

"Are you making all this up?" demanded Wyndham colouring.

Riddell took no notice of the inquiry, but continued rather more earnestly, "Now I'd like your advice, Wyndham, old fellow. I want to do this fellow a good turn. Which do you suppose would be the best turn to do him; to pitch into the fellows that are always doing him harm? or to try to persuade him to stick up for himself and not let them do just what they like with him, eh?"

Wyndham had seen it all before the question was ended, and hung down his head in silence.

Riddell did not disturb him, but waited quietly, and, if truth be told, anxiously, till he should reply.

Presently the boy looked up with a troubled face, and said, "I know I'm an awful fool, Riddell."

"But you're not obliged to be," said the captain, cheerily.

"I'll try not to be, I really will," said Wyndham. "Only—"

"Only what?" asked Riddell, after a pause.

"Only somehow I never think of it at the time."

"I know," said Riddell, kindly.

"Why only this afternoon," said Wyndham, drawn out by the sympathy of his companion, "I tried to object to going down to the town, and they made up some excuse, so that I would have seemed like a regular prig to hold out, and so I went. I'm awfully sorry now. I know I'm a coward, Riddell; I ought to have stuck out."

"I think you ought," said Riddell; "they would probably have laughed at you, and possibly tried to bully you a bit. But you can take care of yourself, I fancy, when it comes to that, eh?"

"I can about the bullying," said Wyndham.

"And so," said Riddell, "you really advise me to say to this fellow I was telling you about, to stand up for himself and not let himself be led about by any one?"

"Except you, Riddell," said the boy.

"No," said Riddell, "not even me. *I* can't profess to tell you all you ought to do."

"I should like to know who can, if you can't?" said Wyndham.

"I think we both know," said Riddell, gravely.

The conversation ended here. For an hour and a half after that each boy was busy over his work, and neither spoke a word. Their thoughts may not all have been in the books before them; in fact it may safely be said they were not. But they were thoughts that did not require words. Only when Wyndham rose to go, and wished his friend good-night, Riddell indirectly referred to the subject of their talk.

"By the way, Wyndham, Isaacs has given up the school librarianship; I suppose you know. How would you like to take it?"

"What has a fellow got to do?" asked Wyndham.

"You have to issue the new books every Monday and collect the old ones every Saturday. There are about one hundred boys subscribe, and they order the new book when they give up the old, so it's simple enough."

"Takes a lot of time, doesn't it?" said Wyndham.

"No, not very much, I believe. Isaacs shirked it a good deal, and you'd have to keep the lists rather better than he did. But I fancy you'd enjoy it rather; and," he added, "it will be an excuse for seeing less of some not very nice friends."

Wyndham said he would take the post, and went off happier in his own mind than he had been for a long time, and leaving Riddell happier too, despite all his failures and vexations elsewhere, than he had been since he became captain of Willoughby.

But, though happy, he could hardly be elated. His effort that evening had certainly been a success, but how long would its effects last?

Riddell was not fool enough to imagine that his promise to old Wyndham was now discharged by that one evening's talk. He knew the boy well enough to be sure that the task was only just begun. And his thankfulness at having made a beginning was tempered with many anxieties for the future. And he might well be anxious!

For a day or two Wyndham was an altered boy. He surprised his masters by his attention in class, and his schoolfellows—all except Riddell—by the steadiness of his behaviour. He avoided his former companions, and devoted himself with enthusiasm to his new duties as librarian, to which the doctor, at Riddell's suggestion, had appointed him.

This alteration, approved of as it was in many quarters, was by no means appreciated by two boys at Willoughby. It was not that they cared twopence about the society of their young Limpet, or that they had any moral objection to good behaviour and steady work. What irritated Gilks and Silk over the business was that they saw in it the hand of an enemy, and felt that the present change in their *protégé* was due to Riddell's influence in opposition to their own. The two monitors felt hurt at this; it was like a direct snub aimed at them, and, considering the quarter from which it came, they did not like it at all.

"This sort of thing won't do," said Gilks to his friend one day, shortly after Riddell's talk with Wyndham. "The young 'un's cut our acquaintance."

"Hope we shall recover in time," said Silk, sneering. "Yes; he's gone decidedly 'pi.' the last week."

"It's all that reverend prig's doing!" growled Gilks. "I mean to spoil his little game for him, though," added he. "How'll you do it?" asked Silk. "That's just it! I wish I knew," said Gilks.

"Oh! leave it to me, I'll get at him somehow. I don't suppose he's too far gone yet."

Accordingly Silk took an early opportunity of meeting his young friend.

"Ah! Wyndham," said he, casually; "don't see much of you now."

"No," said Wyndham, shortly; "I'm busy with the library."

"Oh! I'm afraid, though, you're rather glad of an excuse to cut Silks and me after the row we got you into last week."

"You didn't get me into any row," said Wyndham. "What! didn't he lick you for it? Ah! I see how it is. He's afraid you'd let out on him for being down too. Rather a good dodge too. Gilks and I half thought of reporting him, but we didn't."

"He had a permit, hadn't he?"

"Oh, yes—rather! I don't doubt that. Just like Brown's, the town boy's excuses. Writes them himself."

"I'm certain Riddell wouldn't do such a thing," said Wyndham, warming.

"I never said he would," replied Silk, seeing he was going a little too far. "You see, captains don't want permits. There's no one to pull them up. But I say, I'm awfully sorry about last week."

"Oh! it doesn't matter," said Wyndham, who could not help being rather gratified to hear a monitor making apologies to him; "only I don't mean to go down again."

"No, of course not; and if Gilks suggests it I'll back you up. By the way," he added, in tones of feigned alarm, "I suppose you didn't tell him about going to Beamish's, did you?"

"No," said Wyndham, whose conscience had already reproached him several times for not having confessed the fact.

"I'm awfully glad of that," said Silk, apparently much relieved. "Whatever you do, keep that quiet."

"Why?" said Wyndham, rather concerned.

"My dear fellow, if that got out—well, I don't know what would happen."

"Why, is it a bad place, then?"

43

"Oh, no, not at all," laughed Silk with a mysterious wink. "All serene for follows like Gilks; but if it was known we'd taken *you* there, we'd be done for."

Wyndham began to feel he had had a narrow escape of "doing" for his two patrons without knowing it.

"Promise you won't tell anybody," said Silk.

"Of course I won't," said Wyndham, rather scornful at the idea of telling tales of a schoolfellow.

"Thanks; and I'll take care and say nothing about you, and Gilks won't either, I know. So it'll be all right. I don't know what possessed the fellow to suggest going in there."

All this was somewhat perplexing to Wyndham. He had never imagined Beamish's was such a terrible place, or that the penalty of being found there was so severe. He felt that he had had a fortunate escape, and was glad Silk had put him up to it before he had let it out.

He became more friendly with his ally after this. There is always a bond of attraction where a common danger threatens, and Wyndham felt that, however determined he was not to be led away any more by these friends of his, it was just as well to be civil to them.

So he even accepted an invitation to come and have tea in Silk's room that evening, to look at a volume of "Punch" the latter had got from home, and to talk over the coming boat-race.

Had he overheard a hurried conversation which took place between Silk and Gilks shortly afterwards in the Sixth Form room he would have looked forward to that evening with anything but eagerness.

"Well?" asked Gilks.

"Hooked him, I fancy," said Silk. "He's coming to tea this evening."

"Good man. How did you manage it?"

"Oh, and by the way," said Silk, "that going to Beamish's last week was no end of a crime. If it's found out it's expulsion, remember. He believes it all. I've told him we won't let out on him, and he's promised not to say a word about it. Fancy we've rather a pull on him there."

"You're a jolly clever fellow, Silk," said Gilks, admiringly.

"May be, but I'm not such a nice boy as you are, Gilks."

Chapter Eleven.

The Schoolhouse Boat at Work.

Giles and his ally knew their business well enough to see that they must go to work "gingerly" to recover their lost Limpet. Consequently when Wyndham, according to promise, turned up to tea in Silk's study, nothing was said or done in any way likely to offend his lately awakened scruples.

The tea was a good one, the volume of "Punch" was amusing, and the talk confined itself almost altogether to school affairs, and chiefly to the coming boat-race.

This last subject was one of intense interest to young Wyndham. As brother to the old captain, he was naturally eager to see his brother's boat retain its old position on the river; and as an ardent schoolhouse boy himself, he had a further reason for wishing the same result.

"You know," said he, "I think our fellows are looking up, don't you, Gilks?"

"So fellows say," replied Gilks; "of course, being in the boat myself, it's hard to tell."

"But doesn't the boat seem to be going better?" asked Wyndham. "It looks to be going a lot better from the bank."

"But you don't mean to say, young un," said Silk, "you ever expect the schoolhouse will beat Parrett's?"

"I'm afraid they are rather strong," said Wyndham, regretfully.

"Strong!" said Silk; "they're the finest crew Willoughby's turned out for years. Better even than the one your brother stroked last races."

"And they mean winning, too," said Gilks, "from all I hear. They're specially set on it because they think they've been snubbed over the captaincy, and mean to show they *are* the cock house, though the doctor won't own it."

"Well," said Silk, "as I've not much faith in the Welchers' boat—in fact, I'm not sure if they'll be able to get up a crew at all—I feel delightfully impartial."

"I hope you'll back us," said Wyndham, earnestly.

"Of course, old Gilks is one of your crew," said Silk.

"You know," said the boy, "I'd give anything for our boat to win. It would be such a score for us, after all that has been said, wouldn't it, Gilks?"

"Well, fellows haven't been very complimentary about the schoolhouse lately, certainly," said Gilks.

"No, they certainly haven't," replied Wyndham. "By the way, Gilks, what sort of cox does Riddell make?"

"Rather an amusing one, from all I can hear," said Gilks. "He's not steered the four yet; but he's had some tub practice, and is beginning to find out that the natural place for a boat is between the banks instead of on them."

"Oh," said Wyndham, "I heard Fairbairn say he promised very well. He's a light-weight, you know, and as the juniors are all stopped river-play, we shall have to get a cox. And if Riddell will do, it won't be a bad thing any way."

"I'm rather surprised they didn't try you for it," said Gilks. "You're well-known, you know, and used to the river."

"Oh, I'd rather Riddell did it if he can," said Wyndham. "I know he's awfully anxious to get it up."

The talk went on like this, and trenched on no uncomfortable topic. The only reference to anything of the sort was when Silk said, just as Wyndham was going, "Oh, Wyndham, I've told Gilks here that you've promised not to let out about Beamish's—"

"Yes," said Gilks, "I wouldn't care for that to get about, young un."

"Oh, of course I won't say anything," said Wyndham.

"Thanks, no more will we; will we, Silk?" replied Gilks.

Silk assented and their visitor departed.

"Young fool!" said Gilks, when he and his friend were left alone. "He's not worth bothering about."

"If it weren't for the other prig I'd agree with you," said Silk. "But don't you think we can hit at his reverence occasionally through his disciple?"

"I dare say," said Gilks. "The young prig had an innocent enough time of it to-night to suit even him. How he does talk!"

"Yes, and isn't he hot about the race? I say, Gilks, I hope there'll be no mistake about Parrett's winning. I've a lot of money on them."

"Never fear," said Gilks. "It'll be rather a rum thing if I, rowing in the schoolhouse boat, can't put the drag on them somehow. I don't expect for a moment it will be wanted; but if it is, Gilks will be under the painful necessity of catching a crab!"

"I don't mind how you do it as long as there's no mistake about it," said Silk. With which ungenerous admission Gilks produced a couple of cigar-ends from his pocket, and these two nice boys proceeded to spend a dissipated evening.

The reader will have guessed from what has already been said that the coming boat-race was every day becoming a more and more exciting topic in Willoughby. Under any circumstances the race was, along with the May sports and the cricket-match against Rockshire, one of the events of the year. But this year, ever since it had come somehow to be mixed up with the squabble about the captaincy, and the jealousy between Parrett's and the schoolhouse, it had become more important than ever.

Old Wyndham had, of course, left the schoolhouse boat at the head of the river, but there was scarcely a boy (even in the schoolhouse itself) who seriously expected it would remain there over the coming regatta.

The Parrett's fellows were already crowing in anticipation, and the victory of Bloomfield's boat was only waited for as a final ground for resisting the authority of any captain but their own. Their boat was certainly one of the best which the school had turned out, and compared with their competitors' it seemed as if nothing short of a miracle could prevent its triumph.

But the schoolhouse fellows, little as they expected to win, were meaning to make a hot fight of it. They were on their mettle quite as much as their rivals. Ever since Wyndham had left, the schoolhouse had been sneered at as having no pretensions left to any athletic distinction. They meant to put themselves right in this particular—if not in victory, at any rate in a gallant attempt.

And so the schoolhouse boat might be seen out early and late, doing honest hard work, and doing it well too. Strict training was the order of the day, and scarcely a day passed without some one of the crew adding to his usual labours a cross-country run, or a hard grind in the big tub, to better his form. These extraordinary exertions were a source of amusement to their opponents, who felt their own superiority all the more by witnessing the efforts put forth to cope with it; and even in the schoolhouse there were not a few who regarded all the work as labour thrown away, and as only adding in prospect to the glorification of the enemy.

However, Fairbairn was not the man to be moved by small considerations such as these. He did not care what fellows said, or how much they laughed, as long as Porter swung out well at the reach forward, and Coates straightened his back, and Gilks pulled his oar better through from beginning to end. To secure these ends he himself was game for any amount of work and trouble, and no cold water could damp either his ardour or his hopefulness.

But the chief sensation with regard to the training of the schoolhouse boat was the sudden appearance of Riddell as its coxswain. As the reader has heard, the new captain had already been out once or twice "on the quiet" in the pair-oar, and during these expeditions he had learned all he knew of the art of navigation. The idea of his steering the schoolhouse boat had never occurred either to himself or Fairbairn when he first undertook these practices at the solicitation of his friend. But after a lesson or two he showed such promise that the idea did strike Fairbairn, who mentioned it to one or two of his set and asked their advice.

These judges were horrified naturally at the idea. Riddell was too heavy, too clumsy, too nervous. But Fairbairn was loth to give up his idea; so he went to Mr Parrett, and asked him if he would mind running with the schoolhouse pair-oar during the next morning's spin, and watching the steering of the new captain. Mr Parrett did so; and was not a little pleased with the performance, but advised Fairbairn to try him in the four-oar before deciding.

Fairbairn, delighted, immediately broached the subject to his friend. Poor Riddell was astounded at such a notion.

He cox the schoolhouse boat in the regatta!

"My dear fellow," said he to Fairbairn. "I'm not a very exalted personage in Willoughby as it is—but this would be the finishing stroke!"

"What do you mean—that it's *infra dig.* to cox the boat?"

"Oh no!" said Riddell, "anything but that. But it might be *infra dig.* for the boat to be steered into the bank in the middle of the race."

"Humbug, if that's your only reason. Anyhow, old man, come down and try your hand in the four to-morrow morning."

Riddell protested that the idea was absurd, and that he wouldn't hear of it. But Fairbairn reasoned him down. He hadn't steered them into the bank since the second morning—he hadn't tried steering the four-oar, how did he know he couldn't do it? Mr Parrett had advised the trial strongly, and so on.

"No," said he, "the only question is your weight. You'd have to run off a bit of that, you know."

"Oh," said Riddell, "as to that, you can take as many pounds off me as you like; but—"

"None of your buts, old man," said Fairbairn. "I say, if we only were to win, with you as cox, what a score it would be!"

"None of your 'ifs,' old man," said Riddell, laughing. "But I'll come to-morrow, if you are determined to have your way."

"Of course I am," said Fairbairn.

This conversation took place the evening that young Wyndham was taking tea with Silk and Gilks in the study of the former.

The intelligence that the new captain was to be taken out to steer the schoolhouse boat mysteriously got wind before the evening was over, and spread over the school like wildfire. Consequently, when Riddell arrived at the boat-house in the morning, he was surprised and horrified to find that nearly all Willoughby was awake and down at the river banks to see him.

It was embarrassing certainly, and when presently the crew got into their seats and a start was made, it became evident the new coxswain was anything but at home in his new position. The boat was a long time getting clear of the landing stage owing to his persistently mistaking in his flurry his right hand for his left, and then when it did get out into mid-stream the same reason prevented him from discovering that the reason why the boat would turn round instead of going straight was because he had his right cord pulled hard the whole time.

This spectacle, as may be imagined, afforded intense gratification to the curious onlookers, and many and hilarious were the shouts which fell on the ears of the unlucky captain.

"Oh, well coxed there!" one voice cried.

"Well steered in a circle!" shouted another.

"Mind you don't knock the bank down," yelled a third.

"Pull your right there!"

"Try him without the rudder. See if he don't steer better that way."

In the midst of these uncomplimentary shouts the boat slowly wended its erratic course up the river, amidst crowds of boys on either bank.

"Riddell, old man," said Fairbairn, leaning forward from his place at stroke, "what's the row?"

It only needed a friendly voice to recall the captain to himself. By an effort he forgot about the crowds and turned a deaf ear to the shouts, and straightening himself, and taking the lines steadily in his hands, looked up quietly at his friend. Richard was himself again.

"Now then!" cried Fairbairn to his men behind, "row all!" and he led them off with a long steady stroke.

For a little distance the boat travelled well. Riddell kept a good course, and the whole crew worked steadily. The scoffers on the bank were perplexed, and their jeers died away feebly. This was not a crew of muffs assuredly. Those first twenty or thirty yards were rowed in a style not very far short of the Parrett's standard, and Parson himself, the best cox of Parrett's house, could hardly have taken the boat down that reach in a better course.

There was something ominous in this. But, to the great relief of the unfriendly critics, this showy lead was not maintained. Before a hundred yards were completed something seemed to go wrong in the boat. It rolled heavily and wavered in its course. What was wrong?

The fault was certainly not in Fairbairn, who kept doggedly to work in perfectly even style. Nor, to all appearance, was it in Riddell. He was evidently puzzled by the sudden unsteadiness of the boat, but no one could lay it to his charge.

"Who's that digging behind?" cried Fairbairn over his shoulder.

None of the other three owned the soft impeachment, and the boat seemed to right itself of its own accord.

Fairbairn, whose temper was never improved by perplexities, quickened his stroke, and gave his men a spell of hard work for a bit to punish them.

This seemed to have a good effect, and once again the onlookers were startled to see how steadily and fast the boat was travelling. But once again the mysterious disturbance interrupted their progress.

This time Fairbairn stopped short, and turning round demanded angrily who it was who was playing the fool, for an effect like this could only be put down to such a course. Porter, Coates, and Gilks all repudiated the suggestion, and once more, amid the ironical cheers of the onlookers, Fairbairn resumed his work and lashed viciously out with his oar.

This last protest of his seemed to have had the desired effect, for during the rest of the journey up to the Willows the boat travelled fairly well, though it was evident plenty of work was needed before the crew could be considered in proper racing trim. But no sooner had they turned and started for the home journey than once again the rolling suddenly became manifest. Fairbairn rowed on a stroke or two without apparently noticing it, then turning sharply round in the middle of a stroke he discovered the reason.

The blade of Gilks's oar was about a foot under the surface, and he himself was lurching over his seat, with the handle of the oar up to about his chin.

"What on earth do you mean by it?" demanded Fairbairn, angrily.

"Mean by what?" asked Gilks.

"By playing the fool like that; that's what I mean," retorted Fairbairn.

"Who was playing the fool?" snarled Gilks. "How can I help catching a crab when he's constantly turning the boat's head in the middle of a stroke?"

"All rot!" said Fairbairn.

"All very well for you at stroke," said Gilks, viciously. "You come and row bow and see if you don't feel it. I'd like to know who could keep his oar straight with such steering."

"If you'd row half as well as he steers," said Fairbairn, "you'd row a precious sight better than you do! You'd better take care, Gilks."

"Take care of what, you fool?" demanded Gilks, whose temper was now fairly gone.

"Ready all, you fellows!" cried Fairbairn, stretching forward.

This brief conversation had been heard only by those in the boat, but its purport had been gathered by those on the bank who had watched the angry looks and heard the angry voices of the speakers.

"Bravo! fight it out!" cried some one, and the news that there was a quarrel in the schoolhouse boat added greatly to the zest of the critics' enjoyment.

Fairbairn's caution—whether purposely, or because he could not help it—was lost upon the offending bow oar. The boat had scarcely started again when Gilks caught another crab, which for the moment nearly upset the crew. Fairbairn rowed on, with thunder in his face, regardless of the incident, and Riddell kept as straight a course as he could, despite the unsteadiness. In due time the unsatisfactory practice came to an end, and the crew stood together again on the steps of the boat-house.

Gilks seemed to expect, and every one else expected, that Fairbairn would once more take the defaulter to task for his performance that morning, and Fairbairn did not disappoint him; though he dealt with the matter in a rather unexpected manner.

"I shall want the tub-pair after third school," said he to the boatman. "Riddell, will you come and cox. Crossfield and me?"

"Who—Crossfield?" asked Coates.

"Yes; I shall try him for bow."

"You mean to say," exclaimed Gilks, taking the matter in, "you're going to turn me out of the boat?"

"Certainly," said Fairbairn, coolly.

"What for?" demanded Gilks, threateningly.

"Because," replied Fairbairn, taking Riddell's arm and walking slowly off—"because we can do better without you."

Gilks stared at him a moment as though he meditated flying at him. If he did, he thought better of it, and turned away, muttering to himself that he would pay them all out, let them see if he did not.

Threats of this sort were not unheard-of things from Gilks, and no one was greatly disturbed by them. On the whole, Fairbairn's decision was approved of by most of the schoolhouse partisans, particularly those who had watched the proceedings of the morning. A few thought Gilks might have been accorded a second chance, but the majority argued that if a fellow caught crabs like that in a practice he would probably do it in the race, and they did not want the risk of that.

As to his excuse about the steering, every one who knew anything about that knew it meant nothing, and Gilks did not repeat it.

As he reached the school Silk met him with angry looks.

"Is it true what I hear," said he, "that you're out of the boat?"

"Yes, it is," growled Gilks.

"Why, you idiot! whatever have you done this for?"

"I did nothing. They wanted to get rid of me, and they did."

"Yes, because you hadn't the ordinary sense to keep up appearances till the race, and must begin to practise your tricks a month beforehand!" said Silk, greatly enraged, for him.

"All very well," said Gilks, sullenly. "I should have liked to see you rowing your best with that puppy steering; thinking he's doing it so wonderfully, the prig!"

"And just because you hadn't the patience to hold out a week or two you go and spoil everything. I didn't think you were such a fool, upon my word."

Gilks was cowed by the wrath of his friend.

"I couldn't help it," he said. "I'm awfully sorry."

"It's done us completely now," said Silk. "For all we know they may win. Who's to take your place?"

"Crossfield."

"Just the man I was afraid. He's the best man they could have picked out. I tell you what, Gilks, you'd better go and apologise and see if you can't get back into the boat. Who could have believed you'd be such a fool! Go at once, for goodness' sake."

Gilks, who saw his own mistake fully as well as his friend, obeyed. He found Fairbairn in his study with Riddell. The former seemed not at all surprised to see him.

"Fairbairn," said Gilks, "I hope you'll let me stay in the boat. I'm sorry I played the fool this morning."

"Then you *were* playing the fool?" demanded Fairbairn, to whom Riddell had just been confiding that perhaps, after all, there had been some fault in the steering to account for it.

"Yes," said Gilks, sullenly.

"Then," said Fairbairn, hotly, "you may be a fool, but I won't be such a big one as to let you stay in the boat another day!"

Gilks glared a moment at the speaker. Evidently it would be no use to argue or plead further; and, smarting with rage and humiliation, none the less keen that Riddell had been present and heard all, he turned away.

"You'll be sorry for this, you two," he growled. "Humbugs!"

"Well rid of him," said Fairbairn, as soon as he had gone.

"Yes. I don't think much of him," said Riddell, thinking as much of young Wyndham and his temptations as of the schoolhouse boat.

"Well, old man," said Fairbairn, after a pause, "you steered awfully well when you once began. Whatever made you so shaky at first?"

"My usual complaint," said Riddell, smiling. "I was thinking what other people were thinking."

"Oh," said Fairbairn, "unless you can give that up you may as well shut up shop altogether."

"Well, if I must do one or the other, I think I'll keep the shop open," said Riddell, cheerily. "By the way," added he, looking at his watch and sighing, "I have to see some juniors in my study in two minutes. Good-bye."

"Be sure you're down for the tub practice this afternoon."

"I'll be there," said Riddell.

Chapter Twelve.

48

Bloomfield In Tribulation.

Bloomfield was beginning to discover already that the new dignity to which he had been raised by his own partisans at Willoughby was anything but a bed of roses. Vain and easily led as he was, he was not a bad fellow by any means; and when the mutiny against the new captain first began, he flattered himself that by allowing himself to be set up in opposition he was really doing a service to Willoughby, and securing the school against a great many disasters which were certain to ensue if Riddell was left supreme.

But in these lofty hopes he was getting to be a trifle disappointed. In his own house, of course, especially among those over whom he was wont to rule in athletic sports, his authority was paramount. But these, after all, constituted only a small section of Willoughby. Over the rest of the school his influence was strangely overlooked, and even the terrors of his arm failed to bring his subjects to obedience.

It was all very well at first, when the one idea was indignation against the doctor's new appointment. But as soon as the malcontents discovered that they had raised one more tyrant over their own heads, they began to find out their mistake, and did their best to correct it. They argued that as they had elected Bloomfield themselves they weren't bound to obey him unless they chose; and when it came to the point of having to give up their own will in obedience to his, they remembered he was not the real captain of Willoughby and had no right to order them!

So poor Bloomfield did not find things quite as comfortable as he had expected.

One of the first rebuffs he got was administered by no less stately a hand than that of Master Telson of the schoolhouse.

This young gentleman ever since his last unfortunate expedition in "Noah's Ark" had been somewhat under a cloud. His forced absence from the river for a whole week had preyed upon his spirits. And when at the end of that period he did revisit his old haunts, armed with a captain's permit, it was only to discover that whatever small chance he ever had of coxing his house's boat at the coming regatta, had vanished under the new arrangement which had brought Riddell into the boat.

It is only fair to say that this disappointment, keen as it was, had no effect on his loyalty. He was as ready as ever to fight any one who spoke ill of the schoolhouse. But it certainly had given him a jar, which resulted in rather strained relations with some of his old allies in Parrett's.

Of course nothing could shake his devotion to Parson. That was secure whatever happened, but towards the other heroes of Parrett's, particularly the seniors, he felt unfriendly. He conceived he must have been the victim of a plot to prevent his steering the schoolhouse boat. It was the only reason he could think of for his ill-luck; and though he never tried to argue it out, it was pretty clear to his own mind some one was at the bottom of it. And if that was so, who more likely than Bloomfield and Game and that lot, who had everything to gain by his being turned out of the rival boat?

This was the state of mind of our aggrieved junior one afternoon not long before the regatta, as he strolled dismally across the "Big" on his way to the river. Parson was not with him. He was down coxing his boat, and the thought of this only reminded Telson of his own bad luck, and added to his ill-temper.

He was roused from his moody reflections by the approach of two boys, who hailed him cheerily.

"What cheer, Telson, old man?" cried King. "How jolly blue you look! What's the row?"

"Nothing," replied Telson.

"We've just been down to see the boats. Awful spree to see old Riddell steering! isn't it, Bosher?"

"Yes," said Bosher; "but he's better than he was."

"Never mind, they won't lick us," said King. "You should have seen our boat! Bless you, those schoolhouse louts—"

"King, I'll fight you!" said Telson, suddenly.

"Oh! beg pardon, old man, I didn't—eh—what?"

This last remark was caused by the fact that Telson was taking off his coat. King, utterly taken aback by these ominous preparations, protested his sorrow, apologised, and generally humiliated himself before the offended schoolhouse junior.

But Telson had been looking out for a cause of quarrel, and now one had come, he was just in the humour for going through with the business. "Do you funk it?" he asked.

"Oh, no; not that, old man," said King, still friendly, and very slowly unbuttoning his jacket; "but I'll apologise, Telson, you know."

"Don't want any apologising; I want to fight," said Telson. "I'll take young Bosher too."

"Oh!" said Bosher, rather alarmed, "I don't want to fight."

"I knew you were a beastly funk!" said Telson, scornfully.

"No, I'm not," said Bosher, meekly.

"Get out of the way!" cried the majestic Telson, brushing past him towards King, who now stood with his coat off and a very apologetic face, ready for the young bantam's disposal.

Telson and King fought there and then. It was not a very sanguinary contest, nor was it particularly scientific. It did Telson good, and it did not do King much harm. The only awkward thing about it was that neither side knew exactly when to stop. Telson claimed the victory after every round, and King respectfully disputed the statement. Telson thereupon taunted his adversary with "funking it," and went at him again, very showy in action, but decidedly feeble in execution. King, by keeping one arm over his face and working the other gently up and down in front of his body, was able to ward off most of the blows aimed, and neither aspired nor aimed to hit out himself.

The "fight" might have lasted a week had not Game, coming up that way from the boats, caught sight of it. As it was neither an exciting combat nor a profitable one, the Parrett's monitor considered it a good case for interfering, as well as for calling in the authority of the popular captain.

"King and Telson," he said, stepping between the combatants, "stop it, and come to Bloomfield's study after chapel. You know fighting in the 'Big' is against rules."

"What are we to go to Bloomfield for?" demanded Telson, whose temper was still disturbed.

"For breaking rules," said Game, as he walked on.

"Shall you go?" said Telson to King as the two slowly put on their coats.

"Yes, I suppose so, or he'll give us a licking."

"I shan't go; he's not the captain," said Telson.

"I say, you'll catch it if you don't," said King, with apprehension in his looks. "They're always down on you if you don't go to the captain when you're told."

"I tell you he's not the captain," replied Telson, testily, "and I shan't go. If they want to report me they'll have to do it to Riddell."

With which virtuous decision he went his way, slightly solaced in his mind by the fight, and still more consoled by the prospects of a row ahead.

Telson was quite cute enough to see he had a strong position to start with, and if only he played his cards well he might score off the enemy with credit.

He therefore declined an invitation to Parson's to partake of shrimps and jam at tea, and kept himself in his own house till the time appointed for reporting himself to the captain. Then, instead of going to Bloomfield, he presented himself before Riddell.

"Well?" said the captain, in his usual half-apologetic tone.

"Oh!" said Telson, "I'm reported, please, Riddell."

"What for? Who reported you?" asked Riddell.

"Game—for fighting," replied Telson.

"He hasn't told me of it. You'd better come in the morning."

"Oh! it's all right," said Telson. "I was fighting King in the 'Big' this afternoon."

Riddell looked perplexed. This was the first case of a boy voluntarily delivering himself up to justice, and he hardly knew what to do.

However, he had found out thus much by this time—that it didn't so much matter what he did as long as he did something.

"You know it's against rules," said he, as severely as he could, "and it's not the first time you've done it. You must do fifty lines of Virgil, and stop in the house on Monday and Tuesday."

"All right! Thanks," said Telson, rapidly departing, and leaving Riddell quite bewildered by the apparent gratitude of his fag.

Telson betook himself quietly to his study and began to write his lines. It was evident from the restless way in which he looked up at every footstep outside he did not expect to remain long undisturbed at this harmless occupation. Nor was he disappointed.

In about ten minutes King entered and said, "I say, Telson, you're in for it! You're to go to Bloomfield directly."

"What's he given you?"

"A licking!" said King; "and stopped my play half a week. But I say, you'd better go—sharp!"

"I'm not going," said Telson.

"What!" exclaimed King, in amazement.

"Cut it," said Telson; "I'm busy."

"He sent me to fetch you," said King.

"Don't I tell you I'm not coming? I'll lick you, King, if you don't cut it!"

King did "cut it" in a considerable state of alarm at the foolhardiness of his youthful comrade.

But Telson knew his business. No sooner had King gone than he took up his Virgil and paper, and repaired once more to Riddell's study.

"Please, Riddell," said he, meekly, "do you mind me writing my lines here?"

"Not a bit," said Riddell, whose study was always open house to his youthful fag.

Telson said "Thank you," and immediately deposited himself at the table, and quietly continued his work, awaiting the result of King's message.

The result was not long in coming.

"Telson!" shouted a voice down the passage in less than five minutes.

Telson went to the door and shouted back, "What's the row?"

"Where are you?" said the voice.

"Here," replied Telson, shutting the door and resuming his work.

"Who's that?" asked Riddell of his fag.

"I don't know, unless it's Game," said Telson.

"Now then, Telson," cried the voice again, "come here."

"I can't—I'm busy!" shouted Telson back from where he sat. At the same moment the door opened, and Game entered in a great state of wrath.

The appearance of a Parrett monitor "on duty" in the schoolhouse was always a strange spectacle; and Game, when he discovered into whose study he had marched, was a trifle embarrassed.

"What is it, Game?" asked Riddell, civilly.

"I want Telson," said Game, who, by the way, had scarcely spoken to the new captain since his appointment.

"What do you want?" said Telson, boldly.

"Why didn't you come when you were sent for?" demanded Game.

"Who sent for me?"

"Bloomfield."

"I'm not Bloomfield's fag," retorted Telson. "I'm Riddell's."

"What did I tell you this afternoon?" said Game, beginning to suspect that he had fallen into a trap.

"Told me to go to the captain after chapel."

"And what do you mean by not going?"

"I did go—I went to Riddell."

"I told you to go to Bloomfield," said Game, growing hot.

"Bloomfield's not the captain," retorted Telson, beginning to enjoy himself. "Riddell's captain."

"You were fighting in the 'Big,'" said Game, looking uneasily at Riddell while he spoke.

"I know I was. Riddell's potted me for it, haven't you, Riddell?"

"I've given Telson fifty lines, and stopped his play two days," said Riddell, quietly.

"Yes, and I'm writing the lines now," said Telson, dipping his pen in the ink, and scarcely smothering a laugh.

Game, now fully aware of his rebuff, was glad of an opportunity of covering his defeat by a diversion.

"Look here," said he, walking up to Telson, "I didn't come here to be cheeked by you, I can tell you."

"Who's cheeking you?" said Telson. "I'm not."

"Yes, you are," said Game. "I'm not going to be humbugged about by you."

"I don't want to humbug you about," replied the junior, defiantly.

"I think there's a mistake, you know," said Riddell, thinking it right to interpose. "I've given him lines for fighting in the 'Big,' and there's really no reason for his going to Bloomfield."

"I told him to come to Bloomfield, and he ought to have come."

"I don't think you had any right to tell him to go to Bloomfield," replied Riddell, with a boldness which astonished himself. "I'm responsible for stopping fights."

"I don't want you to tell me my business," retorted Game, hotly; "who are you?"

Game could have thrashed the captain as easily as he could Telson, and the thought flashed through Riddell's mind as he paused to reply. He would much have preferred saying nothing, but somehow the present seemed to be a sort of crisis in his life. If he gave in now, the chance of asserting himself in Willoughby might never return.

"I'm the captain," he replied, steadily, "and as long as I am captain I'm responsible for the order of the school, and I prefer to do my own work!"

There was something in his look and tone as he uttered these inoffensive words which took Game aback and even startled Telson. It was not at all like what fellows had been used to from Riddell, certainly very unlike the manner he was generally credited with. But neither Telson nor Game were half so amazed at this little outburst as was the speaker himself. He was half frightened the moment he had uttered it. Now he was in for it with a vengeance! It would go out to all Willoughby, he knew, that he meant to stand by his guns. What an awful failure, if, after all, he should not be able to keep his word!

Game, with a forced smile which ill accorded with his inward astonishment, left the study without another word, heedless even of the laugh which Telson could no longer repress.

Of course many perverted stories of their adventure immediately got abroad in Willoughby. Telson's highly-coloured version made it appear that a pitched battle had been fought between Game and the new captain, resulting in the defeat of the former chiefly through Telson's instrumentality and assistance. As, however, this narrative did not appear in the same dress two hours running, it was soon taken for what it was worth, and most fellows preferred to believe the Parretts' version of the story, which stated that Riddell had announced his intention of keeping order in Willoughby without the help of the monitors, and had had the cheek to tell Bloomfield to mind his own business.

The indignation of Parrett's house on hearing such a story may be imagined. It was even past a joke. Bloomfield seriously offered to resign all pretensions to authority and let things take their course.

"It makes me seem," he said, "as if I wanted to stick myself up. If he's so sure of keeping order by himself, I don't see what use it is my pretending to do it too."

"It would serve him right if you did so," said Game. "But it would be so awfully like giving in now, after you have once begun."

This view of the matter decided the question. But Bloomfield all the same was considerably impressed by what had happened.

He knew in his heart that his only title to the position he assumed was the whim of his schoolfellows. He was a usurper, in fact, and however much he tried to persuade himself he was acting solely for the good of Willoughby, he knew those motives were only half sincere. And in spite of all his efforts, the school was as rowdy as ever. If he did thrash a batch of juniors one day, or stop some disorderly Limpets of their play, it never seemed to make much impression. Whereas the one or two rioters whom Riddell had ventured to tackle had somehow distinctly reformed their habits. How was it?

Bloomfield, as he thought the thing over, was not quite happy. He had been happier far last term when, under old Wyndham, he had exerted himself loyally for the good of the school. Was he not exerting himself now? Why should he be unhappy? It was not because he felt himself beaten—he scorned the idea—or that he felt unequal to the task before him. That too was preposterous. And yet, he felt, he certainly needed something. If only now he were first classic as well as captain of the clubs, what a pull he would have!

And as this thought occurred to him, he also recalled Crossfield's famous speech at the last Parliament and the laughter which had greeted it. Could he translate "Balbus hopped over a wall" without the dictionary? Ah! He thought sometimes he would try, just to prove how slanderous Crossfield's insinuation had been. The result of all these cogitations was that Bloomfield began to discover he was not quite such an "all-round" man as his friends had told him. And that being so, had not he better qualify himself like an honest man for his post?

He did not like to confide the idea to his friends for fear of their laughter, but for a week or two at least he actually read rather hard on the sly. The worst of it was, that till the examinations next term there could be nothing to show for it. For the Sixth did not change their places every day as the lower forms did. There was no chance of leaping to the top at a bound by some lucky answer, or even of advancing a single desk. And therefore, however hard he worked this term, he would never rise above eighteenth classic in the eyes of the school, and that was not—well, he would have liked to be a little higher for the sake of Willoughby!

The outlook was not encouraging. Even Wibberly, the toady, and Silk, the Welcher, were better men than he was at classics.

Suppose, instead of spending his energy over classics, he were to get up one or two rousing speeches for the Parliament, which should take the shine out of every one else and carry the school by storm? It was not a bad idea. But the chance would not come. No one could get up a fine speech on such a hackneyed subject as "That Rowing is a finer Sport than Cricket," or that "The Study of Science in Public Schools should be Abolished!" And when he did attempt to prepare an oration on the subject of Compulsory Football, the first friend he showed it to pointed out so many faults in the composition of the first sentence that prudence prompted him to put the effusion in the fire.

Meanwhile his friends and admirers kept him busy. Their delight seemed to be to seize on all the youngsters they could by any pretext lay hands on and hale them to appear before him. By this means they imagined they were making his authority known and dealing a serious blow at the less obtrusive captain in the schoolhouse.

Poor Bloomfield had to administer justice right and left for every imaginable offence, and was so watched and prompted by officious admirers that he was constantly losing his head and making himself ridiculous.

He gave one boy a thrashing for being found with a paper dart in his hand, because Game had reported him; and to another, who had stolen a book, he gave only twenty lines, because he was in the second-eleven. Cusack and Welcher, who was caught climbing the schoolhouse elms one Monday, he sentenced to an hour's detention; and Pilbury, whom he caught in the same act on Tuesday, he deprived of play for a week—that is, he said he was not to leave his house for a week. But Pilbury turned up the very next day in the "Big," under the very nose of the Parrett captain, who did not even observe his presence.

It was this sort of thing which, as the term dragged on, made Bloomfield more and more uncomfortable with his position. It was all very well for Game, and Ashley, and Wibberly to declare that but for him Willoughby would have gone to the dogs— it was all very well of them to make game of and caricature Riddell and his failures. Seeing is believing; and Bloomfield, whose heart was honest, and whose common sense, when left to itself, was not altogether feeble, could not help making the unpleasant discovery that he was not doing very much after all for Willoughby.

But the boat-race was now coming on. There, at any rate, was a sphere in which he need fear no rival. With Parrett's boat at the head of the river, and he its stroke, he would at any rate have one claim on the obedience of Willoughby which nobody could gainsay.

Chapter Thirteen.

Telson and Parson go to an Evening Party.

It was the Saturday before the boat-race, and the excitement of Willoughby was working up every hour. Boys who were generally in the habit of lying in bed till the chapel bell began to ring had been up at six for a week past, to look at the practices on the river. Parliament had adjourned till after the event, and even the doings of the rival captains indoors were forgotten for a while in prospect of the still more exciting contest out of doors.

Everybody—even the Welchers, who at the last moment had given up any attempt to form a crew, and "scratched"—found it hard to think or talk of any other subject, and beyond the school bounds, in Shellport itself, a rumour of the coming race had got wind and attracted many outsiders to the river banks.

But it was not the prospect of the coming race which this Saturday afternoon was agitating the mind of Master Henry Brown.

Brown was a Limpet, belonging to the schoolhouse, who occupied the distinguished position of being the only day-boarder in Willoughby. His parents lived in Shellport, and thus had the benefit of the constant society of their dear Harry; while the school, on the other hand, was deprived of that advantage for a portion of every day in the term.

It was probably to make up for this deprivation that Mr and Mrs Brown made it a practice of giving an evening party once a term, to which the doctor and his ladies were always invited, and also any two of dear Harry's friends he liked to name.

In this way the fond parents not only felt they were doing a polite and neighbourly act to their son's schoolmaster and schoolfellows, but that they were also the means of bringing together teacher and pupil in an easy unconstrained manner which would hardly be possible within the walls of the school itself.

It was the prospect of one of these delightful entertainments that was exhilarating Brown this Saturday afternoon.

And it must be confessed the excitement was due to very opposite emotions in the breast of the day-boarder. The doctor and his ladies were coming! On the last two occasions they had been unfortunately prevented, which had been a great blow to Brown's "pa and ma" but a relief to Brown himself. And now the prospect of meeting these awful dignitaries face to face in his own house put him in a small panic. But on the other hand, he knew there would be jellies, and savoury pie, and strawberries, and tipsy-cake, at home that night. He had seen them arrive from the confectioner's that morning, and, Limpet as he was, Brown smiled inwardly as he meditated thereon. This was a second ground for excitement. And a third, equal to either of the other two, was that Parson and Telson were invited and were coming!

He had tried one or two other fellows first. He had sounded Coates on the subject, but he unfortunately was engaged. He had pressed Wyndham to come, but Wyndham was busy that evening with the library. He had appealed to one or two other schoolhouse Limpets, but all, on hearing that the doctor and Co. were to be present, respectfully declined.

Finally Brown dropped upon Telson, and condescendingly proposed to him to be present as one of his two friends.

Telson thought the matter over and fancied it promised well. He liked the sound of the jellies and the tipsy-cake, and just at present he knew of no special reason for "funking" the doctor. As for the doctor's ladies, Telson had never seen them, so they did not weigh particularly with him.

"Who else is going?" he asked.

"Oh, I don't know yet," said Brown, rather grandly. "I've one or two fellows in my mind."

"Why don't you ask young Parson?" suggested Telson, innocently.

"Parson? he's not a schoolhouse kid."

"I know he's not, but he and I are very chummy, you know. I wouldn't mind coming if he went."

"I'll see," said Brown, mightily, but secretly relieved to know of some one likely to come as his second "friend."

"All right," said Telson. "I've not promised, mind, if he can't come."

"Oh, yes, you have!" replied Brown, severely, as he left the room.

In due time he found Parson and broached the subject to him.

Parson viewed the matter in very much the same light as Telson had. He liked the "tuck-in" better than the company.

It never occurred to him it was odd that Brown should come all the way from the schoolhouse to invite him, a Parrett's junior, to his feast; nor did it occur to him either that the invitation put him under any obligation to his would-be host.

"I tell you what I'll do," said he, in a business-like manner, much as if Brown had asked him to clean out his study for him, "if you ask Telson to come too, I'm game."

Brown half doubted whether these two allies had not been consulting together on the subject, so startling was the similarity of their conditions.

"Oh! Telson's coming," he said, in as offhand a way as he could.

"He is! Then I'm on, old man; rather!" exclaimed the delighted Parson.

"All right! Six-thirty, mind, and chokers!" said Brown, not a little relieved to have scraped up two friends for the festive occasion. At the appointed time—or rather before the appointed time, for they arrived at twenty minutes past six—our two heroes, arrayed in their Sunday jackets and white ties, presented themselves at the house of their host. They had "put it on" considerably in order to get ahead of the doctor's party; for they considered that—as Parson expressed it—"it would be a jolly lot less blushy work" to be there before the head master arrived. There was no doubt about their success in this little manoeuvre, for when the servant opened the door the hall was full of rout seats, and a man, uncommonly like the greengrocer, in a dress coat, was busily unpacking plates out of a small hamper.

Into this scene of confusion Parson and Telson were ushered, and here they were left standing for about five minutes, interested spectators, till the hall was cleared and the domestic had leisure to go and tell Master Harry of their arrival.

Master Harry was dressing, and sent down word they had better go into the shoe-room till he came down. Which they did, and amused themselves during the interval with trying on Mr Brown's Wellingtons, and tying together the laces of all Harry's boots they could discover.

In due time Harry appeared in grand array. "How jolly early you are!" was his hospitable greeting. "You said six-thirty, didn't you?" said Telson. "Yes; it's only just that now. Nobody will be here for a quarter of an hour yet. You had better come in and see ma."

The two guests obeyed cheerfully. Ma was in the drawing-room, busily adjusting the sashes of the three juvenile Misses Brown, with her mouth full of pins. So all she could do was to smile pleasantly at her two visitors and nod her head as they each came up and held out their hands to be shaken.

"Better sit down," suggested Brown.

Parson and Telson thereupon retreated to the sofa, on the edge of which they sat for another five or ten minutes, looking about them complacently, and not attempting to break the silence of the scene.

The silence, however, was soon broken by a loud double knock at the hall door, which was the signal for Mr Brown, senior, to bolt into the room in a guilty way with one cuff not quite buttoned, and stand on the hearthrug with as free-and-easy an air as if he had been waiting there a quarter of an hour at least. Knock followed knock in quick succession, and after the usual amount of fluttering in the hall, the greengrocer flung open the drawing-room door and ushered in Dr and Mrs Patrick, Miss Stringer, and half a dozen other arrivals.

Our two heroes, sitting side by side, unnoticed on the edge of the sofa, had full opportunity to take stock of the various guests, most of whom were strangers to them.

As every one appeared to be about the doctor's age, things promised slowly for Parson and Telson, whose interest in Brown's party decidedly languished when finally they found themselves swept off their perch and helplessly wedged into a corner by an impenetrable phalanx of skirts.

But this was nothing compared with a discovery they made at the same time that they had missed their tea! There was a merry rattle of cups and spoons in a room far off, through the half-open door of which they could catch glimpses of persons drinking tea, and of Brown handing round biscuits and cake. The sight of this was too much to be borne. It was at least worth an effort to retrieve their fatal mistake.

"I say," said Telson, looking for his friend round the skirts of a stately female, "hadn't we better go and help Brown, Parson?"

Luckless youth! The lady in question, hearing the unexpected voice at her side, backed a little and caught sight of the speaker.

"What, dear?" she said, benevolently, taking his hand and sitting down on the sofa; "and who are you, my little man?"

"My little man" was fairly trapped; there was no escaping this seizure. Parson got away safely to the tea-room, and the sight of him dodging about among the cakes and cups only added to the misery of the hapless Telson.

"Who are you, my little dear?" said the lady, who was no other than Miss Stringer herself.

Telson, fortunately for him, was ignorant of the fact—as ignorant, indeed, as Miss Stringer was of the fact that the little dear she was addressing was a Willoughbite.

"Telson, ma'am," said Telson, following Parson with longing eyes.

"Johnny?" said the lady.

"No—Augustus," replied the proud bearer of the name.

Miss Stringer surveyed him benevolently. He was a nice-looking boy, was Telson—and the lady thought so too.

"And will you give me a kiss, Augustus dear?" she said, with her most winning smile.

What could Augustus do? A hundred desperate alternatives darted through his mind. He would bolt into the tea-room; he would shout for help; he would show fight; he would— But while he was making up his mind what he would do, he found himself being kissed on the cheek in the most barefaced manner, before everybody, by this extraordinary female; and, more than that, being actually set down on the sofa beside her! He only hoped Parson or Brown had not seen it.

Well for Miss Stringer she did not guess the wrath that boiled in the bosom of her small companion!

"And do you live here, dear?" inquired she, pleased to have this opportunity of studying the juvenile human nature in which she was so much interested.

"No, I don't," said Telson, surlily; then, suddenly recollecting he was in polite though disagreeable company, he added, "ma'am."

"And where do you go to school, pray?" inquired the spinster.

"Oh, Willoughby," replied Telson, who had gradually given up all hope of tea, and was making up his mind to his fate.

Miss Stringer gave a little start at this piece of information, and was on the point of betraying her identity, but she forbore. "After all," thought she, "he might be more constrained if I were to enlighten him on that subject."

"So you go to Willoughby," she said, with interest. "And how do you like it?"

"Oh, well enough," said Telson, relenting somewhat towards his companion as she showed no further signs of kissing him. "Nice lot of fellows, you know, on the whole."

"Indeed? Let me see, who is the head master?" inquired the lady.

"Oh, Paddy—that old boy there by the fire. And that's Mrs Paddy there with the curls."

Miss Stringer appeared to receive another shock at this piece of information, which, however, Telson, flattered by her evident interest in his remarks, did not take to heart.

"And," said she, presently, with a slight nervousness in her voice, "I hope you like them?"

"Oh," blurted out Telson, "Paddy's not so bad, but the dame's an old beast, you know—at least, so fellows say. I say," added he, "don't you tell her I said so!"

Miss Stringer regarded him with a peculiar smile, which the boy at once took to mean a promise. So he rattled on. "And she's got a sister, or somebody hangs about the place, worse than any of them. Why, when old Wynd—"

"And," said Miss Stringer, suddenly—"and which house are you in—in the schoolhouse?"

"Hullo, then! you know Willoughby?" demanded Telson sharply.

Miss Stringer looked confused, as well she might, but replied, "Ah! all public schools have a schoolhouse, have they not?"

"I suppose so," said Telson. "Yes, I'm a schoolhouse fellow. I'm the captain's fag, you know—old Riddell."

"Mr Riddell is the captain, then?"

"Rather! Do you know him?"

Poor Miss Stringer! How sad it is, to be sure, when once we go astray. She, the Griffin of Willoughby, was as much at the mercy of this honest unconscious fag as if he had caught her in the act of picking a pocket. For how could she reveal herself now?

"I—I think I met him once," she said.

"Where? at his home, was it?" asked Telson, who seemed to be urged by a most fiendish curiosity on the subject.

55

"No," faltered the lady; "it was—er—I think it was at Dr Patrick's."

"Very likely," said Telson. "He was up there to tea, I know, just before he was made captain. But I didn't know any one else was there except Paddy and his hyenas."

"His what, sir!" exclaimed Miss Stringer, in a voice which nearly startled Telson off the sofa.

"I mean, you know, the fellows—?"

"And where do you live at home?" asked Miss Stringer, determined to steer clear of this awkward topic.

"Oh, London," said Telson; "do you know London?"

"Yes—it is indeed a wonderful place," said Miss Stringer, "and whereabouts does your father live?"

"Oh, my governor's in India," began Telson.

"Your who?" said Miss Stringer, with a feeble attempt at severity.

"My dad, you know; and I live with my grandfather. Jolly old boy. He was at Willoughby when he was a boy. Did you know him then? I expect he'll recollect you, you know."

"I do not think," said Miss Stringer, with a very ruffled countenance, "that your grandfather and I ever met."

"Oh, I don't know. He recollects most of the old people down here, you know. I say, there's Parson beckoning; he's my chum, you know. I expect he wants me to help with some of the things."

And so saying off he went, leaving Miss Stringer, so to speak, fairly doubled up, and in a state of mind which may be more easily imagined than described.

Every one observed how singularly silent and retiring Miss Stringer was all that evening. Some attributed it to the heat of the room, others feared she might not be well, others guessed she found the Browns' entertainment very slow; but no one, least of all Telson himself, had a suspicion of the true reason.

That young gentleman and his ally, after finding out that there was not much chance of their services being required to "look after the things"—the greengrocer being quite able to deal with the business single-handed—found themselves once more stranded in the drawing-room, and gradually getting edged back by the skirts, when an unlooked-for distinction rescued them from their perilous situation.

The distinction was none other than a sign of recognition from the doctor and a friendly signal to approach.

Like a pair of small well-trained circus ponies the two friends obeyed the summons and climbed over the intervening skirts.

"Well, Telson and Parson," said the doctor, shaking hands, "I'd no idea you were here—how are you?"

"We got a captain's permit. Quite well, thank you, sir."

"My dear, these are two of our boys, Telson and Parson."

Mrs Patrick regarded the two boys in her usual precise way, and said,—

"Among so many boys under our roof, I find it impossible to remember every face. And which is Master Telson?"

"This is Telson," said Parson. "He's in the schoolhouse, you know—"

"I do not know," said Mrs Patrick, severely.

"Don't you?" said Parson, with genuine astonishment. "He's captain's fag, you know."

"I must repeat I do not know," reiterated Mrs Patrick.

"Oh, well, he's only been that a little time, since the sports, you know, when old Wyndham left. I say, ma'am, are you going to be at the race on Wednesday?"

Mrs Patrick looked somewhat baffled as she replied,—

"I think it very possible."

"It'll be a jolly good race," said Telson. "Old Parson is coxing Parrett's, and it looks like a win for them. Only we aren't so bad, and now Gilks is out of the boat and Riddell's settled as cox we ought to make a race of it. Fairbairn's quite as long a reach as Bloomfield, only he doesn't kick his stretcher so hard—does he, Parson?"

"Rather not," said Parson. "That's where we get the pull of you; besides, I'm a lighter weight than Riddell, though he's boiled down a good bit since he went into training."

"Good deal depends on who gets the inside berth," said Telson, delightfully oblivious of the bewildered Mrs Paddy's presence. "It's a jolly long swing round Willow Point for the outsiders—half a length at least."

"Yes; but it's just as bad round the corner at the finish the other way."

"Ah! talking about the race, I see," said the doctor, returning to the group at this point. "So, Telson, Riddell's to steer your boat after all."

"Yes, sir," said Telson; "it's settled now."

"So that the schoolhouse boat is still the captain's boat, eh? Ah! Parson, though, I suppose, wants the Parrett's boat to win."

"Parson coxes for Parrett's," said Telson.

"Parrett—I mean Mr Parrett—stopped my river-play a week, sir," said Parson, by way of explaining the circumstance; "but I've had captain's leave to row out since, so they kept me in the boat."

This sporting conversation went on for some time longer, Mrs Patrick not venturing again to join in. At last the doctor broke up the conference of his own accord, and our two heroes, once more adrift, went out for a lounge in the hall, as they explained, to cool themselves, but really to be at hand for a bolt into the supper-room whenever the happy moment should arrive.

It did arrive after what seemed to be a week's suspense and then the hardships and perils of the evening were fully compensated for. The two friends got into a snug corner, "far from the madding crowd," where, to put it mildly, they spent a very busy half-hour. They managed it well. Neither boy helped himself—he wouldn't be so greedy; but each helped the other. When Telson saw Parson's plate getting empty of sandwiches, he most attentively fetched him a clean one with a trifle on it; and when Telson had finally got through his jellies (for he had more than one) it was Parson's brotherly hand which assisted him to an ice!

As they sat there they positively wished Brown's "pa and ma" gave a party once a week!

But all good things come to an end, and so did this grand party. Guests began to depart, and among the earliest were the doctor and his ladies. The doctor came up to the boys, and said, kindly, "We're driving up; you two had better come with us, there's plenty of room on the box. Now, my love—now, Miss Stringer."

Miss Stringer! Telson nearly fainted as he saw who it was who answered to the name.

"Let's walk up," he said, entreatingly, to Parson.

"I don't mind, only Paddy—"

"Now then, boys," cried the doctor, "there's room for one inside. Telson, will you come?"

Telson bounded up on to the box without another word, and Parson beside him, and the fly drove off.

"Oh, Parson, old man, I'm a gone coon!" exclaimed Telson, in tones of abject misery, as soon as they were clear of the Browns' premises.

"Why, what's up?"

"Miss Stringer!"

"What about her? Isn't she a cad, eh?"

"Yes, and *I told her so*," groaned Telson; "I didn't know who she was, and I said—"

"Hullo, I say, look there!" exclaimed Parson, suddenly catching his friend by the arm.

They were passing the Aquarium, which at that moment was disgorging its visitors. Among those who emerged exactly as the doctor's fly passed were three boys, whom Telson and Parson recognised in a moment.

They were Silk and Gilks and another younger boy, who seemed to shrink from observation, and whose head was turned another way as the fly passed. The three, immediately on gaining the street, started to run towards Willoughby ahead of the fly.

The two boys on the box pulled their caps over their eyes, and said not a word till the truants were clear. Then Telson said, "That was young Wyndham!"

"I know. I wonder if Paddy saw them?"

"Shouldn't think so. And they didn't see us. I say, will they get in before us?"

"It'll be a shave if they do. What a row there'll be if they don't!"

It was a curious thing that almost immediately after this short dialogue Telson's cap fell off into the road, and the fly had to be pulled up while he and Parson got down and looked for it. It was a dark night, and the cap took some time to find. When finally it was recovered, and progress was resumed, full five minutes had been lost over the search, by which time the truants had got a clear half-mile to the good, and were safe.

Chapter Fourteen.

The Boat-Race.

The few days that intervened between the Saturday of Brown's party and the Wednesday of the great race were days of restless suspense in Willoughby. Even Welch's caught the contagion, and regretted at the last hour that they had withdrawn from the all-important contest. As to the other two Houses, there never had been a year when the excitement ran so high or the rivalry grew so keen. Somehow the entire politics of Willoughby appeared to be mixed up in the contest, and it seemed as if the result of this one struggle was to decide everything.

The crews had worked hard up to the last, watched morning and evening by anxious spectators from the bank. The trials had been carefully noted and times compared, the variations in style had been eagerly criticised, the weights of the rowers had become public property, and in short every detail likely to influence the result was a subject of almost painful interest to the eager partisans on either side.

And every hour seemed to promise a closer race. Not that Parrett's had fallen off. On the contrary, they still remained what they had been all along, the smartest and strongest crew that Willoughby had ever put upon the river. But the schoolhouse boat had made wonderful strides. It was long since it had ceased to be the laughingstock of the hostile juniors, and it was some time since its appearance and work had begun to cause a shade of uneasiness in the minds of a few of the rival house. Fairbairn, far from Bloomfield's match in physique or style, had yet displayed an amount of steady, determined work which had astonished most fellows, and inspired with confidence not only his partisans on the bank, but the three oarsmen at his back. By dint of patient, untiring practice he had worked his crew up to a pitch of training scarcely hoped for, and every day the schoolhouse boat had gained in style and speed.

Had the race been a fortnight or three weeks later few boys would have cared to prophesy definitely as to the result. As it was, though Parrett's was morally bound to win, it was clear the race would be a fierce one, and hardly fought every foot.

Such was the general opinion in Willoughby that Tuesday evening after the last practice had come to an end, and when the boats were finally housed for the night only to reappear next day in racing trim.

Young Wyndham, as he sat in Riddell's study with his books before him, could as soon have done a stroke of work as fly over the schoolhouse elms. Indeed, it was such a farce for him even to make the attempt that he shut up his books and gave up the idea.

"I say, Riddell," he said, presently, addressing the captain, who, though excited too after his own fashion, was poring determinedly over his work.

"Well?" asked he, looking up.

"I say, *do* you think there's any chance of our boat winning?"

The boy asked the question so anxiously that one might have supposed his whole happiness in life depended on the answer.

"It's very hard to say," said Riddell. "I think we have some chance, at any rate."

"You did the course in as good time as Parrett's yesterday, didn't you?" said Wyndham.

"Yes, but we had a better tide," said Riddell.

Wyndham's face clouded, for he knew it was true.

"You *must* win, I say," said he, almost fiercely.

Riddell smiled.

"I mean to oblige you if I can, for one," said he.

"If they win," said Wyndham, "it'll be—"

But what it would be the youthful enthusiast lacked words to express.

Riddell turned again to his writing.

"Hadn't you better finish your work?" said he.

"Oh, I can't!" exclaimed Wyndham. "Who could work just before the race?"

So saying, he got up and gathered together his things.

Riddell was sorry for this. He had hoped the boy would stay. Amid all his fresh duties the new captain had kept his eye on his old friend's brother, and of late he had seen things which made him uneasy. Wyndham was on friendly terms again with his two undesirable patrons, and simultaneously his work in the library and his visits to Riddell's own study had become less regular. It all meant something, Riddell knew; and he knew, too, that that something was not any good. He made one attempt to detain the boy.

"You aren't going?" he said kindly.

"Yes. It's really no use grinding, to-night, Riddell."

"Won't you stop and keep me company, though?" asked the captain.

"You're working," said the boy. "I'll come to-morrow. Good-night."

And he went, leaving Riddell very uncomfortable. Why should he be so eager to go? Why should he always seem so restless now whenever he was in that study? Why should he always avoid any reference to—

Ah! here he was back again. A gleam of hope shot through Riddell's breast as he saw the door open and Wyndham re-enter. Perhaps, after all, the boy was going to stay and give him a chance. But no, Wyndham had come back for his knife, which Riddell had borrowed for sharpening a pencil. That was all he wanted; and having recovered it he departed quickly.

Riddell spent the rest of that evening in low spirits. He had been baulked, and worse than that, he felt other hands were playing their game more successfully, and that amongst them all young Wyndham was going wrong.

So the eve of the great boat-race was anything but a cheerful evening for the new captain.

But with the morning even Riddell could hardly harbour any thoughts outside the event of the day. Morning school that Wednesday was a farce all over Willoughby. Even the doctor seemed absent-minded, while one or two of the junior masters gave up the attempt in despair.

The race was fixed for three o'clock, when the tide would be running up at its fastest, and long before that hour every advantageous point of view on the banks was secured by eager spectators. These were by no means all Willoughby boys, for the school boat-race was always more or less of an event in Shellport itself, whose inhabitants flocked in large numbers to the scene of the contest.

Carnages lined the banks on either side for a considerable distance, and as usual the doctor's party assembled in great force on Willow Point. The towing-path was jealously kept clear for the schoolboys, who trooped down in force the moment after lunch, and took possession of their places along the course. Some crowded at the starting-point. These were chiefly the more athletic heroes of the school, whose flannels and running-shoes bespoke their intention of following the race on foot. Others, less actively inclined, massed at various critical points along the course, some at the finish, but more opposite Willow Point, which being just three-quarters of the way down, and almost within view of the goal, was generally considered the most advantageous point of view of the whole race.

At this point, in a snug corner above the path, with a fine view of the sharp bend of the river, and of the reaches up and down stream which met there, sat Gilks and Silk. They knew probably as well as any one that the crisis of the race was pretty sure to be played out at Willow Corner, and not a few late comers looked up at their commanding perch with envy.

"Where's the young 'un?" said Silk.

"Running with the race," said Gilks. "I couldn't dissuade him. He's gone daft over the thing."

Silk laughed.

"I'm afraid it'll be a blow to him, then. Young fool. I say, he was at his father confessor's last night. I wonder if he'll let out about Saturday night?"

"Not he. That is," said Gilks, viciously, "I don't think he will."

"Well, it might be warmish for him if he did."

"Very warmish," said Gilks, with a scowl, which it was just as well for Wyndham's comfort he did not see.

There was a silence, during which Gilks whistled to himself, and Silk regarded his ally with a smile.

"You are a nice boy!" he broke out presently. And the laugh which greeted this very unoriginal observation closed the conversation for a time.

Meanwhile, down at the boat-house things were getting very lively.

Telson, Philpot, Pilbury, Cusack, King, and other of our juvenile friends, who, with their usual modesty, proposed to run along with the race, and now formed part of the crowd which awaited the start, kept up a boisterous chorus of shouts, some of defiance, some of derision, some of applause, addressed alternately to foe and friend.

The young Welchers especially, having no personal interest in the race, felt themselves delightfully free to make themselves objectionable to all parties, and took full advantage of the circumstance.

They howled at everybody and everything. Whenever King and Bosher greeted the appearance of the Parrett's boat with a friendly cheer they hooted; and no sooner did Telson sing out to welcome the crew of his house, but they caterwauled derisively in the same direction.

"Jolly lot *they* know about rowing!" yelled Cusack.

"Why don't you give them some lessons?" retorted Telson, hotly.

"Boo—hoo! Who got kicked out his boat! Young muller, couldn't steer a tub."

"I'll tub you, young Pilbury, see if I don't, presently," replied Telson.

"Never mind them," shouted King, "can't even make up a boat; pack of funks, all of them!"

"Hullo! who are you?" cried Philpot, rounding on these new assailants. "We'd have a boat, never fear, if there was any chance of fair play."

"Lot of fair play you'd want, to turn the boat round and round and catch crabs every other second!"

"There are our fellows!" cried Wyndham, raising a loud cheer as Fairbairn, Coates, Porter, Crossfield, and Riddell appeared on the landing stage.

"Hurrah! schoolhouse, hurrah!"

"Ye-ow, look at them—there's a lot!" hooted the Welchers.

"There's old Parson!" yelled Telson, Bosher, and King, as the youthful hero in question strutted magnificently down to the landing.

"What cheer, stuck-up jackass?" howled the Welchers, with an insulting laugh; "why don't you grin?"

This remark was suggested by Parson grandly waving his handkerchief and smiling to his admiring friends.

But it is time to quit these friends and make our way to the boats themselves, which now lie waiting for their crews to embark.

This is always a tedious process for onlookers. The shifting of stretchers, the getting-out of oars, the arrangement of rudder strings, and the delicate trimming of the boat, may be interesting enough to the crews themselves, but only feed the impatience of onlookers.

And as usual hitches are bound to occur. Coates has got the oar belonging to Crossfield. And when this mistake has been remedied, Bloomfield in the other boat suddenly discovers that his stretcher is a little weak, and insists on waiting till a new one is brought.

Finally everything is ready, and the two boats slowly swing out into mid-stream. The schoolhouse boat has won the toss, for it takes up the inside berth, amid the triumphant cheers of its partisans.

"Hurrah! you're inside," they cry.

"Mind you put them into the bank," is the derisive echo of the enemy.

"Now, Fairbairn; now, you fellows," cries Wyndham's voice.

"Now, boss Riddell—mind your eye. Pull your left when you want to go right," shout the facetious Welchers.

Riddell had long got past the stage of being flurried by shouts from the bank. He feels nervous undoubtedly, but he does not look it, as he quietly tries his rudder-lines and settles himself on his seat.

Fairbairn is as cool as ever. To look at him he might be just starting for a quiet saunter up-stream. And the crew behind him are equally composed, as they lie on their oars waiting for the start.

But the Parrett's crew, as they come smartly up and take their outside berth, receive an ovation far beyond that of their rivals. They are undoubtedly the popular crew, as well as the favourites.

Every man in the boat has done something for Willoughby in times past, and as the boys see their heroes ready now for a fresh triumph, they forget all about their little tyrannies indoors, and cheer them like mad.

"Bravo Parrett's. Bravo, Bloomfield! Hurrah, captain! You're to win."

Even the Welchers for the moment join in the popular clamour.

"Go it, you cripples!" cries Cusack, encouragingly; "no milksop captains. Two to one on Bloomfield!"

All this time the boats are lying in position. Mr Parrett on the little steam-launch behind surveys them critically, and satisfies himself that all is square. Then he advances to the prow of his boat and shouts the usual question.

The next moment he gives the word, and the two boats dart forward like arrows from a bow, and the race has begun.

Gilks and Silk up above Willow Corner heard the shout which greeted the start, and turned anxiously towards the direction from which it came.

"They're off now!" said Silk, trying to appear more unconcerned than he really was.

"Yes; no mistake about it!" said Gilks, whose anxiety was certainly not less than that of his friend.

"How long before we see them?"

"Three minutes; they ought to get into the School Reach by then."

Neither spoke for a minute. Then Silk said, "What a row the fellows are making!"

"Yes," said Gilks; "there's a bigger crowd than I ever saw down this year."

Another silence. And then presently in the far distance, at the end of the School Reach, they could see first the smoke of Mr Parrett's launch, then a black moving crowd on the bank, and finally two white specks on the water.

"There they are!" said Gilks.

"Can you tell which is which?" asked Silk.

"No, not yet."

An anxious minute followed. The doctor and his party on the point opposite left their tent and came down to the water's edge; spectators who had been getting tired of waiting now freshened up and made final and desperate attempts to improve their position, while those who meant to fall in with the runners buttoned their jackets and turned up their trouser ends.

"Schoolhouse inside!" exclaimed Gilks, suddenly, as the sun momentarily caught the blue oars of the inside boat.

This was all that could be ascertained for the moment. From where they sat the blue and the red flags seemed to be coming towards them exactly abreast.

The crowd advanced with a roar, above which it was impossible to hear the name of the leading crew. But presently, as the two boats approached the corner, a slight turn inwards enabled them to answer the question for themselves.

"We lead!" exclaimed Silk.

Silk was a Welcher and Gilks a schoolhouse boy, but "we" meant Parrett's.

Yes, the red flag was ahead, though only a little.

"How long before they're at the point?"

"Half a minute. I say, how splendidly the schoolhouse are steering, though!"

Silk laughed. "More than Parrett's are! Young Parson's taking them round rather sharp, isn't he?"

"No; he always turns in like that; it's better than the long sweep. Now look out!"

During this brief dialogue the two boats had come on towards the corner. As far as Gilks and Silk could see at present Parrett's led by about half a length, which advantage, however, it stood to lose owing to its outside position at the corner. Parson, however, knew what he was about even better than Riddell, who had kept a magnificent course down the reach, but who now seemed afraid to take full advantage of the sharp corner. The Parrett's coxswain, on the other hand, with his half-length to the good, began turning his boat's head early, even at the risk of running dangerously close on his rival's water, and so saved as much as possible of the lost ground.

It was an anxious moment, for as the boats came round that corner so the race usually depended. The crowd on the banks well knew the crisis, and shouted out their warnings and encouragements to the rival coxswains with redoubled eagerness.

"Now then, Riddell! round you go! Pull your right!"

"Steered indeed, Parrett's! Bravo, Parson!"

The corner was half-turned, the boats lay nearly level, each coxswain pulling hard with his right line, when suddenly there was a shock in the Parrett's boat, followed by a loud shout from Parson, and next moment the boat was shooting helplessly straight towards the bank, from which it was only saved by a prompt order to "Backwater all!" from Bloomfield.

What could it be? The shouts on the bank died away into sudden stillness, and fellows forgot even to keep up with the schoolhouse boat, which, followed by the steam-launch, rowed steadily on towards the winning-post.

What was it? The answer soon became known, when Parson, standing in his boat, waved the broken end of a rudder-line above his head. At the critical point of the race this had failed, and in consequence all the efforts of the rowers were useless, and—and the schoolhouse boat was Head of the River!

The rage, excitement, and disappointment at such an unlooked-for termination to the great struggle was beyond description, as the reader may imagine. A general rush was made for the unlucky boat, and shouts and recriminations and taunts and condolences bore witness to the mixed feelings of the spectators.

Some demanded a fresh race there and then, some suggested foul play, others urged the boat to row on and make the best race they could of it, others boldly claimed the victory for Parrett's, since they led at the moment of the accident.

Amidst all this tumult the unlucky boat slowly backed into mid-stream, and turned towards home, Parson steering no longer by rudder but by word of mouth. As it did so, a distant report announced that the schoolhouse boat had reached the winning-post; whereat the Parrett partisans set up a loud defiant shout, which they maintained during the entire homeward progress of their ill-starred boat.

Among the few who remained on the scene of the accident were Gilks and Silk, both pale and agitated.

The latter, as has been said, was painfully interested in the result of the race. To him the defeat of Parrett's meant more than the mere disappointment of a hope or the humiliation by a rival. It meant the loss of a good deal more money than he possessed, and the miscarriage of a good deal which he had expected with absolute confidence to win. No wonder then that his face was white and his voice trembling as he rounded on his friend.

"You fool!" exclaimed he, with an oath.

It was rather hard surely on Gilks, who may have encouraged his friend to rely on the victory of the Parrett's boat, but who certainly was as much astounded and mortified by the accident as he was.

"There must be another race," said he, hurriedly. "They can't take this as decisive, I tell you. They *must* have another."

"You wouldn't have said so if the right boat had won," said Silk, with a sneer.

"I can't make it out," said Gilks, looking very miserable.

"Fools never can," snarled Silk, turning on his heel.

Chapter Fifteen.

Foul Play.

Willoughby reassembled after the eventful boat-race in a state of fever. The great event which was to settle everything had settled nothing, and the suspense and excitement which was to have been set at rest remained still as unsatisfied as ever, and intensified by a feeling of rage and disappointment.

As boys dropped in in groups from the course, and clustered round the school gate, one might have supposed by their troubled faces that instead of a rudder-line having broken both crews had been capsized and drowned.

The Parrett's partisans particularly were loud in their clamour for a new race, and many of them freely insinuated foul play as the cause of the accident.

The schoolhouse, on the other hand, indignantly repelled the charge, and dared their opponents defiantly to meet them again. And amidst all this wrangling and bickering, the Welchers dispensed their taunts and invectives with even-handed impartiality, and filled in just what was wanted to make the scene one of utter confusion and Babel.

"I tell you we'd have beaten them hollow," shouted Wibberly to the company in general.

"No you wouldn't!" retorted Wyndham; "we were ahead and our men were as fresh as yours, every bit!"

"Ya—boo—cheats! Told you there'd be no fair play with such a pack," shouted the Welchers.

"Look here, who are you calling a cheat?" said Wyndham, very red in the face, edging up to the speaker.

"You, if you like," shouted Pilbury and Cusack.

"I'll knock your heads together when I catch you," said Wyndham, with lofty disgust, not intending to put himself out for two juniors.

A loud laugh greeted the threat.

Meanwhile, fellows were running up every moment. Some who had been waiting for the boats at the winning-post had only just heard the news, and came in red-hot with excitement to learn particulars.

"It's all a vile dodge," howled Wibberly, "to get their boat to the head of the river."

"I'll bet anything the precious captain's at the bottom of it," shouted another. "He'd stick at nothing, I know."

"Yes, and you'll see, now they'll funk another race!"

"Who'll funk another race?" roared the hot-headed Wyndham. "I'll row you myself, you asses, the lot of you."

Another derisive laugh followed at the speaker's expense.

"It's not our fault if your line broke," cried a schoolhouse boy. "It's your lookout. You should have seen it was right before you started."

"Yes. You wouldn't have been so anxious for a new race if it was our line had broken," said Wyndham.

"Yes, we would. We're not afraid of you!"

"Yes, you are."

"No, we aren't. You're a set of cheats. Couldn't win by fair means, so you've tried foul."

"I'll fight any one who says so," retorted Wyndham.

How long the wrangle might have gone on, and to what riot it might have led, cannot be told. It was at its hottest, and a general fight seemed imminent, when a diversion was caused by the sudden appearance of Parson running at full speed up the path from the river.

There was something unusual in the looks and manner of the Parretts' coxswain, which even his misadventure that afternoon was not sufficient to account for. He bore tidings of some sort, it was evident, and by common consent the clamour of the crowd was suspended as he approached.

Among the first to hail him at shouting distance was Telson.

"What's up, old man?" he cried.

Parson rushed on a dozen yards or so before he answered. Then he yelled, in a voice half-choked with excitement, "The line was cut! It's foul play!"

The howl which arose from the agitated crowd at this amazing piece of news—amazing even to those who had most freely raised the cry of foul play—was one the like of which Willoughby never heard before or since. Mingled rage, scorn, incredulity, derision, all found vent in that one shout—and then suddenly died into silence as Parson began again.

"They've looked at the place where it broke," he gasped. "It's a clean cut half-way through. I knew it was foul play!"

Once again the shout drowned his voice.

"Who did it?" shrieked a voice, before Parson could resume.

Parson glared round wrathfully for the speaker.

"I don't know," he replied. "Sorry for him if I did!"

This valiant invective from the honest little fag failed even to appear ludicrous in the midst of the general excitement. Further words were now interrupted by the appearance of the Parretts' crew coming slowly up the walk.

This was the signal for a general cheer and rush in their direction, in the midst of which the defeated heroes with difficulty struggled up to the school. Wrath and indignation were on all their faces. In reply to the hundred inquiries showered upon them they said nothing, but forced their way through the press sullenly, heedless of the cheers of their sympathisers or the silence of their opponents.

The crowd slowly fell back to let them pass, and watched them disappear into the school. Then they turned again towards the path from the river, and waited with grim purpose.

The news announced by Parson and confirmed by the black looks of the injured crew had fallen like a thunderbolt, and for the moment Willoughby was stunned. The boys could not—would not—believe that one of their number could be guilty of such an act. And yet, how could they disbelieve it?

In a few minutes there was a cry of "Here they are!" and at the same moment the schoolhouse crew appeared on the walk. They, victors though they were, looked troubled and dispirited as they approached, talking eagerly among themselves, and unconcerned apparently about the crowd which in ominous silence awaited them.

They certainly did not look like guilty persons, and it is most probable not even the wildest libeller in Willoughby would have cared positively to charge any one of them with the dishonourable deed.

But for all that, they had won in consequence of that deed, and that was quite sufficient to set three-fourths of the crowd against them.

As they came up a loud groan and cries of "Cheats! Foul play!" suddenly arose. Startled by the unexpected demonstration, the five heroes looked up with flushed faces.

"Cheats! Cowards!" reiterated the hostile section, beginning at the same time to surge towards them.

Foremost among these was Tucker of Welch's house and Wibberly of Parrett's, who, as the crowd behind pressed forward, were carried with their abusive taunts on their lips into the midst of the schoolhouse group. The latter, as may be imagined, were in anything but the humour for an assault of this sort, and their leaders instantly resented it in a *very* practical manner.

"Where are you coming to?" demanded Fairbairn, flinging Wibberly from him into the arms of his followers.

Before Wibberly could recover his balance the crowd had closed in by a sudden impulse, and with a loud shout had set upon the crew.

"Have them over, Parrett's!" shouted a voice, as Wibberly staggered back a second time before Fairbairn's stalwart arm, while at the same moment Tucker received a similar rebuff from Crossfield.

The summons was promptly answered, and a dash was made on the five schoolhouse boys with a view to carrying out the threat literally, when Wyndham's voice shouted, "Rescue here! schoolhouse, come on!"

Instantly the whole crowd seemed to resolve itself by magic into two parties, and a short but desperate battle ensued.

The fire had been waiting for weeks for a match, and now the flare-up had come. Nobody knew whom he hit out at or by whom he was attacked that forenoon. The pent-up irritation of half a term found vent in that famous battle in which the schoolhouse boys fought their way inch by inch up to the door of their house.

Luckily for them, the most formidable of their rivals were not upon the field of action, and in due time the compact phalanx of seniors, aided by Wyndham and his band of recruits, forced their way through superior numbers, and finally burst triumphantly through and gained their stronghold.

But the victory was hardly bought, for the slaughter had been great.

Coates had a black eye, and Porter's jacket was torn from his back. Riddell had twice been knocked down and trodden on, while Wyndham, Telson, and others of the rescuing party were barely recognisable through dust and bruises. On the other side the loss had been even greater. Tucker and Wibberly, the only two monitors engaged, were completely doubled up, while the number of maimed and disabled Limpets and juniors was nearly beyond counting.

So ended the great battle at the school gate, and it ended only just in time, for as the schoolhouse boys finally gained their quarters, and the enemy picked itself up and turned surlily schoolwards, the doctor and his party arrived on the scene and gave a finishing touch to the rout.

That evening was a sore one for Willoughby. Sore not only in respect of bruised bodies and swollen faces, but still more in the sense of disappointment, suspicion, and foul play.

Among the most violent of the Parrett's the whole mystery of the thing was perfectly clear. These philosophers could see it all from beginning to end, and were astonished any one else should be so dull as not to see it too.

"Of course, it's a regularly arranged thing," said Wibberly, whose face was enveloped in a handkerchief and whose lips were unusually thick. "They've vowed all along to keep their boat at the head of the river, and they've managed it."

"Yes," said another. "They knew what they had to expect if Bloomfield got there. I can see it all."

"But you don't mean to say," said Strutter, "the Premier," "that you think any one of those fellows would do such a thing as cut our rope?"

"I don't know," said Wibberly. "I don't see why they shouldn't. I don't fancy they'd stick at a trifle, the cads!"

"If Gilks had been in the boat," said another, "I could have believed it of him, but he was as anxious for us to win as we were ourselves."

"No wonder; he and his friend Silk have been betting right and left on us, I hear."

"Well, I suppose there's bound to be a new race," said Strutter.

"I don't know," replied Wibberly. "I'd be just as well pleased if Bloomfield refused. The vile cheats!"

Bloomfield, be it said to his credit, was no party to these reckless accusations. Mortified as he was beyond description, and disappointed by the collapse of his ambition, he yet scouted the idea of any one of his five rivals being guilty of so dirty a trick as the cutting of his boat's rudder-line. At the same time he was as convinced as any one that foul play had been at the bottom of the accident, and the perpetrator of the mean act was undoubtedly a schoolhouse boy. What mortified him most was that he did not feel as positive by any means as others that his boat, without the accident, would have won the race. He had been astonished and even disheartened by the performance of the rival crew, who had stuck to him in a manner he had not looked for, and which had boded seriously for the final result.

It was this reflection, more even than the thought of the broken line, which troubled him that evening. Could it be possible that his luck was deserting him?

His companions were troubled by no such suggestion. Indignation was the uppermost feeling in their breasts. Whoever had done the deed, it was a vile action, and till the culprit was brought to justice the whole schoolhouse was responsible in their eyes.

"I wonder a single one of them can hold up his head," exclaimed Game.

"I hope to goodness Bloomfield won't demand a fresh race. *I* won't row if he does," said Ashley.

"And the worst of it is they'll try to make out now they would have won in any case. I heard one of them say so myself this very afternoon."

"Let them say what they like," said Ashley. "Nobody will believe them."

Perhaps these hot-headed heroes, had they been able to overhear a conversation that was going on at that very time in the captain's study, would have discovered that at any rate it was not the immediate intention of the schoolhouse to insist that the victory was theirs.

Riddell had recovered somewhat from his rough handling that afternoon, but he looked pale and dejected as, along with his friend Fairbairn, he sat and discussed for the twentieth time the event of the day.

"It's quite evident we must offer them a fresh race," said he.

"Yes, I think so," said Fairbairn. "It's hard lines, for I expect it won't be easy to get our men up to the mark again after they are once run down."

"We can't help that," said Riddell. "It's the least we can do."

"Of course. But I don't see, Riddell, old man, that we are bound to hang down our heads over this business. Whoever did it did as mean a trick to us as ever he did to them. I'd like to have him a minute or two, even if he was my own brother."

"Well," said Riddell, "to my mind it seems like a disgrace to the whole house, and the least we can do is to offer to row again."

"Oh, rather; that's settled. I say," added Fairbairn, "I'd give anything to get at the bottom of it. I saw the boats locked up last night, and I was there when they were taken out this morning. I can't imagine how it was done."

"It seemed a clean cut, didn't it?"

"Yes; about three-quarters of the way through. Whoever did it must have been up to his business, for he only touched the right cord on which all the strain comes at the corner."

"It must have been done between five o'clock yesterday and this morning," said Riddell. "If the cut had been there yesterday the line would have given at the corner to a certainty."

"Oh, yes; it must have been done in the night."

"Doesn't the boatman know anything about it?"

"No; I asked him. He says no one opened the door after the boats had gone in except himself and the boat-boy."

"It's horribly mysterious," said Riddell. "But, I say, hadn't we better offer the new race at once?"

"All serene."

"Had we better write?" asked Riddell.

"No; why? What's the use of looking ashamed?" said Fairbairn; "let's go to them. Bloomfield's sure to be in his study."

The two boys went accordingly, and found the Parrett's captain in his study along with Game and Ashley. It was rarely indeed that the schoolhouse seniors penetrated uninvited into the headquarters of their rivals. But on this occasion they had a right cause at heart and honest consciences to back them.

But it was evident at a glance they had fallen on unfriendly society. Game, quite apart from his state of mind with regard to the accident, had not forgotten his repulse at the hands of the new captain a week or two ago, nor had Bloomfield quite got over the indirect snub he had received on the same occasion.

Riddell himself had almost forgotten the circumstance, and attributed the unencouraging aspect of the rival seniors entirely to the day's misadventure.

"Excuse us coming over," said he, feeling that a beginning must be made to the interview, "but we wanted to tell you how sorry our fellows are about the race."

"Have you found out who did it?" asked Bloomfield.

"No," said Riddell, "and we can't even guess."

"But what we came for specially," broke in Fairbairn at this point, "was to say we are quite ready to row you again any day you like."

There was a touch of defiance in the tone of the schoolhouse stroke which was particularly irritating to the Parrett's boys.

"Of course, we would row you—" began Bloomfield.

"But we don't mean to," broke in Game, "till this ugly business is cleared up."

"What do you mean?" asked Fairbairn.

"You know what we mean," said Game, warmly. "As soon as you find out who cut our line we'll go out on the river again."

"Yes; we don't mean to row you till that's done," said Ashley.

"How on earth are we to find out who cut your line any more than you?" said Fairbairn, losing his temper.

"There's no doubt he must be a schoolhouse fellow," said Bloomfield, who but for his friends would have been disposed to accept the challenge.

"I'm afraid he is," said Riddell.

"Well, I won't row again till we know who he is," repeated Ashley.

"Do you suppose *we* know who he is?" demanded Fairbairn.

"You're the proper people to find out, that's all I know," said Ashley.

"Then you mean to say you won't row again?" asked Fairbairn.

"No, if it comes to that," said Bloomfield.

"Why," said Game, "the same thing might happen again."

"If you'd looked to your lines before you started," said Fairbairn, hotly, "it wouldn't have happened."

"We shall certainly make a point of looking at them again when next we row you," said Ashley, with a sneer.

Fairbairn seemed inclined to retort, but a look from Riddell deterred him.

"Then you won't row again?" he repeated once more.

"No."

"Then we claim to-day's race," said Fairbairn.

"You can claim what you like," said Game.

"And our boat remains at the head of the river."

"It doesn't matter to us where it remains," replied Ashley. "You may think what you like and we'll think what we like."

It was evidently useless to attempt further parley, and the two schoolhouse boys accordingly retired, bitterly disappointed to be thwarted of their only chance of righting themselves and their house in the eyes of Willoughby.

It soon got to be known there was to be no second race, and, as usual, all sorts of stories accompanied the rumour. The enemies of the schoolhouse said openly that they had refused Bloomfield's demand for a new race, and intended to stick to their ill-gotten laurels in spite of everybody. On the other side it was as freely asserted that Parrett's had funked it; and some went even so far to hint that the snapping of the rope happened fortunately for the boat, and saved it under cover of an accident from the disgrace of a defeat. The few who knew the real story considered Bloomfield was quite right in refusing another race till the culprit of the first should be brought to justice.

65

But the two fellows on whom the announcement fell most severely were Gilks and Silk. For if the race of that day was to stand, the schoolhouse boat had definitely won the race, and consequently they were both losers to a considerable extent.

They had counted almost certainly on a second race, but now that this had been decided against, their wrath and dismay knew no bounds. They spent the evening in vituperations and angry discussion, and ended it in what was very little short of a downright quarrel. Indeed, if young Wyndham had not opportunely arrived on the scene shortly before bedtime and created a diversion, the quarrel might have come to blows.

Wyndham burst into the room suddenly.

"Has either of you seen my knife?" he enquired; "I've lost it."

"Have you?" inquired Silk.

"Yes; I fancy I left it here last night. I say, have you heard Parrett's won't accept a new race?"

"I wonder why?" asked Silk.

"Because they say they won't have out their boat again till the fellow's found who cut the lines."

"Well, I don't blame them—do you, Gilks?" said Silk. "I suppose there's no idea who he is?"

"Not a bit," said Wyndham; "I wish to goodness there was. Some fool, I expect, who's been betting against Parrett's."

"I could show you a fool who's been betting on Parrett's," said Silk, "and who's decidedly up a tree now! I say, young 'un, I suppose you couldn't lend me a sov. till the end of the term?"

"I've only got half-a-sov. in the world," said Wyndham.

"Well, I'll try and make that do, thanks," said Silk.

Wyndham pulled out his purse rather ruefully and handed him the coin.

"Mind you let me have it back, please," he said, "as I'm saving up for a racket. And I say," added he, leaving, "if you do come across my knife, let's have it, will you?"

Chapter Sixteen.

Bosher, his Diary.

Probably no two boys in all Willoughby were more excited over the result of the famous boat-race than Parson and his dear friend Telson. And it is hardly necessary to state that this agitation arose from totally conflicting reasons.

Parson's indignation found solace in the most sweeping and vehement invectives his vocabulary could afford against the unknown author of the dastardly outrage upon his rudder-line. By an easy effort of imagination he included the whole schoolhouse, root and branch, in his anathemas, and by a very trifling additional effort he discovered that the objects of his censure were guilty, every one of them, not only of this particular crime, but of every crime in the Newgate Calendar, from picking pockets to murder. He fully agreed with the decision of his chiefs to have nothing more to do with such a graceless crew till the injury was atoned for; and meanwhile he felt himself at perfect liberty—nay, it was his painful duty—to insult, abuse, and maltreat, as occasion offered, every one unlucky enough to wear the schoolhouse ribbon on his cap.

This being the case, it may be imagined his friend Telson (who, by the way, had barely recovered from the shock of Brown's party) found himself in a very delicate position. For in the whole of his code of honour two points were paramount with him. One was loyalty to the schoolhouse, the other was loyalty to Parson. How these two duties could be carried out now, at one and the same time, was a source of much anxiety to the perplexed Augustus.

He too was as indignant about the whole affair as his friend. But his wrath was aimed first of all against those who dared to insinuate that any schoolhouse boy could have been guilty of the evil deed, and next against the Parretts' authorities for refusing Riddell's and Fairbairn's offer of a new race.

He and his friend had a long and painful discussion of the whole question an evening or two later in the study of the latter.

"It's all very well," said he, "to say it's a schoolhouse chap has done it—"

"I tell you a schoolhouse chap *must* have done it," said Parson. "Who else would do such a dirty trick?"

"I'll fight you, old man, if you go on like that," observed the schoolhouse fag.

"Oh, beg pardon," said Parson, apologetically. "I mean who else could have done it, you know?"

"A Welcher might," suggested Telson.

"What would be the good to him? They hadn't a boat. Besides, they all go against Riddell, don't they?"

"Well, I mean to say," said Telson, falling back on to the next grievance, "your fellows ought to row us again. We'd have rowed you again like a shot if our line had smashed. *We* don't funk you."

"And do you think we funk you? A pack of—I mean," added Parson, pulling up in time, "do you think we funk you?"

"Why don't you row us again, then?"

"Because there's no honour in the thing while your fellows go in for beastly low dodges like that," replied Parson.

"I tell you," said Telson, finding it very difficult to keep in with his friend, "we did not do it. I say we didn't do it; there!"

"What's the use of your saying that when you know no one but a schoolhouse fellow *could* have done it?" demanded his friend.

"I tell you we didn't do it," repeated Telson, "and you've got to prove we did before you say we did," added he, with triumphant emphasis.

"You've got to prove you didn't," replied Parson, not to be beaten in this line of argument.

"How can I prove we didn't when—when we didn't do it?" cried Telson, making up in noise for what he lacked in logic.

"I knew you couldn't prove it!" said Parson, triumphant in his turn. "I knew it was one of your blackguard—"

"All right, old man, I *shall* fight you," said Telson.

"I didn't mean, old man, really," said Parson. "What I mean to say is—"

"I don't care what you say," said Telson. "What I say is, we did *not* do it!"

"All very well," replied Parson, "but I'm certain you did."

"How are you certain, I'd like to know?"

"Because, I tell you," said Parson, slowly and incisively, "it couldn't have been done by any one else."

"How do you know it couldn't?" asked Telson warmly.

"There you are! If you didn't do it you'd be able to prove it, but you can't, you see."

And so this edifying argument went on, or rather round, very much after the style of a dog trying to catch his tail, and at its close Parson and Telson stood as far from solving the mystery as ever.

This slight difference of opinion, however, could hardly fail to result in a little mutual irritation, and for the first time in their friendship the two boys felt as if they did not love one another exactly like brethren. It was therefore no small relief when further argument was abruptly cut short by the entrance of King, looking particularly cheerful and important.

"Hullo, you two!" exclaimed he. "Guessed I'd find you here. Such a lark!"

"What is it?" asked the two friends, delighted with any diversion.

"Why," exclaimed the delighted King, "you know Bosher?"

"What about him? What's he done?"

"Guess."

"It's not he that cut the rudder-line, is it?" asked Telson.

"No, of course not. But, just fancy, he keeps a diary!"

"What!" exclaimed the other two, laughing, "old Bosher keep a diary! How do you know that?"

King looked very mysterious, and then said, laughing, "I say, what would you give for a squint at it?"

"Have you got it, then?"

"Rather," said King, producing a small notebook from his pocket. "I found it in the Big just now."

The notion of Bosher keeping a diary had been amusing enough, but the chance of looking at such a production was irresistible.

The boys did make one languid protest, more, however, to relieve their consciences than to dissuade one another from the meanness of looking into another boy's diary.

"Rather low, perhaps," said Telson, "to look at a fellow's notes."

"I don't know," said King. "If a fellow keeps a diary he must expect it to be looked at if he leaves it about. I know I should."

"Well, yes, so should I too," said Parson. "Besides, you know, of course we wouldn't tell any one else."

"Rather not," said Telson. "But you know, Parson," he added, seriously, "it's just possible he might have something about the rudder-line in it, and it would be a great thing to clear that up, wouldn't it?"

"So it would," said Parson, seating himself at the table.

Telson and King did the same, and Bosher's diary was forthwith opened.

To all appearance Bosher was the most unlikely boy in all Willoughby to keep a diary. He was not usually credited with overmuch intelligence, and certainly not with much sentiment, and the few remarks he did occasionally offer on things in general were never very weighty. He was a good-tempered, noisy, able-bodied fag, who was at any one's service, and who in all his exploits did about as much work for as little glory as any boy in the school.

The present discovery certainly revealed him in a new and startling light, and it was with a feeling somewhat akin to awe that the three boys who called themselves his friends set themselves to the task of inspecting his private—his very private diary.

The small volume dated from the beginning of the term, and the first entry the trio examined may be taken as a fair specimen of its general contents.

"'May 20. The twentieth of May. I awake at 5:37, and got up at 5:43. My motive is to see the boats. It was a beautiful and fine morning. The early birds were singing gladly wore my flannels for running along with the boat.'"

Bosher was a little shaky occasionally in his punctuation, which will explain any apparent incoherence in the above and following sentences.

"'I sang as I dressed except while washing The Minstrel Boy. Started out at 6:2—met Parson in the Big. Parson thinks too much of himself.'"

"Sharp chap, Bosher," said King.

"I'll pull his nose when I see him," said Parson, who, however, did not appear very deeply affronted so far.

The reading continued.

"'Parson ran on and left me alone. Now that I am alone let me muse on my past life and hope it will be better only the schoolhouse boat was out. I think they or our boat will win. Nice seeing them row Gilks catches a crab'" (this was previous to Gilks's ejection from the boat). "'Entered chapel at 1 to 8. King was there eating toffee.'"

"Hullo, King, *you're* all right. When this diary's published some day, you'll figure all serene," said Telson, laughing.

"Wait a bit," said King, "your turn's coming."

"'At breakfast sit opposite Telson. He eats vulgar. Thou shouldest not talk with thy mouth full, Telson, I prithee.'"

The readers fairly broke down at this point. Telson had to admit that his turn *had* come, and relieved himself by announcing that he would *prithee* his candid chronicler some day in a way which would astonish him.

"'Meditations at breakfast,' continued the diary. 'The world is very big. I am small in the world. I will ambition twenty lines for gross conduct with Harrison—throwing bread I repent entirely. Parson wanted me to do his "Caesar" for him.'"

"Oh, what a whacker!" exclaimed Parson.

"'I declined, owing to not knowing—'"

"I can believe that!" added Parson.

"'Both detained for gross conduct not knowing verbs my home is far away. Let out at 12:28.'"

"What rot it is!" exclaimed Parson, looking up. "What a howling young ass he must be to put it all down!"

"I guess he didn't expect we'd see it," said Telson. "But, I say, we can't read it all. Let's see what he says about the boat-race."

This was agreed to, and the eventful day was turned to.

"'Rose at 7:3,'" began Telson, reading—"oh, we don't want that. Let's see, 'Attended chapel at half a minute to eight. Half a minute more I had been too late. That had been bad alas had I been bad it had been bad for me next to Wyndham in chapel. Wyndham hath lost his knife he requested me had I seen it. I answered nay I had not. He said—' Oh, what frightful bosh it is, I say!"

"So it is; but it would be a spree to see what he says about the race."

"That'll be pages on, at the rate he goes at," said Telson, whipping over a few leaves. "Let's see. 'Gross conduct with King talking in class King meanly tells Parrett he is a beastly sneak.'"

"What does he say?" exclaimed King. "I told Parrett he was a beastly sneak? What crams the fellow tells! Fancy me saying that to Parrett! All I said was I wasn't talking!"

"Why, I see it," said Parson. "He's left out a semi-colon or something; the 'he's a beastly sneak' means *you*, old man. 'King meanly tells Parrett. He (that is, King) is a beastly sneak.' That makes it all right."

"Does it?" cried the indignant King—"does it make it all right! I'll make it all right for him, I can promise him. I never sneaked of him in my life!"

"Wire in, old man, and get to the race," urged Parson impatiently.

"Here, this looks like it," said Telson, reading. "'Being the boat-race no afternoon school I am pleased. A vast mass on the towpath I being in flannels waited twenty-three minutes for the start. Meditating as I stood, how vast is the world.' (Hullo! he had that before; that seems to be his usual meditation.) 'How vast is the world. I am small in the world Parson is a conceited ass.'"

Parson turned very red in the face, of course, at this unexpected turn, which, however, his two companions greatly enjoyed.

"'Parson is a conceited ass—'"

"I say, you needn't go over it twice," expostulated the injured youth.

"'A conceited ass,'" continued Telson, his voice wavering with suppressed laughter. "'He thinks he is a great man but he's little in the world and fond of gross conduct. He and Telson are the conceitedest asses in Willoughby.'"

This double shot fairly broke down the gravity both of reader and audience, and it was some little time before the diary could proceed. The account of the race which followed was evidently not original. It appeared to be copied verbatim from an account of the last University Boat-race, with a few interpolations intended to adapt it to the present circumstances. It began thus:

"'Punctually at half-past eight ("eight" scratched out and "three" substituted) Mr Searle (altered to Mr Parrett) gave the signal to go, and at the word the *sixteen* oars dashed simultaneously into the water. The Oxonians were the first to show a lead, and at the Creek ("Creek" scratched out and nothing substituted) were a foot to the good. The Craydle is a pleasing river with banks running up from the sea to slopes up the Concrete Wall this advantage was fully maintained ("maintained" altered to "lost")—'"

"Oh, skip all that," said Parson impatiently; "go on to the part about Willow Corner."

"'About a mile from home the Oxford stroke ("stroke" altered to "Bloomfield") spurted, and the dark blue flag ("dark blue" altered to "schoolhouse") once more shot ahead. Gross steering by Parson, who I allude to above, who steers his boat into the bank and breaks rudder-line. It is ascertained Fairbairn and others are suspected. After this a ding-dong race ensued to the finish where eventually the dark (altered to "light") blues won by a foot (altered to "mile") Parrett's having given in owing to Parson who is alluded to above.'"

"Oh, I say, this is a drop too much," exclaimed the wrathful Parson, rising. "I'll pay him out for this, see if I don't!"

"Don't be an ass, Parson," said Telson. "Sit down, can't you? You've no business to look at his diary at all, you know, if it comes to that."

Parson sat down with a wrathful countenance, and Telson proceeded.

"We shall not see a new race as I hear Riddell and Bloomfield declining. I spoke to Parson who completely repents. He suspects Telson who he ascertains is the one to do it. It is gross. How many things go wrong. Wyndham hath not found his knife he requested me had I seen it. I answered nay, not so. I have composed these verses which I will set down here as they may recall the past:—

"'My name is Norval (altered to "Bosher"), on the Grampian (altered to "Willoughby") hills. My father (altered to "Doctor Patrick") feeds his flocks (altered to "boys")'."

"Well," said Telson, as he closed the thrilling narrative, and tossed it back to King, "I never thought Bosher was up to much, but I didn't know he was a downright lunatic."

"Oh, I don't know," said King. "It's not so bad. I tried to keep a diary once, but I could never find anything to say."

"Well, I guess Bosher's not hard-up in that line," said Telson, laughing. "But, I say, we ought to give it to him back somehow."

"I'll give it to him back pretty hot!" exclaimed Parson. "I vote we burn the boshy thing."

"Oh, you can't do that. You'd better smuggle it back into his study somehow, King, without his knowing."

"All serene," said King, pocketing the book. "Hallo! who's this coming?"

As he spoke there was a sound of hurrying footsteps in the passage outside, and immediately afterwards the door opened and revealed none other than the sentimental author of Bosher's diary himself.

Just at present, and luckily for him, he did not appear to be in a sentimental mood; his face was a little scared and mysterious-looking as he hurriedly stepped into the room and shut the door after him.

"Look out, I say!" he exclaimed, "the Welchers are coming!"

This magic announcement dispelled in a moment whatever resentment may have lurked in the minds of any of the three students on account of the diary. In the presence of a common danger like this, with the common enemy, so to speak, at the very door, they were all friends and brothers at once.

"Where? How do you know?" demanded the three.

"I was looking for a book I had lost," said Bosher, "in the Big near our door, and I heard Cusack tell Pilbury to wait till he went and saw if the coast was clear. So they'll be here directly."

"Jolly lucky you heard them," said Parson. "What shall we do, you fellows?"

There was a slight interval for reflection, and then Telson said, "Fancy the jug dodge is about the best. They won't be up to it, eh?"

This proposal seemed to meet with general approval, and as time was precious Parson's tin jug, full of water, was forthwith hoisted adroitly over the door, and delicately adjusted with nail and twine so that the opening of the door should be the signal for its tilting over and disgorging its contents on the head of the luckless intruder. It was such an old method of warfare that the conspirators really felt half ashamed to fall back upon it, only time was short and the enemy might come any moment. As an additional precaution, also, a piece of the twine was stretched across the doorway about three inches from the ground, with the considerate purpose of tripping up the expected visitors. And to complete the preparations, each of the besieged armed himself with an appropriate weapon wherewith to greet the intruders, and thus accoutred sat down and waited the event with serene minds.

The event was not long in coming. Before many minutes a stealthy footstep was heard outside, which it was easy to guess belonged to the spy of the attacking party. Parson motioned to the others to be silent, and seated himself at his table, with a book before him, in full view of the key-hole. The little manoeuvre evidently told, for the footsteps were heard stealthily hurrying away, and the watchers knew the main body would soon be here.

It seemed no time before the approaching sounds gladdened their expectant ears. The invaders were evidently walking in step and trying to imitate the heavy walk of some senior, so as to give no suspicion of their purpose.

The besieged smiled knowingly at one another, glanced up at the suspended jug, and then softly rising with their weapons at the ready, calmly awaited the assault.

Whoever knew a set of Parrett's juniors caught napping? The Welchers would have to be a precious deal more cunning than this if they expected to score off them.

The footsteps advanced and reached the door. There was a brief pause, the handle turned, Parson gave the signal, and next moment—Mr Parrett entered the study!

As he opened the door the jug overhead, true to its mechanism, tilted forward and launched a deluge of water over the head and shoulders of the ill-starred master, just as he tripped forward over the string and fell prone into the apartment, while at the same instant, accompanied by a loud howl, one sponge, two slippers, and a knotted towel flew into his face and completed his demolition.

What Mr Parrett's reflections may have been during the few seconds which immediately followed no one ever found out. But, whatever they were, it is safe to say they were as nothing compared with the horror and terror of the youthful malefactors as they looked on and saw what they had done.

With a cry almost piteous in its agony, they rushed towards him and lifted him, dripping and bruised as he was, to his feet, gazing at him with looks of speechless supplication, and feeling crushed with all the guilt of actual murderers.

It spoke volumes for Mr Parrett's self-control that, instead of sitting and gaping foolishly at the scene of the disaster, or instead of suddenly hitting out right and left, as others would have done, he took out his handkerchief and proceeded quietly to dry his face while he collected his scattered thoughts.

At length he said, "Are these elaborate preparations usually kept up here?"

"Oh no, sir!" cried Parson, in tones of misery. "Indeed, sir, we never expected you. We expected—"

His speech was cut short by a fresh noise outside—this time the real enemy, who, little guessing what was going on within, halted a moment outside before commencing proceedings. Then, with a simultaneous war-whoop, they half-opened the door, and, without entering themselves, projected into the centre of the room—a bottle! Pilbury and Cusack had not studied natural science for nothing!

The strange projectile smashed to atoms as it fell, and at the same instant there arose a stench the like of which the nose of Willoughby had never known before.

Mr Parrett and the boys choked and made a dash for the door, but the enemy were hanging on to the handle in full force, and it was at least two minutes before the almost suffocated Parson could gasp, "Open the door! do you hear? Mr Parrett's here; let him out."

"Won't wash, my boy!" cried a mocking voice—"won't wash! Wait a bit, we've got another bottle for you when you're quite ready!"

"Let me out, boys!" cried Mr Parrett as well as he could for choking and holding his nose.

"Tell you it won't wash, my boy!" cried the insulting voice outside. "Try again! Have a little more sulphuretted hydrogen. Jolly stuff, isn't it? Hold on, you fellows, while I chuck it in!"

The idea of another bottle was more than any one could endure.

Mr Parrett groaned and cleared his throat for another summons, but Parson was before him.

"I say," cried he, in positively piteous tones, "we give in. I'll apologise, anything—do you hear?"

"Eh—go down on your knees, then," cried the enemy.

"I am," said Parson.

"Is he? the rest of you? is he on his knees? both of them?"

"Yes, he is," cried Bosher. "Honour bright."

"Well then, say 'I'm a beastly cad, and a funk, and a sneak, and I knuckle under and will never do it any more.'"

"I'm a beastly cad," gasped Parson, choking with shame, anger, and sulphuretted hydrogen, "and a funk, and a sneak, and I knuckle under and will never do it any more."

"Now all the rest of you say it!"

Telson, Bosher, and King obeyed, one after the other.

"Is that all of you?"

"Yes," said Parson, terrified at the prospect of Mr Parrett having to go through the ordeal. "Telson, Bosher, King, and I are the only boys here."

"All serene," cried the jubilant voice outside, "open the door, you fellows!"

We draw a veil over the scene which followed!

Mr Parrett hurried out of the room the moment the door was open, merely turning to say, "Come to me all of you at seven to-night!"

And then with his handkerchief still over his mouth he hurried off.

Chapter Seventeen.

A Surprise in Store.

For a few minutes, as the disconcerted and terrified youngsters stood in a small band at Parson's study-door and watched Mr Parrett slowly retreat down the passage, it seemed as if the final crisis in the career of every one present had arrived.

It would have been bad enough to be caught in the midst of a simple free fight and sent up to the doctor. But the case was far more terrible than that! For Mr Parrett had been fearfully and wonderfully mixed up in the whole affair. A few weeks ago the Parrett's juniors had done their best to drown him; now they had done their best to drown him and break his neck and crack his skull all at one onslaught; and as if that wasn't enough, the Welchers had stepped in at the same moment and added poison and suffocation to the other crimes of which the unlucky master was the victim.

Of course he would think it from the beginning to end one elaborate and fiendish plot against his life. It would not matter to him which boys committed one assault and which another. He had figured as the victim of all parties, and all parties, there could be no doubt, would now be included under one terrific sentence.

In the presence of this common doom, schoolhouse, Parretts, and Welchers for the first time that term showed symptoms of a passing brotherhood.

They stood rooted to the spot and speechless for at least two minutes after the ill-starred master had vanished, then Telson—usually the first to recover his wits—whistled drearily and low, "Whew! we will catch it!"

"Think we'll be expelled?" said Cusack.

"Shouldn't wonder," said Parson, retreating slowly into his study, followed by the rest.

"He'll send us up to the doctor, certain," said King.

There was a long unpleasant pause, at the end of which Cusack said, "Well, it's no use staying here. Come on, you fellows."

"May as well stay," suggested Parson. "We'd better all turn up together."

So it was decided not to break up the party, and that evening the unwonted spectacle of Telson, Parretts, and Welchers, sitting amicably together in one study, might have been noted as one of the greatest wonders of that wonderful term.

Of course boys could not sit and talk of nothing. And of course it was hardly to be expected they would confine their conversation altogether to a review of their misdeeds. The talk gradually became general, and occasionally even animated.

"Guess Pil and I will have to shut up chemistry after this," said Cusack.

Pilbury smiled grimly.

"What do you call the beastly stuff?" asked Telson.

"Sulphuretted hydrogen," said Cusack, briskly. "First of all you take a—"

"Oh, shut up shop! We don't want a chemistry lecture," broke in Parson.

There was a brief pause, then Philpot asked, "I say, is it true then, there's not going to be a new race?"

"Of course not," said Parson; "what's the use when we can't be sure of fair play?"

"Jolly right too," said Cusack, delighted to agree with his old enemy for once; "those schoolhouse cads are cheats, every one of them?"

"All right!" exclaimed Telson jumping up; "I'll fight you, young Cusack, for that!"

Cusack was somewhat taken aback by this unexpected outbreak, but was inclined, nevertheless, to accept the challenge. Parson, however, interfered peremptorily.

"Look here," he said, "we're in quite enough row for one day, without wanting any more. So shut up, you fellows, do you hear?"

"Make him apologise, then," said Telson, wrathfully.

"Oh, all serene. Nobody was hurting you," said Cusack.

"Do you apologise, or do you not?" demanded Telson.

"I didn't say I didn't, did I?"

This was as much as the irascible schoolhouse fag could expect, so he sat down again.

"You know," said Pilbury, anxious to make things *quite* pleasant again, "a lot of the fellows say the schoolhouse would have won in any case."

"I'd like to know who says that," demanded Parson, whose turn it now was to be angry.

"Oh, everybody in our house. They looked like winning, you know, from the very start, didn't they, Pil?"

"Yes, a lot you and your friend Pil know about rowing," sneered Parson.

"Know as much as you do!"

"Pity if you know such a lot you can't put a boat on the river."

"I tell you what we'll do," said Cusack. "Pil and I will row any two of your lot; there now. Funk it, eh?"

Parson looked hard at the speaker, and then glanced at Telson. Telson glanced back at Parson, and then eyed the Welchers grimly.

"You'd promise fair play?" asked Parson.

"Of course we would; we always do."

"You'd *give* us fair play, then?" demanded Parson.

"Yes, honour bright."

"All serene. Telson and I will row you; eh, Telson?"

"Rather!" said Telson, "and give them a start too."

"All very well, you fellows," said King, "but suppose we're all expelled to-morrow."

This unpleasant suggestion took away most of the interest in the proposed race, and it was decided to defer further arrangements till the fate of the parties should be decided.

After this the party waited gloomily till seven o'clock came, and then, in decidedly low spirits, rose in a body and repaired to Mr Parrett's study.

Had they been aware of the actual state of that amiable athlete's mind from the moment they last saw him, handkerchief in mouth, hurrying down the passage, till now, their trepidation would have been considerably relieved. The first thing Mr Parrett had done on regaining his room after that "bad quarter of an hour" with his juniors was to throw himself into a chair and laugh heartily.

The fact was, his sense of humour was inconveniently acute for the master of a public school, so that what would strike other masters as a heinous offence, occurred to him more as a ludicrous chapter of accidents. And to Mr Parrett's mind a more ludicrous chapter of accidents had rarely occurred in his history. He saw the whole matter at once, and the more he thought about it the funnier it all seemed. And yet, funny as it was, it was a painful necessity that discipline must be maintained, and that however much he enjoyed the joke he must be severe on the jokers.

When, therefore, the group of youthful culprits slowly filed into his room, his voice was stern and his countenance betrayed no symptoms of the amusement which lurked beneath.

"Now, you boys," said he, surveying the anxious array carefully, "what have you to say for yourselves?"

"Please, sir," began Parson, Telson, and Cusack, all at a breath.

"Stop," said Mr Parrett; "only one at a time. You, Parson, what have you to say?"

"Please, sir," said Parson, "we're all awfully sorry. It was quite an accident, really."

"What was an accident?" demanded Mr Parrett.

"Why, you getting mauled about like—"

"Tell me, Parson," said Mr Parrett, pinching himself to keep himself grave, "was it an accident that your water-can was hung over the door and the string stretched across the bottom of it?"

"Oh no, sir; not that, but—"

"Was it an accident that you had missiles in your hands and threw them in the direction of the door as it was opened?"

"No, sir."

"Then, sir, what was the accident?"

"You were the accident, please, sir," said Parson, sadly.

"I guessed so. And for whom were these preparations intended, pray?"

"For the Welchers, sir," began Parson, longing to launch out into a full explanation; "and please, sir—"

But again the master pulled him up short, and, turning to Cusack and his brother Welchers, said, "And you—*your* preparations were for—?"

"For the Parretts, sir," broke in Cusack.

"Just so," said Mr Parrett, deliberately. "And now just listen to me. This is not the first time I have had to speak to some of you for this very conduct."

Parson, Telson, Bosher, and the other Parretts looked very dejected at this point.

"And it is by no means the first time this term that all of you have been guilty of similar disturbances. Most of you here look frightened and uneasy enough now. I wish I could believe it was because you know you have been doing wrong and disgracing the school, instead of merely because I happened to have suffered by your bad conduct. But such conduct must be put a stop to. For the remainder of the term each one of you will lose one hour's play a day except Saturdays."

A shudder, half of anguish, half of relief, went round the small assembly at this first clause of Mr Parrett's sentence. The next clause was still more severe.

"For the remainder of this term, too, none of you will be allowed to go into any house except your own, under any pretence, without *my* leave, or the Doctor's."

Telson and Parson looked at one another and groaned inwardly. They could hardly realise what this cruel sentence involved, but they knew it meant that life would hardly be worth living for the next six weeks.

"And," continued Mr Parrett, "I have one more thing to say. Some of you here are in my house, and every one of you, I see, is in my form in Third School. You are most of you idle boys, and, as you know, there are plenty in the same Form better behaved and more industrious than yourselves."

"Oh yes, sir," said Parson, frankly.

"What I shall do during the remainder of the term is this," said Mr Parrett. "If I hear of any other case of disturbance between the boys of different houses, in which any one of you are implicated, I intend to punish the entire Form, and stop every boy's play for one day. It rests with you, therefore, to decide whether such a thing shall take place or not. But if you give me reason, I shall most certainly do it!"

Mr Parrett spoke severely, and looked as good as his word. He had carefully weighed his words beforehand, and he knew tolerably well the boys with whom he had to deal. They were noisy boys, and troublesome boys, and cheeky boys, and idle boys, but they were honest on the whole, and the master calculated pretty shrewdly on the effect which this last decision would have on their conduct.

As long as it was a mere question of getting his own particular self into a row, not one of these boys fixed any precise limit to his disorderly instincts; but when it came to getting a whole lot of other boys into the row too, a new and very embarrassing difficulty arose which was fairly insurmountable.

Mr Parrett dismissed the boys sternly, and then, trusting he had done right, and trusting still more to be able to turn the better qualities of his noisy young pupils to some good purpose, he went straight to the doctor and told him what he had done.

Dr Patrick fully approved of the decision of his colleague, and while on the subject opened his mind to him on the question of the discipline of Willoughby generally.

"Have you been able to judge at all of the order of the school lately, Parrett?" he said.

"Well, sir," said Mr Parrett, "I'm not sure that it is as good as it should be. Of course, it was an experiment making Riddell captain, particularly as he is not generally popular."

"His unpopularity arises from no cause in himself," said the doctor; "if it did I would not have put him in the post. But he will live it down—in fact, he is doing so now, I fancy."

"I think he is," said Mr Parrett. "The great difficulty is to get him to assert himself."

"I trust," said the doctor, after a pause, "there is no truth in the report that Bloomfield and the monitors of your house are trying to set up a counter authority to Riddell's."

"It is true," said Mr Parrett; "and it is the secret of most of the bad order in the school. But I am not sure, sir, whether it is a matter you would do well to notice. It is one of the difficulties which Riddell has to live down, and which bring him out more than anything else. He has made his mark already on the usurpers."

"You are quite right," said the doctor. "I would rather leave a difficulty like that to right itself. And I dare say the reason Riddell is so slow in asserting himself, as you say, is that in his own house he really has not much to do."

"Exactly," said Mr Parrett.

The doctor paused for a moment and then started on an apparently fresh topic.

"I am afraid Welch's house is no better than it was."

"How can it be?" said Mr Parrett. "It has not a single senior of influence or even character in it."

"And more than that," added the doctor, "it contains a few boys—one or two only, I hope—whose influence is distinctly bad."

Mr Parrett nodded.

"A change of some sort must be made," said the doctor. "It has occurred to me, Parrett, quite recently, that Riddell might do better there."

Mr Parrett opened his eyes wide.

"You are astonished," said the doctor. "So was I when I first thought of it. But Riddell is a safe man, if slow, and his influence is just what is wanted in Welch's. Besides, Fairbairn would make an excellent head for the schoolhouse. What do you think?"

"Without doubt Riddell, as far as character goes, is the best boy you could choose. I'm not quite sure, though, whether he has sufficient force."

"But, as you say, his force answers to his difficulties. At any rate I am disposed to try him. A few weeks will show how he gets on. I have not much fear myself."

And so the head master and his lieutenant separated.

Little dreaming of the changes in store for them, Silk and Gilks were sitting together in the study of the latter, furtively consuming cigar-ends and looking decidedly glum as they conversed together in low and mysterious and not very amicable tones.

"Think he'll do it?" said Silk.

"He had a letter from home this morning," replied Gilks, "I know, because he sat next to me at breakfast while he was reading it."

"Did you see what it said," inquired Silk, as naturally as if looking over another fellow's letters were an ordinary proceeding.

"No, but it was from his brother, and it had a post-office order in it."

"It had? that's lucky. How much was it for?"

"I couldn't see," said Gilks.

"Where is he now?" asked Silk, after a pause.

"I don't know. Probably in his Holiness's study—or, no, it's library night—he'll be there."

"What a nuisance that library is. The young beggar's always pottering about there," said Silk. "Think he'll look us up before bedtime?"

"Don't know," said Gilks.

"You'd better know," said Silk. "He must come, and you'd better see he does."

This last was spoken in a somewhat menacing voice, and Gilks sulkily replied, "What are you in such a hurry to-night for? The morning will do, won't it?"

"No," said Silk, "it won't, there; and if it did, I choose to see him to-night."

"I don't know what makes you so precious disagreeable," growled Gilks. "I don't want to be ordered about by you, I can tell you."

Silk sneered. "I'm under great obligations to you, I know," he said.

"Well," said Gilks, who winced visibly under the satire, "however could I help it? It wasn't my fault, I tell you. I'm awfully sorry you lost on the race, but—"

"But you'd better look alive and do what I tell you," said Silk, viciously.

It was curious, to say the least of it, that in so short a time the Welcher should have so completely got the upper hand of his confederate that the latter departed meekly without another word on his errand.

He found Wyndham, as he had expected, in the library, busy getting together the books for distribution next day.

"Hullo!" said Gilks, with a show of cordiality; "here you are again. You seem to live here."

"No, I don't," said Wyndham, looking not very pleased to be interrupted; "but I always have to get ready an evening before the day, or the fellows kick up such a jolly row when they're kept waiting."

"How long shall you be?" asked Gilks.

"I don't know. Why?" asked Wyndham.

"Only Silk wants to speak to you."

Wyndham's face clouded. He had come fresh from Riddell's study an hour ago. His brother's friend had been as kind as ever. In a hundred ways he had shown it without sermon or lecture, and Wyndham had felt stung with a sense of his own ingratitude and dishonesty as he accepted the help and goodness of his mentor.

Now, consequently, this summons to present himself before Silk was more than usually distasteful.

"I can't come, tell him. It will take me all the evening to finish this."

"You'd better go, though," said Gilks.

"I can't. Why had I better go?" asked Wyndham, looking uncomfortable.

"It's something important he wants you for. You'd better go, young un."

Wyndham flung down the book in his hand with a baffled air, and muttering, "I hate the fellow!" walked miserably off. Gilks called him back for a moment.

"I say," he said, "don't you be such a fool as to rile Silk, young un. He could make it precious awkward for you and me too if it came to a row. Take my advice and keep in with him."

Wyndham answered nothing, but went off moodily to Silk. "Ah, Wyndham," said the latter, cordially, as his young *protégé* entered, "I was just wondering if you'd give me a look up."

"Gilks came and said you wanted me; that's why I came," said Wyndham.

"Awfully good of you," said Silk. "Of course I wanted you. The fact is, young un," said he, becoming a little mysterious, "there's rather an awkward thing turned up. I hope it won't come to anything, I'm sure, but it doesn't do to be too sure."

"What do you mean?" demanded Wyndham, looking alarmed. "I mean," said Silk, slowly, "that last time you took Gilks and me down to Beamish's—"

"*I* took you!" exclaimed Wyndham. "*You* took me—you made me go."

Silk laughed.

"Well, the last time we three went to Beamish's, if you like—the Saturday before the race; last Saturday, in fact—somebody saw us, or rather saw you."

"What!" cried Wyndham, turning pale. "Who was it?"

"It wouldn't do you any good to know," said Silk, "but it seems to be a fact."

"Who was it? a master or a monitor, or who?" asked the boy, anxiously.

"Neither. I don't fancy you know the fellow at all; I do, though."

Silk, as he concocted this lie, would probably have been as astonished as any one to discover that the escapade in question had really been witnessed by two boys from the box of the doctor's own fly!

"You know him?" said Wyndham. "Will he let out, do you think?"

"I can't say. I think I could prevent him," said Silk.

"Oh, please do," said the troubled boy, full of exaggerated terror at the consequences of detection.

"I'll see," said Silk, not very assuringly.

"What!" cried Wyndham. "You surely won't leave me in the lurch, Silk?"

Silk looked benevolently at his young friend.

"It depends," said he, coolly.

"Depends! On what? Oh, Silk, what do you mean?"

"Don't alarm yourself," said Silk, smiling. Then he added, confidentially, "The fact is, young un, I'm hard-up. I lost a lot of money on the race, owing to that—that is, because Parrett's lost. The thing is, can you lend me a couple of sovereigns, Wyndham?"

Wyndham's face clouded for a moment, but he replied quickly, "Yes, I can, Silk, if you'll promise to see it doesn't get out about last Saturday."

"Of course I will. You don't suppose I'm such a cad as all that."

"Oh, no," said Wyndham, looking more cheerful, and taking out his purse.

He drew from it a post-office order.

"It's for three pounds," he said. "I was going to change it to-morrow."

"Oh, I'll do that," said Silk. "I'm going into town early. You have signed it, I see. There'll be a sov. to give you out of it, won't there?"

"Yes, please; and the two pounds, and the ten shillings the other day," faltered the boy.

75

"You shall have them back, never fear," said Silk, pocketing the order.

Wyndham, in spite of this assurance, did fear considerably, as he returned with empty purse to his house.

Chapter Eighteen.

The new Captain turned Welcher.

Riddell, who probably felt the sting of the boat-race mishap more sensitively than any boy in Willoughby, was pacing the playground in a dispirited mood a morning or two after, when Dr Patrick suddenly confronted him.

"Ah, Riddell," said the latter, cheerily, "I'm glad I have met you. I want to have a talk. Let me see," said he, pulling out his watch, "there's hardly time now, though. Will you come and have tea with me this evening?"

Riddell turned pale at the bare suggestion, and would probably have invented some wild excuse to get off the dreaded honour had not the doctor continued, "I'm sorry Mrs Patrick and her sister are from home; they take a great interest in you, I can assure you."

"Oh, not at all," cried Riddell, whom the bare mention of those ladies' names was sufficient to confuse hopelessly.

"Come at seven o'clock, will you?" said the doctor, pleasantly, not noticing his head boy's perturbation.

Riddell continued his walk in a state of considerable perplexity. For some moments he could not get beyond the fact that Mrs Patrick and Miss Stringer were from home, and the relief of that reflection was unspeakable. But what could the doctor want him for? Was it to tell him he did not consider him equal to the duties of captain, and to relieve him of his office? Riddell devoutly wished it might be so. And yet he hardly fancied from the head master's manner this was to be the subject of their interview.

Perhaps it was to cross-examine him as to the boat-race. That wretched boat-race! Riddell had hardly had a minute's peace since that afternoon. The burden of the whole affair seemed to rest upon him. The taunts of the disappointed Parretts, which glanced harmless off minds like Fairbairn's and Porter's, wounded him to the quick, and, until the mystery should be solved, Riddell felt almost like a guilty party himself. He rather hoped the doctor did want to talk about this. It would be a relief to unburden his mind, at any rate. But even these troubles were slight compared with Riddell's concern about his old friend's brother. In spite of all his efforts young Wyndham was going wrong. He was getting more irregular in his visits to Riddell's study, and when he did come he was more reserved and secret, and less inclined to confide in his friend than before. It was easy to guess the reason, and Riddell felt baffled and dispirited as he thought about it. To save young Wyndham from his bad friends would be worth to him more even than to secure the order of Willoughby, or to discover the perpetrator of the boat-race outrage.

In this troubled state of mind Riddell passed the day till the time arrived for him to present himself at the doctor's.

He entered warily and suspiciously, as though not quite sure whether, after all, the two ladies might be lying in ambush somewhere for him. But no, there was no deception, only the doctor was there, and he, unrestrained by the presence of his usual bodyguard, was most friendly and cordial.

"Ah, Riddell, glad to see you. Sit down. You find me a bachelor, you see, for once in a way."

Riddell was soon at his ease. The doctor chatted pleasantly over their tea about various Willoughby topics, giving his opinion on some and asking the captain's opinion on others, and so delicately showing his sympathy for the boy in his difficulties and his approval of his efforts for the good of the school, that Riddell was quite won over, and prepared for the serious matter which the doctor presently broached. "Yes," said the latter, in reply to some reference by Riddell to the Welchers. "Yes, I am a good deal concerned about Welch's house, Riddell. I dare say you can understand why."

"I think so, sir. They don't seem to pull together there somehow, or have the sympathy with the good of the school."

"Precisely. That's just what it is," said the doctor, delighted to find his head boy so exactly understanding the nature of the house over which he was to be installed. "They seem to be 'each man for himself, and none for the State,' I fear."

"I think so," said Riddell. "They hold aloof from most of the school doings, unless there's a chance of a row. They had no boat on the river this year, and I don't think they will have a man in the eleven against Rockshire. And they seem to have no ambition to work for the school."

The doctor mused a bit, and then said, with a half-sigh, as if to himself, "And I wish that were the worst of it." Then turning to Riddell, he said, "I am glad to hear your opinion of Welch's house, Riddell, and to find that you seem to understand what is wrong there. What should you say to taking charge of that house in future?"

This was breaking the news suddenly, with a vengeance, and Riddell fairly gaped at the head master as he sat back in his chair, and wondered if he had heard aright.

"What, sir!" at length he gasped; "*I* take charge of Welch's!"

"Yes, my boy," said the doctor, quietly.

"Oh, I could never do it, sir!" exclaimed Riddell, pale at the very notion.

"Try," said the head master. "It may not be so impossible as you think."

"I'm not popular, sir," faltered Riddell, "and I've no influence. Indeed, it would only make things worse. Try some one else, sir. Try Fairbairn."

"I shall want Fairbairn to be the head of the schoolhouse," said the doctor.

"I'm sure it would be a mistake, sir," repeated Riddell. "If there was any chance of my succeeding I would try, but—"

"But," said the doctor, "you have not tried. Listen, Riddell; I know I am not inviting you to a bed of roses. It is a come-down, I know, for the captain of the school and the head of the schoolhouse to go down to Welch's, especially such a Welch's as ours is at present. But the post of danger, you know, is the post of honour. I leave it to you. You need not go unless you wish. I shall not think worse of you if you conscientiously feel you should not go. Think it over. Count all the cost. You have already made a position for yourself in the schoolhouse. You will have to quit that, of course, and start afresh and single-handed in the new house, and it is not likely that those who defy the rules of the school will take at first to a fellow who comes to enforce them. Think it all over, I say, and decide with open eyes."

The doctor's words had a strange inspiriting effect on this shy and diffident boy. The recital of all the difficulties in the way was the most powerful argument to a nature like his, and when at length the doctor wished him good-night and told him to take till the following day to decide, Riddell was already growing accustomed to the prospect of his new duty.

For all that, the day that ensued was anxious and troubled. Not so much on account of Welch's. On that point his mind was pretty nearly made up. It seemed a call of duty, and therefore it was a call of honour, which Riddell dare not disobey. But to leave the schoolhouse just now, when it lay under the reproach caused by the boat-race accident; and worse still, to leave it just when young Wyndham seemed to be drifting from his moorings and yielding with less and less effort to the temptations of bad companions—these were troubles compared with which the perils and difficulties of his new task were but light.

For a long time that night Riddell sat in his study and pondered over the doctor's offer, and looked at it in all its aspects, and counted up all the cost.

Then like a wise man he took counsel of a Friend. Ah! you say, he talked it over with Fairbairn, or Porter, or the acute Crossfield—or, perhaps, he wrote a letter to old Wyndham? No, reader, Riddell had a Friend at Willoughby dearer even than old Wyndham, and nearer than Fairbairn, or Porter, or Crossfield, and that night when all the school was asleep, little dreaming what its captain did, he went to that Friend and told Him all his difficulties about Welch's, and his anxieties about young Wyndham, and even his unhappiness about the boat-race; and in doing so found himself wonderfully cheered and ready to face the new duty, and even hopeful of success.

Next morning he went to the doctor and told him he was ready to enter on his new duties. Dr Patrick was not the man to flatter his head boy or to inspire him with undue hopes; but he was undoubtedly gratified by the decision, and Riddell felt encouraged in the consciousness of his sympathy.

At call-over that evening the Welchers had the pleasure of being informed by the doctor of the new arrangements proposed for their welfare, and, it need hardly be said, were considerably moved thereby.

At first they were disposed to regard the affair as a joke and a capital piece of fun. But when that evening Riddell put in an appearance at supper, in their house, and when Telson was intercepted bringing over his late master's goods and chattels to the study next but one to that of Silk, they began to take the matter in rather more seriously.

For the first time for a long while Welch's house seemed to be of one mind—a mind made up of equal mixtures of resentment and amazement and amusement. Probably, had they been more accustomed to thinking together, they would have summoned a monster meeting, as Parrett's would have done, to discuss the situation. As it was, they resolved themselves into several small groups, each of which dealt with the topic of the hour in its own way.

The juniors of course had a good deal to say on the subject. Pilbury, Cusack, Philpot, Morgan, and a few other kindred spirits held a council of war in the study of the two former immediately after supper.

"Rum start this, eh, Pil!" said Cusack, by way of opening proceedings.

"You know," said Pil, confidentially, "I'm not surprised. He made such a regular mess of it in the schoolhouse."

"Don't know what's the good of his coming here, then," said Philpot; "our fellows aren't a bit quieter than the schoolhouse."

No one was bold enough to dispute this peculiarly modest description of the order of Welch's house.

"I wonder if he's been kicked out of the captaincy as well?" asked Cusack, who was apparently convinced in his own mind that the new move was a degradation for Riddell.

"I don't know," said Morgan; "Paddy said something about it being a good thing for us to get the captain of the school as head of our house."

"Oh, ah—a jolly good thing," said Pilbury; "jolly lookout for us if he's stuck here to pull us up whenever we have a lark."

77

"Bless you, *he* can't pull a fellow up!" said somebody. "They said he used to now and then in the schoolhouse."

"Not he. He's afraid to look at a chap."

"I say," said Cusack, "rather a spree to fetch him, eh, you fellows, and see how he does. Eh?"

"I'm game," said Pilbury; "what shall we do? Smash in his study-door?"

"Oh, no," said Cusack, "no use doing that. Let's give him 'Bouncer' to start with."

"That ought to startle him up," said Philpot, laughing, "if he's not used to it."

"Rather—open the door a bit, Morgan. Now, you fellows, are you all game? All together."

And with that the party struck up at the top of their voices the famous old Willoughby chorus, of which the first verse runs as follows:

"Oh, Bouncer was a Willoughby chap, sir,

Bouncer! Bouncer! Bouncer!

Upon his head he wore his cap, sir,

Bouncer! Bouncer! Bouncer!

Below his cap he wore his head,

His eyes were black and his hair was red,

And he carried his bat for a cool *hundred*,

Bouncer! Bouncer! Bouncer!"

This poetic record of the virtues and accomplishments of their legendary school hero gave ample scope, as the reader may surmise, for spirited declamation; and on the present occasion more Welchers than Riddell were startled by the sudden and vehement outburst of the patriotic hymn. Indeed, as it appeared to be a point of honour with the vocalists to pitch no two voices in the same key, the effect was even alarming, and suggested the sudden letting loose of a menagerie.

The singers waited meekly for a few seconds to see whether their efforts had met with the success they deserved. But as a dead silence reigned, and no one came, they considerately determined to give their audience another chance; and therefore launched forthwith into the second verse, which was delivered with even more dramatic power than the first:

"Old Bouncer stood six foot and an inch, sir,

Bouncer! Bouncer! Bouncer!

And four foot round his chest was a pinch, sir,

Bouncer! Bouncer! Bouncer!

Twelve stone two was his fighting weight,

And he stroked our boat for the champion plate,

And ran his mile in four thirty-eight,

Bouncer! Bouncer! Bouncer!"

This time the heroic efforts of the melodious juniors had their reward. Before the last line was reached the door of the new captain's study opened, and Riddell appeared in the passage. His first appearance in his new capacity was naturally a matter of curiosity on every hand; and as he approached the scene of the noise he became aware that almost every occupant of the passage was standing at his door, watching curiously for what was to happen.

He certainly did not look, as he walked nervously down the corridor, the sort of fellow to quell a riot; and any one might have prophesied that he was not likely to come off any better now than he did when he once went on a similar errand to the stronghold of the Limpets.

And yet the weeks that had elapsed since then had not been thrown away on Riddell. Would the reader like to hear what his thoughts were as he neared the scene of his trial?

"What had I better do? If I get in a rage I shall only make a fool of myself; if I report them to the doctor I shall be shirking my own work; if I remonstrate mildly and do no more, my chances in Welch's are done for, and these fellows who are on the lookout for my failure will get their crow. I *must* get on the right side of these youngsters if I can, so here goes!"

With this reflection he reached the door just as the third verse of "Bouncer" commenced, the performers having carefully turned their backs so as to appear wholly unconscious of a visitor. Verse three referred altogether to the intellectual attainments of the wonderful Bouncer.

"Bouncer was the cock of the school, sir,

Bouncer! Bouncer! Bouncer!

And Socrates to him was a fool, sir,

Bouncer! Bouncer! Bouncer!

He could cross the 'asses' bridge in the dark,

And 'Hic Haec Hoc' he thought a lark.

And swallowed irregular verbs like a shark,

Bouncer! Bouncer! Bouncer!"

Before this spirit-stirring recital had reached its climax one or two of the performers had found it impossible to resist a look round to see how the captain took it. So that the "surprise" at finding him standing there at its conclusion fell rather flat.

Much to the disappointment of the spectators outside, moreover, Riddell shut the door behind him. The juniors eyed him curiously. Contrary to their expectation, he neither looked frightened nor confused, but his face was as cheery as his voice as he said, "You see, I couldn't resist your beautiful music."

Was he in jest or earnest? Did he really mean he had enjoyed the chorus, or was he poking fun at them? They could not quite tell.

"Oh," said Cusack, not quite as defiantly, however, as he could have wished, "that's a song we sing among ourselves, isn't it, you fellows?"

"Ah!" said Riddell, before "the fellows" could chime in, "it's good fun belonging to a musical set—especially for songs like this, that appear to have several tunes all sung at once! You should give a concert."

The boys looked more perplexed than ever. It sounded like chaff, and yet they could scarcely believe it was. So they smiled vacantly at one another, and began to feel the situation a little awkward.

"I suppose," continued Riddell, feeling his way carefully—"I suppose between nine and ten is the usual time for singing in Welch's? I fancied it was before supper!"

"Oh!" said Pilbury, "we do as we like here."

"Do you, really?" replied the captain. "How jolly that must be!"

Cusack and Pilbury could hardly tell why they laughed at this very innocent observation, but they did, and Riddell was quick enough to see his advantage.

"You know, I'd be very sorry to interfere with the beautiful music," he said; "but do you think you could get to like not to sing after supper?"

The boys stared as if they were not quite sure yet how to take it. However, the captain made himself clear without further delay. "The fact is," said he, a trifle nervously, but in his friendliest tones—"the fact is—I don't know what you think, but I'd be awfully glad if you fellows would back me up for a week or two in Welch's. Of course, you know, the doctor's put me here, and I don't suppose you're much alarmed by the move, eh? You needn't be."

"We aren't," said Morgan, in a decidedly mild attempt at heroism.

"I'm glad of that," said the captain; whereat the rest of the company laughed at the unlucky Morgan, who had quite expected the joke to go the other way. "You know," continued Riddell, sitting upon the table and talking as familiarly as though he were in his own study, "I'd rather like if among us we could pull Welch's up a bit before the end of the term. It seems rather a shame, for instance, we didn't have a boat on the river these races, and that there's not a single Welcher in the first eleven."

"It's a beastly shame!" said Philpot. "Bloomfield's down on us, you know; he's got a spite against us."

"Oh! I don't know," said Riddell. "I fancy if we'd got some good enough men he'd be only too glad to put them in. After all, the glory of the school is the chief thing."

"Tucker and Silk will never practise," said Cusack. "I know *I* would if I'd got the chance."

"Well, I don't see why you shouldn't start the House Cricket Club this year, at any rate," said Riddell.

"That's just what Tucker and Silk won't do. We wanted them to do it, didn't we, Pil?"

"Rather!" said Pil; "and they told us to mind our own business."

"Suppose we start it ourselves?" suggested the captain; "I'm a Welcher now, you know. I don't see why, because Tucker and Silk object, the whole house should be done out of its cricket."

"No more do I," said Philpot.

"They'll kick up a jolly row with us, though," said Morgan.

"I don't think so," said Riddell. "At any rate, that's no reason why there shouldn't be a club."

"All serene!" said Cusack, warming up to the notion, and quite forgetting "Bouncer."

"I say, Riddell, couldn't we start it now?"

"Yes, certainly," said Riddell; "why not? I propose Cusack be the secretary."

"Oh, I say!" cried that youth, blushing, half with pleasure and half with embarrassment; "you'd better be that, Riddell."

"Oh, no," said Riddell, laughing, "I don't know the fellows so well as you. If you were secretary, and Pilbury or Philpot treasurer, I'd be president, or something of that sort, if you like."

The idea of the new club took like wildfire, and an enthusiastic consultation followed. It was resolved to summon a meeting next day of all who took an interest in the sport, and to arrange for a trial match at once. Riddell went as warmly into the details as any one, and took every opportunity of working up the patriotic spirit of his younger companions.

"You know," said he, "I don't see at all why we shouldn't be able to get together a team for the junior elevens if we practise hard."

"The nuisance is," said Cusack, "we're stopped an hour a day's play all this term."

"What for?" inquired the captain.

The melancholy story of Mr Parrett and the sulphuretted hydrogen was recounted.

"It's a pity," said he, gravely.

"I wonder if Paddy would mind giving us a licking instead," suggested Pilbury, whose hands were of the horny kind.

Even the others whose palms were less seasoned seemed willing to fall in with this alternative, but Riddell discouraged it.

"No," said he, "he's not likely to do that. But I tell you what I'll do. I'll see him and Parrett and tell them about the club, and undertake that you'll be steady the rest of the term if they'll let you off. Do you think I'd be safe in saying so?"

"Rather! I'll promise, for one," cried Cusack.

"And I'll try," said Pilbury.

"So will we," said the others.

So it was settled. And when next day Riddell in triumph was able to announce that the doctor and Mr Parrett had agreed to withdraw the prohibition, in consideration of the captain's promise on their behalf, great was the jubilation.

Greater still was Riddell's own satisfaction in feeling that he had at least made a good start towards getting on the right side of the juniors of his new house.

Chapter Nineteen.

"Is Willoughby degenerate?"

As might be expected, the new captain's move in attempting to win over the juniors of Welch's only served to increase the irritation of those seniors who had hitherto reigned supreme in the house.

But Riddell had taken this into his calculation, and was therefore not greatly astonished when immediately after the enthusiastic cricket meeting just referred to, Silk followed him to his study in a by no means amiable frame of mind.

Silk was not given to losing his temper, but on the present occasion he was decidedly ruffled. And no wonder.

Any fellow would be ruffled who suddenly found himself deposed from his authority in the manner in which Silk had been. Had he been one of the most conscientious and painstaking of monitors, he might well have been excused flaring up a little, and, indeed, would have shown a poor spirit had he not done so.

But Silk, as the reader knows, was neither painstaking nor conscientious. He did not care a rap about Welch's, still less about Willoughby. As long as he could please himself and annoy his enemies, he did not care what became of his house or the boys in it. It was only when any one ventured to dispute his authority as head of the house that he attached any value to his office. In fact, it was the story of the Dog in the Manger carried out in school life—he would not be troubled doing his duty to Welch's, and he would not if he could help it let any one else do it for him.

Riddell, if truth must be told, was not at all sorry to have an early opportunity of coming to an explanation with Silk.

Silk was one of the very few boys in Willoughby whom the captain positively disliked, and that being so Riddell was troubled with none of the half-apologetic nervousness which he usually felt in the presence of his other fellow-seniors. He looked upon Silk both as an enemy to Willoughby and as the evil genius of young Wyndham, and therefore was by no means disposed to beg his pardon or consult his pleasure in the new order of things at Welch's.

"I hear the juniors have been saying something to you about starting the cricket club," said Silk, in tones which were the reverse of conciliatory.

"Yes," said Riddell; "or, rather, I suggested it to them."

"You did! All I can say is, it's like your impudence. Welch's is come to a pretty pass if *you're* sent here to look after our athletics."

Riddell did not feel called upon to reply to this, and Silk therefore continued, "Don't you know Tucker and I have been captains of the clubs here for the last two years?"

"I was told so."

"Then what business have you to interfere?"

"There was no house club at all this year."

"A lot *you* care about the cricket. I know well enough it's just a canting dodge for snubbing Tucker and me before the fellows, nothing more."

"You're quite mistaken," replied Riddell.

"Oh, of course! You'd like to make out that you care a fig about cricket. You who couldn't even bowl a ball from one end of the wickets to the other!"

There seemed nothing particular to reply to in this, so Riddell remained silent. This only irritated Silk the more, who felt that he was by no means getting the best of it.

"You'd better stop this sort of thing at once," he said, viciously. "You're sent here to look after the morals of the house, not to interfere with what doesn't concern you. Tucker and I can look after the cricket without you."

"Are you and Tucker going to start the old club again, then?" asked Riddell quietly.

"Whatever business of yours is it whether we are or aren't? Find out."

"That's what I'm trying to do. If you are, I'll advise the other fellows to join it and not have two clubs."

"*You* advise the fellows!" sneered Silk; "they don't want a schoolhouse prig like you to advise them."

It was evidently no use trying to conciliate a fellow like this, and Riddell began to get tired of the interview.

"I don't want to offend you or anybody," said he boldly; "but if you and Tucker won't take the trouble to start the club, I don't see that all the house is to be done out of their cricket in consequence. The fellows have little enough to keep them together as it is."

"You are a nice *little thing* to keep them together with, I must say," snarled Silk, "and you've made a good start by setting the juniors against their seniors."

"I've done nothing of the sort," replied Riddell, quietly; "and if you'll excuse me, I've some work to do, and there's really not much use talking on the subject."

So saying, he turned, and began taking his books down from the shelf.

Silk, whose irritation had been gradually getting beyond bounds, was pleased to regard this action as a direct insult to himself, and flared up accordingly.

"Look here, you snivelling, stuck-up, hypocritical prig, you!" exclaimed he, advancing and seizing the captain roughly by the arm, "we'd better come to an understanding at once. If you think you're going to cheek us just as you please here, you're mistaken, I tell you. What do you mean by it?"

"By what?" inquired Riddell, mildly, but quite composedly.

Silk's only reply was a passionate blow in the captain's face, which sent him staggering to the other side of the room.

It was a critical moment. Riddell was no coward, nor was he one of those sickly individuals who, not satisfied to be struck on one cheek only, invite a repetition of the assault on the other side. Physically weak and nervous as he was, he had sufficient British instinct to move him to stand up for himself.

And yet as he stood there a moment irresolute, it flashed across him that whatever the cost he must not enter upon a fight with Silk.

Of course he would be called a coward, and nothing he could say could prove he wasn't. He was no match for Silk, and consequently his refusal to defend himself would be called fear.

"And yet," thought he, "if I fight, my chance in Welch's is gone, even if I were able to beat him. The fellows will have no more respect for me than any other rowdy, and will soon enough make my thrashing an excuse for mutiny."

It was a hard position for any boy, and the courage required to hold him back cost Riddell more effort than had he blindly rushed into the fray and given himself up to be thrashed.

"Will you fight?" shouted Silk, advancing.

"No," said Riddell, as coolly as he could.

"Wretched coward!" exclaimed the bully, "of course you won't. Then take what you deserve. I'll give you the biggest hiding you ever had in your life."

He would probably have carried out his threat, and Riddell would probably before half a minute have given up all further idea of non-resistance, when an opportune diversion occurred in the person of Telson, who appeared with the remainder of his late senior's possessions from the schoolhouse.

"I say, Riddell," he exclaimed, almost before the door was open, "here's a jolly go! I've got to be that beast Gilks's fag, and— Hullo! what's up?"

This remark was caused by Silk's suddenly turning on his heel and hurrying from the study without putting into execution his threat.

"What was he up to?" asked Telson, as the door was shut. "He was going to exterminate me, so he said," replied Riddell, smiling.

"I wish he'd tried, and you'd given him a jolly licking," said Telson. "He's a cad. I wonder what young Wyndham or any one sees to like in him."

"Wyndham likes him, then?" asked the captain. "They always seem jolly thick," said the fag. "By the way, Riddell, were you ever at Beamish's?"

"Beamish's? No!" exclaimed Riddell. "Why?"

"Oh," said Telson, "I only wanted to know what sort of place it was."

"Not a good one. There's a pretty strong rule against it in the school. Bad job for any one caught going there."

"I know, I'm not going; I only wanted to know what sort of place it was. But I'm off, I've got a motion on in Parliament to-morrow. I say, Riddell, I wish you hadn't left the schoolhouse."

And off went the junior, leaving Riddell somewhat perplexed by his chatter, but considerably consoled nevertheless to think that there was any one in the schoolhouse, or anywhere, who was sorry to lose him.

However, the same reason which took Telson away left Riddell also little time to spend in vague reflections. He, too, had a speech to prepare for Parliament to-morrow.

The meeting promised to be an important one in many respects. It was the first after the boat-race, and consequently party feeling was likely to make use of the opportunity to let off a little of its steam. Then, of course, it was the captain's first public appearance as the head of Welch's, and that was sure to excite a good deal of curiosity and interest. And last, but not least, the subject for the evening was a debate on the question, "That Willoughby is Degenerate," to be opened in the affirmative by Ashley, and in the negative by Porter, and on this burning question the debate as well as the division promised to be pretty interesting.

There was the usual lively time before the regular business was reached over "Questions," of which there were a good many on the notice-paper. But it will be best to report the meeting in the usual Parliamentary style, as it would have appeared on the records of the House, had any record been kept at Willoughby:

Mr Bloomfield took the chair at three o'clock.

Mr Merrison (Welcher) gave notice that at the next meeting he would move—"That this House gives its support to the Liberal candidate in the coming election at Shellport, and does all in its power to kick out the Radical." (Loud cheers.)

Mr Pringle (Parrett's) asked the Home Secretary what day the summer holidays were to begin.

Mr Ashley replied that he was not in a position to inform the hon. member, but probably in about six weeks.

Mr Wyndham, jun. (schoolhouse), wished to ask why Parrett's would not row another race when the schoolhouse had offered it? (Great schoolhouse cheers.)

Mr Game (First Lord of the Admiralty), amid equally loud cheers on Parrett's side, replied that as soon as the schoolhouse found out who had been mean enough to cut the Parrett's rudder-line, and gave him up to justice, they would see about it.

Whereupon Mr Wibberly begged to ask the schoolhouse stroke whether he had any information to give the House on the subject.

Mr Fairbairn.—The information I have to give the House is that Mr Riddell and I, directly after the race, went to Mr Bloomfield and said we were sorry for the accident—(ironical laughter from Parrett's)—and offered to row them again any day they liked, and the offer was declined. (Schoolhouse cheers.)

Mr Tipper.—I should like to know if the schoolhouse fellows are making any efforts to discover the culprit by whose assistance they won the race. (Tremendous Parrett's cheers.)

Mr Fairbairn.—I can't say we are. (Derisive cheers of "Of course not!" from Parrett's.) The hon. gentlemen opposite seem to know so much about it, that I think they had better find the culprit themselves. ("Hear, hear," from the schoolhouse.)

The proceedings at this stage became rather noisy, every one being anxious to express his opinion on the question. It was not till after the President had threatened to "adjourn the House" that silence was at length restored.

Bloomfield took the sensible course, also, of announcing that, as quite enough questions had been asked about the race, he should not allow any more on that subject.

Whereupon Mr Tucker, the Welcher, rose and put a question on another matter. He wanted to know the reason why Mr Riddell had become a Welcher; whether it was true that he had been turned out of the schoolhouse for being incompetent; and whether he had been kicked out of the captaincy as well.

Mr Crossfield said he had been requested to reply. And first he must congratulate the hon. member on having succeeded in asking a question which any one could understand. (Laughter.)

In reply, he understood Mr Riddell had been sent to Welch's in order to study the virtues of a fellow called Tucker, who was—

Mr Tucker, rising: Mr Chairman, I didn't put my question in order to be insulted by Crossfield or any one. (Laughter.)

Mr Crossfield.—I apologise to the hon. gentleman. I will not insult him by supposing he has any virtues. I should say Mr Riddell has gone to take a few lessons in the art of keeping a house in order, which no one can so well teach him as Mr Tucker. (Loud laughter.) In reply to the gentleman's second question—

Mr Tucker.—I don't want any more. (Laughter.)

Mr Crossfield.—In reply to the gentleman's second question, I am sorry to inform him that his impressions are about as correct and intelligent as they usually are. (Renewed cheers and laughter, in the midst of which Tucker subsided in a state of mind hardly amiable.)

As soon as silence was restored, Mr Porter wished to ask the captain of the eleven whether the team to play against Rockshire was yet settled.

Mr Bloomfield.—Not quite. Nine names are fixed—Game, Tipper, Ashley, Wibberly, and myself from Parrett's house, and Fairbairn, Porter, Coates, and Crossfield from the schoolhouse. (Cheers and counter-cheers, and loud cries of "What about the Welchers?") What about the Welchers? That's what everybody wants to know! (Loud cheers.)

Hereupon Mr Cusack rose in his place and asked if the House was aware that the Welchers' cricket club was started again; that he was the secretary; and old Mr Pil the treasurer, and Mr Riddell the president, that the subscription was two shillings and sixpence in advance, and that— But here the enthusiastic secretary's announcement was drowned in the general laughter of the assembly, led by the Parrett's juniors, who roared as if they'd never heard such a joke in their lives. "Won't be a joke when we smash you in one innings," shouted Cusack, standing on his seat to give emphasis to the challenge. "Ho, ho! when's that to be?"

"When you like," cried the Welchers. "Do you funk it?"

"Unless those juniors there hold their row," interposed Bloomfield, "I shall have them turned out of the meeting." Whereat the little breeze calmed down.

The President then called upon Mr Ashley to move the resolution standing in his name, which he did in a rather feeble speech.

"I really don't think it necessary to say much to prove that the school is degenerate. Look at the clubs! They aren't nearly as good as they were in old Wyndham's time. Parrett's clubs, thanks to Mr Bloomfield, keep up; but where are the others? Then the rows. (Hear, hear.) I'm sure there have been more rows in the school this term than all the rest of the year put together. The juniors seem to do what they like,"—("Hear, hear," from Telson, Parson, and Co.)—"and no one seems to know who has a right to keep any one else in order. Now, why is all this? (Loud cheers from Bosher.) You know as well as I do. The captain of the school always used to be a fellow the boys could look up to. Old Wyndham and the captain before him were something like fellows. (Loud Parrett's cheers.) *They* weren't afraid to look any one in the face—(cheers)—and *they* didn't, when they got tired of one house—(cheers)—ask the doctor to move them to another. (Terrific applause from the Parrett's and Welchers.) Why, if this boat-race affair had happened in old Wyndham's time, do you suppose he wouldn't have made it right, and found out the fellow, even if it was his own brother? (Loud cheers, amidst which young Wyndham blushed a great deal at this unexpected piece of notoriety.) I'm not going to say any more." ("Hear, hear," from Fairbairn.)

Mr Porter rose to open the debate on the other side. He wasn't going to give in that Willoughby was going down. It was unpatriotic. (Cheers.) He meant to say if the school did go down it was the fellows' own fault, and not all to be blamed on one boy. Mr Riddell would probably answer for himself—(laughter)—but he (Mr Porter) was pretty sure the school would not degenerate under him. The fellows seemed to think the only thing in the world was brute strength. He had no objection to brute strength—(cheers and laughter)—in fact he fancied he had a little of his own—("Hear, hear," from Telson whose ears Porter had boxed only that morning)—but Willoughby wanted something better than that; and he meant to say there were plenty of fellows in the school who didn't make much noise, but who did as much to keep up the school as all the rowdies put together. And when things have quieted down, as he hoped they would, these fellows would get more thanks than they did now. (Cheers from a few, who apparently considered this last allusion referred specially to them.)

Porter was not a good speaker, and the little he did say was a good deal bungled. Still there was a manly ring about his speech which pleased the better disposed section of his audience, some of whom did not even belong to the same house.

Silk followed. The Welcher monitor was clever to a certain degree, and although he never chose to devote his cleverness to good purposes, he usually managed to get himself listened to when he chose to take the trouble. And at present, his peculiar position as the deposed head of Welch's gave a certain interest to what he had to say. Bitter enough it was.

"What chance is there of the school not going down, I should like to know," said he, "when cant is the order of the day? (Hear, hear.) Of course the school is going down. What interests can any one have in his house when some one comes and begins by setting the juniors against the seniors and then turning up the whites of his eyes and saying, 'What a shocking state of disorder the house is in?' Why, before 'the little stranger'—(loud laughter)—came to Welch's, the seniors and juniors never fell out," ("Hear, hear," from several quarters), "but now there's a regular mutiny. And what's bad for one house is bad for the school. I don't care who's head of Welch's. He's welcome to the honour if he likes, but let him act above-board, that's what I say, and not snivel and look pious while all the time he's doing a dirty trick." (Cheers from Tucker and one or two more, which, however, instantly died out when Crossfield rose.)

Crossfield was the plague of the senior Welchers' lives!

"I was much affected by the beautiful speech of the gentleman who has just sat down," he began. "It is always so sweet to hear conscious innocence asserting itself. After the gentleman's noble efforts for the good of his house (laughter)—and the splendid example he has set of rectitude—(laughter)—and high moral principle—(laughter)—it is truly touching to find him put on one side for an interloper who is villainous enough to tell the juniors they need not walk in his saintly footsteps! (Laughter.) But that is not what I wanted to say, and as the gentleman appears to be overcome by his emotions—(Silk was at that moment angrily leaving the room)—I don't think we need trouble any more about him. (Cheers and laughter.) All I wished to say was this: I always understood from the gentlemen of Parrett's that Mr Bloomfield was captain of Willoughby," (Loud cries of "So he is!"), "and that nobody cared a straw for Mr Riddell." ("No more they do!"). "Then, I don't think Mr Ashley is very complimentary to Mr Bloomfield when he says the fault of all the mischief is that the captain is not an all-round man. For all that he's quite correct. Mr Bloomfield is a well-meaning man, no doubt, but he certainly is not an all-round man." (Uproar.)

Riddell then rose, and his rising was the signal for a great demonstration of party feeling. Parrett's of course went against him, and a large section of Welch's, but the schoolhouse, aided by Cusack, Pilbury, and Co., backed him up. He spoke nervously but boldly.

"I am sorry to have to support the motion of Mr Ashley. I agree with him that Willoughby is not what it was, and not what it should be. (Cheers.) And I also agree with him in thinking that the school might have a good deal better captain than it has." (Cries of "No!" from the schoolhouse.) "However, I do not want to say a word about myself. What I do want to say is this—it's one thing to discover that we are degenerate, and another to try to put ourselves right again. And are we likely to do that as long as we are all at sixes and sevens, pulling different ways, caring far more about our own gratifications than the good of the whole school? I don't think so, and I don't believe Mr Bloomfield does either. Every fellow worth the name of a Willoughbite must be sorry to see things as they are. (Hear, hear.) Why should they remain so? Surely the good of the school is more important than squabbling about who is captain and which is the best house. Of course, we all back up our own house, and, as a Welcher now, I mean to try if our house can't give a good account of itself before the term's over. (Loud cheers from Pilbury, Cusack, Philpot, etcetera.) And if each house pulls itself up, not at the expense of a rival house—(Hear, hear)—but for the glory of the school—(Hear, hear)—we shan't have to complain of Willoughby being degenerate much longer. You remember what old Wyndham said the night before he left. As long as the fellows think first of the school and then of themselves Willoughby will be all right. Depend upon it he was right. We cheered him loud enough then, why not take his advice still?" (Loud cheers.)

This spirited address roused the applause of all the better-minded section, whose cheers were not wholly unmingled with self-reproach. Bloomfield himself, it was plain, felt its force, and as to the more vehement members of Parrett's, it considerably damped their ardour.

84

"Old man," said Fairbairn that evening to his friend the captain, "you struck a really good blow for the school this afternoon. I don't know how you managed to pitch on just the right thing to say, as you did. Things will come all right, take my word for it. They're beginning already."

Alas, there is many a slip 'twixt the cup and the lip, as Willoughby had yet to discover.

Chapter Twenty.

Is Willoughby Mad?

Things did not mend all at once at Willoughby. No one expected they would. And within a few days after the "debate in Parliament" it seemed as if the school had finally abandoned all ideas of order and discipline.

The reader will remember that more than once mention had been made of an approaching election for the free and enlightened borough of Shellport, which was occupying the attention not only of the town, and of the doctor and his ladies, but also of the boys themselves. And the cheers with which Morrison's notice of motion, mentioned in the last chapter, was received, showed plainly enough how things were going.

By long tradition Willoughby had been a Whig school. Fellows did not exactly know what Whig meant, but they knew it was the opposite of Tory on one side and Radical on the other, and they went accordingly. On the present occasion, moreover, they had a sort of personal interest in the event, for the Whig candidate, Sir George Pony, had been discovered to be a sort of second uncle a few times removed of Pringle, one of the Parrett's fags, whereas the Radical, Mr Cheeseman, was a nobody!

For all these reasons Willoughby felt it had a great stake in the contest, and tacitly determined to make its voice heard.

Small election meetings were held by the more enthusiastic politicians of the school, for the purpose of giving vent to their anti-radical sympathies. At these one boy was usually compelled to represent the Whig and another to figure as the unpopular Radical. And the cheering of the one and the hooting of the other was an immense consolation to the young patriots; and when, as usually happened, the meeting proceeded to poll for the candidates, and it was announced that the Whig had got 15,999 votes (there were just 16,000 inhabitants in Shellport), and the Radical only one (polled by himself), the applause would become simply deafening.

Even the seniors, in a more dignified way, took up the Whig cause, and wore the Whig colours; and woe betide the rash boy who sported the opposition badge!

The juniors were hardly the boys to let an occasion like this slip, and many and glorious were the demonstrations in which they engaged. They broke out into a blaze of yellow, and insisted on wearing their colours even in bed. Pringle was a regular hero, and cheered whenever he showed his face; whereas Brown, the town boy, whose father was suspected of being a Radical, was daily and almost hourly mobbed till his life became a burden to him. All other distinctions and quarrels were forgotten in this enthusiastic and glorious outburst of patriotic feeling.

Two days before the election a mass meeting of juniors and Limpets of all houses and ages, summoned by proclamation, was held in a corner of the playground, "to hear addresses by the candidates, and elect a member for Shellport." Pringle, of course, was to figure as his distant uncle, and upon the unhappy Bosher had fallen the lot of assuming the unpopular *rôle* of Mr Cheeseman. The meeting, though only professing to be a juniors' assembly, attracted a good many seniors also, whose curiosity and sense of humour were by no means disappointed at the proceedings.

The chairman, Parson, standing on the top of two cricket-boxes, with a yellow band round his hat, a yellow rosette on each side of his jacket, and a yellow tie round his neck, said they were met to choose a member, and knew who was their man. (Loud cheers for "Pringle.") "They didn't want any Radical cads—(cheers)—and didn't know what they wanted down here." (Cheers.) (Bosher: "*I* don't want to be a Radical, you know.")—(Loud cries of "Shut up!" "Turn him out!") He'd like to know what that young ass Curtis was grinning at? He'd have him turned out if he had any of his cheek. He always suspected Curtis was a Radical. (Curtis: "No, I'm not—I'm for Pony.") There, he knew he was, because Radicals always told crams! Whereat Parson resumed the level ground. Pringle, who had about as much idea of public speaking as he had of Chinese, was then hoisted up on to the platform amid terrific applause.

He smiled vacantly, and nodded his head, and waved his hand, and occasionally, when he caught sight of some particularly familiar friend, brought it up vertically near his nose.

"Silence! Shut up! Hold your row for Pony!" yelled the chairman.

"Go ahead, Pringle!" cried the candidate's supporters.

"Speak out!" shouted the crowd.

"All right," said the unhappy orator, "what have I got to say, though?"

"Oh, anything—fire ahead. Any bosh will do."

Pringle ruminated a bit, then, impelled to it by the cheers of his audience, he shouted, for lack of anything better to say, all he could remember of his English history lesson of that morning.

"Gentlemen—(cheers)—the first thing Edward III did on ascending the crown—(terrific applause, in which the seniors present joined)—was to behead the two favourite ministers—(prolonged cheers)—of his mother." (Applause, amidst which Pringle suddenly disappeared from view, and Morrison, the Limpet, mounted the cricket-box. Morrison was a politician after Willoughby's own heart.)

"I beg to move that Sir George Pony is a fit and proper member for Willoughby," he screamed. "I think the Radicals ought all to be hung. (Cheers.) They're worse than the Tories. (Counter-cheers.) One's about as bad as the other. (United cheers.) We're all Whigs here. (Applause.) I say down with everybody that isn't. (Cheers.) If the Radical gets in I don't mind if the Constitution gets smashed." ("Nor do we!") "It will serve them right for allowing the Radicals in." (Mighty applause.)

I am not going to continue the report of this animated and intellectual meeting. It lasted till call-over, was renewed again directly after tea, and continued long after the speakers and audience were in bed. Bosher got dreadfully mobbed, besides being hit on the ear with a stone and hunted several times round the playground by the anti-Radicals.

Altogether Willoughby had gone a little "off its head," so to speak, on the subject of the election. Riddell found himself powerless to control the excitement, and the other monitors were most of them too much interested in the event themselves to be of much service. The practice for the Rockshire match, as well as the play of the newly-started Welchers' club, was for the time completely suspended; and it was evident that until the election was over there was no prospect of seeing the school in its right mind again.

The day before the event was a busy and anxious one for the captain. All day long fellows came applying to him on the wildest of pretexts for "permits" the following afternoon to go into town. Pilbury, Cusack, and Philpot wanted to get their hair cut. King and Wakefield had to get measured for boots, and to-morrow afternoon was the only time they could fix for the ceremony. Parson and Telson suddenly recollected that they had never called to pay their respects at Brown's after the pleasant evening they had spent there a few weeks ago. Strutter, Tedbury, and a few other Limpets were anxious to study geology that afternoon at the Town Museum, Pringle wanted to see how his "uncle" was getting on, etcetera, etcetera.

All which ingenious pretexts the captain very naturally saw through and firmly declined, much to the mortification of the applicants—who many of them returned to the charge with fresh and still more ingenious arguments for making an exception in their particular case. But all to no effect. About midday the captain's study was empty, and the following notice pasted on the door told its own story.

Notice.

By the Doctor's order, no permits will be allowed to-morrow. Call-over will be at four instead of five.

A. Riddell, Capt.

In other words, the authorities were determined that Willoughby should take no part in the election, and to make things quite sure had fixed call-over for the very hour when the poll would be closing. Of course poor Riddell came in for all the blame of this unpopular announcement, and had a bad time of it in consequence. It was at first reported that the captain was a Radical, and that that was the reason of the prohibition, but this story was contradicted by his appearance that same evening with a yellow ribbon in his buttonhole. It was next insinuated that as he had not been allowed to go down himself he was determined no one else should, and Willoughby, having once taken up the idea, convinced itself this was the truth. However, when a good many of the disappointed applicants went to Bloomfield, and were met by him with a similar refusal, it began to dawn upon them that after all the doctor might be at the bottom of this plot to thwart them of their patriotic desires, and this discovery, though it by no means allayed their discontent, appeared to keep their resentment within some sort of bounds.

The juniors, disappointed in the hope of publicly displaying their anti-radical sentiments before all Shellport, looked about for consolation indoors that evening, and found it in a demonstration against the unlucky Bosher, who, against his will, had been forced to personate the Radical at the recent meeting, and now found it impossible to retrieve his reputation. He was hissed all round the playground, and finally had to barricade himself in his study to escape further persecution. But even there he was not safe. The youthful Whigs forced their way into his stronghold, and after much vituperation and reproach, proceeded to still more violent measures. "Howling young Radical cad!" exclaimed Telson, who, carried away by the excitement of the hour, had forgotten all Mr Parrett's prohibitions, and had come to visit his old allies; "you ought to be ashamed of yourself."

"Indeed, I'm Yellow," pleaded the unhappy Bosher. "They forced me to be Cheeseman at the meeting, but it wasn't my fault."

"Don't tell crams," cried the others. "It's bad enough to be a Radical without trying to deceive us."

"I'm not trying to deceive you, really I'm not," protested Bosher.

"I'll be anything you like. I hate the Radicals. Oh, I say, don't be cads, you fellows. Let me be a Whig, do!"

"No," cried the virtuous Parson. "We'll have no Radical cads on our side."

"But I'm not a Radical cad," cried Bosher; "at least not a Radical."

At that moment King made a sudden grab at a small black book which lay on the mantelpiece.

"Oh, you fellows," cried he, "here's a lark. Here's his diary."

A mighty Whig cheer followed the discovery, amidst which Bosher's wild protests and entreaties were quite drowned.

"His diary!" exclaimed Parson. "That'll show if he's a Radical or not. Hand it over, King. That'll show up his jolly gross conduct, eh?"

"No, no!" cried Bosher. "Give it up, you fellows; it's mine. Don't be cads, I say; it's private." And he made a wild dash for his treasure.

But it was no use. Parson gravely addressed his prisoner.

"Look here, young Bosher, it's no use making a row. We must look at the diary to see if you're really a Radical or not. It's our painful duty, so you'd better be quiet. We're sorry to have to do it, you know, but it can't be helped. If we find nothing Radical in the diary we'll let you off."

It was no use protesting, and poor Bosher had to submit with the best grace he could to hear his inmost thoughts read out in public.

"Here, Telson, old man," said Parson, "you read it. Speak out, mind. Better go backwards; start at yesterday."

Telson took the precious volume solemnly and began, frequently interrupted by the protests of the author, and more frequently by the laughter of his audience.

"'Thursday, the 4th day of the week.'" ("I always thought it was the fifth," observed Cusack).—"Rose at 6:13. Time forbad to shave down in the Big. N.B.—The world is big, I am small in the world, I sawest Riddell who is now in Welch's playing cricket with the little boys. Pilbury sported too, ugly in the face. (Here all but Pilbury seemed greatly amused.) Also Cusack, who thinks a great deal,"—("Hear, hear," from Cusack)—"about himself. (Laughter.) I attend an election at 10:2 in the Big. Parson taketh the chair. Parson is a f—l and two between."

"Oh!" broke in the outraged Parson. "I knew he was a Radical cad. All right, Bosher, my boy; you'll catch it! Steam away, Telson!"

"'It was a gross meeting, Pringle being much stuck-up. He maketh a speech. Meditations while Pringle is making a speech. The grass is very green. (Great laughter at Pringle's expense.) I will aspire up Telson thinketh he is much, but thou ist not oh, Telson, much at all I spoke boldly and to the point. I am the Radical.'"

"There you are!" exclaimed Parson, triumphantly: "didn't I tell you so? Bosher! What do you mean by telling such howling crams, Bosher?"

"I only meant—"

"Shut up! Fire away, Telson!"

"'I am the Radical. I desire to smash everything the little Welchers make noises. Meditations: let me be noble dinner at 3:1 stew. The turnips are gross. I request leave of Riddell to go to the town to-morrow but he sayeth no. I am roused'—that's all of yesterday."

"About enough too!" exclaimed the wrathful Parson. "Just read the day before, before we start hiding him."

"Oh, please don't lick me!" cried the unhappy author: "I'll apologise, you know, Parson, Telson; please don't!"

"'Wednesday—rose at 8:13. Sang as I shaved the Vicar of Bray. I shall now describe my fellows which are all ugly and gross. Parson is the worst.'"

"Eh?" exclaimed the wrathful owner of that name.

"'Parson is the worst,'" read Telson, with evident glee, "'and—and—' oh, let's see," he added, hurriedly turning over the page.

"No, no; read fair; do you hear?" cried Parson. "No skipping."

"I'll crack your skull, Bosher," said Telson, indignantly, handing the diary across to Parson and pointing to the passage.

"'—And Telson is the most conceited ignorant schoolhouse frog I ever saw at breakfast got thirty lines for gross conduct with the abominable King.'"

"There!" exclaimed Telson, in a red heat; "what does he mean by it? Of course, I don't care for myself; it's about the schoolhouse."

"What's that he says about me?" said King.

"'The abominable King,'" cried Telson, reading with great relish; "'thirty lines for gross conduct with the abominable King.'"

"Oh, I say, this is too much, you fellows," cried King.

"Not a bit too much. Just finish that day, Telson," said Parson, handing back the diary.

"Please give it up," pleaded Bosher, but he was immediately sat upon by his outraged companions, and forced to listen to the rest of the chronicle.

"'Wyndham hath not found his knife. I grieve for Wyndham thinking Cusack and the little Welchers to be the thiefs. I smile when Cusack goes to prison in the Parliament a gross speech is made by Riddell I reply in noble speech for the Radicals.'"

"That'll do, that's enough; he *is* a Radical then; he says so himself!" cried Telson, shutting up the book, and flinging it across the room at Bosher, who was standing near the door and just dodged it in time. A regular scramble ensued to secure the "gross" volume, in the midst of which the unhappy author, seeing his chance, slipped from the room, and bolted for his life down the passage.

His persecutors did not trouble to pursue him, and a sudden rumour shortly afterwards that Mr Parrett was prowling about sent Telson and the few Welchers slinking back to their quarters. And so ended the eve of the great election.

The next morning Riddell and those interested in the discipline of the school were surprised to see that the excitement was apparently abated, instead of, as might have been expected, increased. The attendance at morning chapel and call-over was most punctual, and between breakfast and first school only two boys came to him to ask for permits to go into town. One of these was young Wyndham, whom Riddell had seen very little of since leaving the schoolhouse.

Wyndham's desire to go down into town had, as it happened, no connection at all with the election. He was as much interested in that, of course, as the rest of Willoughby, but the reason he wanted to go to Shellport this afternoon was to see an old home chum of his, from whom he had just heard that he would be passing in the train through Shellport that afternoon.

Great, therefore, was his disappointment when Riddell told him that no permits were allowed that afternoon.

"What?" exclaimed the boy. "I've not seen Evans for a year, and he'll think it so awfully low, after writing to me, if I don't show up at the station."

"I'm awfully sorry, Wyndham," said Riddell, who had heard so many wild pretexts for getting leave during the last two days that he even doubted how far Wyndham's might be true or not; "the doctor says no one is to go down, and I can't give any permits."

"But I tell you all I want is to see Evans—there's no harm in that."

"Of course not, and you should get the permit at once if any were allowed."

"You could give me one if you chose."

"But if I gave to one I should have to give to all."

"I don't see that you need tell everybody," said Wyndham, nettled.

"I'm sorry it can't be done, Wyndham; I can't make any exceptions," said the captain, firmly.

"You could well enough if you chose," said Wyndham, sorely disappointed and aggrieved. "The fact is, I don't know why, I believe you've got a spite against me of late."

"You know I haven't, Wyndham," said Riddell, kindly.

Wyndham did know, and at any other time would have felt reproached by the consciousness of his own injustice. But he was just now so bitterly disappointed that he smothered every other feeling, and answered angrily, "Yes, you have, and I don't care if you have; I suppose it's because I'm friends with Silk. I can tell you Silk's a good deal more brickish to me than you are!"

Poor Riddell! This, then, was the end of his hopes of winning over his old friend's brother. The words struck him like a knife. He would almost sooner break all the rules in the school, so he felt that moment, than drive this one boy to throw in his lot with fellows like Silk!

"Wyndham!" he said, almost appealingly.

But Wyndham was gone, and the chance was lost.

The rest of that day passed miserably for the captain. An ominous silence and order seemed to hang over morning school. No further applicants molested him. No case of disorder was reported during the morning, and at dinner the boys were so quiet they might have been in church.

Just after morning school, and before dinner, as he crossed the playground, Wyndham passed him, talking and laughing with Silk; and neither of them noticed him.

The captain retired to his study, dejected and miserable, and, as his only comfort, buried himself in his books. For an hour at least before the early call-over he might forget his trouble in hard work.

But before that hour was half-over Riddell closed his book with a start and a sense of something unusual. This unearthly stillness all over the place—he never remembered anything of the sort before. Not a sound rose from the neighbouring studies, and when he looked out the playground was as deserted as if it had been the middle of the summer holidays. What did it all mean?

Then suddenly the truth flashed upon him. What could it mean, but that Willoughby had mutinied, and, in open defiance of his authority, gone down without leave to Shellport!

He hurried out of his room. There was scarcely a sound in the house. He went into the playground—only one boy, Gilks, was prowling about there, half-mad with toothache, and either unable or unwilling to give him any information. He looked in at Parrett's, no one was there, and even the schoolhouse seemed desolate.

The captain returned to his study and waited in anything but a placid frame of mind. He felt utterly humbled and crestfallen. It had really seemed of late as if he was making some headway in his uphill task of ruling Willoughby, but this was a shock he had never expected. It seemed to point to a combination all over the school to thwart him, and in face of such a feeling further effort seemed hopeless.

Riddell imagined too much. Would it have pained him to know that three-quarters of those who, politics-mad, had thus broken bounds that afternoon had never so much as given him a thought in the matter, and in fact had gone off, not to defy him, but simply to please themselves?

The bell for call-over rang, and Riddell went despondingly to the big hall. Only about a score of fellows, including Bloomfield, Porter, Fairbairn, Coates, and Wibberly (who, by the way, always did as Bloomfield did), answered to their names amid a good deal of wonder and a little laughter.

Bloomfield, who had also regarded the afternoon's business as a test of his authority, looked as crestfallen as the real captain, and for the first time that term he and Riddell approached one another with a common interest.

"There'll be an awful row about this," said he.

"There will," said Riddell; "will you report your fellows, or shall I send up the whole list to the doctor?"

"You send up all the names," said Bloomfield, "that is, unless Fairbairn wants to report the schoolhouse himself."

"No," said Fairbairn, "you send up the list, Riddell."

And so Riddell's captaincy received its first undisputed acknowledgment that term, and he sent up his formidable list to the doctor, and with mingled curiosity, impatience, and despondency waited the result.

Chapter Twenty One.

The new Captain to the Rescue.

There was something more than toothache the matter with Gilks that afternoon.

The fact was his spirits were a good deal worse than his teeth. Things had been going wrong with him for some time, ever since the day he was politely turned out of the schoolhouse boat. He had lost caste among his fellows, and what little influence he ever had among the juniors had also vanished.

Still, if that had been all, Gilks would scarcely have been moping up at Willoughby among the virtuous few that afternoon, while the rest of the school were running mad down in Shellport.

He had a greater trouble than this. Silk, in whose genial friendship he had basked for so many months, had not treated him well. Indeed, it was a well-known fact in Willoughby that between these two precious friends there had been some sort of unpleasantness bordering on a row; and it was also reported that Gilks had come off worst in the affair.

This was the secret of that unfortunate youth's toothache—he had been jilted by his familiar friend. Who would not feel sad under the circumstances?

And yet Gilks's frame of mind was, so to speak, a good deal more black than blue. As he paced up and down the playground, rather like a wolf in a cage waiting for dinner, he was far more exercised to devise some way of making his faithless friend smart for his cruelty than to win back his affection.

When two good fellows fall out it is bad enough, but when two bad fellows fall out it may be even worse, for whereas in the former case one of the two is probably in the right, in the latter both are pretty certain to be in the wrong.

No one knew exactly what the quarrel had been about, or what, if any, were its merits, or whether it was a breaking off of all friendship or merely a passing breeze. Whatever it was, it was enough to give Gilks the "toothache" on this particular afternoon and keep him at Willoughby.

The hour that elapsed after call-over dragged heavily for every one. The three heads of houses, after their brief consultation, went their several ways—at least Bloomfield went his, while Riddell and Fairbairn solaced themselves in one another's society.

"What is the use of keeping up this farce?" exclaimed Riddell, when they were back in his study. "*Isn't* it a farce?"

"Not a bit of it. I don't think much of this affair at all. Of course there'll be a row, but it seems to me a case of temporary lunacy that we can't be responsible for."

"But the doctor holds me responsible."

"You may be sure he won't be down on you for this."

"And then, isn't it just a proof to the whole school that I've no more authority than the smallest junior? Look at that miserable notice there on the door. Who has cared a rap about it?"

"My dear fellow, you're always flying off to despair whenever you get the chance. The same thing might have happened to any captain."

"I wish some one else was captain," said Riddell. "The fellows will mind what I say less than ever now. I'm sure I would gladly give it up to Bloomfield."

"All bosh. You know you wouldn't. And when you've got your head back you'll laugh at yourself for thinking it. Besides, wasn't Bloomfield every bit as much cut up about it as you or me? But," added Fairbairn, "to change the subject, do you see much of young Wyndham now you've left us?"

"Not much. What about him?" asked Riddell, eagerly.

"Only I fancy he's not all straight," said Fairbairn. "He's fallen into bad hands I'm afraid."

"That's an old story," said Riddell; "but what has he done?"

"Nothing particular. I caught him coming home one night late, long after call-over. I ought to have reported him for it, but I thought I'd tell you first. It's a pity for him, for he's not a bad fellow."

"I'd give anything to get him away from Silk!" said Riddell. "It seems a sort of infatuation with him, for he knows well enough Silk means him no good, and yet he's thick with him. And now I expect he'll cut me altogether since I refused him a permit to the town this afternoon."

"He's gone down all the same," said Fairbairn.

"Yes, and not alone either," replied Riddell.

"Hullo!" exclaimed Fairbairn just then, as a sudden sound broke the unwonted stillness of the deserted school, "that sounds like some of the fellows coming back."

He was right. As the two seniors stood leaning out of the window, the sounds which at first had been little more than a distant murmur increased to a roar.

Willoughby was evidently returning in force, and anything but peacefully.

Cries of "Now then, school!"

"Hack it through, there!"

"Down with the Radicals!"

"Pony for ever!" mingled with yells and cheers and coarser shouts of "Down with the schoolboys!" indicated clearly enough that a lively battle was in progress, and that Willoughby was fighting its way home.

The whole town seemed to be coming at their heels, and more than once a pitched battle had to be decided before any progress could be made. But slowly and surely the discipline of the schoolboys, animated by the familiar words of command of the football-field, asserted itself above the ill-conditioned force of their assailants, and at every forward step the triumphant shout of "Pony for ever!" rose with a mighty cheer, which deafened all opposition cries.

In due time the playground gate was reached, amid tremendous cheering, and next moment, driving before them some of their demoralised opponents, the vanguard of the school burst in.

Even Riddell and Fairbairn, as they looked down on the scene, could hardly forbear a little natural pride on witnessing this triumphant charge home of their truant schoolfellows.

That the battle had been sore and desperate was evident by the limping gait, the torn clothes, and the damaged faces of some of the combatants as they swarmed in in an irresistible tide, amid the applause of their comrades and the howls of the baffled enemy, who raged vainly without like so many wild beasts robbed of their prey.

Among the last to fight their way in were Game, Ashley, Tipper, and a few other seniors, who, truants as they were, had yet, to their credit, assumed the place of danger in the rear, where the crowd pressed thickest and with most violence. A sorry spectacle were some of these heroes when finally they plunged into the playground and then turned at bay at the gate.

"All in!" shouted a voice, and immediately a rush was made to close the gates and prevent further entrance, when a loud cry of "Hold on, Willoughby! Rescue here!" held them back.

Riddell started at the sound, and next moment had vaulted from the low window to the ground, closely followed by Fairbairn.

"Rescue! rescue! Man down!" cried the school within.

"Keep them in!—shut them in!" cried the roughs without.

"It's young Wyndham!" said Riddell, rushing wildly to the front; "he'll be murdered!"

"Scrag him!—scrag the schoolboy!" yelled the roughs, making a rush in the direction of the cries.

Not a moment was to be lost; in another minute it might be too late to do any good, and, with a tremendous shout of "Rescue, Willoughby!" the school turned as wildly to get out of the playground as it had just now struggled to get in.

The captain and Fairbairn were the first to get through the gate, followed closely by the other seniors. Riddell was conscious of seeing young Wyndham lying a few yards off among the feet of the roughs, and of being himself carried forward to within reach of him; then of a blow from behind, which sent him forward, half-stunned, right on to the top of his young friend.

After that Riddell was only dimly conscious of what passed, and it was not until he found himself once more in the playground, being helped along by Fairbairn towards the house, that he took in the fact that the rescue had been accomplished, and that the battle was at an end.

"Did they get Wyndham in all right?" he asked.

"Yes."

"Was he much damaged?"

"Very little. You got it worse than he did."

"Some fellow got behind me and sent me over," said Riddell.

"Some fellow did," said Fairbairn, fiercely, "and I know who."

"Who?"

"Silk."

"What! are you sure?"

"I was as close to you at the time as I am now—I'm quite sure."

"The coward! Did any one else see it?"

"No, I think not."

The two walked on in silence to Welch's house, and once more reached the study they had so abruptly quitted.

"Are you badly hurt?" asked Fairbairn.

"Not a bit; my shin is a little barked, that's all."

"What a bulldog you can be when you like, old man," said Fairbairn, laughing. "I never saw any one go into battle so gamely. Why, the whole glory of the rescue belongs to you."

"What bosh! You had to rescue me as well as Wyndham. But I'm thankful he's safe."

"You're awfully sweet about that precious youngster," said Fairbairn. "I hope he'll be grateful to you, that's all."

Riddell said nothing, and shortly afterwards Fairbairn said he must go. As he was leaving Riddell called him back.

"I say, Fairbairn," said he, in his half-nervous way, "you needn't say anything about Silk, there's a good fellow; it wouldn't do any good."

"He deserves a good thrashing," said Fairbairn, wrathfully.

"Never mind; don't say anything about it, please."

And Fairbairn promised and went.

It was quite a novel sensation for the captain to find himself figuring in the eyes of Willoughby as a "bulldog." He knew he was about the last person to deserve the proud title, and yet such are the freaks of fortune, the exaggerated stories of the rescue, differing as they did in nearly every other particular, agreed in this, that he had performed prodigies of valour in the engagement, and had, in fact, rescued Wyndham single-handed.

More than one fellow dropped in during the evening to inquire how he was, and to confirm his new reputation.

Pilbury and Cusack were among the first.

"Is it true your leg's broken?" cried the latter, as he entered the study, in tones of unfeigned concern.

"No, of course not," replied the captain, laughing. "What made you think so?"

"The fellows said so. Pil and I were too far behind to back you up, you know, or we would have, wouldn't we, Pil?"

"Rather," replied Pil.

"Why," said the captain, catching sight of the bruised and ragged condition of these young men of war—"why, you've been knocked about a great deal more than I have."

"Oh," said Cusack, "that was in the run up from Shellport, you know. We did get it a little hot at first until we pulled together and came up in a body."

"Never mind," said Pilbury, "it was a jolly fine show-up for Pony. He's sure to get in; the Radicals were nowhere."

"And what are you going to say to the doctor in the morning?" asked Riddell.

"Eh? oh, I suppose we shall catch it. Never mind, there'll be lots to keep us company. And we've given Pony a stunning leg-up."

And so the two heroes, highly delighted with themselves, and still far too excited to feel ashamed of their mutinous conduct, departed to talk over the day's doings with the rest of their set, and rejoice in the glorious "leg-up" they had given to the Whig candidate.

Other fellows looked in, and bit by bit Riddell picked up the whole history of that eventful afternoon.

It did not appear whether the wholesale breaking of bounds had been a preconcerted act or a spontaneous and infectious impulse on the part of the whole school. Whichever it was, directly dinner was over and the monitors had retired to their houses, a general stampede had been made for Shellport, and almost before many of the truants knew where they were they were in the thick of the election crowd.

At first each set vented its loyalty in its own peculiar way. Some stood in the streets and cheered everything yellow they could discover; others crowded round the polling places and groaned the Radicals; some went off to look for the candidates themselves, and when at last Sir George Pony appeared on the scene in his carriage his enthusiastic young supporters set up a cheer enough to frighten the good old gentleman out of his wits, and, but for the active interference of the police, would have insisted on taking out the horses and dragging the triumphal car themselves round the town.

For a considerable time these juvenile demonstrations were allowed to pass with good-humoured forbearance by the town; but when presently, emboldened by their immunity, the schoolboys proceeded not only to hoot but occasionally to molest the opposite side, the young Shellporters began to resent the invasion. A few scuffles ensued, and the temper of both parties rose. The schoolboys waxed more and more outrageous, and the town boys more and more indignant, so that just about the time when the poll was closing, and when call-over was being sounded up at the school, a free fight had begun in the streets of Shellport.

At the first alarm the school had rallied from all sides, and concentrated its forces on the enemy, who seemed determined to dispute every inch of the ground between the town and the school.

How that battle ended, and how finally the schoolboys got home, we have already seen.

Riddell did not feel it his duty under present circumstances to read his visitors a lecture on the wickedness of breaking bounds. He said it was a wonder they had all got up as safely as they had, and that no more damage had been done. As to the penalties, he advised them to turn up at call-over in the morning and hear all about that from the doctor.

Early next morning, just as Riddell was dressed, there was a knock at his door, and young Wyndham entered.

He looked dejected and uncomfortable, but otherwise appeared to have recovered from the effects of yesterday's ill-usage.

"I say," said he, going up to the captain and holding out his hand, "I'm awfully sorry I was such a cad to you yesterday."

"Not a bit, old fellow," said Riddell, seizing his hand, and glowing with pleasure at this unexpected visit. "Everybody was a bit riled, and no wonder."

"But I've no excuse, I know, after all your brickishness to me, and now, after your helping me out as you did in the scrimmage yesterday, I'm awfully ashamed of being such a low cad."

This was evidently no put-on apology for the occasion, and Wyndham, as he spoke, looked as penitent as his words.

"Oh, nonsense!" said Riddell, who could never stand being apologised to, and always felt more uncomfortable at such times than the apologiser. "But I say, were you much hurt?"

"No, not much. I got down among their feet somehow and couldn't get up. But if you hadn't turned up when you did I might have got it hot."

"It was Fairbairn pulled us both out, I think," said Riddell, "for I was down too."

"Yes, I hear you got an awful hack."

"Nothing much at all."

"I say, Riddell," said Wyndham, nervously, after a pause, "I mean to break with Silk; I wish I'd never taken up with him. I shouldn't have gone down to the town at all yesterday if it hadn't been for him."

"I think you'd be ever so much better without him," said Riddell.

"I know I would. Do you recollect lecturing me about sticking up for myself that night last month? I've been uncomfortable about chumming with him ever since, but somehow he seemed to have a pull on me."

"What sort of pull?"

"Oh," said the boy, becoming still more uncomfortable, and afraid of breaking his promise to say nothing about Beamish's, "a good many things of one sort or another. I've gone wrong, I know."

Wyndham would have given much to be free to make a full confession of all his "going wrong" to the sympathetic Riddell, but, heartily weary as he was of Silk and Gilks, he had promised them to keep their secrets, and young Wyndham, whatever his faults, was honest.

Riddell was quick enough to see that there was something of the sort, and did not press to know more. It was too good news to hear from the boy's own lips that he was determined to break loose from these bad friends, to need to know any more.

"I don't know how it is," said Wyndham, after another pause. "It seems so much easier for some fellows to keep square than for others. I've made up my mind I'd do right a dozen times this term, but it's never come off."

"It's hard work, I know," said Riddell, sympathisingly.

"Yet it seems easy enough to you. I say, I wish you'd look sharp after me for a week or so, Riddell, till I get a good start."

Riddell laughed.

"A lot of good that would do you! The best person to look sharp after young Wyndham is young Wyndham himself."

"Of course I know," said the boy, "but I've sort of lost confidence in myself."

"We can't any of us stand by ourselves," said the captain. "I know I can't. But the help is easy to get, isn't it?"

I need not repeat all the talk that took place that morning between the two boys. What they said was meant for no ears but their own. How one in his quiet manly way tried to help the younger boy, and how the other with all sorts of fears and hopes listened and took courage, was known only to the two friends themselves, and to One other from Whom no secrets—not even the secrets of a schoolboy—are hid.

The bell for call-over put an end to their talk, and with lighter hearts than most in Willoughby they walked across to the Great Hall and heard the doctor's sentence on the truants of yesterday.

It was not very formidable. No half-holiday next Wednesday, and for the seniors a hundred lines of Greek to write out; for the Limpets a hundred lines of Latin, and for the juniors fifty lines of Latin. The doctor had evidently taken a lenient view of the case, regarding the escapade more as a case of temporary insanity than of determined disobedience. However, he relieved his mind by a good round lecture, to which the school listened most resignedly.

There was, however, one part of the punishment which fell heavily on a few of those present. Among the truants had been no less than five monitors—Game, Tipper, Ashley, Silk, and Tucker.

"It would be a farce," said the doctor, severely, "after what has happened, to allow you to retain the posts of confidence you have held in the school. Your blame is all the greater in proportion as your influence was greater too. For the remainder of this term you cease to be monitors. It depends entirely on yourselves whether next term you are reinstated."

Chapter Twenty Two.

A Mysterious Letter.

It was hardly to be expected that the political excitement of Willoughby would altogether disappear until the result of the election was made known. And for some reason or other a whole day had to elapse before the tidings found their way up to the school.

After what had happened no one had the hardihood to ask leave to go down into the town, and none of the butcher's or baker's boys that Parson and Telson intercepted in the grounds could give any information. The hopes of Willoughby centred on Brown, the town boy, whose arrival the next morning was awaited with as much excitement and impatience as if he had been a general returning home from a victorious campaign.

Fully aware of his importance, and feeling popularity to be too unusual a luxury to be lightly given up, he behaved himself at first with aggravating reserve.

"Who's in!" shouted Parson from the school gate, the moment Brown appeared about a quarter of a mile down the road.

Brown, of course, could not hear.

The question was repeated with greater vehemence as he approached, until at last he had no excuse for not hearing.

"Do you hear, you old badger, who's in?" yelled Parson and Telson.

"Look here, you kids," said Brown, loftily, "who are you calling a badger? I'll knock your cheeky heads together if you don't look out."

"Oh I say, who's in! can't you speak?" reiterated the youths, who at this moment possessed only one idea between them.

"Who is it? Who's got in?" repeated some Limpets, who were as eager every bit to hear as the juniors.

"In where?" replied the aggravating Brown, shouldering his way in at the gate and intoxicated with his own importance. "What are you talking about?"

"Why, who's been elected for Shellport? Is Pony in?" shouted the boys, impatiently.

"Pony!" rejoined Brown, half-contemptuously, "do you suppose they'd have an old stick like him!"

"What," exclaimed Merrison. "Is Cheeseman in after all, then?"

"Eh?"

"Is Cheeseman in, can't you hear?"

"I never said he was," replied Brown, majestically.

This was rather too much, and a simultaneous rush was made for the pompous town boy, and the secret forcibly extracted in double quick time.

"Now," cried one of the Limpets, giving his arm a premonitory screw, "out with it, or I'm sorry for you."

"Here, let go my arm, you cad, I say; oh! you hurt! let go, I—oh! oh! Cheeseman's in!"

The arm was flung away in disgust as a simultaneous groan greeted the announcement.

"How much by?" demanded the inquisitors, once more preparing to apply the screw.

But Brown had had quite enough of it, and answered glibly, "Eight hundred and twenty-five majority!"

This was a terrible blow, and in the general dismay which followed, Brown was temporarily overlooked.

"Eight hundred and twenty-five!" exclaimed Merrison. "Why, it's an awful licking. Every one was sure Pony would be five hundred ahead."

"It's foul play and bribery, depend on it," said another.

"Or they've counted wrong."

"Or Brown is telling lies!"

Now, if Brown had been a wise boy he would have taken advantage of the excitement which immediately followed his announcement to retreat quietly and rapidly up to the school, and he reproached himself greatly that he had not. For the ill-temper of the assembly was only too ready to fix on some object upon which to vent itself, and this last suggestion, coupled with the suspicion that Brown's father had been one of the backers of the Radical candidate, brought the town boy once more into most uncomfortable notoriety.

He was hunted almost for his life round the playground and up to the school. It was no use for him to protest that he was out-and-out yellow, that his father had been on Pony's committee. He was far too valuable a scapegoat to be let off; and when at last he managed to bolt headlong into the school and seek shelter in the master's cloak-room, it is safe to say that though he himself felt rather the worse for the adventure, Willoughby on the whole felt rather better.

In due time the news was confirmed, and the school settled rather viciously down to its ordinary work. It was almost a relief when first school was over, and all those who had impositions to write were ordered to keep their places and begin their tasks.

What venom of wrath and disappointment could they not put into those unlucky lines! If the paper had only been the skin of the Radical Cheeseman, and the pens needles, *how* they would have delighted in their penalty!

Scarcely had they begun work, however, when the school messenger came round unexpectedly to summon the whole school to assemble in the Great Hall. What could it be? Was it another lecture? or had the doctor repented of letting them off so easy? Or was there to be another change in the captaincy? or what?

The hall soon filled, and every one waited impatiently for the doctor. He arrived presently, with a letter in his hand and a somewhat important look on his face.

"The last time I spoke in this room," said he, "I had to discharge the painful duty of punishing the whole school for a serious and inexcusable act of insubordination."

"Why do they always call it a *painful* duty?" inquired the artless Telson of his ally; "I'm sure it doesn't hurt *them*."

"Silence! whoever is speaking!" said the doctor, sternly. "I hope what was said then will not be forgotten. An act of that kind could not possibly be allowed to pass without punishment, and any repetition of it would entail the severest measures. However, I say no more of that at present. I have called you together to read to you a letter I have just received from the newly-elected Member for Shellport, Mr Cheeseman."

As the doctor pronounced this unpopular name, one hardy junior, quite mistaking the gravity of the occasion, began a low hiss.

Before the infection could spread the doctor suddenly laid down the letter, and with a voice of thunder demanded, "Who is that? Stand up, sir, in your place!"

The luckless form of the youthful Lawkins, pale and scared, rose from a back bench.

"Leave the room, sir!" said the doctor, wrathfully, "and write out your imposition double, and come to me after third school!"

Poor Lawkins retired, and the assembly, being warned by his awful example, heard the doctor out without further interruption.

"Mr Cheeseman writes as follows:—

"'Dear Dr Patrick,—I hope I need no apology for writing to you on a matter affecting the boys under your charge. A large number of these young politicians, as you are aware, took a somewhat active part in the recent election, in which it was not my good fortune to be their favourite candidate. I understand that their crusade into the town was not only without your permission, but in direct opposition to your wishes; and I conclude, that being so, the offenders have merited the punishment due for such escapades. The election, as you know, is now decided, and I am anxious that one of my first acts in my new capacity should be one of intercession with you to take as lenient a view as you can of this schoolboy freak; and if you should find it consistent with your duty to remit any penalty that may have been inflicted, I shall be as grateful to you as no doubt your boys will be.'

"'I am, dear doctor,'

"'Yours faithfully,'

"'A. Cheeseman.'"

The doctor laid down the letter amidst ominous silence, which even the feeble cheers of Bosher, Brown, and a few others barely disturbed.

"In consideration of this generous letter," he continued, "I have decided to remit the impositions I gave on Saturday, and also to withdraw the prohibition about the half-holiday. The matter of the monitors I cannot reconsider. I may suggest that, after what has happened, it would be a graceful act on the part of the boys to send Mr Cheeseman a letter of thanks, at any rate, if not of apology. You are now dismissed."

It was quite evident that the majority of the boys were at a loss how to take this strange and unexpected announcement. True, they hated the Radicals, but they also hated impositions and detention, and the probability is that, if left to themselves, they would quietly have availed themselves of Mr Cheeseman's clemency.

But to the small band of hot-headed enthusiasts the very notion of being under an obligation to the Radical was repulsive. They could scarcely wait till the doctor had departed before they vehemently denounced the idea.

"Well," said Merrison, "if that's not what you call adding insult to injury, I don't know what you do! I know *I* mean to write every letter of my impot if it was a thousand lines instead of a hundred!"

"So shall I; and I'll not stir out of doors all Wednesday afternoon either," said another.

"Of course not; no honourable fellow would."

"I suppose he thinks he's going to bribe us, the cad. Perhaps he hopes we'll give *him* a leg-up next election?"

"I vote we put on a spurt with the impots and get them all done together," said another. "Paddy shall see which way we go, at any rate."

And so, sorely to the disappointment of some of the juniors, who had been rejoicing prematurely in the removal of their penalties, the order went round in all the houses that every boy was expected in honour to finish his imposition by next day, and also to remain in on Wednesday afternoon, as a protest against "Radical cheek," and this was an appeal no loyal Whig could resist.

It was at least an unusual spectacle in Willoughby to see nearly the whole school insisting on performing a task which no one required of them; each boy not only doing it himself, but seeing that his neighbour did it too!

Several of the small boys and a few lazy seniors protested, but they were coerced with most terrific threats.

The Wednesday half-holiday was spent in determined seclusion, scarcely a boy showing his face in the playground. Even those who had not broken bounds on election-day, and who, therefore, in no case came under the penalty, felt quite out of it, and half ashamed of themselves in the presence of this general burst of political devotion; and it was rumoured that one or two of the weakest-minded of these actually stayed in and wrote out the imposition too!

The following morning was an impressive one in the annals of Willoughby. The doctor, as he stood in the Great Hall speaking to Mr Parrett after morning prayers, was, much to his amazement, waylaid by the school in a body. Every boy carried in his hand a sheet of paper, and wore on his face a most self-satisfied expression.

"What is all this?" inquired the doctor, sharply, a little bit frightened, perhaps, at this sudden and mysterious invasion of his privacy.

Merrison was pushed forward by the crowd, and advancing paper in hand, replied for the company generally.

"Please, sir," said he, "we've brought the impositions."

"Eh?" said the doctor.

"The impositions, sir. We didn't want to be let off, so we stayed in yesterday afternoon, all of us, and wrote them."

From the tones in which Merrison uttered this explanation one might have supposed he expected the doctor to fall on his neck and shed tears of joy over the lofty virtue of his pupils.

Dr Patrick was quick enough to take in the state of affairs at once, and was wise enough to make the best of the situation.

"Ah," said he, coolly, taking Morrison's proffered imposition and glancing his eyes down it. "I am glad to see you desire to make amends for what occurred on Saturday. You can leave the impositions on this table."

"Please, sir, it's not that," said Merrison, hurriedly, alarmed at being suspected of anything like contrition. "It's not that; we—"

"You can leave the impositions on the table," said the doctor, sternly, turning at the same time to continue his conversation with Mr Parrett, which the arrival of the visitors had interrupted.

It was a sad blow for Willoughby, this! They had expected better things. They had meant their act of self-devotion to be a crushing defiance to the Radical, and even a mild rebuke to the doctor himself. But it had turned out neither.

Slowly and sorrowfully they filed past the table and laid their sacrifices thereon, and then departed, dejected and crestfallen. The doctor, with his back turned, never noticed them, and no one had the hardihood to attempt further to attract his attention.

So ended the election episode at Willoughby.

"I hope you've enjoyed yourselves," said Crossfield to Tedbury the Limpet, that afternoon. "Jolly time you've had of it."

"It's all that young ass Morrison's doing," growled Tedbury.

"Never mind," said Crossfield, laughing; "I'm sure it's done you all good. You all wanted something of the sort, and you'll be better of it."

"You're always trying to make a fool of me, Crossfield," said Tedbury, wrathfully.

"My dear fellow, there's not much chance of that. You are far too good a hand at making a fool of yourself to put any one else to the trouble. Ta, ta. Shall you be down at the cricket practice again now?"

This last was a pertinent question. For in the midst of all the late political excitement cricket had decidedly languished at the school, and the Rockshire match as well as the house matches were getting alarmingly near.

However, on the first afternoon after Willoughby had returned to its senses a general rush took place once more to the Big, and it was evident during the week which followed that the fellows intended to make up for lost time.

Nowhere was this activity more observed than in the newly-revived Welchers' club, presided over by the captain, and enlivened by the countenances of that ardent trio, Cusack, Pilbury, and Philpot.

During the week preceding the election they had worked with unabated enthusiasm. You might have seen practice going on any morning at half-past six in the Welchers' corner of the Big. The other houses at first regarded it as a good joke, and the earliest practices of the new club were usually performed in the presence of a large and facetious audience, who appeared to derive infinite delight from every ball that was bowled and every run that was made. But the Welchers were not to be snuffed out. Riddell watched over the fortunes of the new club with most paternal interest, losing no opportunity of firing its enthusiasm, and throwing himself heart and soul into its work. Indeed, as a cricketer the captain came out in quite a new light, which astonished even himself.

He had always taken for granted he was utterly incapable of any athletic achievement, but, with the steady practice now entailed upon him, it began to dawn, not only upon himself, but other people, that as a fielder—at slip or cover-slip—he was decidedly useful, while as a batsman he exhibited a certain style of his own that usually brought together a few runs for his side.

But even his own success was less than that of the club generally. Every member of that small fraternity was intent on the glory of the club, and worked hammer and tongs to secure it. Mr Parrett, kindly jack-of-all-trades as he was, was easily persuaded by Riddell to come down occasionally and bowl them a few balls, and give them a few hints as to style generally. And every time he came down he was more encouraging. Even Bloomfield and a few of the First Eleven magnates thought it worth their while to saunter round once or twice and watch the practice of this promising club.

It may be judged that, in proportion as the young Welchers found themselves succeeding, their enthusiasm for their club and its president increased. The club grew daily. Some Limpets joined it, and even a few seniors. There was some talk of a first eleven to play in the house matches, while by this time the second-eleven was an accomplished fact, its members thirsting for the day when they should match their prowess against the Parretts or schoolhouse juniors.

The election, as I have said, had rudely interrupted all this healthy preparation, and for a moment it seemed to Riddell as if all his new hold on his boys had disappeared. But that event once over, great was his relief to find that they returned to the sport with unabated and even increased ardour.

That week Welch's had out for the first time two sets of wickets, and even thus could hardly keep going all who wanted to play.

"I tell you what," said Bloomfield, one afternoon, as, with his friend Ashley, he was quietly looking on, while pretending not to do so, "say what you will, Riddell doesn't do badly at slip. Watch this over."

As it happened, Mr Parrett was bowling down some rather swift balls to the boy who was batting, with a little break from the off, which the batsman seemed unable to play in any manner but by sending them among the slips. So that, during the over, Riddell, blissfully unconscious of the critical eyes that were upon him, had a busy time of it. And so well did he pick the balls up that the two spies stayed to watch another over, and after that another, at the close of which Bloomfield said, "Upon my word, it's not half bad. And a slip's the very man we want to make up the eleven for Rockshire."

"My dear fellow," said Ashley, in tones almost of alarm, "you're surely not thinking of putting a fellow like that into the eleven."

"I don't care much who goes in so long as he can play," said Bloomfield.

"But fancy the fellow's bumptiousness if he gets stuck into the team! He's bad enough as it is," said Ashley.

"We've got the schoolhouse fellows to look at," said Bloomfield, "*come* along. If they've any one better we'll take him, but we *must* get hold of the best man."

So off they went, and the Welchers' practice continued gaily till the bell for call-over sounded.

"Riddell," said Cusack, who had become captain's fag since the migration to Welch's, "there's a letter for you."

"Where?" asked the captain.

"On your table. I saw it there when I was sticking away your pens just now."

"You may as well bring it," said Riddell; "I am going to the library."

So Cusack went off, and presently reappeared in the library with the letter.

Riddell was busy at the moment searching through the catalogue, and consequently let the letter lie unopened for some little time beside him. In due time, however, he turned and took it up.

It was a strangely directed letter, at any rate—not in ordinary handwriting, but in printed characters, evidently to disguise the authorship.

Riddell hastily tore open the envelope of this mysterious missive and read the contents, which were also written like printing, in characters quite unrecognisable.

The letter was as follows:

"Riddel,—If you want to get to the bottom of that boat-race affair, you had better see what Tom the boat-boy has to say. That's all."

Chapter Twenty Three.

Tom the Boat-boy earns four-and-sixpence.

Riddell, as he read over and over again the mysterious document in his hand, hardly knew what to make of it.

It looked like a clue, certainly. But who had sent it? Was it a friend or an enemy; and if the latter, might it not just as likely be a hoax as not?

He examined the disguised writing letter for letter, but failed to recognise in it the hand of any one he knew. He called back Cusack and cross-examined him as to how and when the letter was brought to his study; but Cusack could tell him nothing. All he knew was that when he went in to look after Riddell's tea that afternoon, it was lying there on the table. He couldn't say how long it had been there. He hadn't been in the room since dinner, nor had Riddell.

Cusack was very curious to know what the letter was about concerning which the captain seemed so much excited; but Riddell declined to gratify him on this point, and put the paper away in his pocket and returned to his work.

"No," said he to himself, "if it's a hoax there's no object in making it public property, and still less reason if there's anything in it."

Of one thing he was determined—he must go down to-morrow morning and have an interview with Tom the boat-boy. The thing *might* all be a hoax, but if there was the remotest chance of its being otherwise it was clearly his duty to do what he could to find out the miscreant who had brought such disgrace upon Willoughby. So he spent a somewhat uneasy evening, and even appeared absent-minded when young Wyndham, now a constant visitor to his study, paid his usual evening call.

"I say," said the boy, with beaming face, as he entered, "isn't it prime, Riddell? Bloomfield's going to try me in the second-eleven, he says. You know I've been grinding at cricket like a horse lately, and he came down and watched me this afternoon, and I was in, and made no end of a lucky score off Dobson's bowling. And then Bloomfield said he'd bowl me an over. My eye! what a funk I was in. I could hardly hold the bat. But I straightened up somehow, and his first ball went by. The next was frightfully swift, and dead on, but it broke a bit to the leg, and I was just in time to get at it and send it right away between long-leg and long-stop in the elms—a safe five if we'd been running. And old Bloomfield laughed and said he couldn't wait till the ball was sent up, and said I could turn up at the second-eleven Big practice to-morrow and see how I got on there. I say, isn't it prime, Riddell? I tell you, I shall stand on my head if I get into the team."

Riddell had only partially heard this jubilant speech, for at that moment Tom the boat-boy was more in his thoughts even than Wyndham the Limpet. However, he had heard enough to gather from it that his young *protégé* was in a vast state of joy and content, and as usual he was ready with any amount of sympathy.

"It will be splendid if you do get in," said he.

"Yes. They've only got eight places actually fixed, I hear, so I've three chances. I say, Riddell, I like Bloomfield, do you know? I think he's an awfully good captain."

Riddell could not help smiling at this artless outburst from the young candidate for cricket honours, and replied, "I like him too, for he came and watched our practice too, here at Welch's."

"Did he bowl you any balls?" demanded Wyndham.

"No, happily," said Riddell; "but some one told me he told somebody else that I might possibly squeeze into the eleven against Rockshire if I practised hard."

"What!" exclaimed Wyndham, in most uncomplimentary astonishment. "*You* in the first eleven! I say, it must be a mistake."

"I'm afraid they'll think it a mistake," said Riddell, laughing; "but I certainly have heard something of the sort."

"Why, you usen't to play at all in our house," said Wyndham.

"No more I did; but since I came here I've been going in for it rather more, though I never dreamt of such rapid promotion."

"Well," said Wyndham, quite patronisingly, "I'm jolly glad to hear it; but I wish you were in the schoolhouse instead of Welch's. By the way, how are the 'kids' in your house getting on?"

"The 'kids' are getting on very well, I fancy," said the captain. "They've a match with the Parrett's juniors fixed already, and mean to challenge the schoolhouse too, I fancy."

"I say, that's coming it rather strong," said Wyndham, half incredulously.

"It's a fact, though," said Riddell, "and what's more, I have it on Parrett's authority that they are getting to play very well together, and any eleven that plays them will have to look out for itself if it is to beat them."

"Ho, ho! I guess our fellows will be able to manage that. Of course, you know, if I'm in the second-eleven, I shan't be able to play with my house juniors."

"That will be a calamity!" said Riddell, laughing, as he began to get out his books and settle himself for the evening's work.

Despite all the boy's juvenile conceit and self-assurance, Riddell rejoiced to find him grown enthusiastic about anything so harmless as cricket. Wyndham had been working hard the last week or so in a double sense—working hard not only at cricket, but in striving to act up to the better resolutions which, with Riddell's help, he had formed. And he had succeeded so far in both. Indeed, the cricket had helped the good resolutions, and the good resolutions had helped the cricket. As long as every spare moment was occupied with his congenial sport, and a place in the second-eleven was a prize within reach, he had neither time nor inclination to fall back on the society of Silk or Gilks, or any of their set. And as long as the good resolutions continued to fire his breast, he was only too glad to find refuge from temptation in the steady pursuit of so honourable an ambition as cricket.

He was, if truth must be told, more enthusiastic about his cricket than about his studies, and that evening it was a good while before Wyndham could get his mind detached from bats and balls and concentrated on Livy.

Riddell himself, too, found work more than ordinarily difficult that night, but his thoughts were wandering on far less congenial ground than cricket.

Supposing that letter did mean something, how ought he to act? It was no pleasant responsibility to have thrown on his shoulders the duty of bringing a criminal to justice, and possibly of being the means of his expulsion. And yet the honour of Willoughby was at stake, and no squeamishness ought to interfere with that. He wished, true or untrue, that the wretched letter had been left anywhere but in his study.

"I say," said young Wyndham, after about an hour's spell of work, and strangely enough starting the very topic with which Riddell's mind was full—"I say, I think that boat-race business is blowing over, do you know? You don't hear nearly so much about it now."

"The thing is, ought it to blow over?" said the captain, gravely.

"Why, of course! Besides, after all it may have been an accident. I broke a bit of cord the other day, and it looked just as if it had been partly cut through. Anyhow, it's just as much the Parretts business as ours, and they aren't doing anything, I know."

"It would be a good deal more satisfactory to have it cleared up," said Riddell.

"It would do just as well to have a new race, and settle the thing right off—even if they were to lick us."

Wyndham went soon afterwards. Riddell was too much occupied with his own perplexities to think much just then of the boy's views on this burning question. And after all, had he thought of them, he would probably have guessed, as the reader may have done, that Wyndham's present cricket mania made him dread any reopening of the old soreness between Parrett's and the schoolhouse, which would be sure to result, among other things, in his exclusion, as a member of the latter fraternity, from the coveted place in the second-eleven.

The next morning the captain was up early, and on his way to the boat-house. Ever since the race the river had been almost deserted, at any rate in the early mornings.

Consequently when Riddell arrived at the boat-house he found no one up. After a good deal of knocking he managed to rouse the boatman.

"I want Tom," he said, "to steer me up to the Willows."

"You might have let me known you'd want the gig yesterday," said the man, rather surlily; "I'd have left it out for you overnight."

Had it been Bloomfield or Fairbairn, or any other of the boating heroes of Willoughby, Blades the boatman would have sung a very different song. But a boatman does not know anything about senior classics.

"You'll find a boat moored by the landing there," said that functionary; "and give a call for young Alf, he'll do to steer you."

But this would not suit Riddell at all. "No," said he; "I want Tom, please, and tell him to be quick."

The man went off surlily, and Riddell was left to kick his heels for twenty minutes in a state of very uncomfortable suspense.

At length, to his relief, Tom, a knowing youth of about fourteen, appeared, with a cushion over one shoulder and a pair of sculls over the other, and the embarkation was duly effected.

Tom was a privileged person at Willoughby. In consideration of not objecting to an occasional licking, he was permitted to be as impudent and familiar as he pleased to the young gentlemen in whose service he laboured. Being a professional waterman, he considered it his right to patronise everybody. Even old Wyndham last season had received most fatherly encouragement from this irreverent youngster, while any one who could make no pretensions to skill with the oars was simply at his mercy.

This being so, Riddell had made up his mind for a trying time of it, and was not disappointed.

"What! so you're a-goin' in for scullin' then?" demanded the young waterman as the boat put off.

"Yes; I want to try my hand," said the captain.

"*You'll* never do no good at it, I can tell yer, before yer begins," said the boy.

So it seemed. What with inexperience of the sculls, and nervousness under the eye of this ruthless young critic, and uneasiness as to the outcome of this strange interview, Riddell made a very bad performance.

"Ya-ow! I thought it would come to that!" jeered Tom when, after a few strokes, the captain got his sculls hopelessly feathered under water and could not get them up again. "There you are! That comes of diggin'! Always the way with you chaps!"

"Suppose, instead of going on like that," said Riddell, getting up the blades of his sculls with a huge effort, "you show me the way to do it properly!"

"What's the use of showing you? You could never learn, I can see it by the looks of you!"

After this particularly complimentary speech Riddell rowed ploddingly on for a little distance, Tom whistling shrilly in the stern all the way in a manner most discouraging for conversation.

But Riddell was determined, come what would, he would broach the unpleasant subject. Consequently, after some further progress up-stream, he rested on his oars, and said, "I've not been out on the water since the day of the boat-race."

"Aren't you, though?" said Tom.

A pause.

"That was a queer thing, the rudder-line breaking that day," said Riddell, looking hard at his young companion.

Tom apparently did not quite like it. Either it seemed as if Riddell thought *he* knew something about the affair, or else his conscience was not quite easy.

"In course it was," replied he, surlily. "I knows nothink about it."

Riddell, for a quiet, nervous boy, was shrewd for his age, and there was something in Tom's constrained and uncomfortable manner as he made this disclaimer that convinced him that after all the mysterious letter *had* something in it.

It was a bold step to take, he knew, and it might end in a failure, but he would chance it at any rate.

"You do know something about it, Tom!" said he, sternly, and with a searching look at the young waterman.

Tom did! He didn't say so! Indeed he violently denied that he did, and broke out into a state of most virtuous indignation.

"Well I ever, if that ain't a nice thing to say to a chap. I tell you, I knows nothink about it. The idea! What 'ud I know anythink about it for? I tell you you're out, governor. You're come to the wrong shop—do you hear?"

Riddell did hear; and watching the boy's manner as he hurried out these protests, he was satisfied that he was on the right tack.

It had never occurred to him before. Perhaps the culprit was Tom himself; perhaps it was he who, for some reason of his own, had cut the line and caused all the mischief.

If that were so, what a relief and what a satisfaction it would be! Riddell felt that if Tom himself were the wrong-doer he could almost embrace him, so great would be his joy at knowing that no Willoughby boy was guilty of the crime. But it was too good a notion to be true, and Tom soon dispelled it.

"I tell you," continued he, vehemently, but looking down so as to avoid the captain's eye. "I tell you I aren't done it, there. It's no use your trying to fix it on me. Do you suppose I wouldn't know if I'd done it? You blame the right parties, governor, do you hear? I *ain't* done it."

"I never said you did," replied Riddell, feeling he had by this time got the upper hand in the argument, "but you know who did."

"There you go. How do I know? I don't know, and I ain't done it."

"Do you mean to tell me," said Riddell, "the lines could have been cut and you not know it? Don't you sleep in the boat-house?"

"In course I do—but I ain't done it, there!"

"Don't be a young fool, Tom," said Riddell, sternly. "What I want to know is who did do it."

"How do you suppose I know?" demanded the boy.

"Who did do it?" again repeated Riddell.

"I don't know, there!" retorted Tom. "I never see his face."

"Then some one did come to the boat-house that night?" said Riddell.

"How do I know? Suppose they did?"

"Suppose they did? I want to know who it was."

"I tell you I don't know. It was pitch dark, and I ain't seen his face, there; and what's more, I don't know the chap."

"But you let him into the boat-house?"

"No, I didn't," said Tom, whose strong point was evidently not in standing cross-examination. "That's where you're wrong again. You're all wrong."

"You knew he was there, at any rate," said Riddell.

"No, I didn't. You're wrong agin. You don't know what you're talkin' about. How could I know he was there, when I worn't there myself?"

"What! did he get in while you were away?"

"In course he did. Do you suppose I goes to bed like you kids at eight o'clock? No fear. Why, I don't get my supper at Joe Blades's till ten."

"Then you found some one in the boat-house when you went there, after supper, to go to bed?"

"There you are, all wrong agin. How do you suppose I'd find him when he got out of the window?"

"Then he came in and went out by the window?" asked Riddell.

"Why, you don't suppose he could come down the chimbley, do you?" retorted Tom, scornfully, "and there's no way else."

"You had the key of the door all the time, of course," said Riddell.

"In course. Do you suppose we leaves the boat'us open for anybody as likes to come in without leave?"

"Then it was seeing the window open made you know some one had been in?" continued the captain.

"Wrong agin! Why, you aren't been right once yet."

"Do you mean you really saw some one there?"

"How *could* I see him when he was a-hoppin' out of the winder just as I comes in? I tell you I didn't see him. You couldn't have sor him either, not with all your learnin'."

"Then you've no idea who it was?"

"Ain't I? that's all you know."

"Why, you say you never saw him. Did you hear his voice?"

"No, I didn't."

"Has some one told you? Has he come and told you himself?"

"No, he ain't. Wrong agin."

"Did he leave anything behind that you would know him by, then?"

The boy looked up sharply at Riddell, who saw that he had made a point, and followed it up.

"What did he leave behind? His cap?" he asked.

"His cap! Do you suppose chaps cut strings with their caps? Why, you must be a flat."

"His knife, was it?" exclaimed Riddell, excitedly. "Was it his knife?"

"There you go; you're so clever. I as good as tell yer, and then you go on as if you guessed it yourself! You ain't got as much learnin' as you think, governor."

"But was it his knife he left behind?" inquired Riddell, too eager to attend to the sarcasms of his companion.

"What could it 'a been, unless it might be a razor. You don't cut ropes with your thumb-nails, do you? Of course it was his knife."

"And have you got it still, Tom?"

Here Tom began to get shy. As long as it was only information that the captain wanted to get at he didn't so much mind being cross-examined, but directly it looked as if his knife was in peril he bristled up.

"That'll do," said he gruffly; "my knife's nothink to do with you."

"I know it isn't, and I don't want to take it from you. I only want to look at it."

"Oh, yes; all very fine. And you mean to make out as it's yourn and you was the chap I saw hoppin' out of the winder, do yer? I know better. He weren't your cut, so you needn't try to make that out."

"Of course it wasn't I," said Riddell, horrified even at the bare suspicion, still more at the idea of any one confessing to such a crime for the sake of getting a paltry knife.

Still Tom was obdurate and would not produce his treasure. In vain Riddell assured him that he made no claim to it, and, even if the knife were his own, would not dream of depriving the boy of it now. Tom listened to it all with an incredulous scowl, and Riddell was beginning to despair of ever setting eyes on the knife, when the boy solved the difficulty of his own accord.

"What do you want to look at it for?" he demanded. "Only to see if I knew whose it was once."

"Well, I ain't a-goin' to let yer see it unless you lay a half-a-crown down on that there seat. There! I ain't a-going to be done by you or any of your scholars."

Riddell gladly put down the money and had the satisfaction at last of seeing Tom fumble in his pockets for the precious weapon.

It was a long time coming to light, and meanwhile the boy kept a suspicious eye on the money, evidently not quite sure whether, after all, he was safe.

At length from the deepest depth of his trouser pocket his hand emerged, bringing with it the knife.

Had Tom not been so intent on the half-crown which lay on the seat he would have been amazed at the sudden pallor which overspread the captain's face and the half-suppressed gasp which he gave as his eyes fell on—*young Wyndham's knife*!

There was no mistaking it. Riddell knew it well. Wyndham when first he possessed it was never tired of flourishing it proudly before all his acquaintances, and finding some pretext for using it or lending it every five minutes of the day.

Riddell had often had it pressed upon him. Yes, and now, with a shock that was almost sickening, he recollected that he had had it in his hand that very night before the boat-race.

And with the thought there rushed in upon him the whole memory of that evening. How excited, how restless the boy had been, how impossible he had found it to work, how wildly he had talked about the coming race, and how he had set his mind on the schoolhouse boat winning. Riddell remembered every word of it now, and how Wyndham's excitement had baulked him of his desire for a serious talk that evening. And then he remembered how abruptly the boy had left him, returning hurriedly a moment after for his knife—this very knife which less than two hours afterwards had been dropped on the boat-house floor in the culprit's hurried retreat by the window!

Riddell felt literally sick as it all rushed through his mind at the sight of the knife in Tom's hand.

"Have you seen it enough?" demanded the youth, still eyeing the half-crown.

"Yes," murmured Riddell. And surely he never uttered a truer word.

Tom, startled by his voice, looked up.

"Hullo," said he, "what's up? One would think you'd never saw a knife afore!"

Riddell tried feebly to smile and recover himself.

"Tell you what," said Tom, struck with a brilliant idea—"tell you what, governor. You lay another two bob on the top of that there half-a-crown and it's your's. Come!"

Riddell mechanically took out his purse and produced the florin. It was almost the last coin that remained of his pocket-money for that term, but he was too miserable even to think of that.

Tom grabbed at the money eagerly, and deposited the knife in Riddell's hand in exchange.

Then, with a load on his heart such as he had never felt before, the captain turned the boat's head and rowed slowly back to Willoughby.

Chapter Twenty Four.

The Rockshire Match.

Riddell was not destined to have much leisure during the next few days for indulging his misery or making up his mind in what direction his duty lay.

As he reached the school after his memorable excursion on the river, he was met by Fairbairn, who had evidently been on the lookout for him.

"Why, where have you been? and what's wrong?" he exclaimed, as he observed his friend's dejected looks.

"I've been a turn on the river," replied Riddell, making a desperate effort to recover his wits and look cheerful.

"You look every bit as if you were just starting there to drown yourself," said Fairbairn; "but, I say, I've got a message for you."

"From whom?" inquired Riddell, who had had quite enough "messages" during the last few days to last him for the rest of the term.

"You'd scarcely guess—from Bloomfield. The thing is, he has two places yet to fill up in the eleven for Saturday, and he wants you to play for one."

Despite his trouble, Riddell could hardly conceal a smile of pleasure at this honour, which, though not exactly unexpected, he had hardly realised till now.

"Oh, I say," said he, "I'm certain there are lots of better fellows."

"You may be quite sure if there had been Bloomfield would have picked them up," said Fairbairn. "As it happens, we want a slip, and I heard Bloomfield say himself that you are awfully good there. You seem to have hidden your light under a bushel, old man, while in the schoolhouse."

"I may have been lucky while Bloomfield was watching," said Riddell.

"All gammon. You needn't fancy he's doing this to compliment you, old man. Game and that lot are awfully down on him about it. They'd like to make up the team entirely of Parretts, but it seems they can't do without us for once! Of course you'll play."

"Oh, yes," said Riddell; "he's captain of the eleven; I must."

"Hurrah. Well, you'll have to turn up at the Big practices, of course, during the next three days. There's one at three this afternoon and another at 6:30, and if you like to come down for an hour after first school I'll give you some balls at the nets."

This was Tuesday. The Rockshire match was to come off on Saturday, and between now and then, as Riddell well knew, every spare moment he could call his own would have to be devoted to cricket.

Personally, with the burden of the secret of young Wyndham's knife upon him, he would have been glad enough of some excuse for avoiding the honour even of a place in the first eleven. But there was no such excuse. On the contrary, his duty pointed clearly to his making the best of the opportunity. As captain of the school, even a humble place in the first eleven would be an undoubted gain to his influence; while to Welch's—demoralised Welch's—the knowledge that once more one of their number was "playing for the school" might be of real service.

Till Saturday, at any rate, he must try to banish the hideous nightmare from his mind, and give himself up wholly to the calls of cricket.

It is easier to resolve to give up one's mind to a pursuit than it is to do it, and for the first day or two Riddell found himself but a halfhearted cricketer. However, as the eventful day drew near things grew more serious, not to say critical.

It was a nervous occasion for the captain the first time he presented himself at a Big practice, and he could not help feeling that the eyes which watched his performance were more than ordinarily critical, and many of them less than ordinarily friendly.

Still he managed not to disgrace himself, and on the next occasion, having partially recovered his presence of mind, he was able to do himself even more justice. Every one had to admit that Riddell was a long way off being a fine cricketer—he would have been the first to admit it himself—but for all that, what with a quick eye, and much perseverance, and sound judgment, he possessed more than one of the qualities which go to make up a useful member of any team.

"He ought to do," said Bloomfield to Game on the Friday evening after the last of the practices. "He stood up to Fairbairn's bowling not at all badly."

"Shouldn't wonder," said Game, whose prejudice was stronger than his judgment, "if Fairbairn bowled down easy to him on purpose; they're awfully thick, you know."

"But I didn't bowl down to him easy," replied Bloomfield; "and he cut me for two twice running."

Game could not answer this argument, and was bound to admit a worse man might have been put into the odd place.

"It's a pity, though; they'll be so jolly cocky, all that set, there'll be no enduring it. I only hope our fellows will do most of the scoring to-morrow, and not leave them a chance of saying they won the match for us."

Bloomfield laughed. "Not much fear of that," said he; "but if they did, I suppose you'd sooner beat Rockshire with their help than be thrashed?"

Game was not quite sure, and said nothing.

One might have supposed that an occasion like the present, when the picked eleven Willoughby was to play the picked eleven of Rockshire, that there would have been no place left for party rivalry, or any feeling but one of patriotic ardour for the victory of the old school. But so deeply was the disease of party spirit rooted in Willoughby that even this match came to be looked on quite as much as a struggle between rival houses as between the school and an outside team.

The discovery was made that the eleven consisted of five schoolhouse players, five Parrett's players, and one Welcher. More than that, the ingenious noted the fact that the two best bowlers of the eleven were Bloomfield and Fairbairn, one from each house, who could also both field as wicket-keepers when not bowling. And the two second bowlers were Game and Porter, also one from each house. This minute analysis might doubtless have been continued down to the cover-points. At any rate, it was manifest the two houses were very evenly divided, both as regarded merit and place, and it would therefore be easy to see which contributed most to the service of the school.

The Rockshire men arrived by the ten o'clock train, and were met as usual by the Willoughby omnibus at the station. As they alighted and proceeded to stroll in a long procession across the Big to their tent, they were regarded with much awe and curiosity by the small boys assembled to witness their advent, some of whom were quite at a loss to understand how boys like themselves could ever expect not to be beaten by great whiskered heroes like these. Even the young Welchers, who had contrived to be practising close to the line of march, felt awed in their presence, and made a most hideous hash of the little exhibition with which they had intended to astonish their visitors.

The self-confident ease of these Rockshire men was even a trifle discouraging for a few of the school heroes themselves, who looked on nervously as their rivals coolly went up and inspected the wickets and criticised the pitch, and then proceeded, laughing among themselves, towards the pavilion. Things like this are more or less terrifying, and an old team that comes down to play a young one ought to be more considerate.

It was fortunate for the school team that all its members were not as shy and diffident as others, or the operation of tossing for innings and other matters of form would never have been got through.

Mr Parrett, however, as an old 'Varsity blue, was as great a hero in the sight of Rockshire as Rockshire was in the sight of Willoughby, and with his aid the preliminaries were all arranged, and Willoughby went out first to field.

The Big was never so crowded with boys, masters, or the outside public, as it was on this bright June day. The exploits of the school at the recent election may have had something to do with the number of townsfolk who flocked up to see the game, but apart from that the Rockshire match was always one of the great events of the season.

Last year, thanks to old Wyndham's prowess, the school had won; but before that, back almost to the days of the mythical Bouncer, the fates had been the other way; and this year, good as the team was, no one had the hardihood to predict with any confidence a victory for the boys.

Just as Riddell was leaving the tent to take his place in the field, young Wyndham came up and clapped him cheerily on the back.

"Go in and win, I say," he cried, gaily. "I back you, old man."

It was the first time the two had met since Riddell's interview with Tom the boat-boy, and the sight of his old friend's brother, and the sound of his voice just now, gave the captain a shock which for the moment almost unmanned him.

He turned pale as he looked at the boy, and thought of that knife.

"Oh, I say," said Wyndham, noticing his perturbation, "pull yourself together, old man; you'll get on all serene. I was funky the first time I showed up for the second-eleven, you know, but it's all right now!"

"Now, Riddell!" cried Bloomfield, impatiently, from the wickets; and off the captain hurried to his post, with a load of trouble at his heart, and feeling anything but a jubilant athlete.

Wyndham, little dreaming what was passing through his patron's mind, settled himself cross-legged at the door of the scorer's tent, and thought of nothing for the next few hours but the match.

The two Rockshire men, upon whom devolved the duty of "opening the ball," strolled slowly up to the wickets, and a minute later the match had begun.

As usual, the first few overs were uneventful. The bowlers were trying what the batsmen were made of, and the batsmen were trying what the bowlers were made of. Riddell was thankful for his part that no ball came his way, and the spectators generally seemed to regard two maiden overs as a sort of necessary infliction at the opening of any big match.

But when Bloomfield took the ball again it was evident things were to grow a little brisker. His first ball was very neatly patted towards square-leg for two, amid the cheers which always greet "the first blood," and his next ball slipped past the long-stop for a bye. Wyndham and some other enthusiasts sighed, as if those three runs had settled the fate of Willoughby. But his sigh was abruptly turned into a cheer when next moment the Rockshire man's wicket tumbled all of a heap, and one of the foe was out for three.

Willoughby began to breathe again. When they had seen those two portentous heroes go in, the prospect of their ever going out had seemed fearfully remote. But now, if one man was got rid of for only three runs, why should not ten men go for only thirty? At which arithmetical discovery the school immediately leapt from the depths of despondency to the heights of confidence, and considered the match as good as won before it was fairly begun.

However, during the next half-hour they had time to seek the happy mean between the two extremes. The newcomer was a tough customer, and should certainly have gone in first. For he was one of those aggravating batsmen who keep a steady bat at everything, who never aspire to a slog, never walk out to a slow, never step back to a yorker, are never too soon for a lob, or too late for a shooter—in fact, who play the safe plodding game in the face of all temptation.

The one comfort was, he did not make many runs. Still, this sort of business is demoralising for bowlers and slow for the field, and a change of bowlers was consequently decided upon after about half an hour's play, when the score was at twenty-one.

Game and Porter were the two new hands, the latter being the first to officiate with a very neat maiden over, loudly cheered from the school tent. Game who followed, was not so fortunate. The Rockshire man who had gone in first cut him hard for three on his second ball—the first hard hit of the match. And this the steady man followed up with a quiet two neatly placed between point and mid-off. Then came another ball, which the same player turned off sharply into the slips.

It was a fairly difficult ball to field, but Riddell picked it up smartly and returned it to the wickets in time to prevent a run being made.

"Well fielded indeed, sir!" cried Wyndham's voice from the tent. Little thought he how strangely those words of encouragement missed their mark. Riddell had just been forgetting his trouble and warming up to the game, and now they came once more to remind him of that hated knife and Tom the boat-boy's story.

The next ball the Rockshire man also "slipped," but this time, though it was within easier reach, and for a first-rate fielder was even a possible catch, Riddell missed it, and two runs were made. "Look out there!" cried Bloomfield severely. "Well tried, sir!" cried some one, sarcastically. "Well missed, sir!" cried some one else, with painful truthfulness. Riddell saw the crisis. Another miss like that, a few more taunts like those, and he might as well retire from the field.

Not for the first time in his life he pulled himself together with a vehement effort and shook off every thought but the one duty that claimed him.

And only just in time.

The last ball of the over was played again into slip, this time very smartly. The school shivered as they saw it whiz straight for the weak point. But they might have spared themselves their agitation, for Riddell had it—all but a catch—before the shiver was over, and had returned it to Fairbairn at the wickets promptly enough to make the Rockshire man feel he had had a narrow escape of a run-out.

"Fielded, sir!" said Bloomfield, as the players crossed over; and this commendation was more encouraging than all the shouts of the schoolhouse partisans.

Porter's next over disposed of the first Rockshire man, amid great school rejoicing, which was only tempered by the reflection among the Parretts that it was a wicket to the credit of the schoolhouse half of the eleven.

Then followed a succession of short but smart innings, during which the Rockshire score crawled up to seventy, despite of a further change of bowlers and very careful all-round fielding by the school.

All this time the steady man hung on obstinately; nothing seemed to puzzle him or tempt him out of his caution.

At length, in sheer desperation, Coates was put on to bowl; anything seemed better than this hopeless deadlock. And so it turned out. Coates's first ball came down temptingly towards the off stump. Any enterprising player would have cut it for a safe four, but this cautious hand, who seemed to smell a rat in everything, was evidently determined not to be taken in by first appearances, and turned it off, half contemptuously, to his favourite quarter among the slips, thinking possibly he might punish the next rather more freely. But the next was not to come for him. Coates's ball was rising a bit as the batsman touched it, and though he did not hit it up, it yet spun a foot or so above the ground, an easy catch, straight into Riddell's hand, who held it fast, much to his own surprise, and greatly to the jubilation of all Willoughby.

"Well caught, sir! Caught, indeed! Played up, Riddell!" were the cries which on all hands greeted the achievement, Wyndham's call being longest and loudest of them all.

But this time Riddell suffered no harm from the sound of that familiar voice. He had steeled himself against it for a few hours at least, and it was to him but one out of many.

Rockshire's first innings terminated shortly with no further event of note. The last wicket fell for ninety-two, a respectable total, of which fifty-nine had been made off the Parretts' batsmen, and thirty-three off the schoolhouse. Indeed, the advantage of the schoolhouse did not end there. Out of three catches—not counting Riddell's—they had made two, while of the five wickets which had been taken by the bowling, they claimed three against their rivals' two.

Great was the dismay of Parrett's as these results were made known. They buoyed themselves up greatly, however, with the prospect of the batting, where it would be strange indeed if they did not score better than the schoolhouse. And after all, it is the runs that win a match.

Bloomfield himself, be it said to his credit, allowed no petty considerations of party rivalry to influence him in sending in the best men at the right time. However much in some ways he might lend himself to the whims of his more energetic comrades, in a matter like the Rockshire match, where he was in sole command, and responsible for the glory of the school, he acted with the sole object of winning the match.

It would have been easy to send in Fairbairn and Porter last, when they would have no chance of scoring; or Coates, who was a rash hitter, and never was safe until the back of the bowling had been somewhat broken, might have been sent in first.

But such an arrangement Bloomfield knew would be fatal for the chances of the school, and it therefore never entered his head to contrive it. And his fairness in this respect was fully justified, for the school put together a hundred and twelve runs— just twenty more than their opponents—a performance which not even the most sanguine Willoughbite had dared to anticipate. Towards this total Riddell, who had gone in last and carried his bat, had contributed seven, not a little to his own surprise and the delight of the onlooking Welchers. But the most remarkable thing about the innings was that, contrary to all calculation, the five schoolhouse fellows had contributed no less than sixty-four runs to the total, while the Parretts' united score only amounted to forty-one.

The second innings of Rockshire differed very little from the first. The steady man went in first, and bothered every bowler the school could bring against him; and, having had one lesson, he took good care not to give himself another, and rather avoided slip for the future. So that Riddell had a quiet time of it, fielding the few balls that came to him steadily and promptly, but otherwise not figuring prominently in the downfall of any wicket.

It was half-past four before Rockshire finally retired with a total for their second innings of ninety-nine, leaving the school boys with eighty runs to obtain to win.

It was not a formidable total after their first-innings performance, but at the outset a calamity happened enough to depress the hopes of any Willoughbite.

Bloomfield had gone in first with every intention of breaking the ice effectually for his side. What, therefore, was the consternation of everybody when, after neatly blocking the first ball, he was clean bowled for a duck's-egg by the second! Willoughby literally howled with disappointment, and gave itself up to despair as it saw its captain and champion retreating slowly back to the tent, trailing his bat behind him, and not daring to look up at the hideous "0" on the telegraph board.

But hope was at hand, though Parrett's was not to supply it. Coates and Crossfield, who were now together, made a most unexpected and stubborn stand. They even scored freely, and the longer they held together the harder it was to part them. The reviving hopes of the Rockshire partisans gradually died out before this awkward combination, and Game and Ashley and Tipper, as they sat and watched this spirited performance by the two schoolhouse boys, felt their triumph for the school utterly swamped in the still more signal victory which the despised house was achieving over them.

The score, amid terrific cheering, went up to fifty-two before a separation could be effected. Then Coates was caught at long-leg, and retired, covered with glory, in favour of Tipper.

Alas for Parrett's! Tipper, in whom their forlorn hopes rested, was run out during his first over, while attempting to snatch a bye!

It was an anxious moment while Bloomfield was deciding whom next to send in. There was still thirty runs to make, but unless he took care the whole innings might be muddled away in the getting of them.

"You go in, Fairbairn," said the captain.

The Parretts felt their fate to be sealed hopelessly. Had Game been sent in he might still have done something for Parrett's, but now his chance might never come.

105

It did not come. Fairbairn joined Crossfield, and the two did just what they liked with the bowling. As the score shot up from fifty to sixty and from sixty to seventy, the school became perfectly hoarse with cheering. Even most of the partisans of Parrett's, sorely as the match was going against them, could not help joining in the applause now that the prospect of the school winning by seven wickets had become a probability.

Up went the score—another three for Fairbairn—another two for Crossfield—seventy-five—then next moment a terrific cheer greeted a four by Fairbairn, which brought the numbers equal; and before the figures were well registered another drive settled the question, and Willoughby had beaten Rockshire by seven wickets!

Chapter Twenty Five.

"Am I My Brother's Keeper?"

The evening of the Rockshire match was one of strangely conflicting emotions in Willoughby.

In the schoolhouse the jubilation was beyond bounds, and the victory of the school was swallowed up in the glorious exploits of the five schoolhouse heroes, who had, so their admirers declared, as good as won the match among them, and had vindicated themselves from the reproach of degeneracy, and once for all wiped away the hateful stigma of the boat-race. The night was spent till bedtime in one prolonged cheer in honour of their heroes, who were glad enough to hide anywhere to escape the mobbing they came in for whenever they showed their faces.

In Parrett's house the festivities were of a far more subdued order. As Willoughbites they were, of course, bound to rejoice in the victory of the old school. But at what cost did they do it? For had not that very victory meant also the overthrow of their reign in Willoughby. No reasoning or excusing could do away with the fact that after all their boasting, and all their assumed superiority, they had taken considerably less than half the wickets, secured considerably less than a third of the catches, and scored considerably less than a quarter of the runs by which the match had been won. Their captain had been bowled for a duck's-egg. Their best bowlers had been knocked about by the very batsmen whom the schoolhouse bowlers had dispatched with ease.

It was vain to attempt to account for it, to assert that the schoolhouse had had the best of the luck: that the light had favoured them; or that just when they happened to bowl the Rockshire men had got careless. Even such stick-at-nothing enthusiasts as Parson, Bosher, and Co., couldn't make a case of it, and were forced to admit with deep mortification that the glory had departed from Parrett's, at any rate for a season.

Perhaps the most patriotic rejoicings that evening were in Welch's house. They cared but little about the rivalry between Parrett's, and the schoolhouse, and were therefore free to exult as Willoughbites pure and simple, bestowing, of course, a special cheer on their own man, Riddell, who, though not having performed prodigies, had yet done honest work for his eleven, and at any rate made one smart catch.

"I tell you what," said Fairbairn, who along with Coates and Porter had escaped from the violent applause of the schoolhouse and sought refuge that evening in the captain's study—"I tell you what, I'm getting perfectly sick of this everlasting schoolhouse against Parrett business."

"So am I," said Porter. "As if they need go into the sulks because our fellows did better than they did!"

"They've brought it on themselves, anyhow," said Coates, "and it may do them good to have to sing small for once."

"I'm afraid if it had been the other way our fellows would have been just as much cut up as theirs are," said Fairbairn. "Upon my word I half envy you, Riddell, old man, being a Welcher."

Riddell smiled.

"Our fellows certainly consider themselves free to abuse or cheer all round, without the least partiality. Listen to them now."

And certainly the hubbub that was going on was a trifle outrageous, even for Welchers.

Indeed it was so outrageous that Riddell was obliged to ask his visitors to excuse him for a moment while he went and quieted them.

As he opened the door of the preparation-room, where the house was assembled, a louder cheer than ever arose in his honour; and then those who waited in the study heard a general lull in the noise, which continued in subdued animation after he had left the scene and returned to his friends.

This casual illustration of the captain's influence in his new house was quite a revelation to the three schoolhouse monitors.

"Why, what do you do to them to shut them up like that?" asked Coates, with something like envy in his tones. "It takes half an hour's bawling to stop a row like that in our house, and a licking or two into the bargain; doesn't it, you fellows?"

Riddell laughed.

"They are cricket-mad at present," said he, "and I suppose they're afraid of having their match against Parrett's stopped."

It was a modest way, no doubt, of accounting for their obedience to his authority; but whatever the reason might be, it was certain the captain had no further occasion to interfere that evening.

"There's one comfort about this match," said Fairbairn, after a pause, "we probably shall not hear any more of that wretched boat-race now."

Whatever induced him to start this most unfortunate topic at this time of all others?

Riddell, who amid all the excitement of the match had contrived partially to forget the burden that lay on his spirit, started uncomfortably at the words, and his face changed to one of undisguised trouble. The others could hardly help noticing it.

"No, we're never likely to get at the bottom of it," said Porter; "so the sooner it drops the better."

"It's very odd, all the same," said Fairbairn, "that there's not been a single hint as to who did it. I wonder if, perhaps, we were wrong in taking for granted it was more than an accident."

This last question was addressed to Riddell, who replied, nervously and uneasily, "No, that is, yes. It can't have been. I'm sure it wasn't an accident."

His three friends looked perplexed by his sudden confusion and change of manner, and Porter had the presence of mind to change the subject.

"I hear there's a jolly row on between Silk and Gilks," said he. "No one knows exactly why."

"I heard it was a bet," said Coates.

"At any rate they've had a split," said Porter.

"They never did much good while they were in partnership," said Coates. "Young Wyndham got rather drawn in by them, I heard."

"Rather!" said Fairbairn. "He was precious near going to the dogs altogether if old Riddell here hadn't pulled him up."

Riddell seemed to lack spirit to join in the conversation, which continued without him.

"Yes, the young 'un cuts them dead now," said Porter, "but he's a bit afraid of them still, I fancy."

"I suppose they could let out upon him about some scrape or other," said Coates, "and that's what gives them a pull."

"Anyhow, it's a good job he has pulled up," said Fairbairn, "for he's not a bad youngster. He's got into the second-eleven just lately, and is tremendously proud of it. He's vowed he'll get old Wyndham to come down and umpire in the match with Templeton second-eleven next month."

All this talk was anything but pleasant for poor Riddell. Little did the speakers dream of the connection between the boat-race and young Wyndham; in fact, the latter topic, as he knew quite well, had been started on purpose to get over the awkwardness which his own confusion about the former had caused.

But to Riddell, with that knife burning in his pocket, it was all one prolonged torture, so that he was heartily glad when at length his friends rose to depart.

He excused himself from walking across the quadrangle with them, and said good-night in a spiritless way, very different from the cheery manner in which he had welcomed them an hour ago.

"I never saw such a rum fellow as Riddell," said Coates, as the three strolled over. "Did you see how cut up he got when something was said about the boat-race?"

"He's a little cracked on that subject," said Fairbairn. "I do believe, until the culprit is found out, he considers himself responsible for the whole affair."

"Well, to judge by his looks he might have been the culprit himself," said Porter, laughing. "Hullo, here's young Wyndham."

"Where are you off to?" asked Fairbairn, with due monitorial solemnity, of that flighty youth; "don't you know it's nearly eight?"

"Oh, do you mind my going across to Riddell's?" asked the boy; "he'll think I've cut him if I don't show up. I've not been to his room for half a week."

"It's a curious thing he has survived it so long," said Fairbairn, laughing. "Mind you are back by 8:30, though, for I'll have lock-up punctual to-night, while there's so much row going on."

"Thanks, Fairbairn," said Wyndham. "I say, what a stunning score our house knocked up in the second innings. Why, we—"

"Cut off," cried Fairbairn, "and tell Riddell all about it. Come on, you fellows."

Wyndham hurried on full of the prospect of a talk over the match with Riddell.

Just at the door of Welch's, however, he met Silk.

The two had scarcely met since the day of the election, when Wyndham, to spite Riddell, had joined himself to this bad friend, and yielded to his persuasion to go down, against leave, to Shellport.

"Oh, young 'un," said Silk, in friendly tones, "you turned up? I'd almost given you up for good."

"I'm going to Riddell's," said Wyndham, determined for once to stand by his colours and have nothing more to do with this tempter.

Silk's face fell, as it always did when Riddell's name was mentioned. He had imagined the boy was coming to see him, and it did not please him to find himself mistaken.

"Are you?" said he. "Come along to my study first, though; I want to speak to you."

"I can't come, thank you," said Wyndham.

"Can't! Why ever not?" exclaimed Silk.

"I don't want to come, that's why," said Wyndham, doggedly, and attempting to move past.

But this by no means suited Silk.

"Suppose I tell you you *must* come," demanded he, stepping in front of the boy with a menacing air.

"Please let me go by," repeated Wyndham, making another attempt.

"Not till you tell me what you mean by saying you won't do as I tell you."

"I mean that I'm not going to your study," said young Wyndham.

"Oh, very well," said Silk, standing back to let him pass.

There was something in his tone and manner as he said the words which made Wyndham uneasy. He had made up his mind at all costs he would break with Silk; yet now he could not help remembering he was at the fellow's mercy.

So, instead of going on, he stood where he was, and said, rather less defiantly, "Can't you say what you've got to say here?"

"Oh, of course. I can easily tell the whole school of your—"

"Oh, hush, please!" cried the boy in alarm; "you promised you wouldn't tell any one. I'll come to your study."

Silk, with a triumphant sneer, turned and led the way, followed by his chafing victim, who devoutly wished he had never thought of coming to see Riddell at all.

When they were in the study, Silk turned and said, "All I want to say is, that, I don't choose for you to be going such a lot to Riddell. I don't like him, and you'd better keep away."

"Why?" faltered Wyndham. "It doesn't do you any harm."

"How do I know you don't blab all my secrets to him, eh?"

"Oh, I wouldn't do it for anything. I promised you and Gilks."

"Bah! what's the use of that? You go and tell him everything you do yourself, and of course he knows it means us as well as you."

"No, he doesn't—really. I've never said a word to him about—about Beamish's."

"It's a good job you haven't; and you'd better not, I can tell you."

"I won't," said the boy.

"I don't choose to have my concerns talked about to anybody," said Silk, "I suppose it was he put you up to cutting me."

"No—that is," said Wyndham, "yes, he did advise me not to be so much with Gilks and you."

"He did?" exclaimed Silk, in a rage. "I thought so; and you—"

Fortunately at this moment Tucker and one or two other of the noisy Welchers broke into the room; and in the diversion so created Wyndham was thankful to slip away.

This, then, was the end of his good resolutions and the hopes they had fostered! He was as much in the power of this bad friend as ever—nay, more, for had he not that very evening been forced to renew the one promise which kept him from confiding everything to Riddell?

He proceeded dejectedly to the captain's study, his cricket enthusiasm strangely damped, and the load of his old short-comings heavy upon him.

Riddell, who was pacing the room moodily, stopped in a half-startled way as his visitor entered.

"Do you want me?" he said.

"No," said Wyndham. "I only just came across to see you, because I thought you'd wonder what had become of me."

"Yes," said Riddell, trying to compose himself, "with all this cricket practice there's not been much chance of seeing one another."

"No," replied Wyndham, whom the very mention of cricket was enough to excite. "I say, wasn't it an awfully fine licking we gave them? Our fellows are crowing like anything, and, you know, if it hadn't been for your catch it might have been a much more narrow affair."

"Ah, well! it's all over now," said Riddell; "so I suppose you'll come and see me oftener?"

"I hope so. Of course, there's the second-eleven practices still going on for the Templeton match, but I'll turn up here all the same."

Riddell took a turn or two in silence. What was he to do? A word from him, he felt, could ruin this boy before all Willoughby, and possibly disgrace him for life.

He, Riddell, as captain of the school, seemed to have a clear duty in the matter. Had the culprit been any *one else*—had it been Silk, for instance, or Gilks—would he have hung back? He knew he would not, painful as the task would be. The honour of the school was in question, and he had no right to palter with that.

Yet how could he deal thus with young Wyndham?—his friend's brother, the fellow he cared for most in Willoughby, over whose struggles he had watched so anxiously, and for whom, now, better resolves and honest ambitions were opening up so cheery a prospect. How could he do it?

Was there no chance that after all he might be mistaken? Alas! that cruel knife and the memory of that evening crushed out the hope. What could he do? To do nothing would be simply adding his own crime to that of another. If only the boy would confess voluntarily! Could that have possibly been the object which brought him there that evening? The last time they had talked together, even in the midst of his contrition, he had been strangely reserved about something in the past. Might not this be the very secret he had now come to confide?

"How have you been getting on the last week?" he asked, gravely. "Have you been able to keep pretty straight?"

"Yes, I hope so," said Wyndham. "You see, this cricket doesn't give a fellow much chance of going wrong."

"No; but of course one needs to do more than merely not go wrong," said the captain.

"What do you mean?"

"I suppose when any of us *has* done wrong we ought to try to make up for it somehow."

"Oh, yes, of course," said Wyndham, feeling a little uncomfortable. "The worst of it is, you can't always do that except by keeping right in future."

"Supposing you had owed some fellow a sovereign last term, you would consider that all you had to do was not to owe him any more this term?" said Riddell.

"No; of course not! I'd have to pay him, I know," said Wyndham.

"Well, what I mean," said the captain, "is that—that—why, the fact is, Wyndham," said he, "I'm afraid you have still some old scores you ought to clear up."

Wyndham looked hard at the captain, and coloured.

"I see what you mean," he said, in a low voice. "I know you're right. I wish I could do it."

"You wish!" exclaimed Riddell. "Wishing will not do it."

Wyndham looked hard at him once more, and answered, in agitated tones.

"I say, Riddell. Do you know about it, then?"

"I think I do."

At that moment a bell began to sound across the quadrangle.

"That's lock-up; I must go!" exclaimed Wyndham, wildly. "For goodness' sake, don't tell any one, Riddell! Oh what a fool I have been!"

And next moment he was gone.

Riddell continued to pace the room, half stupefied with bewilderment and misery.

"For goodness' sake, don't tell any one!" The cry rang in his ears till it drove him nearly mad.

Poor Wyndham! What must his state of mind be? What must it have been all this time, with that miserable secret lurking there and poisoning his whole life? And yet the chance had been given him, and he had clung to the secret still, and in the face of discovery had no other cry than this, "For goodness' sake, don't tell any one!"

That evening, so jubilant all over Willoughby, was one of the most wretched Riddell ever spent.

Chapter Twenty Six.

An Explosion of "SkyRockets."

Parson, Bosher, King, and the other Parrett's juniors were in bad spirits. It was not so much the Rockshire match that was preying on the brotherhood, grievous as that blow had been. Nor were they at the present suffering under any particular infliction, or smarting under any special sense of injustice. Their healths and digestions were all tolerably good, and the mutual friendship in which they had been wont to rejoice showed no signs of immediate dissolution.

The fact was, they didn't know exactly what was the matter with themselves. They could not pretend that it was remorse for the little amount of work they had done during the term, for they stoutly denied that they had done little. On the contrary, they insisted that they were being crammed to a shameful extent.

Nor was their conscience reproaching them for their past transgressions. Of course, they could not help admitting that they had occasionally got into rows lately, but, as every one knew, it was never *their* fault. It had always been owing to some accident or piece of bad luck, and it was quite enough to get punished for it, without being expected to reproach themselves for it.

No. When they came to think of it they didn't see that they had anything to reproach themselves with. On the whole, they were more to be pitied than blamed. They invariably meant well, but they never got any credit for their good intentions, while they were everlastingly getting into trouble on account of their ill-luck!

The fact of the matter was, these virtuous young gentlemen were suffering from that most painful of maladies—dulness.

They had nothing to do—that is, they had nothing to do but work and play cricket. The latter was all very well, but even cricket, when it means three practices a day presided over by a strict senior, gets to be a little wearisome.

As for the work—they groaned as they thought of it. It hadn't been so bad at the beginning of the term, when Bosher's crib to the Caesar and Wakefield's key to Colenso's arithmetic had lent them their genial aid. But ever since Mr Parrett, in the vindictiveness of his heart, had suddenly started Eutropius in the place of Caesar, and Todhunter in the place of Colenso, life had barely been worth living.

It was this last grievance which was the special topic of discussion at an informal tea-party held, about a week after the Rockshire match, in Parson's study.

The company solaced their wounded feelings with unlimited bloater-paste and red-currant jam, and under the soothing influence of these condiments, aided by the watery contents of Parson's teapot, their sorrows found relief in words.

"I bet anything he pitched on Eutropius," said Parson, with his cup to his lips, "because he knows nobody ever wrote a crib to him."

"I don't suppose any one could make him out enough," said King. "It's awful rot."

"Yes, and Ashley says it's awfully bad Latin."

Parson laughed satirically.

"Jolly lot they care what sort of Latin it is as long as they can do us over it."

"I believe," said Bosher, "Gilks has a key to Todhunter."

"He has? Young Telson had better collar it, then," said King, whose opinions on the laws of property as regarded cribs were lax.

"Bah! What's the use of bothering?" cried Parson, pouring himself out his eighth cup of tea. "If he pulls me up for not doing the beastly things I shall tell him they're too hard, straight out."

"Tell him it's jolly gross conduct," cried a voice at the door, followed immediately by Telson, who, contrary to all rules, had slipped across to pay a friendly visit.

He was welcomed with the usual rejoicing, and duly installed at the festive board.

"It's all right if I am caught," said he. "Gilks sent me a message to Wibberly, and I just dropped in here on the way. I say, who's going to lick, you or Welch's?"

"Welch's!" exclaimed the company, in general contempt. "It's like their cheek to challenge us. We mean to give them a lesson."

"Mind you do," said Telson, "or it'll be jolly rough on Parrett's. No end of a poor show you made at the Rockshire."

"Look here, Telson," said Parson, gravely, "suppose we don't talk about that. We were just wondering if Gilks had got a key to Todhunter somewhere."

Telson laughed.

"Wonder if he hadn't! He's got more cribs than school books, I think."

"I say," said King, most persuasively, "could you collar it, do you think, old man!"

"Eh? No," said Telson; "I draw the line at that sort of thing, you know."

"Well, then," said King, evidently in a state of desperate mental agitation, "could you ever find out the answer for Number 13 in Exercise 8, and let me know it in the morning? I'd be awfully obliged."

Telson said he would see, whereat King was most profuse in his gratitude, and Telson received several other commissions of a similar nature.

These little matters of business being satisfactorily settled, the company proceeded to the discussion of more general topics.

"Fearful slow term this," said Parson, with a yawn.

"Yes," said Telson, spreading a piece of bread with about a quarter-of-an-inch layer of jam; "we're somehow done out of everything this term."

"Yes. We can't go out on the river; we can't go into town; we can't go and have a lark in Welch's; you can't come over to see us—"

"No; that's a howling shame!" said Telson.

"We can't do anything, in fact," continued Parson (now at cup Number 9). "Why, we haven't had a spree for weeks."

"You seemed to think my diary was a spree," said Bosher, meekly.

There was a general laugh at this.

"By the way, have you got it here?"

"No fear! I'll take good care you don't see it again, you cads!"

"Eh? By the way, that reminds me we never paid Bosher out for being a Radical, you fellows," said Parson.

"Oh, no—oh, yes, you did!" cried Bosher. "I apologise, you fellows. I'll let you see the diary, you know, some day. Really, I'm not a Radical."

Fortunately for Bosher, the political excitement at Willoughby had quite worn away, so that no one now felt it his duty to execute the sentence of the law upon him and, after being made to apologise on his knees to each of the company in turn, he was solemnly let off.

"You see," said Parson, returning to the point, "we've been up before Parrett twice this term; that's the mischief. We might have chanced a spree of some sort, only if we get pulled up again he may expel us."

There was some force in this argument, and it was generally agreed it would be better for Willoughby that the risk of a calamity like this should not be incurred.

"Fact is," said Telson, cutting another slice of bread, "Willoughby's going to the dogs as hard as it can. The seniors in our house are down on you if you do anything. I even got pulled up the other day for having a duel with young Payne with elastics. Awful spree it was! We gave one another six yards, and six shots each. I got on to his face four times, and once on his ear, and he only hit me twice. One of mine was right in his eye, and there was a shindy made, and I got sixty lines from Fairbairn."

"What a frightful shame!" cried the company. "Yes," said King; "and it's just as bad here. The new monitors pull you up for everything. You can't even chuck boots about in the passage but they are down on you. It was bad enough when Game and that lot were monitors, but ever since they've been turned out and the new chaps stuck in it's worse."

"And they say it's just as bad in Welch's," said Wakefield. "You know," said Parson, profoundly, pouring himself out a fresh cup—"you know, if Riddell and Bloomfield ever took it into their heads to pull together, we'd have an awful time of it."

The bare possibility of such a calamity was enough to sober even the wildest spirit present.

"These seniors are a nuisance," said Telson, after a pause; "and the worst of it is, we can't well pay them out."

"Not in school, or in the Big either," said King. "We might stick nettles in their beds, you know," suggested Bosher, "or something of that sort."

"Rather low, that," said Parson, "and not much fun."

"Would leeches be better?" said Bosher, who had lately been giving himself to scientific investigation.

It was considered leeches might not be bad, but there was rather too much uncertainty about their mode of action. That was a sort of thing more in Cusack's and the Welchers' line than the present company's.

"I tell you what," said Telson, struck with an idea, "we might get at them in Parliament; they're always so jolly fond of talking about fair play there, and every one being equal. Do you know, I think we might have a little fling there!"

"Not at all a bad idea," said Parson, admiringly—"jolly fine idea! We can do what those cads do in the newspapers—obstruct the business! Rattling idea!"

"Yes; and fancy Messrs Telson, Parson, Bosher, and Co. being suspended," said King.

"They couldn't do it, I tell you," said Bosher; "we'd kick up a shine about freedom of speech, and all that. Anyhow, it would be rather a spree, whether we were kicked out or not. We'd be a 'party' you know!"

The idea took, and an animated consultation took place. Parson, for a junior, was very well up in the "rules of the House," and at his suggestion the notice-paper for to-morrow's assembly was got hold of and filled with "amendments."

111

"Call them amendments," said he, "and they can't say anything."

"Oh, all serene," said Telson, who had implicit confidence in his friend.

"For instance, here you are," said Parson. "'Mr Coates to move that Classics is a nobler study than Mathematics.' Amendment proposed: 'Instead of "nobler" say "viler."' Proposed by Bosher, further amendment: 'Instead of "nobler" say "beastlier."' Proposed by Telson—('Hear, hear,' from Telson)—further amendment: 'Instead of "nobler" say "more idiotic."' You see it can easily be worked, and when we've done with 'nobler' we can start on the 'is' and amend it to 'are,' do you twig? There'll have to be a division over each. I say it'll be an awful lark!"

Little dreaming of the delightful treat in store for it, Willoughby assembled next afternoon, expecting nothing better than a dull debate on the well-worn question of classics *versus* mathematics. They were destined to experience more than one surprise before the meeting was over.

Riddell, who had spent a dismal day, not knowing what to do or think, and vainly hoping that Wyndham might by his own free confession solve the bitter problem, came to the meeting. It was the least wretched thing he could do. Anything was better than sitting alone and brooding over his secret.

For the first time he received a cheer as he entered and took his accustomed place. Willoughby was grateful to him for that catch in the Rockshire match. How, at any other time, the captain would have rejoiced over that cheer! But now he hardly heard it.

All the other heroes of the match received a similar ovation in proportion to the service they had done, and when, just at the last moment, Fairbairn, Coates, and Crossfield came in together, the "House" rose at them and cheered tremendously.

The business was preceded by the usual questions, none of which, however, were very important. After the captain's performance last week, and perhaps still more after his speech in the House a week or two ago, honourable men had shown themselves less active in "baiting" him and asking him offensive questions, and on this occasion he was only interrogated once, and that was by Cusack, who wanted to know whether they were not going to get a whole holiday in honour of the Rockshire match? The captain replied that he had heard nothing about it.

Bosher was put up to ask Bloomfield whether he considered Eutropius fit reading for young boys? Loud cheers from all the small boys in question greeted the inquiry, in the midst of which Bloomfield cunningly replied that the honourable member had better give notice of the question for next time.

Then rose Telson, with all the dignity of office, and solemnly inquired of Mr Stutter, the Premier, whether he was aware that a new party had lately been formed in the House, consisting of Messrs Telson, Parson, Bosher, King, and Wakefield, called the "Skyrockets," whose object was to look after the interests of the juniors all over the school, and who would be glad to receive fresh members at one shilling a head?

Stutter, who was scarcely heard in the uproar which followed this sensational announcement, meekly replied that he had not heard a word about it, an answer which, for some reason or other, provoked almost as much laughter as the question.

"All very well for them to grin," growled Telson, who had expected a somewhat different reception to his important question: "wait till we start on the amendments."

The opportunity soon arrived. Coates being called upon to open the debate, let off the speech he had prepared, and if he did not convince the House that classics was a nobler study than mathematics, he at least showed that he had convinced himself.

The "Skyrockets" had barely the patience to hear him out, and the moment he had done, Parson started to his feet, and shouted, "Mr Chairman and gentlemen, I beg to move an amendment—"

Here Bloomfield, whom the sight of the notice-paper had prepared for what was coming, interposed, "When I am ready for the honourable member I will call on him. The motion is not yet seconded."

"No, no! That won't wash, will it, you fellows?" cried Parson, excitedly, planting himself firmly in his place, and evidently seeing through the deep designs of the enemy. "Bother seconding! I mean to move my amendment, if I stick here all night! (Terrific Skyrocket cheers.) We kids have been snubbed long enough, and we're going to make a stand!" ("Question," "Order.") "All very well for you to sing out 'Order'—"

The Chairman:

"Will the honourable member—"

"No, he won't!" screamed Parson, with the steam well up; "and he's not going to! I've got a right to be heard—we've all got a right to be heard, and we're going to be heard, what's more! (Tremendous cheers from the club.) We're all equal here, aren't we, you chaps?" ("Rather!")

Here Fairbairn rose to order, but Parson was too quick for him.

"No, no!" he cried, "we don't want any of your jaw! We're not going to be shut up by you! We're a party, I tell you, and we're bound to stick out!" ("Hear, hear," from Bosher.) "We expected you'd be trying to sit on us, but we made up our minds we won't be sat on! (Prolonged cheers.) I've not begun my speech yet—(laughter)—and I don't mean to till you hold your rows!"

Here there were loud cries of "Order" from various parts of the House, which, however, only served to inspirit the speaker, who proceeded at the top of his voice, "It's no use your going on like that. (I say, you chaps," added he, turning round to his companions, "back me up, I'm getting husky.) You think we're a lot of fools—"

("We're a lot of fools!" chimed in the chorus, by way of backing up their orator.)

"But we're not as green as we look!"

("Green as we look!")

"You all seem to think it funny!"

("Think it funny!")

"But you needn't think you'll shut *us* up!"

("Shut us up!")

Here another attempt was made on the part of the chairman to reduce the meeting to order. Above the laughter and cheering and hooting he cried at the top of his voice, "Unless you stop your foolery, Parson, I'll have you turned out!"

"Will you? Who's going to stop my foolery?" yelled Parson.

("Stop my foolery?") howled the chorus.

"Try it on, that's all! You don't think we funk you!"

("We funk you!")

"Do you suppose we don't know what we're doing?"

("We don't know what we're doing?")

"Look out, you fellows! Hold on!"

This last remark was caused by a rush upon the devoted band, with a view to carry out the edict of the chairman.

Parson went on with his oration till he was secured, hand and foot, and carried forcibly to the door, and even then continued to address the house, struggling and kicking between every syllable. His backers, equally determined, clung on to the forms and desks, and continued to shout and scream and caterwaul till they were one by one ejected.

Even then they maintained their noble stand for freedom of speech by howling through the key-hole and kicking at the door, till finally a select band of volunteers was dispatched "to clear the approaches to the House" and drive the Skyrockets to their own distant studies, where they organised a few brawls on their own account, and ended the afternoon very hoarse, very tired, but by no means cast down.

"Jolly spree, wasn't it?" said Parson, when it was all over, fanning himself with a copybook and readjusting his collar.

"Stunning!" said Telson; "never thought they'd stand it so long. No end of a speech, that of yours!"

"Yes," said Parson, complacently; "most of it impromptu, too! Managed to spin it out, I fancy!"

"Rather," said King, admiringly. "I began to make mine after you'd got kicked out, but couldn't get out much of it."

"Well, all I can say is it was a jolly lark. I feel quite hungry after it," said Telson. "Any of that jam left, old man?"

And so these heroes appropriately celebrated their glorious field-day with a no less glorious banquet, which amply compensated for all the little inconveniences they had had to endure in the course of the afternoon's entertainment.

Meanwhile, rather more serious work was going on in the Great Hall.

The Skyrockets being ejected, the house proceeded in a somewhat humdrum fashion to discuss the relative merits of classics and mathematics. Several of the seniors and a few Limpets had prepared speeches, which they duly delivered. Contrary to the expectation of most present, Riddell took no part in the discussion. As head classic, a speech from him had been quite counted on; but not even the calls of the one side or the taunts of the other could get him on to his feet.

The fact was, he only half heard what was going on. His thoughts were far away, busied with a far more serious inward debate than that on the notice-paper.

At length he could remain idle no longer. He must go and find out Wyndham, or see the doctor, or pay another visit to Tom the boat-boy—anything rather than this suspense and misery and inaction.

He took advantage of a more than ordinarily dreary speech from Tedbury to rise and make his retreat quietly from the room.

But before he had reached the door Tedbury's voice abruptly ceased and Wibberly's was heard saying, "Mr Chairman, I see Mr Riddell is leaving the meeting. Will you allow me to ask him a question before he goes?"

There was something strange about this interruption, and also in the manner in which the question was asked, which drew the sudden attention of the House, and all eyes were turned on the captain.

He stopped and turned in his usual nervous, half-inquiring way, apparently not quite sure what had been said or who had spoken.

"Mr Wibberly," said Bloomfield, "wishes to ask a question of Mr Riddell."

"It is merely this," said Wibberly, rapidly, and giving no time for any objection to be raised on the point of order. "I wish to ask Mr Riddell whether he has found out yet who cut the rudder-line of Parrett's boat at the boat-race, or whether he suspects anybody, and, if so, whom?"

At this unlooked-for question a hubbub immediately arose. Several schoolhouse fellows protested against the proceedings being interrupted in this way, and even Bloomfield exclaimed across the table, "For goodness' sake, Wibberly, don't bring up that wretched subject again."

But those who had watched Riddell had seen him turn suddenly pale at the question, and for a moment make as though he would rush from the room. But he stopped himself, and turned like a hunted deer on the questioner.

A dead silence fell on the assembly, as Wibberly coolly said, "I will repeat the questions. Has Mr Riddell found out who cut the rudder-lines? or does he suspect any one? and, if so, who is it?"

Every eye turned on Riddell. The brief pause had given him time to collect himself and fight out the inward battle; and now he answered steadily, "I do suspect some one. But until I am perfectly sure I shall not say who it is."

So saying, he quietly left the room.

Chapter Twenty Seven.

Everything gone wrong.

Riddell was fairly committed to his task now. Like the good old general who burned his ships when he landed on the enemy's shores, he had cut off from himself the slightest possibility of a retreat, and must now either go right through with the matter or confess himself a miserable failure.

The consciousness of this nerved him with unlooked-for courage, and he walked from the Parliament that afternoon a very different being from the boy who had entered it. He had entered it cowed, irresolute, wretched; he left it indeed still wretched, but with his spirit roused and his mind made up. His duty lay clear before him, and whatever it cost he must do it.

Whether Wibberly was himself the writer of the mysterious letter, or whether some one had prompted him to ask the question, or whether his asking it just at this time was a mere coincidence, he did not trouble to decide.

He felt rather grateful to him than otherwise for having asked it, just as one is occasionally grateful to the thunder-clap for clearing the air.

The first thing without doubt was to find Wyndham, and come to a clear understanding as to whether or not he was the culprit; and the captain lost no time in attempting to put this resolve into practice.

It would not do, he knew, immediately after the scene in the Parliament, when everybody would be on the tip-toe of curiosity, to be seen holding a secret interview with any particular boy. He therefore decided wisely to wait till the usual time when Wyndham was in the habit of coming to his study to do his lessons. Meanwhile, to make sure of his coming, he sent him a message by Cusack to tell him to be sure and turn up.

Cusack, little suspecting the importance of this simple message, delivered it glibly, and being of course brimful of the excitement of the hour, he remained a little to regale Wyndham with a history of the afternoon's events.

"Oh, I say," said he, "you weren't at Parliament this afternoon. There was no end of a shine on."

"Was there?" asked Wyndham.

"Rather. What do you think, those young Parrett's cads came down in a body and kicked up the biggest row you ever saw—said they were a club, and made no end of beasts of themselves, and got kicked out at last, and serve them right too."

"They're always fooling about at something," said Wyndham.

"That they are. They want a good taking down, and we mean to do it next week in the junior house match."

"Ah," said Wyndham, who amid all his recent troubles could never forget that he was a second-eleven man. "Ah, I heard the juniors' match was to come off. What day is it to be?"

"Thursday."

"Oh, I must come and have a look at you. Is Welch's going to win?"

"Going to try, and I fancy we're pretty fair. They've been lazy, you know, in Parrett's, and so we get a pull there. Oh, but I was saving that row with the kids wasn't all this afternoon. Just at the end that cad Wibberly got up and asked Riddell some more about the boat-race—they're always hammering away at that, and what do you think Riddell said—guess!"

"I can't," said Wyndham.

"Why he said he knew who the chap was who had cut the strings, or fancied he did!"

"Who is it?" exclaimed Wyndham, excitedly.

"That's what he won't say. And of course there's an awful row on. They say they'll make him tell, or kick him out of the school or something. They're in no end of a rage."

"Why doesn't he tell who it is?" asked Wyndham.

"Oh, he says he's not sure, or something like that. But I dare say he'll tell you all about it this evening. You're to be sure and turn up, he says, at preparation time."

And off went this vivacious messenger, leaving Wyndham in a considerable state of astonishment and perturbation.

What did Riddell want him for? He had not seen him since that evening, a week ago, when he had so nearly confessed to him about Beamish's. He hardly liked not to go now, although he knew it would be hard to avoid letting out the wretched secret which he had promised Gilks and Silk to keep.

Besides, uneasy as he was about this, he could not help feeling excited about what Cusack had just told him of the boat-race affair. And most likely, when he came to consider, Riddell would be so full of that that he might perhaps not say any more about Beamish's. So Wyndham decided to go, and in due time presented himself with his books at the captain's study.

He could see at once that Riddell was in one of his serious moods, and his heart sank, for he had no doubt what was coming, and felt that, unless he were to break his promise, matters were sure to be made worse.

"I'm glad you've come," said Riddell; "you went off so suddenly the other evening."

"Yes," said Wyndham; "the lock-up bell rang, and I was bound to be in my house before it stopped."

"You know what I want to see you about now, Wyndham?" said the captain, nervously.

"Yes," replied the boy, doggedly; "I suppose I do."

There was a long, uncomfortable pause, at the end of which Riddell said, "Surely, Wyndham, you are not going to leave it to me to clear up this matter?"

"What do you mean?" asked the boy, burying his face in his hands, and utterly unnerved by the tones of his friend's voice.

"I mean this," said Riddell, as firmly as he could, "that there are only two courses open. Either you must confess what you have done, of your own accord, or it will be my duty to do it for you."

"I don't see how it's your duty to tell everybody," said the boy. "I should get expelled to a dead certainty!"

"It must either be one or the other," said the captain.

"Oh, Riddell!" exclaimed the boy, springing to his feet, "don't say that! I know I've been a cad, and let myself be led into it; but surely it's not so bad as all that! You've always been a brick to me, I know, and I've not been half grateful enough. But do let us off this time! please do! I can't tell you anything; I would gladly, only I've promised. You wouldn't have me break my promise? If you tell of me I shall be expelled I know I shall! Do help me out this time!"

"Poor fellow!" said Riddell, who was not proof against this sort of appeal from any one, least of all from one he loved.

The boy was quick in the energy of his despair to follow up his advantage.

"I'd make it good any other way—any way you like—but don't have me expelled, Riddell. Think of them all at home, what a state they would be in! I know I deserve it; but can't you get me out of it?"

"If you were to go to the doctor and tell him everything—" began Riddell.

"Oh, that's just what I can't do!" exclaimed Wyndham. "I'd do it like a shot if it was only myself in it. I don't know how you found it all out, I'm sure; but I can't go and tell the doctor, even if it was to get me off being expelled."

It was no use going on like this. Riddell was getting unmanned every moment, and Wyndham by these wild appeals was only prolonging the agony.

"Wyndham, old fellow," said the captain, in tones full of sympathy and pity, "if I had dreamt all this was to happen I would never have come to Willoughby at all. I know what troubles you have had this term, and how bravely you have been trying to turn over a new leaf. I'd give anything to be able to help you out of this, but I tell you plainly I don't see how to do it. If you like, I'll go with you to the doctor, and—"

"No, no!" exclaimed Wyndham, wildly, "I can't do that! I can't do that!"

"Then," said Riddell, gravely, "I must go to him by myself."

Wyndham looked up and tried to speak, and then fairly broke down.

"If the honour of the whole school were not involved—"

Wyndham looked up in a startled way. "The honour of the school? What has it got to do with my going to—"

What strange fatality was there about Riddell's study-door that it always opened at the most inopportune times?

Just as Wyndham began to speak it opened again, and Bloomfield, of all persons, appeared.

"I want to speak to you, Riddell," he said.

The words were uttered before he had noticed that the captain was not alone, or that his visitor was young Wyndham, in a state of great distress—hardly greater than that of Riddell himself.

As soon as he did perceive it he drew back, and said, "I beg your pardon; I didn't know any one was here."

"I'll go," said Wyndham, hurriedly, going to the door, and hardly lifting his eyes from the ground as he passed.

Bloomfield could hardly help noticing his strange appearance, or wondering at it.

"Anything wrong with young Wyndham?" said he, not sorry to have some way of breaking the ice.

"He's in trouble," said the captain. "Won't you sit down?"

It was a very long time since the head of Parrett's and the captain of the school had met in this polite way. But Bloomfield for some time past had shown signs of coming round to see that the position which had been forced upon him, and which he had been very ready at first to accept, was not a satisfactory one. And, greatly to the disgust of some of his fellow-monitors, he had shown this more than once by friendly advances towards his rival. But, so far, he had never got to the length of calling upon him in his study.

Riddell was scarcely surprised to see him, although he was quite unprepared for the very amicable way in which he began.

"I'm sorry to interrupt you," said Bloomfield, "but I've been intending to come over the last day or two."

"It's very good of you," said Riddell.

"The fact is," said Bloomfield, a little nervously, "ever since that debate in Parliament some weeks ago, when you spoke about all pulling together, I've felt that our fellows haven't done as much as they ought in that way—I know I haven't."

Riddell did not exactly know what to say. He could not say that the Parrett's fellows *had* "pulled together" for the good of the school, so he said nothing.

"I'm getting rather sick of it," continued Bloomfield, digging his hands in his pockets.

"So am I," said the captain.

"You know," said Bloomfield, "it was that wretched boat-race affair which made things as bad as they were. Our fellows wouldn't have kept it up so long if that hadn't happened."

Riddell began to get more and more uneasy. He had expected this was coming, and there was no escaping it.

"It was an awfully ugly business, of course," continued Bloomfield; "and though no one suspected fellows like you and Fairbairn of such a thing, our fellows, you know, were pretty sure some one was at the bottom of it."

Riddell could not help thinking, in the midst of his uneasiness, how very sagacious the Parrett's fellows had been to make the discovery!

"And now," said Bloomfield, looking up, and feeling relieved to have his speech nearly done—"now that you've found out who it is, and it's all going to be cleared up, I think things ought to come all right."

It was a painful situation for the captain of Willoughby. The bribe which Bloomfield offered for his secret was what had been the wish of his heart the whole term. If he accepted it now there would be an end to all the wretched squabbles which had worked such mischief in the school the last few months, and the one object of his ambition as head of the school would be realised.

Surely, now, he could hold back no longer. His duty, his interest, the honour of the school, all demanded his secret of him; whereas if he held it back things would be worse than ever before. And yet he hesitated.

That last wild half-finished exclamation of Wyndham's lingered in his mind and perplexed him. Suppose there should be some mistake? With that knife in his pocket, and the poor boy's whole conduct and demeanour to corroborate its story, he could scarcely hope it. But *suppose* there was a doubt, or even the shadow of a doubt, what right had he to accuse him, or even to breathe his name?

"I hope it will be cleared up before long," said he. "Why, you said you knew who it was!" said Bloomfield. "I said I suspected somebody."

"Who is it?" asked Bloomfield.

"I can't tell you," replied Riddell. "I'm not sure; I may be wrong."

"But surely you're not going to keep a thing like this to yourself!" exclaimed Bloomfield, warmly; "it concerns everybody in the school. I've a right, at any rate, as stroke of the Parrett's boat, to know who it is."

"Of course, you have; and if I was quite sure I was right I would tell you."

"But you can tell me whom you suspect," said Bloomfield, who had not anticipated this difficulty. "No, I cannot," replied the captain. "In confidence, at any rate," said Bloomfield. "No, not till I am sure. I really cannot."

Bloomfield's manner changed. This rebuff was not what he had expected. He had come here partly out of curiosity partly from a desire to be friendly, and partly owing to the eagerness of his companions to have an explanation. He had never doubted but that he would succeed; nay, even that Riddell would be glad to meet him more than half-way. But now it seemed this was not to be, and Bloomfield lost his temper.

"You mean to say," said he, angrily, "you're going to keep it to yourself?"

"Yes, till I am sure."

"Till you are sure! What are you going to do to make it sure, I'd like to know?"

"Everything I can."

"You know, I suppose, what everybody says about you and the whole concern?" said Bloomfield.

"I can't help what they say," said the captain. "They say that if you chose you could tell straight out like an honest man who it is."

Riddell looked quickly up at the speaker, and Bloomfield felt half ashamed of the taunt directly it escaped his lips.

"I say that's what the fellows think," said he, "and it's in your own interest to clear yourself. They think you are shielding some one."

The captain's face changed colour rapidly, and Bloomfield was quick enough to see it.

"It's hardly what fellows had been led to expect of you," said he, with a touch of sarcasm in his voice. "Anyhow it knocks on the head any idea of our pulling together as I had hoped. I certainly shall do nothing towards it as long as this ugly business is going on."

"Bloomfield, I've told you—" began Riddell.

"You've told me a great deal," said Bloomfield, "but you can't deny that you are sheltering the cad, whoever he is, under the pretext of not being quite sure."

Riddell said nothing, and Bloomfield, seeing nothing could come of this altercation, left the room.

At the door, however, a thought struck him. Could that agitated scene between Riddell and young Wyndham, which he had interrupted by his arrival, have had anything to do with this mystery?

He recollected now what a state of distress both had been in; and, now he thought of it, surely he had heard Wyndham's voice saying something in tones of very eager appeal at the moment the door was open. Besides Wyndham had been very "down" for a week past. Bloomfield had noticed it at the cricket practices; and more than one fellow had spoken of it in his hearing. He knew too how thick the boy was with the captain, and with what almost brotherly concern Riddell watched over all his interests; every one in Willoughby knew it.

Bloomfield was only a moderately clever youth, but he knew enough to put two and two together; and, as he stood there at the door, the state of the case flashed across his mind. He might get at the secret after all!

"You forget that other people can suspect besides you, Riddell," he said, turning back. "Suppose I was to suspect that precious young friend of yours who stood blubbering here just now?"

It was well for the captain that his back was turned as Bloomfield said this, otherwise the least doubt as to the correctness of his guess would have been instantly dispelled.

The last strait in which Riddell found himself was worse than any that had gone before. For he could not deny, and to say nothing would be the same as assenting. The secret was out, and what could he do? The only thing seemed to be to appeal to Bloomfield's generosity, to explain all to him, and to implore him, for a day or two at least, to keep sacred the confidence.

And yet—it was the old question—suppose he were wrong, and suppose after all Wyndham were not the culprit, what grievous wrong would he be doing him by admitting even his suspicion! He composed himself with an effort, and turning, replied, "Excuse me, Bloomfield, I've told you I can say nothing at present, and it is really useless to say any more about it."

Bloomfield departed, perplexed and angry. His anger was partly because he could not help feeling that Riddell was in the right; and his perplexity was to know what to think of it all, and whether his guess about young Wyndham was near the mark or not.

"Well," inquired Game, who with one or two of the most ardent Parretts was eagerly waiting his return. "Have you got it out of him?"

"No," said Bloomfield, "he won't tell me."

"The cad!" exclaimed Game. "Why ever not?"

"He says he's not sure, that's why," said Bloomfield; "but it's my private opinion he's shielding some one or other."

"Of course he is," said Ashley. "I shouldn't wonder if he's known who it is all along."

"Anyhow," said Tipper, "he ought to be made to clear it up, or else pay up for it. I know I'll cut him dead next time I see him."

"So shall we," replied one or two others.

"He won't afflict himself much about that," said Bloomfield; "if I were sure he didn't want to shirk it I'd be inclined to give him a day or two before doing anything."

"What's the use? Of course he wants to shirk it," said Game, "and thinks it will blow over if it goes long enough. I'll take precious good care it doesn't, though."

"Upon my honour," said Ashley, "I never expected Willoughby would *come* to this pass. It was bad enough to have a coward and a fool as captain, but it's rather too much when he turns out to be a cheat too!"

"And to think that he ever got stuck in the first eleven," said Tipper. "I told you, Bloomfield, he'd be no credit to you."

"He caught out that best man of theirs," said Bloomfield.

"Bah! I'd sooner have lost the match twice over," exclaimed Game, "than win it with his help!"

And so these estimable young gentlemen, satisfied that they alone were the glory and support of Willoughby, disposed in their own minds of their wicked captain, and thanked their lucky stars they were made of nobler stuff and loftier principle.

Chapter Twenty Eight.

Wyndham makes a final Venture.

If any proof had been needed that young Wyndham was "down," as the Parrett's fellows termed it, the fact that he did not put in appearance at the second-eleven practice next day supplied it.

Bloomfield, who in ordinary course had strolled round to watch the play, noticed his absence, and drew his own conclusions from it.

To Bloomfield's credit be it said that, whatever his own suspicions may have been, he had been as reluctant as Riddell himself, as long as any doubt existed, to name Wyndham publicly as the culprit for whom all Willoughby was on the lookout. He had been very angry with Riddell for his reserve, but when it came to the point of publishing his own suspicions or not, his better feeling prevented him, and led him to copy the captain's example.

For Riddell's reply to the suggestion of Wyndham's name had neither confirmed or denied its correctness. He had merely declined to say anything about the matter, so that as far as Bloomfield was concerned it was no more than a guess, and that being so, he too was wise enough to keep it to himself.

However, now that he noticed Wyndham's unwonted absence from the cricket practice, he felt more than ever convinced something was wrong in that quarter.

And so there was.

Wyndham, with a drawn sword, so to speak, over his head, was fit for nothing.

He dared not go back to Riddell. As long as his tongue was tied any explanation was impossible, and unless he could explain, it was worse than useless to talk to the captain.

Equally out of the question was a confession to the doctor, or a letter explaining all to his brother. The only thing was either to make up his mind to his fate, or else, by getting Silk and Gilks to release him from his promise, to get his tongue free to make a full confession of his own delinquencies, and throw himself entirely on the doctor's mercy.

This last chance seemed feeble enough. But a drowning man will clutch at a straw, and so Wyndham, as his last hope, faced the unpromising task of working on the generosity of his two old patrons.

He began with Gilks. Gilks was in his own house, and had always seemed to be the least vicious, as he was also the least clever of the two. Besides, of late it was notorious Gilks and Silk were no longer the friends they had been. There was a mystery about their recent quarrel; but as Gilks had been down in the mouth ever since, while Silk showed no signs of dejection, it was safe to assume the former had come off second best.

Wyndham therefore selected Gilks for his first attempt as being on the whole the less formidable of the two.

He found him in his study listlessly turning over the pages of a novel, which evidently must either have been a very stupid one or else not nearly as engrossing as the reader's own reflections.

He looked up with some surprise to see Wyndham, who since he had somewhat ostentatiously cut his and Silk's acquaintance some weeks ago, had never been near him.

"What do you want here?" he demanded, not very encouragingly.

"I know you've not much reason to be friendly with me," began the boy, "but I want to speak to you, if I may."

"What about?" said Gilks, roughly.

The poor boy seemed suddenly to realise the hopeless nature of the task he had undertaken, and he nearly broke down completely as he answered, "I'm in awful trouble, Gilks."

"What's that to do with me?" asked Gilks.

Wyndham struggled hard to shake off the weakness that had come over him, and replied, "It's about those visits to—to Beamish's. They—that is, Riddell—I don't know how or who told him—but he seems to have found out about it."

"Riddell!" cried Gilks, scornfully; "who cares for him?"

"Oh, but," continued Wyndham, tremulously, "he means to report me for it."

"What? report you? I thought you and he were such dear pious friends," sneered Gilks.

"We are friends; but he says it is his duty to do it."

Gilks laughed scornfully.

"Of course, it is! It only needs for a thing to be mean and low, and it will always be his duty to do it. Bah! the hypocrite!"

Wyndham was proof against this invective. Nay, bitterly as the captain's sense of duty affected him, he could not help a passing feeling of indignation on his friend's behalf at Gilk's words.

But he was prudent enough to keep his feelings to himself.

"Of course," said he, "if he does report me for it, I shall be expelled."

"You may be sure of that," replied Gilks, "but what's all this got to do with me?"

Wyndham looked up in surprise.

"Why," said he rather nervously. "Of course you know, we, that is you and I and Silk, are all sort of in the same boat over this affair. That is, if it all came out. But I fancy Riddell only suspects me."

"Well, if he does," said Gilks, "it's all the less any concern of mine."

"I promised, you know," said Wyndham, "to you and Silk to say nothing about it."

"Of course you did," said Gilks, "and you'd better stick to it, or it'll be the worse for you!"

"I think," continued the boy, "and Riddell says so—if I were to go and tell the Doctor about it, only about myself, you know, he might perhaps not expel me."

"Well?" said Gilks.

"Well," said Wyndham, "of course I couldn't do it after promising you and Silk. But I thought if I promised not to say anything about you and make out that it was all my fault, you wouldn't mind my telling Paddy."

Gilks looked at the boy in perplexity. This was a code of morality decidedly beyond him, and for a moment he looked as if he half doubted whether it was not a jest.

"What on earth do you mean, you young muff?" he exclaimed. "I mean, may I go and tell him that I went those two times to Beamish's? I promise to say nothing about you." Gilks laughed once more.

"What do I care what you go and tell him?" he said. "If you want to get expelled as badly as all that I don't want to prevent you, I'm sure."

"Then I really may?" exclaimed poor Wyndham, scarcely believing his own ears.

"Of course, if you keep me out of it, what on earth do I care what you tell him? You may tell him you murdered somebody there for all I care."

"Oh, thanks, thanks," cried Wyndham with a positively beaming face. "I give you my word I won't even mention you or Silk."

"As long as you don't mention me, that's all *I* care for," said Gilks; "and upon my word," added he, with a sigh half to himself, "I don't much care whether you do or not!"

Wyndham was too delighted and relieved to pay any heed to this last dreary remark, and gratefully took his leave, feeling that though the battle was anything but won yet he was at least a good deal nearer hope than he had been an hour ago.

But he very soon checked the reviving flow of his spirits as the prospect of an interview with Silk began to loom out ahead.

He had not seen Silk since the evening of the Rockshire match, when, as the reader will remember the meeting was anything but a pleasant one, and, but for the timely arrival of a third party, might have ended severely for the younger boy.

The recollection of this did not certainly add to the hopefulness of his present undertaking; but young Wyndham was a boy of such a sanguine temper, and such elastic spirits, that he could not help hoping something would turn up in his favour even now. He had got on far better than he had dared to hope with Gilks, why not also with Silk?

Besides, when all was said, it was his only chance, and therefore, whether he hoped anything or nothing, he must try it.

He wandered about during the hour between first and second school with the idea of coming across his man in the quadrangle or the playground. He could not make up his mind to beard the lion in his den; indeed at present he had every reason to fight shy of Welch's.

Second and third school passed before he was able to renew his search, and this time he was successful.

Just as he was beginning to give up hope, and was meditating a show-up for appearance's sake at the cricket practice, he caught sight of Silk lolling on a bench in a distant corner of the Big.

His heart sunk as he made the discovery, but it was no time for consulting his inclinations.

He moved timidly over in the direction of the bench, taking care to approach it from behind, so as to be spared the discomfort of a long inspection on the way.

Silk blissfully unconscious of the visit in store, was peacefully performing a few simple addition sums on the back of an envelope, and calculating how with six shillings he should be able to pay debts amounting to twenty-six, when Wyndham's shadow suddenly presented itself between him and his figures and gave him quite a start.

"Ah!" said he, in his usual friendly style, and to all appearances quite forgetful of the incidents of his last interview with this visitor. "Ah, Wyndham, so you've come back?"

"I wanted to see you very particularly," said the boy.

"Plenty of room on the seat," said Silk.

Wyndham, feeling far more uncomfortable at this civility than he had done at Gilk's roughness, sat down.

"Nice weather," said Silk, mockingly, after the pause had lasted some little time.

"I want to ask you a favour—a great favour," said Wyndham, feeling that a beginning must be made.

"Very kind of you," replied Silk, going on with his sums, and whistling softly to himself.

Wyndham did not feel encouraged. He had half a mind to back out of the venture even now, but desperation urged him on.

"You know I promised you never to say a word about Beamish's," he faltered, at length.

"So you did," replied Silk, drily.

"Would you mind letting me off that promise?"

"What?" exclaimed Silk, putting down his paper and pencil and staring at the boy.

"I mean only as far as I'm concerned," said Wyndham, hurriedly, trying to avert a storm.

"As far as you are concerned! What on earth are you talking about?" exclaimed the other.

"I want to confess to the doctor that I went those two times," said the boy. "I wouldn't mention your name or Gilk's. I only want to tell him about myself."

"Have you gone mad, or what?" cried Silk, utterly perplexed, as Gilks had been, to understand the boy's meaning.

Wyndham explained to him as best he could how the matter stood. How Riddell appeared to have discovered his delinquencies, and was resolved to report him. Of the certain result of such an exposure, and of the one hope he had, by voluntarily confessing all to the doctor, of averting his expulsion.

Silk listened to it all with a sneer, and when it was done, replied, "And you mean to say you've got the impudence to come to me to help to get you out of a scrape?"

"Please, Silk," said the boy, "I would be so grateful."

"Bah!" snarled Silk, "have you forgotten, then, the nice row you kicked up in my study a week ago? and the way you've treated me all this term? because if you have, I haven't."

"I know it's a lot to ask," pleaded the boy.

"It's a precious lot too much," said Silk; "and no one who hadn't got your cheek would do it!"

And he took up his paper and pencil again, and turned his back on the boy.

"Won't you do it, then?" once more urged Wyndham.

"Not likely!" rejoined Silk. "If you want favours you'd better go to your precious friend Riddell; and you can go as soon as you like. I don't want you here!"

"If you'd only do it," said Wyndham, "I'd—"

"Do you hear what I say?"

"I'd never ask you for the money you borrowed," said the boy quickly.

Silk laughed as he turned once more on his victim, and said, "Wouldn't you really? How awfully considerate! Upon my word, the generosity of some people is quite touching. Let's see, how much was it?"

"Thirty shillings," said Wyndham, "and the change out of the post-office order, two pounds."

"Which makes," said Silk, putting the figures down on his paper, "three pounds ten, doesn't it? and you think what you ask is worth three pounds ten, do you?"

"It's worth far more to me," said the boy, "because it's the only thing can save me from being expelled."

Silk mused a bit over his figures, and then replied, "And what would happen if I didn't pay you back?"

"I wouldn't say a word about it," cried the boy, eagerly, "if only you'd let me off the promise!"

"And suppose I told you I consider the promise worth just double what you do?"

Wyndham's face fell for a moment; he had not dared to write home about the loss of his last pocket-money, and saw very little chance of raising the wind for so large an amount again. Yet it seemed his only hope.

"Would that make it all right?" he asked.

"I might think about it," said Silk, with a sweet smile—"under conditions."

"I don't know how I can manage it," said Wyndham; "but I'll try. And you won't mind, then, my going to the doctor?"

"What! do you suppose I'm fool enough to let you do it before I have the money?" exclaimed Silk. "You must have a nice opinion of me!"

It was no use urging further; Wyndham saw he had got all he could hope for. It was little better than nothing, for before he could get the money—if he got it at all—the explosion might have come, and he would be expelled. If only Riddell, now, would wait a little longer!

As the thought crossed his mind he became aware that the captain was slowly approaching the bench on which he and Silk were sitting. It was anything but pleasant for the boy, after all that had happened, to be discovered thus, in close companionship with the very fellow he had promised to avoid, and whom he had all along acknowledged to be the cause of his troubles.

His instinct was to spring from his place and either escape or meet Riddell. But Silk saw the intention in time and forbade it.

"No," said he, with a laugh; "don't run away as if you were ashamed of it. Stay where you are; let him see you keep good company now and then."

"Oh, I must go!" exclaimed the boy; "he'll think all sorts of things. He'll think I'm such a hypocrite after what I promised him. Oh, do let me go!"

His agitation only increased the amusement of his tormentor, who, with a view to give the captain as vivid an impression as possible, laid his hand affectionately on the boy's arm and beamed most benignantly upon him. It was no use for Wyndham to resist. After all, suspicious as it might appear, he was doing nothing wrong.

And yet, what *would* Riddell think?

The captain was pacing the Big in a moody, abstracted manner, and at first appeared not to notice either the bench or its occupants. Wyndham, as he sat and trembled in Silk's clutches, wildly hoped something might cause him to turn aside or back. But no, he came straight on, and in doing so suddenly caught sight of the two boys.

He started and flushed quickly, and for a moment it looked as if he were inclined to make a wild dash to rescue the younger boy from the companionship in which he found him. But another glance changed that intention, if intention it had been.

His face fell, and he walked past with averted eyes, apparently recognising neither boy, and paying no heed to Wyndham's feebly attempted salute.

Before he was out of hearing Silk broke into a loud laugh. "Upon my word, it's as good as a play!" cried he. "You did it splendidly, young 'un! Looked as guilty as a dog, every bit! He'll give you up for lost now, with a vengeance!"

Wyndham's misery would have moved the pity of any one but Silk. The new hopes which had risen within him had been cruelly dashed by this unhappy accident, and he felt no further care as to what happened to him. Riddell would have lost all faith in him now; he would appear little better than an ungrateful hypocrite and impostor. The last motive for sparing him would be swept away, and—so the boy thought—the duty of reporting him would now become a satisfaction.

He tore himself from the seat, and exclaimed, "Let me go, you brute!"

Silk looked at him in astonishment; then, relapsing into a smile, said, "Oh, indeed! a brute, am I?"

"Yes, you are!"

"And, let's see; I forget what the little favour was you wanted the brute to do for you?"

"I want you to do *no* favour!" cried Wyndham, passionately.

"No? Not even to allow you to go to the doctor and tell him about Beamish's?"

"No; not even that! I wouldn't do it now. He may now find out what he likes."

"It might interest him if I went and told him a few things about you?" said Silk.

"Go! as soon as you like—and tell him anything you like," cried Wyndham. "I don't care."

"You wouldn't even care to have back your three pound ten?"

"No," said the boy, "not even if you ever thought of paying it back."

Silk all this time had been growing furious. The last thing he had expected was that this boy, whom he supposed to be utterly in his power, should thus rise in revolt and shake off every shred of his old allegiance. But he found he had gone too far for once, and this last defiant taunt of his late victim cut him to the quick.

He sprang from the seat and made a wild dash at the boy, but Wyndham was too quick for him, and escaped, leaving his adversary baffled as he had never been before, and almost doubting whether he had not been and still was dreaming.

Wyndham ran as fast as he could in the direction of the school, and would have probably gone *on* running till he reached his own study, had not the sight of Riddell slowly going the same way ahead of him suddenly checked his progress.

As it was, he almost ran over him before he perceived who it was. For Riddell just at that moment had halted in his walk, and stooped to pick up a book that lay on the path.

121

However, when Wyndham saw who it was, he swerved hurriedly in another direction, and got to his destination by a roundabout way, feeling as he reached it about as miserable and hopeless as it was possible for a boy to be.

Chapter Twenty Nine.

A Select Party at the Doctor's.

Young Wyndham, had he only known what was in the captain's mind as he walked that afternoon across the Big, would probably have thought twice before he went such a long way round to avoid him.

Silk's little piece of pantomime had not had the effect the author intended. In the quick glance which Riddell had given towards the bench and its occupants he had taken in pretty accurately the real state of the case.

"Poor fellow!" said he to himself; "he's surely in trouble enough without being laid hold of by that cad. Silk thinks I shall fancy he has captured my old favourite. Let him! But if he has captured him he doesn't seem very sure of him, or he wouldn't hold him down on the seat like that. I wonder what brings them together here? and I wonder if I had better go and interfere? No, I think I won't just now."

And so he walked on, troubled enough to be sure, but not concluding quite as much from what he saw as Wyndham feared or Silk hoped.

As he walked on fellows glared at him from a distance, and others passing closer cut him dead. A few of the most ardent Parrett's juniors took the liberty of hissing him and one ventured to call out, pointedly, "Who cut the rudder-lines?"

Riddell, however, though he winced under these insults, took little notice of them. He was as determined as ever to wait the confirmation of his suspicions before he unmasked the culprit, and equally convinced that duty and honour both demanded that he should lose not a moment in coming to a conclusion.

It was in the midst of these reflections that the small book which Wyndham had seen him pick up caught his eye. He picked it up mechanically, and after noticing that it appeared to be a notebook, and had no owner's name in the beginning, carried it with him, and forgot all about it till he reached his study.

Even here it was some time before it again attracted his attention, as its importance was wholly eclipsed by the contents of a note which he found lying on his table, and which ran as follows:

"Dear Riddell,—Will you join us at tea this evening at seven? I expect Fairbairn and Bloomfield.

"Yours faithfully,—

"R. Patrick."

Riddell groaned. Had he not had trouble, and humiliation, and misery enough? What had he done to deserve this crowning torture? Tea with the Griffins!

He sat down and wrote, as in politeness bound, that he would have much pleasure in accepting the doctor's kind invitation, and, sending the note off by Cusack, resigned himself to the awful prospect, which for a time shut out everything else.

However, he had no right, he felt, to be idle. He must finish his work now, so as to be free for the evening's "entertainment," and for the other equally grave duties which lay before him.

But somehow he could not work; his mind was too full to be able to settle steadily on any one thing, and finally he pushed away the books and gave up the attempt.

It was at that moment that the small black book he had found caught his eye.

He took it up, intending, if possible, to ascertain whose property it was, and, failing that, to send Cusack to "cry" it round the school.

But the first thing that met his eye on the front page roused his curiosity. It was evidently a quotation:

"Pass me not, oh! reader, by,

Read my pages tenderly ('tenderly' altered to 'on the sly');

All that's writ is writ for thee,

Open now and you shall see."

After such a cordial invitation, even Riddell could hardly feel much qualm about dipping farther into this mysterious manuscript.

It appeared to be a diary, which, but for the announcement at the beginning, one would have been inclined to regard as a private document. And the first entry Riddell encountered was certainly of that character:

"Friday, the fifth day of the week.—My birthday. Rose at 6:59½. I am old. I am 24 (and ten off) some one had taken my soap. Meditations As I dressed me. The world is very large I am small in the world I will aspire as I go to chapel I view Riddell who toucheth his hat. Gross conduct of my father sending me only half a crown breakfast at 7:33. Disturbance with the evil Telson whereby I obtained lines."

This was quite enough for one day, and Riddell, greatly mystified, turned a few pages farther on to see if the narrative became more lucid as it progressed.

"I am now a skyrocket. Meditations on being a skyrocket. The world is very large, etcetera. Gross meeting of Parliament Riddell the little captain sitteth on his seat. I made a noble speech gross conduct of Parson, who is kicked out. Eloquence of Bloomfield who crieth Order under the form I see Telson hanging on. I hang too and am removed speaking nobly. Large tea at Parson's the cake being beastly. Riddell it seems hath cut the rudder-lines. I indignate and cut him with a razor I remove two corns from my nether foot."

More in this strain followed, and lower down the diary proceeded:

"Wyndham the junior thinketh much of himself he is ugly in the face and in the second-eleven. I have writ a poem on Wyndham.

"'I do not like thee, Dr Fell (altered to "Wyndham junior")

The reason why I cannot tell (altered to "say");

But this I know, and know full well (altered to "ill")

I do not like thee, Dr Fell (altered to "Wyndham junior").'

"I over hear much of Wyndham the gross Telson and the evil Parson not knowing I am by the little boys say they have seen the ugly Wyndham come from Beamish's. Oh evil Wyndham being taken by Silk and Gilks. No one knows and Wyndham is to be expelled. I joy much Riddell knoweth it. Telson telleth Parson that Riddell is gross expelling for Beamish's and Wyndham weepeth in private. I smile at the practice Mr Parrett bowleth me balls. I taketh them and am out."

If Bosher could have seen the effect of this elegant extract upon the captain he would probably have "joyed" with infinite self-satisfaction. Riddell's colour changed as he read and re-read and re-read again these few lines of idiotic jargon.

He lay down the book half a dozen times, and as often took it up again, and scrutinised the entry, and as he did so quick looks of perplexity, or joy, or shame, even of humour, chased one another across his face.

The truth with all its new meaning slowly dawned upon him. It had been reserved to Bosher's diary, of all agencies in the world, to explain everything, and cast a flood of light upon what had hitherto been incomprehensible!

Of course he could see it all now. If this diary was to be believed—but was it? Might it not be a hoax purposely put in his way to delude him?

Yet he could not believe that this laboriously written record could have been compiled for his sole benefit; and this one entry which he had lit upon by mere chance was only one of hundreds of stupid, absurd entries, most of which meant nothing at all, and which seemed more like the symptoms of a disease than the healthy productions of a sane boy.

In this one case, however, there seemed to be some method in the author's madness, and he had given a clue so important that Riddell, in pondering over it that evening and calculating its true value, was very nearly being late for the doctor's tea at seven o'clock.

However, he came to himself just in time to decorate his person, and hurry across the quadrangle before the clock struck.

On his way over he met Parson and Telson, walking arm-in-arm. Although the same spectacle had met his eyes on an average twice every day that term, and was about the commonest "show" in Willoughby, the sight of the faithful pair at this particular time when the revelations of Bosher's diary were tingling in his ears impressed the captain. Indeed, it impressed him so much that, at the imminent risk of being late for the doctor's tea, he pulled up to speak to them.

Parson, as became a loyal Parrett, made as though he would pass on, but Telson held him back.

"I say, you two," said Riddell, "will you come to breakfast with me to-morrow morning after chapel?"

And without so much as waiting for a reply, he bolted off, leaving his two would-be guests a trifle concerned as to his sanity.

The clock was beginning to strike as Riddell knocked at the doctor's door, and began at length to realise what he was in for.

He did not know whether to be thankful or not that Bloomfield and Fairbairn would be there to share his misery. They would be but two extra witnesses to his sufferings, and their tribulations were hardly likely to relieve his.

However, there was one comfort. He might have a chance before the evening was over of telling Bloomfield that he now had every reason to believe his suspicions about the culprit had been wrong.

How thankful he was he had held out against the temptation to name poor Wyndham two days ago!

"Well, Riddell, how are you?" said the doctor, in his usual genial fashion. "I think you have met these ladies before. Mr Riddell—my dear—Miss Stringer. These gentlemen you have probably seen before also. Ha! ha!"

Riddell saluted the ladies very much as he would have saluted two mad dogs, and nodded the usual Willoughby nod to his two fellow-monitors, who having already got over the introductions had retreated to a safe distance.

A common suffering is the surest bond of sympathy, and Riddell positively beamed on his rival in recognition of his salute.

"I trust your mother," said Mrs Patrick, "whose indisposition we were regretting on the last occasion when you were here, is now better?"

"Very well indeed, I hope," replied the captain, hardly knowing what he said. "Thank you."

"And I trust, Mr Riddell," chimed in Miss Stringer, "that you were gratified by the result of the election."

"No, thank you," replied Riddell, beginning to shake in his shoes.

"Indeed? If I remember right you professed yourself to be a Liberal?"

"Yes—that is—the Radical got in," faltered Riddell, wondering why in common charity no one came to his rescue.

"And pray, Mr Riddell," continued Miss Stringer, ruthlessly, "can you tell us the difference between a Liberal and a Radical? I have often longed to know—and you I have no doubt are an authority?"

Riddell at this point seriously meditated a forced retreat, and there is no saying what desperate act he might have committed had not the doctor providentially come to the rescue.

"The election altogether," said he, laughing, "is rather a sore point in the school. I told you, my dear, about the manner in which Mr Cheeseman's letter was received?"

"You did," replied Mrs Patrick, who for some few moments had had her eyes upon Bloomfield, with a view to draw him out.

"Now do you really suppose, Mr Bloomfield, that the boys in your house, for instance, attached any true importance at all to the issue of the contest?"

Bloomfield, who had not been aware till this question was half over that it had been addressed to him, started and said—the most fatal observation he could have made—

"Eh? I beg your pardon, that is."

"I inquired," said Mrs Patrick, fixing him with her eye, "whether you really supposed that the boys in your house, for instance, attached any true importance at all to the issue of the contest?"

Bloomfield received this ponderous question meekly, and made a feeble effort to turn it over in his mind, and then dreading to hear it repeated once more, answered, "Oh, decidedly, ma'am."

"In what respect?" inquired the lady, settling herself down on the settee, and awaiting, with raised eyebrows, her victim's answer.

Poor Bloomfield was no match for this deliberate style of tactics.

"They were all yellow," he replied, feebly.

"All what, sir?" demanded Mrs Patrick.

"All Whig, I mean," he said.

"Exactly. What I mean to know is, do they any of them appreciate the distinction between a Whig (or, as Mr Riddell terms it, a Liberal)—"

Riddell winced.

"—Between a Whig and a Radical?"

"Oh, certainly not," replied Bloomfield, wildly. "And yet you say that they decidedly attached a true importance to the issue of the contest? That is very extraordinary!"

And Mrs Patrick rose majestically to take her seat at the table, leaving Bloomfield writhing and turned mentally inside out, to recover as best he could from this interesting political discussion!

"The Rockshire match was a great triumph," said the doctor, cheerily, as the company established itself at the festive board—"and a surprise too, surely—was it not?"

"Yes, sir," said Fairbairn, who, seeing that Bloomfield was not yet in a condition to discourse, felt it incumbent on him to reply—"we never expected to win by so much."

"It was quite an event," said the doctor, "the heads of the three houses all playing together in the same eleven."

"Yes, sir," replied Fairbairn, "Bloomfield here was most impartial."

Bloomfield said something which sounded like "Not at all."

"I was especially glad to see the Welchers coming out again," said the doctor, with a friendly nod to Riddell.

"Yes," said Fairbairn, who appeared to be alarmingly at his ease; "and Welch's did good service too; that catch of Riddell's saved us a wicket or two, didn't it, Bloomfield?"

"Yes," replied Bloomfield.

"Was Rockshire a specially weak team this year?" asked the doctor.

"I don't think so, sir," replied Fairbairn, politely handing the toast to Miss Stringer as he spoke; "but they evidently weren't so well together as our men."

"And what, Mr Fairbairn," asked Miss Stringer at this point, in her most stately tones—"what, pray, is the exact meaning of the expression 'well together,' as applied to a company of youths?"

Bloomfield and Riddell groaned inwardly for their comrade. They had seen what was coming, and had marked his rash approach to the mouth of the volcano with growing apprehension. They had been helpless to hold him back, and now his turn was come—he had met his fate.

So, at least, they imagined. What, then, was their amazement when he turned not a hair at the question, but replied, stirring his tea complacently as he did so, "You see, each of the Rockshire men may have been a good cricketer, and yet if they had not been used to playing together, as our fellows have been, we should have a decided pull on them."

Miss Stringer regarded the speaker critically. She had not been used to have her problems so readily answered, and appeared to discover a suspicion of rudeness in the boy's speech which called for a set-down.

"I do not understand what you mean by a 'pull,' Mr Fairbairn," said she, sternly.

"Why," replied Fairbairn, who was really interested in the subject, and quite pleased to be drawn out on so congenial a topic, "it's almost as important to get to know the play of your own men as to know the play of your opponents. For instance, when we all know Bloomfield's balls break a bit to the off, we generally know whereabouts in the field to expect them if they are taken; and when Porter goes on with slows every one knows to stand in close and look out for catches."

"Yes," said Bloomfield, gaining sudden courage by the example of his comrade, "that's just where Rockshire were weak. They were always shifting about their field and bowlers. I'm certain they had scarcely played together once."

"And," added Riddell, also taking heart of grace, and entering into the humour of the situation—"and they seemed to save up their good bowlers for the end, instead of beginning with them. All our hitting men got the easy bowling, and the others, who were never expected to score in any case, were put out by the good."

"In this respect, you see," continued Fairbairn, addressing Miss Stringer, "a school eleven always get the pull of a scratch team."

Miss Stringer, who during this conversation had been growing manifestly uncomfortable, vouchsafed no reply, but, turning to her sister, said, with marked formality, "My dear, were the Browns at home when you called this afternoon?"

"I regret to say they were out," replied Mrs Patrick, with a withering glance round the table.

"Of course, it depends, too," said Bloomfield, replying to Fairbairn's last question and giving him an imperceptible sly kick under the table, "on whether it's early or late in the season. If we were to play them in August they would know their own play as well as we know ours."

"Only," chimed in Riddell, "these county teams don't stick to the same elevens as regularly as a school does."

"My dear, have you done your tea?" inquired Mrs Patrick's voice across the table.

"Yes. Shall I ring?" said the doctor.

"Allow me," said Fairbairn, rising hastily, and nearly knocking over Miss Stringer in his eagerness.

The spinster, who had already received in her own opinion sufficient affront for one evening, put the worst construction possible on this accident, and answered with evident ill-temper, "You are very clumsy, sir!"

"I beg your pardon, indeed!" said Fairbairn. "I hope you are not hurt?"

"Be silent, sir!"

Fairbairn, quite taken aback by this unexpected exclamation, did not know what to say, and looked round inquiringly at the doctor, as much as to ask if the lady was often taken this way.

The doctor, however, volunteered no explanation, but looked uncomfortable and coughed.

"If you will excuse me," said Miss Stringer to her sister, with a forced severity of tone, "I will go to my room."

"You are not well, I fear," said Mrs Patrick. "I will go with you"; and next moment the enemy was gone, and the doctor and his boys were together.

Dr Patrick, who, to tell the truth, seemed scarcely less relieved than his visitors, made no attempt to apologise for Miss Stringer's sudden indisposition, and embarked at once on a friendly talk about school affairs.

This had been his only object in inviting the boys. He had nothing momentous to say, and no important change to propose. Indeed, his object appeared to be more to get them to talk among themselves on matters of common interest to the school, and to let them see that his sympathy was with them in their efforts for the public good.

No reference was made to the state of affairs in Parrett's, or to the rivalries of the two captains. That the doctor knew all about these matters no one doubted, but he took the wise course of leaving them to right themselves, and at the same time of making it very clear what his opinions were of the effect of disunion and divided interest in a great public school.

Altogether the evening was profitably and pleasantly spent, and when at length the boys took their leave it was with increased respect for the head master and one another.

The ladies, greatly to their relief, did not return to the scene.

"Miss Stringer," said Fairbairn, as the three walked together across the quadrangle, "doesn't seem to appreciate cricket."

The others laughed.

"I say," said Bloomfield, "you put your foot into it awfully! She thought you were chaffing her all the time."

"Did she? What a pity!" replied Fairbairn.

"Of course, we were bound to help you out when you were once in," continued Bloomfield. "But I don't fancy we three will be asked up there again in a hurry."

They came to the schoolhouse gate, and Fairbairn said good-night. Riddell and Bloomfield walked on together towards Parrett's.

"Oh, Bloomfield!" said the captain, nervously, "I just wanted to tell you that I believe I have been all wrong in my guess about the boat-race affair. The boy I suspected, I now fancy, had nothing to do with it."

"You are still determined to keep it all to yourself, then?" asked Bloomfield, somewhat coldly.

"Of course," replied the captain.

At this point they reached Parrett's. Neither boy had any inclination to pursue the unpleasant topic—all the more unpleasant because it was the one bar to a friendship which both desired.

"Good-night," said Bloomfield, stiffly.

"Good-night," replied the captain.

Chapter Thirty.

New Lights on old Questions.

Fairbairn was startled next morning while engaged over his toilet by a sudden visit from the captain.

What could be wrong to bring him there at this hour, with a face full of anxiety and a voice full of concern, as he inquired, "Will you do me a favour, old man?"

Fairbairn knew his friend had been in trouble for some time past, and was sore beset on many hands. He had not attempted to intrude into his secrets or to volunteer any aid. For he knew Riddell would ask him if he wanted it. In proof of which here he was.

"Of course, I will," replied he, "if I can."

"Do you happen to have a pot of jam you could lend me?"

Fairbairn fairly staggered at this unexpected request. He had imagined he was to be asked at the very least to accompany his friend on some matter of moment to the doctor's study, or to share some tremendous secret affecting the honour of Willoughby. And to be asked now for the loan of a pot of jam was too great a shock for his gravity, and he burst out laughing.

"A pot of jam!" he exclaimed. "Whatever do you mean?"

"Oh, any sort you've got," said the captain, eagerly; "and I suppose you haven't got a pie of any sort, or some muffins?"

Fairbairn gaped at his visitor with something like apprehension as he came out with this extraordinary request. The captain's voice was grave, and *no* suspicion of a jest lurked in his face. Could he possibly have succumbed to the mental strain of the past term, and taken leave of his wits?

"What *are* you talking about, Riddell?" asked Fairbairn, in tones almost of pity. "Has anything happened to you?"

Riddell looked at the speaker inquisitively for a moment, then broke out into a laugh.

"What an ass I am! I forgot to tell you what I wanted them for. The fact is, I asked two kids to breakfast this morning, and I just remembered I had nothing but tea and toast to offer them; and it's too early to get anything in. I'd be awfully obliged if you could help me out with it."

Fairbairn's merriment broke out afresh as the truth revealed itself, and it was some time before he could attend to business. He then offered Riddell anything he could find in his cupboard, and the captain thereupon gratefully availed himself of the offer to secure a pot of red-currant jam, a small pot of potted meat, two or three apples, and a considerable section of a plum cake. All these he promised to replace without delay, and triumphantly hurried back with them in his pocket and under his jacket, in time to deposit them on his table before the bell began to ring for chapel. He also sent Cusack round to the school larder to order three new laid eggs and some extra butter to be delivered at once.

These grand preparations being duly made, he breathed again, and went hopefully to chapel.

As it happened, he had been very near reckoning without his host, or I should say his guests. For Parson and Telson had been some time before they could make up their minds to accept the hurried invitation of the previous evening.

"It's a row," Telson had said, as the captain disappeared.

"Of course it is. I'm not going," said Parson.

"Wonder what about?"

"Oh, that Skyrocket affair, I suppose."

"Do you think he'll give us impots if we don't go?"

"Don't know—most likely."

"Rum, his asking us to breakfast, though," said Telson.

"All a dodge, I expect," said Parson. "By the way, what sort of breakfasts does he go in for?"

"Not bad when he likes," said Telson, with the authority of an old fag.

"Bacon?" asked Parson.

"Sometimes," said Telson.

"Jam?" inquired Parson.

"Generally," replied Telson.

There was a pause. Then Parson said, "Fancy we'd better turn up. It's only civil, when he asked us."

"All serene," said Telson; "if it is a row, of course it will come off in any case. And we may as well get our breakfast somewhere."

With which philosophical resolve the matter had been settled, and the amiable pair parted to meet next morning after chapel.

Riddell spared himself the embarrassment of waiting to escort his guests to the festive board, and hurried off in advance to see that the preparations were duly made in their honour.

He caught Cusack wistfully eyeing the unwonted array of good things on the table, and evidently speculating as to who the favoured guests were to be. It was with some difficulty that the captain got him sent off to his own breakfast in the big hall, half bribed thereto by the promise of a reversion of the coming feast.

Then, feeling quite exhausted by his morning's excitement, he sat down and awaited his visitors.

They arrived in due time; still, to judge of their leisurely approach and their languid knock, a little suspicious of the whole affair. But the moment the door opened, and their eyes fell on the table, their manner changed to one of the most amiable briskness.

"Good-morning," said Riddell, who, in the presence of the greater attractions on the table, ran considerable risk of being overlooked altogether.

"Good-morning," cried the boys, suddenly roused by his voice to a sense of their social duty.

"Awfully brickish of you to ask us round," said Telson.

"Rather," chimed in Parson.

"I'm glad you came," said the captain. "We may as well have breakfast. Telson, have you forgotten how to boil eggs?"

Telson said emphatically he had not, and proceeded forthwith to give practical proof of his cunning, while Parson volunteered his aid in cutting up the bread, and buttering the toast.

In due time the preliminaries were all got through, and the trio sat down to partake of the reward of their toil.

Riddell could not thank his stars sufficiently that he had thought of embellishing his feast with the few luxuries from Fairbairn's cupboard. Nothing could exceed the good-humour of the two juniors as one delicacy after another unfolded its charms and invited their attention. They accompanied their exertions with a running fire of chat and chaff, which left Riddell very little to do except gently to steer the conversation round towards the point for which this merry meeting was designed.

"Frightful job to get old Parson to turn up," said Telson, taking his fourth go-in of potted meat; "he thought you were going to row him about that shindy in the Parliament!"

"No, I didn't," rejoined Parson, pushing up his cup for more tea. "It was you said that about blowing up us Skyrockets."

"What a howling cram," said Telson. "I never make bad jokes. You know, Riddell, it was Parson stuck us up to that business. He's always at the bottom of the rows."

Parson laughed at this compliment.

"You mean I always *get* into the rows," said he.

"Anyhow, I don't suppose the Skyrockets will show up again this term," said Telson.

"They certainly did not get much encouragement last time," said Riddell, laughing. "You know I don't think you fellows do yourselves justice in things like that. Fellows get to think the only thing you're good at is a row."

"Fact is," said Parson, "Telson thought we'd been so frightfully snubbed this term, we kids, that he said we ought to stick up for ourselves."

"I said that?" cried Telson. "Why, you know it was you said it!"

"By the way," said Parson, "wasn't there to be a special meeting of the House to-day, for something or other?"

Telson looked rather uncomfortable, and then said, "Yes, I heard so. I fancy it's about you, somehow," added he, addressing Riddell.

"About me?" asked the captain.

"Yes—to kick you out, or something," said Telson; "but Parson and I mean to go and vote against it."

This was news to Riddell, and rather astonishing news too.

"To kick me out?" he asked. "What for?"

"Oh, you know," said Parson. "It's some bosh about that boat-race affair. Some of the chaps think you are mixed up in it, but of course it's all a cram. I've told them so more than once."

"It's all those Parrett's cads," said Telson, taking up the matter from a schoolhouse point of view. "They're riled about the race, and about the cricket-match, and everything else, and try to make out every one's cheating."

"Well, some one must have been cheating," said Parson, a trifle warmly, "when he cut my rudder-lines; and he's not likely to be one of *our* fellows—much more likely to be a schoolhouse cad!"

"I'll fight you, you know, Parson!" put in Telson.

Riddell saw it was time to interfere. The conversation was drifting into an unprofitable channel, from which it would scarcely work its way out unassisted.

What he wanted was to find out whether there was any truth in the explanation which the diary afforded of young Wyndham's conduct, and he was a long way from that yet.

"Have some more cake, Telson," said he, by way of changing the subject.

Telson cheerfully accepted the invitation, while Parson, to spare his host the trouble of pressing him to take an apple, helped himself.

Then when they were well started once more the captain said, "Who's going to win the juniors' match, Parson? Our fellows quite think they are."

"Yes," said Parson, contemptuously; "I heard they had cheek enough to say so. But they'll be disappointed for once."

"Well," said Riddell, "they've been practising pretty steadily of late. They're not to be despised. Whatever has become of the juniors' eleven in the schoolhouse, Telson?"

"Can't make out," replied Telson; "they're an awful set of louts this year; only one or two good men in the lot. I don't think they can scrape up an eleven."

"Ah!" said the captain, seeing his chance; "you've lost a good many good fellows. Wyndham, for one, has got up into the second-eleven, I hear."

"Yes," said Parson; "and jolly cocky he is about it, too!"

"He's not been down at the practices lately, though," said Telson, colouring slightly, and for no apparent reason.

"Why? Is he seedy?" said the captain.

"Eh! No; I don't think so. Wyndham's not seedy, is he, should you think, Parson?"

"No," said Parson, exchanging uncomfortable glances with his ally; "not exactly seedy."

"It'll be a pity if he doesn't get playing in the Templeton match," said Riddell.

Would the fish bite? If the diary had spoken true, these two boys were at present very full of Wyndham's affair, and a trifle indignant with the captain himself for his supposed intention of reporting that youth's transgression at headquarters. If that were so, Riddell considered it possible that, after their honest fashion, they might take upon themselves to give him a piece of their mind, which was exactly what he wanted.

"The fact is," said Telson, "Parson and I both think he's down in the mouth."

"Indeed?" asked the captain, busily buttering a fresh slice of toast.

"Yes. Haven't you seen it?" asked Parson.

"He's in a funk about something or other," said Telson.

It was getting near now!

"What about, do you know?" asked the captain.

"Why, you know," said Telson. "About being expelled, you know."

"Expelled! What for?" asked Riddell; and the boy's reply gave him a satisfaction quite out of proportion to its merits.

"About Beamish's, you know," said Telson, confidentially; "he thinks you're going to report him."

"And he's bound to get expelled if you do," said Parson.

"And how do you know about it?" asked the captain, quietly.

"Oh! you know, Parson and I spotted them—that is, Gilks and Silk and him—that night of Brown's party. But we never told anybody, and don't mean to, so I don't know how it came out."

"Anyhow," said Parson, "if he's to be expelled, Silk and Gilks ought to catch it too. I bet anything they took him there. Thanks! a little piece."

This last sentence was in reply to an invitation to take some more cake.

Under cover of this diversion, Riddell, with thankful heart, continued to steer the talk out again into the main channel of school affairs, of which the affair of Wyndham junior was but one of many.

Before the meal was over it had got as far Eutropius, and he fairly won his guests' hearts by announcing that he did not consider that historian's Latin nearly as good as Caesar's, an opinion which they endorsed with considerable heat.

All good things come to an end at last, and so did this breakfast, the end of which found the boys in as great good-humour as at the beginning. They thanked the captain most profusely for his hospitality, which they never doubted was meant as a recognition of their own sterling merits, and of the few attempts they had lately made to behave themselves; and, after inviting him to come to a concert they were about to give on the evening of the juniors' match, took their departure.

"By the way," said Riddell, as they were going, "do either of you know to whom this book belongs? I found it in the playground yesterday."

A merry laugh greeted the appearance of Bosher's diary, which the pair recognised as a very old friend.

"It's old Bosher's diary," said Telson. "He's always dropping it about. I believe he does it on purpose. I say, isn't it frightful bosh?"

"It isn't very clear in parts," said the captain.

"Did he call you 'evil,' or 'gross,' or 'ugly in the face,' in the part you looked at?" asked Telson; "because, if so, we may as well lick him for you."

"No, don't do that," said Riddell; "you had better give it him back, though, and advise him from me not to drop it about more than he can help. Good-bye."

With a great weight off his mind, Riddell went down to first school that day a thankful though a humbled man.

What a narrow escape he had had of doing the boy he cared for most in Willoughby a grievous injustice. Indeed, by suspecting him privately he had done him injustice enough as it was, for which he could not too soon atone.

In the midst of his relief about the boat-race he could scarcely bring himself to regard seriously the boy's real offence, bad as that had been; and, indeed, it was not until Wyndham himself referred to it that afternoon that its gravity occurred to him.

Just as the special meeting of the Parliament (convened by private invitation of Game and Ashley to a select few of their own way of thinking) was assembling, Wyndham, in compliance with a message from the captain, strolled out into the Big towards the *very* bench where yesterday he had had his memorable talk with Silk.

Riddell was waiting there for him, and as the boy approached, his wretched, haggard looks smote the captain's heart with remorse.

He had scarcely the spirit to return Riddell's salute as he seated himself beside him on the bench and waited for what was to come.

"Old fellow," said Riddell, "don't look so wretched. Things mayn't be so bad as you think."

"How could they be anything else?" said Wyndham, dolefully.

"If you'll listen to me, and not look so frightfully down," said the captain, "I'll tell you."

Wyndham made a feeble attempt to rouse himself, and turned to hear what the captain had to say.

"You wonder," said Riddell, "how I came to know about that visit to Beamish's. Would it astonish you to hear that till this time yesterday I never knew about it at all?"

"What!" exclaimed Wyndham, incredulously; "you were talking to me about it two or three days before."

"So you thought. You thought when I said it was my duty to report it, and that the honour of the school was involved in it, and all that, that I was talking about that scrape at Beamish's."

"Of course you were," said Wyndham. "What else could you have been talking about? I confessed it to you myself."

"And you couldn't see what the honour of the school had to do with your going to Beamish's, could you?" asked Riddell.

"Well, no. Perhaps it has, but I didn't see it at the time."

"Of course not," said the captain, "and if I had been thinking of Beamish's I should never have said such a stupid thing."

"Why, what *do* you mean?" said Wyndham, puzzled.

"Why, this. In all our talks you never once mentioned Beamish's. You concluded what I suspected you of was this, and I concluded that the scrape you were confessing was the one I suspected you of."

"What do you suspect me of, then?" inquired Wyndham, "if it wasn't that?"

"I'm ashamed to say," said the captain, "I suspected you of having cut the lines of Parrett's rudder at the boat-race."

Wyndham, in the shock of this announcement, broke out into an almost hysterical laugh.

"Suspected me of cutting the rudder-lines!" he gasped.

"Yes," said Riddell, sorrowfully. "I'm ashamed to say it."

"Why, however could you?" exclaimed the boy, in strange bewilderment.

Riddell quietly told him the whole story. Of the mysterious letter, of his visit to Tom the boat-boy, of the knife, of the recollection of Wyndham's movements on the night in question, and then of his supposed admission of his guilt.

Wyndham listened to it all with breathless attention and wonder, and when it was all done sighed as he replied, "Why, Riddell, it's like a story, isn't it?"

"It is," said the captain, "and rather a pitiful story as far as I am concerned."

"Not a bit," replied the boy, as sympathetically as if Riddell was the person to be pitied and he was the person who had wronged him. "It was all a misunderstanding. How on earth could you have helped suspecting me? Any one would have done the same.

"But," added he, after a pause, "what ought I to do about Beamish's? Of course that was no end of a scrape, and the mischief is, I promised those two cads never to say a word about it. By the way, you saw me with Silk on this bench yesterday afternoon?"

"Yes," said Riddell; "you didn't seem to be enjoying yourself."

"I should think I wasn't. I'd been trying to get him to let me off that promise, and he had offered to do it for seven pounds, under condition. I might have closed with him if you hadn't come past just then. He held me down to rile you, and I got so wild I rounded on him and made him in a frightful rage, and it's very likely now he may tell Paddy if you don't."

"Not he," said Riddell. "You're well out of his clutches, old man, and it strikes me the best way you can atone for that affair is by keeping out of it for the future, and having no more to do with fellows like that."

"What on earth should I have done," said the boy, "without you to look after me? I'd have gone to the dogs, to a dead certainty."

"It seems I can look after you rather too much sometimes," said the captain. "Ah, there's Silk coming this way. We needn't stop, here to give him a return match. Come on."

And the two friends rose and strolled off happily arm-in-arm.

Chapter Thirty One.

Welch's versus Parrett's Juniors.

"Of course," said Riddell, as he and Wyndham strolled down by the river that afternoon, "now that your mystery is all cleared up we are as far off as ever finding out who really cut the rudder-lines."

"Yes. My knife is the only clue, and that proves nothing, for I was always leaving it about, or lending it, or losing it. I don't suppose I kept it one entire week in my pocket all the time I had it. And, for the matter of that, it's not at all impossible I may have dropped it in the boat-house myself some time. I often used to change my jacket there."

Riddell had half expected Wyndham would be able to afford some clue as to who had borrowed or taken the knife at that particular time. He was rather relieved to find that he could not.

"Tom the boat-boy," said he, "distinctly says that the fellow who was getting out of the window dropped the knife as he did so. Of course that may be his fancy. Anyhow, I don't want the knife any more, so you may as well take it."

So saying he produced the knife from his pocket, and handed it to his companion.

"I don't want the beastly thing," cried Wyndham, taking it and pitching it into the middle of the river. "Goodness knows it's done mischief enough! But, I say, whoever wrote that note must have known something about it."

"Of course," said the captain, "but he evidently intends the thing to be found out without his help."

"Never mind," said Wyndham, cheerily, "give yourself a little rest, old man, and come down and see the second-eleven practise. I've been too much up a tree to turn up lately, but I mean to do so this evening. I say, won't it be jolly if my brother can come down to umpire in the match."

"It *will*," said Riddell, and the pair forthwith launched out into a discussion of the virtues of Wyndham senior, in which one was scarcely more enthusiastic than the other.

On their way back to the Big they met Parson and Telson, trotting down to the bathing sheds.

The faces of these two young gentlemen looked considerably perplexed as they saw the captain and his supposed victim walking arm-in-arm. However, with the delightful simplicity of youth they thought it must be all right somehow, and having important news of some sort to relate, they made no scruple about intruding on the interview.

"Oh, I say, Riddell," began Telson, "we've just come from the Parliament. No end of a row. Last time was nothing to it!"

"What happened?" asked the captain.

"Why, you know," said Parson, "it was Game and Ashley's affair summoning this meeting. They sent round a private note or something telling the fellows there would be a special meeting, signed by Game, First Lord of the Admiralty, and Ashley, Home Secretary. A lot of the fellows were taken in by it and turned up, and of course they had taken good care not to summon anybody that was sweet on you. So it was a packed meeting. At least they thought so. But Telson and I showed up, and the whole lot of the Skyrockets, and gave them a lively time of it."

"You see," said Telson, eagerly taking up the narrative, "they didn't guess we'd cut up rough, because we've been in rows of that sort once or twice before."

Wyndham broke out laughing at this point.

"Have you, really?" he exclaimed.

"Well," continued Telson, too full of his story to heed the interruption, "they stuck Game in the chair, and he made a frightfully rambling speech about you and that boat-race business. He said you knew who the chap was, and were sheltering him and all that, and that you were as bad every bit as if you'd done it yourself, and didn't care a hang about the honour of the school, and a whole lot of bosh of that sort. We sung out 'Oh, oh,' and 'Question,' once or twice, but, you know, we were saving ourselves up. So Ashley got up and said he was awfully astonished to hear about it—howling cram, of course, for he knew about it as much as any one did—and he considered it a disgrace to the school, and the only thing to do was to kick you out, and he proposed it."

"Then the shindy began," said Parson. "We sent young Lawkins off to tell Crossfield what was going on, and directly Ashley sat down old Telson got up and moved an amendment. They tried to cry him down, but they couldn't do it, could they?"

"Rather not," said Telson, proudly. "I stuck there like a leech, and the fellows all yelled too, so that nobody could hear any one speak. We kept on singing out 'Hole in the corner! Hole in the corner!' for about twenty minutes, and there weren't enough of them to turn us out. Then they tried to get round us by being civil, but we were up to that dodge. Parson went on after me, and then old Bosher, and then King, and then Wakefield, and when he'd done I started again."

"You should have seen how jolly wild they got!" cried Parson. "A lot of the fellows laughed, and joined us too. Old Game and Ashley were regularly mad! They came round and bawled in our ears that they gave us a thousand lines each, and we'd be detained all the rest of the term. But we didn't hear it; and when they tried to get at us we hit out with rulers, and they couldn't do it. You never saw such a lark!"

"And presently Crossfield turned up," said Telson. "My eye! you should have seen how yellow and green they looked when he dropped in and walked up to his usual place! We shut up for a bit as soon as he came—and, you know, I fancy they'd have sooner we kept it up. They were bound to say something when the row stopped. So Game tried to rush the thing through, and get the fellows to vote before Crossfield knew what was up. But he wasn't to be done that way."

"'I didn't quite hear what the motion was?' says he, as solemn as a judge.

"'Oh! it's about the honour of the school. Riddell—'

"'Excuse me, Mr Deputy-Chairman and ex-monitor,' says Crossfield, and there was a regular laugh at that hit, because, of course, Game had no more right in the chair, now he's not a monitor, than I had. 'If it's anything to do with the honour of the school, of course it couldn't be in better hands than yours, who have summoned the meeting on the sly, and taken such care to select a nice little party!'

"They tried to stop him at that.

"'You can't stop the business now. We were just going to take the vote when you came in,' said Game.

"'Exactly!' says Crossfield, propping himself up comfortably against the back of the form as if he was going to stay all night; 'that's just why I came, and that's just why Bloomfield, and Porter, and Coates, and Fairbairn, and a few other gentlemen who have a sort of mild interest in the honour of the school—although it's nothing, of course, to yours—are coming on too. They'll be here before I've done my speech. By the way, one of you kids,' said he, with a wink our way, 'might go and fetch Riddell; he'd like to be here too.'

"We shoved young Wakefield out of the door to make believe to go and fetch you. But they'd had quite enough of it, and shut up the meeting all of a sudden.

"'I adjourn the meeting!' cried Game, as red as a turkey-cock.

"'All right! that will suit me just as well,' says Crossfield, grinning. 'Is it to any particular day, or shall we get notice as before?'

"Of course they didn't stop to answer, and so we gave no end of a cheer for old Crossfield, and then came on here."

And having delivered themselves of this full, true, and particular account of the afternoon's adventures, these two small heroes continued their trot down to the river to refresh their honest limbs after the day's labours.

Their version of the proceedings was very little exaggerated, and, as Crossfield and several others who were present each entertained his own particular circle of friends with the same story, the whole affair became a joke against the luckless Game and Ashley.

Even their own house did not spare them, and as for Bloomfield, he evinced his displeasure in a way which surprised the two heroes.

"What's all this foolery you've been up to, you two?" said he, coming into the preparation-room after tea, where most of the senior Parretts were assembled.

It was not flattering certainly to the two in question to have their noble protest for the honour of the school thus designated, and Game answered, rather sheepishly, "We've been up to no foolery!"

"You may not call it foolery," said Bloomfield, who was in anything but a good temper, "but I do! Making the whole house ridiculous! Goodness knows there's been quite enough done in that way without wanting your help to do more!"

"What's the use of going on like that?" said Ashley. "You don't suppose we did it to amuse ourselves, do you?"

"If you didn't amuse yourselves you amused every one else," growled Bloomfield. "Everybody's laughing at us."

"We felt something ought to be done about Riddell—" began Game.

"Felt! You'd no business to feel, if that's the best you can show for it," said Bloomfield. "*You'll* never set things right!"

"Look here," said Game, quickly, losing his temper; "you know well enough it was meant for the best, and you needn't come and kick up a row like this before everybody! If you don't care to have Riddell shown up, it is no reason why we shouldn't!"

"A precious lot you've shown him up! If you'd wanted to get every one on his side, you couldn't have done better. You don't suppose any one would be frightened out of his skin by anything a couple of asses who'd been kicked out of the monitorship had to say?"

Bloomfield certainly had the habit of expressing himself warmly at times, and on the present occasion he may have done so rather more warmly than the case deserved. But he was put out and angry at the ridiculous performance of the Parrett's boys, in which he felt the entire house was more or less compromised.

As to Riddell, Bloomfield still kept his own private opinion of him, but the difference between him and his more ardent comrades was that he had the sense to keep what he thought to himself.

At any rate, he gave deep offence now to Game and Ashley, who retired in high dudgeon and greatly crestfallen to proclaim their wrongs to a small and sympathetic knot of admirers.

Perhaps the most serious blow these officious young gentlemen had received—hardly second to their snubbing by the Parretts' captain—had been the mutiny of their own juniors, on whose cooperation they had calculated to a dead certainty.

To find Parson, Bosher, King, and Co. standing up in defence of Riddell against *them* was a phenomenon so wonderful, when they came to think of it, that they were inclined to imagine they themselves were the only sane boys left out of a house of lunatics. And this was the only consolation that mixed with the affair at all.

As to these juniors, they had far more to think about. In three days the match with Welch's would be upon them, and a panic ensued on the discovery.

132

They had been contemptuously confident of their superior prowess, and it was not until one or two of them had actually been down to inspect the play of the rival team, and Bloomfield had come down to one of their own practices and declared publicly that they were safe to be beaten hollow, that they regarded the coming contest seriously.

Then they went to work in grim earnest. Having broken with Game, on whom they had usually depended for "instruction and reproof," they boldly claimed the services of Bloomfield, and even pressed the willing Mr Parrett into the service.

Mr Parrett pulled a very long face the first afternoon he came down to look at them. He had been coaching the Welchers for a week or two past, and therefore knew pretty well what their opponents ought to be. And he was bound to admit that the young Parretts were very much below the mark.

They had a few good men. Parson was a fair bat, and King bowled moderately; but the "tail" of the eleven was in a shocking condition. Everything that could be done during the next few days was done. But cricket is not a study which can be "crammed" up, like Virgil or Euclid; and, despite the united efforts of Bloomfield and Mr Parrett, and a few other authorities, the team was pronounced to be a "shady" one at best as it took its place on the field of battle.

Riddell had kept his men steadily at it to the last. With a generosity very few appreciated, he forbore to claim Mr Parrett's assistance at all during the last few days of practice, but he got Fairbairn and one or two of the schoolhouse seniors instead, and with their help kept up the courage and hopes of the young Welchers, wisely taking care, however, by a little occasional judicious snubbing, to prevent them from becoming too cocky or sure of the result.

It was quite an event to see the Welchers' flag hoisted once more on the cricket-ground. Indeed, it was such an event that the doctor himself came down to watch the play, while the muster of schoolboys was almost as large as at a senior house match.

Among all the spectators, none were more interested in the event than the seniors, who had taken upon themselves the responsibility of "coaching" their respective teams.

Riddell was quite excited and nervous as he watched his men go out to field, while Bloomfield, though he would have been the last to own it, felt decidedly fidgety for the fate of his young champions.

However, Parretts, who went in first, began better than any one expected. Parson and King went boldly—not to say rashly—to work from the outset, and knocked the bowling about considerably before a lucky ball from Philpot got round the bat of the former and demolished his wicket.

Wakefield followed, and he too managed to put a few runs together; but as soon as his wicket fell a dismal quarter of an hour followed for the Parretts. Boy after boy, in all the finery of spotless flannel and pads and gloves, swaggered up to the wicket, and, after taking "middle" in magnificent style, and giving a lordly glance round the field, as though to select the best point for placing their strokes, lifted their bats miserably at the first ball that came, and had no chance of lifting it at another.

It was a melancholy spectacle, and far more calculated to excite pity than amusement. Bloomfield chafed and growled for some time, and then, unable to stand it any longer, went off in disgust, leaving the young reprobates to their fate.

Scarcely less remarkable than the collapse of Parrett's was the steadiness of Welch's in the field. Although they had little to do, they did what there was to do neatly and well, and, unlike many junior elevens, did it quietly. The junior matches at Willoughby had usually been more famous for noise than cricket, but on this occasion the order of things was reversed, and Riddell, as he looked on and heard the compliments from all quarters bestowed on his young heroes, might be excused if he felt rewarded for all the labour and patience of the past month.

It offended him not at all to hear this good result attributed generally to Mr Parrett's instructions. He knew it was true. Mr Parrett himself took care to disclaim any but a small amount of merit in the matter.

"It's a wonder to me," said he to Fairbairn, in the hearing of a good many seniors, who were wont to treat anything he had to say on athletic matters as authoritative—"it's a wonder to me how Riddell, who is only a moderate player himself, has turned out such a first-rate eleven. He's about the best cricket coach we have had, and I have seen several in my time. He has worked on their enthusiasm without stint, and next best to that, he has not so much hammered into them what they ought to do, as he has hammered out of them what they ought not to do. Three fellows out of five never think of that."

"I'm sure they don't," said Fairbairn.

"See how steady they were all the innings, too!" continued Mr Parrett. "Three coaches out of five wouldn't lay that down as the first rule of cricket; but it is, especially with youngsters. Be steady first, and be expert next. That's the right order, and Riddell has discovered it. I would even back a steady eleven of moderate players against a rickety eleven of good ones. In fact, a boy can't be a cricketer at all, or anything else, unless he's steady. Now, you see, unless I am mistaken, they will give quite as good an account of themselves at the wickets as they did on the field."

And off strolled the honest Mr Parrett, bat in hand, to umpire, leaving his hearers not a little impressed with the force of his views on the first principles of cricket.

The master's prophecy was correct. The Welchers, notwithstanding the fact that they had only twenty-five runs to get to equal their rivals' first innings, played a steady and careful innings, in which they just trebled the Parretts' score. The bowling against them was not strong certainly, but they took no liberties with it. Indeed, both the captain and Mr Parrett had so ruthlessly denounced and snubbed anything like "fancy hitting," that their batting was inclined to err on the side of the over-cautious, and more runs might doubtless have been made by a little freer swing of the bats. However, the authorities were well satisfied. Cusack carried his bat for eighteen, much to his own gratification; and of his companions, Pilbury, Philpot, and Walker each made double figures.

It required all Riddell's authority, in the face of this splendid achievement, to keep his men from jeopardising their second innings in the field by yielding prematurely to elation.

"For goodness' sake don't hulloa till you're out of the wood!" he said; "they may catch up on you yet. Seventy-five isn't such a big score after all. If you don't look out you'll muddle your chance away, and then how small you'll look!"

With such advice to hold them in check, they went out as soberly as before to field, and devoted their whole energies to the task of disposing of their enemies' wickets for the fewest possible runs.

And they succeeded quite as well as before. Indeed, the second innings of the Parretts was a feeble imitation of their first melancholy performance. Parson, King, and Wakefield were the only three who made any stand, and even they fared worse than before. All the side could put together was twenty-one runs, and about this, even, they had great trouble.

When it became known that the Welchers had won the match by an innings and twenty-nine runs, great was the amazement of all Willoughby, and greater still was the mortification of the unlucky Parretts. No more was said about the grand concert in which they intended to celebrate their triumph. They evidently felt they had not much to be proud of, and, consequently, avoiding a public entry into their house, they slunk in quietly, and, shutting out the distant sounds of revelry and rejoicing in the victorious house, mingled their tears over a sympathetic pot of tea, to which even Telson was not invited.

Chapter Thirty Two.

A Climax to Everything.
Among the few Willoughbites who took no interest at all in the juniors' match was Gilks.

It was hardly to be wondered at that he, a schoolhouse boy, should not concern himself much about a contest between the fags of Welch's and Parrett's. And yet, if truth were known, it would have been just the same had the match been the greatest event of the season, for Gilks, from some cause or other, was in no condition to care about anything.

He wandered about listlessly that afternoon, avoiding the crowded Big, and bending his steps rather to the unfrequented meadows by the river. What he was thinking about as he paced along none of the very few boys who met him that afternoon could guess, but that it was nothing pleasant was very evident.

At the beginning of this very term Gilks had been one of the noisiest and liveliest fellows in Willoughby. Although his principles had never been lofty, his spirits always used to be excellent, and those who knew him best could scarcely recognise now in the anxious, spiritless monitor the companion whose shout and laugh had been so familiar only a few months ago.

Among those who met him this afternoon was Wibberly. Wibberly, like Gilks, felt very little interest in the juniors' match. He was one of the small party who yesterday had come in for such a smart snubbing from Bloomfield, and the only way to show his sense of the ingratitude of such treatment, especially towards an old toady like himself, was to profess no interest in an event which was notoriously interesting the Parretts' captain.

So Wibberly strolled down that afternoon to the river, and naturally met Gilks.

The two were not by any means chums—indeed, they were scarcely to be called friends. But they had one considerable bond of sympathy in a common dislike for the schoolhouse, and still more for Riddell. Gilks, as the reader knows, was anything but a loyal schoolhouse man, and ever since he became a monitor had cast in his lot with the rival house. So that he was generally considered, and considered himself to be, quite as much of a Parrett as a "schoolhouser."

"So you are not down looking at the little boys?" said Wibberly.

"No," said Gilks.

"Awful rot," said Wibberly, "making all that fuss about them!"

"Pleases them and doesn't hurt us," replied Gilks.

"In my opinion it's all a bit of vanity on the part of Riddell. He'd like to make every one think he has been coaching his kids, and this is just a show-off."

"Well, let him show off; who cares?" growled Gilks.

"All very well. He ought to be hooted round the school instead of flashing it there in the Big, the hypocritical cad!"

"Well, why don't you go and do it?" said Gilks; "you'd get plenty to join you."

"Would I? No, I wouldn't. Even Bloomfield's taking his part—he's gammoned him somehow."

"Well, that doesn't prevent your going and hooting him, does it?" said Gilks, with a sneer. "You've a right to enjoy yourself as well as any one else."

"What! have you come round to worship his holiness too?" asked Wibberly, who had at least expected some sympathy from Gilks.

"Not exactly!" said Gilks, bitterly; "but I've come round to letting the cad alone. What's the good of bothering?"

"And you mean to say you'd let him go on knowing who the fellow is who cut the rudder-lines of our boat, and not make him say who it is?"

"I expect that's all stuff about his knowing at all," said Gilks.

"Not it! Between you and me, I fancy he's had a tip from somewhere."

"He has? Bah! don't you believe it. He'd like to make believe he knows all about it. It would pay, you know."

"But every one thinks he knows."

"Not he! He would have told the fellow's name long ago. Whatever object would he have in keeping it back?"

"Oh! I don't know. He says some gammon about not being quite sure. But he's had time enough to be sure by now."

Gilks walked on in silence for a little, and then inquired, "And suppose you did get to know who it was, what would be the use?"

"The use!" exclaimed Wibberly, in amazement. "Why, what do you mean? By Jove, I'm sorry for the fellow when he turns up. He'll soon find out the use of it."

Gilks said nothing, but walked on evidently out of humour, and Wibberly having nothing better to do accompanied him.

"By the way," said the latter, presently, seeing his companion was not disposed to continue the former conversation, "what's up between you and Silk? Is it true you've had a row?"

Gilks growled out something which sounded very like an oath, and replied, "Yes."

"What about?" inquired the inquisitive Wibberly, who seemed to have the knack of hitting upon unwelcome topics.

"It wouldn't do you any good to know," growled Gilks.

"I heard it was some betting row, or something of that sort," said Wibberly.

"Eh?—yes—something of that sort," said Gilks.

"Well," said Wibberly, "I never cared much for Silk. He always seemed to know a little too much for me. I wouldn't break my heart if I were you."

"I don't mean to," said Gilks, but in a tone which belied the words, and even struck Wibberly by its wretchedness.

"I say," said he, "you're awfully down in the mouth these times. What's wrong?"

"What makes you think anything's wrong? I'm all right, I tell you," said Gilks, half angrily.

Wibberly was half inclined to say that he would not have thought it if he had not been told so, but judging from his companion's looks that this little pleasantry would not be appreciated, he forbore and walked on in silence.

It was a relief when Wibberly at length discovered that it was time for him to be going back. Gilks wanted nobody's company, and was glad to be left alone.

And yet he would gladly have escaped even from his own company, which to judge by his miserable looks as he walked on alone was less pleasant than any.

He was sorry now he had not gone to watch the juniors, where at least he would have heard something less hateful than his own thoughts, and seen something less hateful than the dreary creations of his own troubled imagination.

"What's the use of keeping it up?" said he, bitterly, to himself. "I don't care! Things can't be worse than they are. Down in the mouth! He'd be down in the mouth if he were!—the fool! I've a good mind to— And yet I daren't face it. What's the use of trusting to a fellow like Silk! Bah! how I hate him. He'll betray me as soon as ever it suits him, and—and—oh, I don't care. Let him!"

Gilks had reached this dismal climax in his reflections, when he suddenly became aware that the object of his meditations was approaching him.

Silk had his own reasons for not joining the throng that was looking on at the juniors' match. It may have been mere lack of interest, or it may have been a special desire to take this walk. Whichever it was, his presence now was about as unwelcome an apparition as Gilks could have encountered, and the smile on the intruder's face showed pretty clearly that he was aware of the fact.

"What are you prowling about here for?" said he as he came up, with all the insolence of a warder addressing a convict.

"I've a right to walk here if I choose," replied Gilks, sulkily; "what are you here for?"

"To find you. I want to speak to you," replied Silk.

"I don't want to speak to you," replied Gilks, moving on.

"Don't you?" replied Silk, with a sneer. "You'll have to do it whether you want or not, my boy."

There was something about the Welcher which had the effect of cowing his companion, and Gilks, fuming inwardly, and with a face as black as thunder, said, "Well—say what you've got to say, and be done with it."

Silk laughed.

"Thank you. I'll take my time, not yours. Which way are you going?"

"No way at all," said Gilks, standing still.

"Very well. I'm going this way. Come with me."

And he began to walk on, Gilks sullenly following.

"You saw Wyndham the other day?" said Silk.

"Suppose I did?"

"What did he want?"

"I don't know—some foolery or other. I didn't listen to him."

"You needn't tell lies. What did he want, I say?"

"How should I know?" retorted Gilks.

"What did he want? do you hear?" repeated the other.

"He wanted me to let him blab about something—about Beamish's it was."

"And did you tell him he might?"

"Yes. I said he might blab about me too for all I cared. And so he may. I wish to goodness he would."

"And whatever business had you to tell him he might say a word about it?" demanded Silk, angrily.

"What business? A good deal more business than you've got to ask me questions."

"Do you know what he's done?"

"No, I don't; and I don't care."

"Don't you care?" snarled Silk, fast losing his temper; "that foolery of yours has spoiled everything."

"So much the better. *I* don't care."

"But *I* care!" exclaimed Silk, furiously, "and I'll see you care too, you fool!"

"What's happened, then?" asked Gilks.

"Why, Riddell—"

"For goodness' sake don't start on him!" cried Gilks, viciously; "he's nothing to do with it."

"Hasn't he? That's all you know, you blockhead! He suspected Wyndham of that boat-race business. I can't make out how, but he did. And the young fool all along thought it was Beamish's he was in a row about. But Riddell wouldn't have known it to this day if you hadn't given the young idiot leave to go and blab, and so clear it up."

"Let him blab. I wish he'd clear up everything," growled, or rather groaned, Gilks.

"Look here!" said Silk, stopping short in his walk and rounding on his victim. "I've had quite enough of this, and you'd better shut up. You know I could make you sorry for it if I chose."

Gilks said nothing, but walked on sullenly.

"And the worse thing about it," continued Silk, "is that now Wyndham and Riddell are as thick as brothers, and the young toady's sure to tell him everything."

"And suppose he does?"

"There's no suppose about it. I don't choose to have it, I tell you."

"How can you help it?" said Gilks.

"We must get hold of the young 'un again," said Silk, "and you'll have to manage it."

"Who?—I?" said Gilks, with a bitter laugh.

"Yes, you. And don't talk so loud, do you hear? You'll have to manage it, and I think I can put you up to a way for getting hold of him."

"You can spare yourself the trouble," said Gilks, stopping short and folding his arms doggedly. "I won't do it."

"What!" cried Silk, in a passion.

It was the second time in one week that Silk had been thus defied—each time by a boy whom he had imagined to be completely in his power. Wyndham's mutiny had not wholly surprised him, but from Gilks he had never expected it.

"I won't do it, there!" said Gilks, now fairly at bay and determined enough.

Silk glared at him for a moment, then laughed scornfully.

136

"You won't? You know what you are saying?"

"Yes, I know," said Gilks.

"And you know what I shall do?"

"Yes, you'll tell—"

Silk's face fell. He was beginning to discover that once more he had overdone his part, and that the ground was taken from under him. But he made one last effort to recover himself.

"I say, Gilks," said he, half coaxing, half warning, "don't be a fool. Don't ruin yourself. I didn't mean to be offensive. You know it's as much in your interest as mine. If we can get hold of young Wyndham again—"

"If you want him, get him yourself, I'm not going to do it," once more said Gilks, with pale face and clenched teeth.

Silk's manner changed once more. His face became livid, and his eyes flashed, as he sprang at Gilks, and with a sudden blow, exclaimed, "Take that, then!"

It was as good as proclaiming that the game was over. As Gilks's guilty confidant he had retained to the last some sort of influence; but now, with that blow, the last shred of his superiority had gone, and he stood there beaten before ever the fight began.

Gilks had expected the blow, but had not been prepared for its suddenness. It struck him full on the cheek, and for a moment staggered him—but only for a moment. Wasting no words, he returned it vehemently, and next moment the fight had begun.

That fight was not the growth of a day or a week. For many weeks it had been getting nearer and nearer, sometimes by rapid strides, sometimes by imperceptible steps; but always getting nearer, until now it had suddenly reached its climax; and the cry, "A fight—Gilks and Silk!" spread like wildfire over Willoughby.

The Welchers, in the heyday of their triumph, heard it above even the chorus of the glorious Bouncer; and hearing it, forsook their revelry and hurried towards it. The Parretts quitted their melancholy teapot, and rushed with one accord to the spot. And ere they reached it Telson was there, and many a schoolhouse Limpet, and Game, and Ashley, and Wibberly, from Parrett's; and Tucker, and I know not what crowds from Welch's. And they crowded round, and took sides, and speculated on the result, and cheered impartially every hit.

Far be it from me to describe that fight. It was no different from twenty other fights that same term, except from the one fact that the combatants were seniors. No one cared an atom about the quarrels or its merits. It was quite enough that it was an even match—that there was plenty of straight hitting and smart parrying, and that it lasted over a quarter of an hour.

It was a wonder it lasted so long. Not that the men could not stay, but because no monitor with power to stop it appeared on the scene. Indeed, the only monitor present was Gilks himself, and he took no steps to end the conflict.

At length, however, while the result was still undecided, a cry of "*Cave!*" was raised.

"Look out, here's Riddell!" cried some small boy.

A round was just beginning, and neither combatant evinced any desire to desist on account of the captain's approach.

Riddell was not alone, Fairbairn was with him, and, being naturally attracted by the crowd and shouting, they both hurried up in time to see the end of the round.

As soon as it was over they pushed their way in among the crowd and entered the ring.

"Stop the fight!" said Riddell.

The two combatants glared at him angrily, and Gilks replied, "Who says so?"

"I say so," said Riddell, quietly.

The days were long gone by when the captain issued his orders in an apologetic voice and a diffident manner. He had learned enough during this term to discover the value of a little self-confidence, and had profited by the discovery. Willoughby was far more docile to an order than to a request, and on the present occasion neither Gilks nor Silk seemed disposed to argue the matter.

They put on their jackets sulkily, and, without further words to one another or to the monitors, betook their battered selves to their several quarters.

Willoughby, perceiving that the matter was at an end, also dispersed and returned to its several quarters. The Welchers resumed their interrupted revel with unabated rejoicing; the melancholy Parretts called for more hot water to eke out the consolations of their teapot; the Limpets turned in again to their preparation, and the seniors to their studies—every one criticising the fight, and wondering how it would have ended, but scarcely one troubling himself much about its merit, and less still about its consequences.

One of these consequences the principals in the engagement were not long in learning. A message arrived for each, before the evening was over, that they were reported to the doctor, and were to go to his room at nine next morning.

Silk did not get the message till late, as he had been absent most of the evening in Tucker's study, who was an expert at repairing the damage incurred in a pugilistic encounter.

When about bedtime he returned to his own study and found the captain's note lying on the table, he broke out into a state of fury which, to say the least of it, it was well there was no one at hand to witness.

Late as the hour was, he went at once to Riddell's study.

Riddell was half-undressed as his visitor entered. "What do you want?" he inquired.

"I want you! Do you mean to say you've reported me to the doctor?"

"Of course. It was a fight. I'm bound to report it."

"*Bound* to report it. You snivelling humbug! Have you sent the name up yet?"

"Why do you want to know?" said Riddell, who had ceased to be in bodily fear of Silk for some time past.

"Because I want to know. Have you sent it up?"

"I have."

"All right, you'll be sorry for it," said Silk.

"I *am* sorry for it," replied the captain.

Silk saw at a glance that the captain was not to be bullied, and changed his tone.

"I suppose you know," said he, "we shall both be expelled?"

"The doctor doesn't usually expel for fighting," said the captain.

"Of course not. But you remember getting a note from me a little time ago."

"From you? No; I never had a note from you."

"What, not one telling you to go down and see Tom the boat-boy?"

"Was that from you?" exclaimed Riddell, in astonishment.

"Of course it was. And of course you know now what I mean."

"I don't. I could discover nothing," said the captain.

"You mean to say you don't know who cut the rudder-lines?"

"No; who?"

"Gilks!"

Chapter Thirty Three.

A Treaty of Peace.

The captain's first impulse on receiving from Silk this astounding piece of information was to go at once to the schoolhouse and confront Gilks with his accuser.

But his second impulse was to doubt the whole story and look upon it as a mere fabrication got up in the vague hope of preventing him from reporting the fight to the doctor.

It was absurd to suppose Gilks had cut the rudder-lines. Not that it was an action of which he would be incapable. On that score the accusation was likely enough. But then, Riddell remembered, Gilks, though a schoolhouse boy, had all along been a strong partisan of the Parretts' boat, and, ever since he had been turned out of his own boat, had made no secret of his hope that Parrett's might win. He had even, if rumours spoke truly, lost money on the race. How was it likely, then, he would do such an absurd thing as cut the rudder-lines of the very boat he wanted to win, and on whose success he had even made a bet?

It was much more likely that Silk had made this wild charge for the sake of embarrassing the captain, and leading him to reconsider his determination to report the fight.

And what followed partly confirmed this idea.

"You don't want to get both Gilks and me expelled?" said Silk, with a half-whine very different from his late bullying tones.

"The doctor never expels fellows for fighting."

"But he will when he finds out all this other business," said Silk.

"I really can't help that," said the captain, not quite seeing how the two offences were involved one with another.

"It's bound to come out," continued Silk, "and Gilks will bring me into it too. I say, can't you get back the names?"

"Certainly not," said the captain.

"You were glad enough to hush it all up when you thought it was young Wyndham had done it," said Silk.

The captain winced, and Silk was quick enough to see it.

"You profess to be fair and honest. Do you call it fair to shelter one fellow because he's your friend, and tell about another because he isn't? Eh, Riddell?"

It was not a bad move on Silk's part. The question thrust home, and had he been content to leave the matter there, it might have been some time before the captain, with his own scrupulous way of regarding things, would have detected its fallacies. But, not for the first time, Silk overdid it.

"Besides," said he, seeing he had made an impression, and foolishly thinking to follow it up—"besides, young Wyndham's a long way from being out of the wood himself yet. Of course I don't want to do it, but I could make it rather awkward for him if I chose."

The captain fired up scornfully, but Silk did not notice it, and continued, "You wouldn't like to see him expelled, would you? If I were to tell all I know about him, he would be, to a certainty."

Riddell, on whom these incautious words had acted with a result wholly different from what was intended, could scarcely contain himself to talk coolly as he replied, "Please leave my room. I don't want you here." Silk looked round in a startled way at the words, and his face changed colour.

"What?" he demanded. "Please leave my room," replied the captain. "Not till you promise to get back the names."

"I shall do nothing of the sort."

"You won't? You know the consequence?" Riddell said nothing. "I shall tell of Wyndham," said Silk. "Please leave my room," once more said the captain. Silk glared at him, and took a step forward as though he meant to try one last method for extorting the promise.

But Riddell stood his ground boldly, and the spirit of the bully faltered.

"You'll be sorry for it," snarled the latter. Riddell said nothing, but waited patiently for him to go. Seeing that nothing more was to be gained, and baffled on all points—even on the point where he made sure of having his enemy, Silk turned on his heel and went, slamming the door viciously behind him.

Riddell had rarely felt such a sense of relief as he experienced on being thus left to himself.

The suddenness of Silk's disclosure and the strange way in which it had been followed up had disconcerted him. But now he had time to think calmly over the whole affair.

And two things seemed pretty clear. One was that, strange as it seemed, there must be something in Silk's story. He could hardly have invented it and stuck to it in the way he had for no other purpose than embarrassing the captain; and the pressure he had applied to get Riddell to withdraw the names before the doctor saw them, confirmed this idea.

The other point made clear was that his duty, at whatever cost, even at the cost of young Wyndham himself, was to report the fight and make no terms with the offenders. If the result was what Silk threatened, he could only hope the doctor would deal leniently with the boy.

One other thing was clear too. He must see both Wyndham and Bloomfield in the morning.

With which resolve, and not without a prayer for wisdom better than his own to act in this crisis, he retired to bed.

Early next morning, before almost any sign of life showed itself in Willoughby, the captain was up and dressed.

The magic that so often attends on a night's sleep had done its work on him, and as he walked across the quadrangle that fresh summer morning his head was clear and his mind made up.

The outer door of the schoolhouse was still unopened, and he paced outside, as it seemed to him, for half an hour before he could get in.

He went at once to Wyndham's study, and found that young athlete arraying himself in his cricket flannels.

"Hullo, Riddell!" cried he, as the captain entered; "have you come to see the practice? We're going to play a scratch match with some of the seniors. You play too, will you?"

The captain did not reply to this invitation, and his serious face convinced Wyndham something must be wrong.

"What's up, I say?" he inquired, looking concerned.

"Nothing very pleasant," said Riddell. "You heard of the fight last night?"

"Eh? between Silk and Gilks? Yes. I half guessed it would come to that. They've been quarrelling a lot lately."

"I reported them, and they are to go to the doctor's after breakfast," said Riddell.

"They'll catch it, I expect," said Wyndham. "Paddy's sure to be down on them because they're seniors."

"They expect to catch it. At least, Silk says so. He came to me last night and tried to get me to withdraw the names. And when I said I couldn't be threatened to tell about you, and get you into a row."

Wyndham's face changed colour.

"What? I say, do you think he really will?" he exclaimed.

"I think it's very likely," said the captain.

"Of course, you can't withdraw the names?" said the boy.

"I've no right to do it—no, I can't," replied the captain.

"Oh, of course. But I say, what had I better do?" faltered the boy. "I hoped that bother was all over."

"I would advise you to go to the doctor before chapel and tell him yourself."

The boy's face fell.

"How can I? I promised I wouldn't, and Silk wouldn't let me off when I asked him."

"But he is going to tell of you, he says. You had much better let the doctor hear it from you than from him."

"If only I could!" exclaimed the boy; "but how can I?"

"I don't want to persuade you to break a promise," said the captain, "but I'm sorry for it."

"I suppose I'm sure to get expelled," said the boy, dismally; "they're sure to make it as bad against me as they can."

Riddell reflected a little, and then said, "Perhaps it's only a threat, and no more. At any rate, if the doctor is told he is sure to give you a chance of telling him everything, so don't give up hope, old man."

Poor Wyndham did not look or feel very hopeful certainly as he thought over the situation.

"Thanks for telling me about it, anyhow," said he. "I say, shall you be there to hear what they say?"

"I don't know. I don't think so. But if you are sent for let me know, and I'll go with you."

With this grain of comfort the captain went, leaving Wyndham anything but disposed to show up at the cricket practice. Indeed, for a little while he gave up all thought of going out, and it was not till a messenger arrived to tell him he was keeping everybody waiting that he screwed himself up to the effort and went.

Riddell meanwhile, with the other half of his mission still to execute, went over to Parrett's. Parson was lounging about at the door, with a towel over his arm, waiting, as any one might have guessed, for Telson.

"Has Bloomfield gone out?" asked the captain of this youthful hero.

Parson, who ever since the famous breakfast in Riddell's room had looked upon the captain with eyes of favour, replied, "No, I don't think so, I'll go and see if you like."

"Thanks. If he's in, tell him I want to speak to him."

"All serene. Hold my towel, do you mind? It's Bosher's, and he may try to collar it if he sees me. And tell Telson I'll be back in a second."

And off he went, leaving the captain in charge of Bosher's towel.

He soon returned with a message that Bloomfield was getting up, and would be out in a minute or two.

"I say," said he, after the two had waited impatiently some time, each for his own expected schoolfellow, "did you see much of the fight last night?"

"No," said Riddell, "I didn't see it at all."

"Oh, hard lines. I got there late, as I went to tell Telson. Gilks used his right too much, you know. We both thought so. He keeps no guard to speak of, and— Hullo! where on earth have you been all this time?"

This last exclamation was in honour of Telson, who appeared on the scene at that moment, and with whom the speaker joyfully departed, leaving Riddell only half informed as to the scientific defects in Gilks's style of boxing.

In due time Bloomfield appeared, not a little curious to know the object of this early interview.

Riddell, too, was embarrassed, for the last time they met they had parted on anything but cordial terms. However, that had nothing to do with his duty now.

"Good-morning," he said, in reply to Bloomfield's nod. "Do you mind taking a turn? I want to tell you something."

Bloomfield obeyed, and that morning any one who looked out might have witnessed the unusual spectacle of the Willoughby captains walking together round the quadrangle in eager conversation.

"You heard of the fight?" said Riddell.

"Yes; what about it?" inquired Bloomfield.

"I've reported it. And last night Silk came to me and asked me to get back the names."

"You won't do it, will you?" asked Bloomfield.

"No. But the reason why Silk wanted it was because he was afraid of something else coming out. He says it was Gilks who cut the rudder-lines."

"What! Gilks?" exclaimed Bloomfield, standing still in astonishment. "It can't be! Gilks was one of us. He backed our boat all along!"

"That's just what I can't make out," said the captain; "and I wanted to see what you think had better be done."

"Have you asked Gilks?" inquired Bloomfield.

"No. I thought perhaps the best thing was to wait till they had been up to the doctor. They may let out about it to him, if there's anything in it. If they don't, we should see what Gilks says."

"If it had been your lines that were cut," said Bloomfield, "I could have believed it. He had a spite against all your fellows, and especially you, since he was kicked out of the boat. But he had betted over a sovereign on us, I know."

"I shouldn't have believed it at all," said Riddell, "if Silk hadn't sent me an anonymous note a week or two ago. Here it is, by the way."

Bloomfield read the note.

"Did you go and see the boat-boy?" he asked.

"Yes; and all I could get out of him was that some one had got into the boat-house that night, and scrambled out of the window just in time to avoid being seen. But the fellow, whoever he was, dropped a knife, which I managed to get from Tom, and which turned out to be one young Wyndham had lost."

"Young Wyndham! Then it was true you suspected him?"

"It was true."

And then the captain told his companion the story of the complication of misunderstandings which had led him almost to the point of denouncing the boy as the culprit; at the end of which Bloomfield said, in a more friendly tone than he had yet assumed, "It was a shave, certainly. Young Wyndham ought to be grateful to you. He'd have found it not so easy to clear himself if you'd reported him at once."

"I dare say it would have been hard," said Riddell.

"I'm rather ashamed of myself now for trying to make you do it," said Bloomfield.

"Oh, not at all," said Riddell, dreading as he always did this sort of talk. "But, I say, what do you think ought to be done?"

"I think we'd better wait, as you say, till they've been to Paddy. Then if nothing has come out, you ought to see Gilks."

"I think so, but I wish you'd be there too. As captain of the clubs, you've really more to do with it than I have."

"You're captain of the school, though," said Bloomfield, "but I'll be there too, if you like."

"Thanks," said Riddell.

And the two walked on discussing the situation, and drifting from it into other topics in so natural a way that it occurred to neither of them at the time to wonder how they two, of all boys, should have so much in common.

"I shall be awfully glad when it's all cleared up," said Riddell.

"So shall I. If it is cleared up the credit of it will belong to you, I say."

"Not much credit in getting a fellow expelled," said Riddell.

"Anyhow, it was to your credit sticking by young Wyndham as you did."

"I was going to report him for it, though, the very day the matter was explained."

"Well, all the more credit for making up your mind to an unpleasant duty like that when you might have shirked it."

The bell for chapel began to ring at this point.

"There goes the bell," said Bloomfield. "I say, how should you like to ask me to breakfast with you? I'd ask you to my room, only our fellows would be so inquisitive."

Riddell jumped at the hint with the utmost delight, and to all the marvels of that wonderful term was added this other, of the two Willoughby captains breakfasting *tête-à-tête*, partaking of coffee out of the same pot and toast cut off the same loaf.

They talked far more than they ate or drank. It was more like the talk of two friends who had just met after a long separation, than of two schoolfellows who had sat shoulder to shoulder in the same class-room for weeks. Bloomfield confided all his troubles, and failures, and disappointments, and Riddell confessed his mistakes, and discouragements, and anxieties. And the Parrett's captain marvelled to think how he could have gone on all this term without finding out what a much finer fellow the captain of the school was than himself. And Riddell reproached himself inwardly for never having made more serious efforts to secure the friendship of this honest, kind-hearted athlete, and gradually these secret thoughts oozed out in words.

Bloomfield, as was only natural and only right, took to himself most of the blame, although Riddell chivalrously insisted on claiming as much as ever he could. And when at last this wonderful meal ended, a revolution had taken place in Willoughby which the unsuspecting school, as it breakfasted elsewhere, little dreamed of.

"Upon my honour we *have* been fools," said Bloomfield: "that is, I have. But we'll astonish the fellows soon, I fancy. Do you know I've a good mind to break bounds or have a fight with some one just to make you give me an impot!"

"As long as you don't do anything which calls for personal chastisement," said the captain, laughing, "I'll promise to oblige you."

"I say," said Bloomfield, as the bell for first school was beginning to ring, "I'm glad we—that is I—have come to our senses before old Wyndham comes down. His young brother has persuaded him to come and umpire for the school in the Templeton match."

Riddell's face became troubled.

"I hope young Wyndham may be here himself. You know, Silk threatened that unless I withdrew the names he would tell the doctor about that affair of Beamish's and get Wyndham expelled to spite me."

Bloomfield laughed.

"Not he. It's all brag, depend on it. But why on earth doesn't the young 'un go and make a clean breast to the doctor, before he gets to know of it any other way?"

"That's just the worst of it. They made him promise he wouldn't say a word about it to any one, and he's such an honest young beggar that even though Silk tells of him, he won't tell of Silk."

"That's awkward," said Bloomfield, musing. "Did he tell you about it, then?"

"No. His mouth was shut, you see. If I hadn't found out about it from Parson and Telson, who saw the three of them coming out, I shouldn't have known it till now."

Bloomfield's face brightened.

"Then you found it out quite independently?" asked he.

"To be sure."

"All right. Then the best thing you can do is to report him for it at once."

"What?" exclaimed Riddell, aghast, "report him?"

"Yes. And then you can go to Paddy and tell him all about it, and explain how he was led into it, and he's sure not to be very down on it."

"Upon my word," said Riddell, struck with the idea, "I do believe you are right. It's the very best thing I could do. What a donkey I was never to think of it before."

So it was decided that young Wyndham was forthwith to be reported for his transgression, and as the time had now arrived when all the school but Gilks and Silk were due in class, the two captains hurried off to their places, each feeling that he had discovered a friend; and in that friend a hope for Willoughby, of which he had scarcely even dreamed till now.

Chapter Thirty Four.

A Busy Day for the Doctor.

Riddell had not been many minutes in class before a message came from the doctor summoning him to the library.

On his arrival there he found, to his surprise, Silk standing alone in the middle of the room, while the doctor was quietly writing at his table.

"Riddell," said the doctor, as the captain entered, "you reported two boys to me. Only one is here."

"I told Gilks he was to be here at nine o'clock, sir," said the captain.

"You had better go and see why he is not here."

Riddell obeyed, and found on inquiry at the schoolhouse that Gilks was on the sick-list, and had obtained leave from the matron to remain in bed till after dinner.

The captain had his private doubts as to the seriousness of the invalid's case, especially as, of the two, he was the less damaged in yesterday's fight. However, he had no right to question the matron's decision, and returned accordingly to report the matter to the doctor.

"Humph!" said the doctor, who also evidently considered it a curious coincidence that Gilks should be taken unwell the very morning when his presence was required in the library; "he had better have come. You say he is to be up after dinner?"

"Yes, sir."

"Then let him know he is to come here at four o'clock, and you, Silk, come too at that hour."

Silk, who had evidently screwed himself up for the present interview, looked disappointed.

"I should like just to say, sir—" began he, with a glance at Riddell.

But the doctor interrupted.

"Not now, Silk. Go to your class now, and come here at four o'clock."

"But it's not about—"

"Do you hear me, sir?" said the doctor, sternly.

Silk went.

The captain was about to follow his example, when it occurred to him he might not have so favourable an opportunity again that day for acting on Bloomfield's advice respecting Wyndham.

"Can you spare a few minutes, sir?" said he, turning back.

"Yes, what is it?" said the doctor.

"It's about young Wyndham, sir."

"Ah! Nothing wrong, I hope. He has seemed a good deal steadier than he was, of late."

"So he is, sir. But this is about something he did some time ago."

The doctor settled himself judicially in his chair, and waited for the captain's report.

"He got into bad company early in the term, sir, and was tempted down into the town without leave, and once let himself be taken to Beamish's Aquarium."

The doctor gave a grunt of displeasure, which sounded rather ominous.

"How long ago was this?"

"A few days before the boat-race, sir. It has been weighing on his mind ever since."

"Did he tell you of it?" asked the doctor.

"No, I found it out accidentally. When I spoke to him about it he admitted it and seemed very sorry."

"And why did he not come to me himself at once?"

"That's just it, sir," said the captain. "I advised him to do it, and he told me he had promised the—the companions with whom he went never to mention the matter to anybody, and this prevented his coming. He even went to them, and begged them to let him off the promise so that he might come and confess to you, but he did not succeed."

"Did he ask you, then, to come and tell me?"

"No, sir. But he is in constant dread of your hearing about it from any one else, so that I thought it would be the best thing to tell you of it myself."

The doctor nodded his head.

"He does not know, of course, of your doing this?"

"Oh no, sir."

"And who were the companions who you say took him to this place?"

Riddell coloured up and felt very uncomfortable.

"Do you mind me not telling you, sir?" he said. "Wyndham only wanted you to know about his part in it. I'll tell you if you wish," added he, "but I'd rather not if you do not mind."

"You need not do so at present," said the doctor, greatly to the captain's relief, "but you had better send Wyndham to me."

"Yes, sir," said Riddell, turning to go, but lingering for one final word. "I hope, sir—you—that is, if you can—you will take a lenient view of it. Young Wyndham's very steady now."

"I must see Wyndham before I can decide," said the doctor, "but you have acted rightly in the matter—quite rightly."

The captain went to find Wyndham, hoping for the best, but decidedly anxious.

That young gentleman was engaged in the agonies of Euclid when the school messenger entered, and announced that the doctor wanted to see him at once. His face fell, and his heart beat fast as he heard the summons. It needed not much effort to guess what it all meant. Gilks and Silk had of course been up before the doctor, and the latter had carried out the threat of which Riddell had told him; and now he was summoned to hear his fate!

At the schoolhouse door he found Riddell waiting for him.

"Oh, Riddell, I say!" exclaimed he, in tones of misery, "I've to go to the doctor at once. Silk has told about me. I say, do come with me."

"Silk hasn't told about you at all," said the captain; "I've reported you myself."

"You!" cried Wyndham, in tones of mingled amazement and reproach; "oh, why?"

"Wouldn't you sooner have had me do it than Silk?" asked Riddell.

The boy saw his meaning at once, and as usual flew from one extreme to the other.

"Oh, of course! What a brute I was not to see it. Thanks awfully, old man. What awful grief I should have come to if it hadn't been for you!"

143

"I don't know at all what view the doctor takes of the matter," said the captain, gravely; "you had better not expect too much."

Wyndham groaned.

"If only I'm not expelled!" said he. "I suppose you can't come too?"

"No. The doctor wants to see you alone, I think."

"Well, here goes. By the way, of course, you didn't mention the other fellows' names?" he added.

The manner in which he said this made Riddell feel doubly glad that the doctor had not insisted on his telling.

"No—I didn't," he said.

And off went Wyndham, dismally, to the doctor's study.

It was an anxious morning for the captain. Wyndham had not returned before first school was over, and Riddell felt he could not rest till he knew his fate.

He told Bloomfield of his morning's proceedings, but even this new friend's encouragement failed to shake off the suspense that weighed upon him.

Presently when he could wait patiently no longer, it occurred to him Wyndham might possibly have gone back to his study unobserved, and be waiting there for him. So he went across to the schoolhouse to find out.

But nearly all the studies in the schoolhouse, Wyndham's included, were empty, as they almost always were at this hour of the day during summer; and the captain was about to return, more uncomfortable than ever, to the Big, when a door at the end of the passage opened, and some one called his name.

It was Gilks, who, as he was dressed, had evidently recovered from his indisposition earlier than was expected.

He beckoned as the captain looked round; and Riddell, inwardly wondering when his work as a police-officer would cease, and he would be able to retire again into private life, turned and entered his study.

Gilks shut the door carefully behind him. He had a haggard look about him which may have been the result of his ailment, or may have been caused by mental trouble, but which certainly was not the expression to which the captain had been used.

"I'm to go to the doctor at four?" he asked.

"Yes. He put it off, as you were reported on the sick-list."

"Of course he thinks I was shamming?"

"I don't know."

"I was—and I wasn't. I couldn't make out what to do, that was it, so I stayed in bed. Was Silk there?"

"Yes."

"Did he say anything?"

"No; the doctor told him to come again at four."

Gilks took one or two uncomfortable turns up and down the room, and then said, "I may as well tell you, it's no use keeping it back any longer, for it's sure to come out. I was the fellow who cut the rudder-line. Did you know that?"

"I had heard it."

"Who told you—Silk?"

"Yes."

"I thought so. I knew he would. And he'll tell Paddy this afternoon. I don't care if he does."

"I scarcely believed it when he said so," said Riddell.

"Eh? I suppose you thought it was rather too low even for me. So it would have been once," he said, bitterly.

"But you backed the Parrett's boat all along," said Riddell. "Oh, that. If that's all that puzzled you it's easily explained. Perhaps if you were doing a thing like that in the dark, expecting to be caught out every moment, you might make a mistake too."

"Then you meant to cut *our* lines?" asked the captain, seeing the whole mystery explained at last.

"Of course I did; and so I should have done if the rudders hadn't been shifted, and Parrett's put into the schoolhouse boat." He took a few more turns, and then continued, "You may fancy what a pleasant state of mind I've been in since. I daresay you'll be glad to hear I've been miserable day and night."

"I'm very sorry for you," said Riddell, so sympathetically that the unhappy boy started.

"You wouldn't be if you knew it was all to spite you. I was as bad as Silk in that, though it was his idea about cutting the lines. The accident turned out well for us in one way—nobody suspected either of us. But Silk has led me the life of a dog ever since. I've not known what minute it might all come out. He was always holding it over my head, and I had to do anything he told me. I can tell you I've thought of bolting more than once, or telling Paddy."

144

"It must have been a dreadful time for you," said Riddell. "So it was. But I'm glad it's all over now. I shall be glad to be expelled. I've been ashamed to look any one in the face for weeks. I used to be happy enough before I knew Silk, but I don't expect ever to be happy again now."

There was a tremble in his voice as he said this, which went to the captain's heart.

"I hope it's not so bad as that," said he, quietly. "Everybody here hates me, and they'll hate me all the more now," said Gilks. "You and young Wyndham are the only fellows that have been good to me, and I've done both of you nothing but mischief."

"I think," said Riddell, "the fellows will soon forgive. They would, I know, if they guessed how you have suffered already."

"You are right. I have suffered," said Gilks. Another long pause followed, during which the minds of both were full.

The one sensation in the captain's heart was pity. He forgot all about the crime in commiseration of the wretchedness of the criminal. Yet he knew it was useless to hold out any hope of a reprieve, even if that had been to be desired. All he could do was to let the poor fellow know at least that he was not friendless; and this sign of sympathy Gilks gratefully appreciated.

"I don't know why you should trouble yourself about me," he said, after some further talk. "You owe me less than anybody. I've been nothing less than a brute to you."

"Oh, no," said Riddell; "but, do you know, I think it would be well to go to the doctor at once?"

"I mean to go at once. Do you think he'll let me go off this afternoon, I say? I wouldn't dare to face the fellows. I've got most of my things packed up."

"I expect he would. But you stay till the morning. You can have my study. It's quieter than this."

Perhaps no more hospitable invitation had been issued in Willoughby, and Gilks knew it. And it was too welcome not to be accepted gratefully.

The captain soon afterwards departed, leaving the penitent behind him, subdued and softened, not by any sermon or moral lecture, which at such a time Riddell felt would be only out of place, but by sheer force of kindness—that virtue which costs so little, yet achieves so much.

In this new excitement the captain had for the moment forgotten young Wyndham, but he was soon reminded of that afflicted youth's existence on reaching the Big.

He was there, waiting impatiently. A glance sufficed to show that at any rate the worst had not happened, but Wyndham's face was such a mixture of relief and woe that the captain felt some misgivings as he inquired eagerly what was the news.

"He was frightfully kind," said Wyndham, "and talked to me like a father. I never felt so ashamed of myself. I'm certain it's what you said made him let me off so easy—that is, so what he means for easy. He said nothing about expelling, even when I couldn't tell him the names of those two fellows. But he's gated me till the end of the term! I may only go out for the half-hour after first school, and half an hour after half-past five. And you know what that means," he added, with a groan.

"What?" asked Riddell, too rejoiced that his friend was safe to be over-curious as to the exact consequence of his sentence.

"Why!" exclaimed Wyndham, "it's all up with the second-eleven!"

It was a blow undoubtedly—perhaps the next hardest blow to expulsion—but so much less hard that not even the boy himself could for long regard it as a crushing infliction.

He had had his lesson, and after the suspense of the last few weeks he was ready to expiate his transgression manfully, if sorrowfully.

"Anyhow," said he, after pouring out all his disappointment into the captain's sympathetic ear, "it's not as bad as being sent off home. And if it hadn't been for you that's what might have happened. I say, and think of my brother coming down to umpire, too! What a fool I shall look! Never mind; it can't be helped. I'm sure to get into the eleven next season. I say, by the way, I've no right to be standing out here. I shall have to go in."

And so ended the story of young Wyndham's transgressions.

Riddell had to officiate at yet one more investigation that eventful day.

Scarcely had Wyndham disappeared when a message reached him that the doctor wished to see him again.

With no doubt this time as to the purport of the summons, he obeyed.

He found Gilks standing in the doctor's presence, where Silk had stood an hour or so earlier.

"Riddell," said the doctor, whose face was grave, and whose voice was more than unusually solemn, "Gilks here has just been making a very serious statement about an accident that happened early in the term—the breaking of the line at the boat-race, which he confesses was his doing. I wish you to hear it."

"Gilks told me of it just before he came to you, sir," said the captain.

"I never expected to hear such a confession from a Willoughby boy," said the doctor. "The honour of the whole school has suffered by this disgraceful action, and if I were to allow it to pass without the severest possible punishment I should not be doing my duty. Gilks has done the one thing possible to him to show his remorse for what has occurred. He has confessed it voluntarily, but I have told him he must leave the school to-morrow morning."

Gilks remained where he was, with his eyes on the ground, while the doctor was speaking, and attempted no plea to mitigate the sentence against him.

"I find," continued the doctor, "that if he tells the truth he has not been the only, and perhaps not the principal, culprit. He says he did what he did at the suggestion of Silk. Perhaps you will send for Silk now, Riddell."

Riddell went off to discharge the errand. When he returned Gilks looked up and said, nervously, "Need I stay, sir? I don't want to see Silk."

The doctor looked at him doubtfully, and replied, "Yes, you must stay."

A long, uncomfortable pause followed, during which no one spoke or stirred. At length the silence was broken by a knock on the door, and Silk entered.

He glanced hurriedly round, and seemed to take in the position of affairs with moderate readiness, though he was evidently not quite sure whether Gilks or the captain was his accuser.

The doctor, however, soon made that clear.

"Silk," he said, "Gilks accuses you of being a party to the cutting of the rudder-links of one of the boats in the race last May. Repeat your story, Gilks."

"He needn't do it," said Silk, "I've heard it already."

"He says you suggested it," said the doctor.

"That's a lie," said Silk sullenly; "I never heard of it till afterwards."

"You know you did," said Gilks. "When I was turned out of the boat, and couldn't baulk the race that way, it was you suggested cutting the lines, and I was glad enough to do it."

"So you were," snarled Silk, incautiously—"precious glad."

"Then you did suggest it?" said the doctor, sharply.

Silk saw his mistake, and tried to cover it, but his confusion only made the case against him worse.

"No, I didn't—he told me about it afterwards—that is, I heard about it—I never suggested it. He said he knew how to get at the boats, and I said—"

"Then you did speak about it beforehand?" said the doctor.

"No—that is—we only said—"

"Silk," said the doctor, sternly, "you're not speaking the truth. Let me implore you not to make your fault greater by this denial."

Silk gave in. He knew that his case was hopeless, and that when Gilks had said all, Riddell could corroborate it with what had been said last night.

"Well—yes, I did know of it," said he, doggedly.

"Yes," said the doctor; "I'm glad at least you do not persist in denying it. You must quit Willoughby, Silk; I shall telegraph to your father this afternoon. You must be ready to leave by this time to-morrow."

Silk hesitated for a moment, then with a look round at Riddell, he said, "Before I go, sir, I think you ought to know that Wyndham junior—"

"What about him?" asked the doctor, coldly.

"He is in the habit, as Riddell here knows, of frequenting low places of amusement in Shellport. I have not mentioned it before; but now I am leaving, and Riddell is not likely to tell you of it, I think you ought to know of it, sir."

"The matter has already been reported," said the doctor, almost contemptuously. "You can go, Silk."

The game was fairly played out at last, and Silk slunk off, followed shortly afterwards by the captain and Gilks.

Chapter Thirty Five.

A Transformation Scene.

Willoughby little dreamed that night, as it went to bed, of the revolutions and changes of the day which had just passed.

It knew that Silk and Gilks had been reported for fighting, and naturally concluded that they had also been punished. It had heard, too, a rumour of young Wyndham's having been "gated" for breaking bounds.

But beyond that it knew nothing. Nothing of the treaty of peace between the two captains, of the discovery of the boat-race mystery, of the double expulsion that was impending.

And still less did it dream of the unwonted scene which was taking place that evening in the captain's study.

Riddell and Gilks sat and talked far into the night.

I am not going to describe that talk. Let the reader imagine it.

Let him imagine all that a sympathetic and honest fellow like Riddell could say to cheer and encourage a broken-down penitent like Gilks. And let him imagine all that that forlorn, expelled boy, who had only just discovered that he had a friend in Willoughby, would have to say on this last night at the old school.

It was a relief to him to unburden his mind, and Riddell encouraged him to do it. He told all the sad history of the failures, and follies, and sins which had reached their catastrophe that day; and the captain, on his side, in his quiet manly way, strove all he could to infuse some hope for the future, and courage to bear his present punishment.

Whether he succeeded or not he could hardly tell; but when the evening ended, and the two finally betook themselves to bed in anticipation of Gilks's early start in the morning, it was with a feeling of comfort and relief on both sides.

"If only I had known you before!" said Gilks. "I don't know why you should be so kind to me. And now it's too late to be friends."

"I hope not," said Riddell, cheerily. "We needn't stop being friends because you're going away."

"Needn't we!—will you write to me now and then?" asked Gilks, eagerly.

"Of course I will, and you must do the same. I'll let you know all the news here."

Gilks sighed.

"I'm afraid the news here won't be very pleasant for me to hear," said he. "What a fury the fellows will be in when they hear about it. I say, Riddell, if you get a chance tell them how ashamed and miserable I was, will you?"

"I will, I promise you," replied Riddell.

"And, I say, will you say something to young Wyndham? Tell him how I hate myself for all the mischief I did to him, and how thankful I am he had you to keep him straight when I was trying to lead him all wrong. Will you tell him that?"

"I'll try," said the captain, with a smile, "part of it. But we ought to be turning in now, or we shall not be up in time."

"All right," said Gilks. "Good-night, Riddell."

"Good-night, old fellow."

Bloomfield was up early next morning. He had only received the evening before the melancholy notification of the fact that young Wyndham, owing to circumstances over which he had no control, would be unable to play in the second-eleven match next week; and he had it on his mind consequently to find a successor without delay.

Probably, on the principle that the early bird gets the worm, he determined to be out in good time this morning. But for once in a way the bird was too early for the worm, and Bloomfield prowled about for a good quarter of an hour before the aspiring youth of Willoughby mustered at the wickets.

It was during this early prowl, while the hands of the clock were between half-past six and seven, that he received something like a shock from seeing the captain alight at the school gate from the town omnibus.

"Why, whatever's up? Where have you been?" inquired Bloomfield.

"I have just been to see poor Gilks off," said the captain.

"What! then it was true?"

"Yes, I hadn't time to tell you yesterday. He's been expelled."

"The cad!" cried Bloomfield. "It's lucky for him he was able to slink off unnoticed."

"Oh! don't be too down on him," said the captain. "You'd have been sorry for him if you'd have seen how cut up and ashamed he was. After all, he was little better than a tool in somebody else's hands."

"Silk's you mean?" said Bloomfield. "And I suppose he gets off scot-free?"

"No; he is expelled too. He had to confess that he suggested the whole thing, and he is to go this morning."

"That's a comfort! But why on earth did they cut our lines instead of yours?"

"That was a blunder. Gilks, in his flurry, got hold of the wrong rudder. I really think that's why it wasn't found out long ago."

"Very likely. But what a nice pair of consciences they must have had ever since! I suppose the doctor will announce that they've been expelled?"

"I don't know. But I hope he won't be too hard on Gilks if he does. I never saw a fellow so broken-down and sorry. He quite broke down just now at the station as he was starting."

"Poor fellow!" said Bloomfield. "The fellows won't take the trouble to abuse him much now he's gone."

147

At this point two Parrett's juniors came past. They were Lawkins and Pringle, two of the noisiest and most impudent of their respectable fraternity.

Among their innocent amusements, that of hooting the captain had long been a favourite, and at the sight of him now, as they concluded, in altercation with their own hero, they thought they detected a magnificent opening for a little demonstration.

"Hullo! Booh! Fiddle de Riddell!" cried Pringle, jocosely, from a safe distance.

"Who cut the rudder-lines? Cheat! Kick him out!" echoed Lawkins.

The captain, who was accustomed to elegant compliments of this kind from the infant lips of Willoughby, took about as much notice of them now as he usually did. In other words, he took no notice at all.

But Bloomfield turned wrathfully, and shouted to the two boys, "Come here, you two!"

"Oh, yes; we'll come to *you*!" cried Lawkins.

"You're our captain; we'll obey *you*!" said Pringle, with a withering look at Riddell.

"What's that you said just now?" demanded Bloomfield.

"I only said, 'Kick him out!'" said Lawkins, somewhat doubtfully, as he noticed the black looks on the Parrett's captain's face.

Bloomfield made a grab at the two luckless youths, and shook them very much as a big dog shakes her refractory puppies.

"And what do you mean by it, you young cubs!" demanded he, in a rage.

"Why, we weren't speaking to *you*," whined the juniors.

"No, you weren't; but I'm speaking to you! Take that, for being howling young cads, both of you!" and he knocked their two ill-starred heads together with a vigour which made the epithet "howling" painfully accurate. "Now beg Riddell's pardon at once!" said he.

They obeyed with most abject eagerness.

"Mind I don't catch you calling my friends names like that any more," said Bloomfield. "Riddell's captain here, and if you don't look out for yourselves you'll find yourselves in the wrong box, I can tell you! And you can tell the rest of your pack, unless they want a hiding from me, they'd better not cheek the captain!"

So saying, he allowed the two terrified youngsters to depart; which they did, shaking in their shoes and marvelling inwardly what wonder was to happen next.

The morning passed, and before it was over, while all the school was busy in class, Silk left Willoughby. His father had arrived by an early train, and after a long interview with the doctor had returned taking his boy with him. No one saw him before he went, and for none of those whom he had wronged and misled did he leave behind any message of regret or contrition. He simply dropped out of Willoughby life, lamented by none, and missed only by a few who had suffered under his influence and were now far better without him.

After morning classes the doctor summoned the school to the great hall, and there briefly announced the changes that had taken place.

"Two boys," said he, "are absent to-day—absent because they have left Willoughby for good. Now that they are gone, I need not dwell on the harm they have done, except to warn any boys present, who may be tempted to follow in their steps, of the disgrace and shame which always follow vice and dishonesty."

There was a great stir and looking round as the doctor reached this point. He had not yet announced the names, though most present were able to guess them.

"It's not you two, then?" whispered Telson across the bench to where Cusack and Pilbury sat in mutual perplexity.

"Two things at least are comforting in what has passed," continued the doctor. "One is that by the confession of these two boys a very unpleasant mystery, which affected the honour of the whole school, has been cleared up; I mean, of course, the accident at the boat-race early in the term."

It was then, that! Willoughby bristled up with startled eagerness to hear the rest, and even Telson found no joke ready to hand.

"The other consolation is that one of the boys, Gilks—"

There was a sudden half-suppressed exclamation as the name was announced, which disconcerted the doctor for a moment.

"Gilks," pursued he, "expressed deep contrition for what he had done, and wished, when leaving, that the school should know of his shame and sorrow. He left here a softened and, I hope, a changed boy; and I feel sure this appeal to the generosity of his old schoolfellows will secure for him what he most desires—your forgiveness."

There was a silence, and every face was grave, as the doctor concluded, "I wish I could say as much of his companion, and I fear, leader in wrong—Silk."

There was another start, but less of surprise than assent this time. For when Gilks had been named as one culprit every one knew the name of the other.

"I have no message for you from him," said the doctor, with a voice in which a faint tremble was discernible; "but on his behalf we may at least hope that in new scenes, and under more favourable conditions, he may be able to recover the character he lost here. An event like this carries its own lesson. Do not be too ready to blame them, but let their example be humbly taken by each one of you as a warning against the first approach of temptation, from which none of us is free, and which by God's help only can any of us hope ever to resist or overcome."

The doctor's words did not fail to make a deep impression on those present. There were not a few whose consciences told them that after all the difference between them and the expelled boys was not very great, and it had needed a warning like this to arouse them.

The rest of the day a subdued atmosphere hung over Willoughby. A good many boys thought more than was their wont, and even the noisiest shrunk from indulging their high spirits to their customary extent.

But the chief feeling that day was one of relief. Not that two bad boys had been expelled, but because the hateful boat-race mystery had been finally cleared up, and with it the reproach on the honour of Willoughby had been removed. As long as it had hung like a black cloud over the term, boys had lacked spirit and encouragement to rally for the good of the school. House had been divided against house, set against set, captain against captain, and the order and discipline of the school had gone down to a miserable pitch.

Against all these opposing influences the new captain, as we have seen, had struggled gallantly, and not wholly without success; but even his influence could not disperse all the suspicions, and heartburnings, and jealousies that centred round that unlucky race. Now, however, the clearing up of that mystery, and, still more, the new alliance, rumours of which were spreading fast, between the two captains, opened new hopes for the old school.

There were not a few who at first treated the rumours of the new alliance with sceptical derision, but they had soon cause to discover that it was more than a joke.

Stutter and Wibberly, two of the sceptics, happened to be caught that very afternoon by Bloomfield in the act of "skulking" dinner—that is, of answering to their names at the call-over, and then slipping off unobserved to enjoy a rather more elaborate clandestine meal in their own study. It was not a very uncommon offence, or perhaps a very terrible one, but it was an offence which monitors were bound to report.

"Where are you off to?" demanded Bloomfield, encountering these two deserters.

"Oh, it's all right," said Wibberly, "we've been called over. We're only going to Stutter's study."

"Go back at once," said Bloomfield, "and go to the captain after six."

Wibberly laughed.

"You're joking surely," said he; "you usen't to mind the extra feeds now and then."

"If I shirked my duty once it's no reason I should do it for ever. Go back, do you hear? at once."

"What, won't you let us go this time?" said Wibberly, quite bewildered by this unexpected sternness on the part of his old patron.

"Do you hear what I say?" thundered Bloomfield. "Do you want to be licked into the bargain?"

"Oh, very well," said Wibberly, with a last fond thought of Stutter's good bill of fare. "But, I say, you needn't give us lines, Bloomfield."

"I've nothing to do with giving you lines. That's the captain's affair."

"What do you mean? Do you mean to say you'll report us to Riddell?"

"Of course. He's the captain."

"Oh, look here!" cried Wibberly, quite convinced now that the rumours were no joke. "We'll go back, and we'll do lines for you, but for goodness' sake don't send us up to him."

"We had no warning, you see," said Stutter, "that things were changed."

"Go back, then," said Bloomfield, "and make up your minds unless you keep rules you'll get treated just the same as any other rowdies. I won't report you this time, but you'd better take care what you do."

This little incident made a remarkable impression, not only on the two boys immediately concerned, but on the school generally. For it soon got noised about, and no public proclamation could have made the state of Bloomfield's mind clearer.

But a day or two later the last glimmer of doubt was removed by the proceedings which took place in that august assembly, the Willoughby Parliament.

Honourable members assembled in large numbers, as they always did after any special school excitement, and even had this inducement been lacking, the significant sentence, "Resignation of Mr Bloomfield—Election of President," on the notice-board would have sufficed to pack the house.

Riddell had implored Bloomfield not to take this step, or at least to defer it to the beginning of the next term. But he might as well have pleaded with a lamp-post. The Parrett's captain was inexorable.

"No," said he; "if it was the last day of the term I'd do it. It would serve me right if I was kicked round the school for sticking there so long."

Before the business began Crossfield rose and asked to be allowed to put a question. This was the signal for a general buzz of anticipation which was not lessened by the sight of Messrs Game and Ashley looking very uncomfortable where they sat.

"I should like to ask Mr Game, whom I see present, if he will kindly report to the House the proceedings of the last special meeting, which he summoned in the interests of the honour of the school. I hope the gentleman will speak out, as we are all anxious to hear him."

Game blushed up to the roots of his hair, and dug his hands in his pocket, and tried to look as unconcerned as possible at the laughter which greeted this innocent question.

As he made no offer to reply, Crossfield thereupon regaled the House with a highly facetious report of that famous meeting, amid much laughter and cheers, not a few of which were directed to the heroic "Skyrockets." This little diversion being at an end, it was suggested by the Chair that perhaps the matter might now drop, which, greatly to the relief of the discomfited ex-monitors, it accordingly did, and after a few other questions the orders of the day were reached.

"Gentlemen," said Bloomfield, rising and speaking nervously, but resolutely, "you will see by the notice-paper that I am going to resign the office of President of the Willoughby Parliament. (No, no.) Gentlemen, there's a proverb which says, 'It's never too late to mend.' That's the principle on which I am doing this now. I've been in this chair under false pretences. (No, no.) I was elected here under false pretences. (No, no.) I was a fool to let myself be elected, and I'm ashamed of myself now. Gentlemen, I am *not* the captain of Willoughby! I never was; and I had no more right to be than any fag present. (Loud cheers from Parson, Telson, Cusack, and others.) The only thing I can do now, gentlemen, to show how ashamed I am, is to resign. And I do resign. For goodness' sake, gentlemen, let's be done with the folly that's been working the very mischief in Willoughby all this term. I know I've been as bad as any one, so I've no right to abuse any one. But we've time to pull ourselves right yet. It wants three clear weeks to the holidays. (Groans from Bosher.) In three weeks, if we choose, we can make the old school what it was the day old Wyndham left. (Cheers.) We've had more than folly among us this term. We've had foul play—thank goodness no one here was concerned in that. We don't want to kick fellows that are down, but now they've gone our chance of pulling up is all the better, and we'll do it. (Cheers.) I said the only thing I could do to atone for my folly was to resign. No, gentlemen, there is something else I can do, and will do. I propose that the captain of Willoughby be elected our President! (Cheers.) He's a jolly good fellow, gentlemen—(cheers)—and I can tell you this (and I'm not given to romancing), if it hadn't been for him, gentlemen, there would have been scarcely anything of Willoughby left to pick up."

Bloomfield, whose spirited address had carried his audience by storm, as only a genuine, hearty outburst can, sat down amid tremendous cheers. The school had fast been coming round to his way of thinking, but it had wanted some one to give it utterance. Riddell, in his speech a week or two ago, had hit the right nail on the head, and now Bloomfield had driven it home.

When presently the applause subsided, young Wyndham was discovered, all excitement and eagerness, trying to be heard.

"I want to second that!" he cried, in a voice that positively trembled. "I'm only a Limpet, and I've been in lots of rows, but you none of you know what a brick he is. Gentlemen, he's worth the lot of us put together! I mean it. If you only knew what he's done for me, you'd say so. I'm in a row now." ("Hear! hear!" from Cusack.) "I'm detained all the rest of the term. (Cheers from Bosher.) I can't play in the second-eleven next week—(loud laughter)—but, gentlemen, I don't care a hang now old Riddell's put where he ought to be, at the head of the school—(applause)—and I'm proud to be allowed to second it."

This was no ordinary meeting truly. No sooner was Wyndham done, but Telson leapt on his form, and shouted,—

"On behalf of the kids—(laughter)—I third that. (Laughter.) I don't know what you're grinning at—(laughter)—but, I can tell you, we all mean to back him up. (Loud cheers.) That's all I've got to say!"

Other speeches followed, equally cordial, from Fairbairn and the captain's old schoolhouse friends, and even from some unexpected quarters where every one supposed the old partisanship still lurked.

Amid much enthusiasm Riddell was elected President, and duly installed by his old rival.

Then there were loud calls for "A speech!" from the captain. It was long before he could sufficiently overcome his nervousness to attempt it, but at last he said—or rather stammered—amidst the enthusiasm of the meeting, "I am much obliged, gentlemen. I wish Bloomfield had kept the post. I'm afraid I sha'n't make a good President. Gentlemen, if we go on as we have begun to-day the captain of Willoughby will have nothing to do. The old school is looking up fast. (Cheers.) Now we are all pulling one way, I should like to see what can stop us! But I really can't make a speech now. If you knew all I feel—but there, I shall only break down if I try to go on, so I'd better stop."

And thus Willoughby returned once more to her right mind.

Chapter Thirty Six.

Willoughby herself again.

It was the day of the Templeton match, and all Willoughby had once more turned out into the Big to watch the achievements of its heroes.

Yet it was not so much the cricket that fellows crowded out to see. Of course, the contest between the second-eleven and Templeton was moderately interesting. But it was not of the first importance, and Willoughby might have survived had it been deprived of the pleasure of witnessing it.

But the pleasure of witnessing old Wyndham umpiring for the old school in the very Big where his own mighty victories had been achieved, was quite another matter; and in honour of this event it was that Willoughby turned out in a body and watched the Templeton match.

The old captain had not much altered in the few weeks since he had left Willoughby. His whiskers had not had time to grow, and he even wore the same flannel jacket he had on at the athletic sports in May. But in the eyes of the boys he might have been no longer a man, but a demi-god, with such awe and reverence did they behold him.

He had lately scored one hundred and five for the Colts of his county, and had even been selected to play in the eleven against M.C.C. next week. What he might not achieve when he went up to Oxford in the autumn no one could say, but that he would be stroke of the eight and captain of the fifteen, and carry off all the events in the next University athletics, no one at the school ventured to doubt for a moment.

The Templeton boys hardly knew what to make of all this demonstration in favour of their opponents' umpire, and it added considerably to their nervousness to hear loud cries of "Well umpired, sir!" when any one was given out.

Parson and Telson, having taken the precaution to send Bosher and Lawkins early in the day to keep seats for them on the round bench under the schoolhouse elms, viewed the match luxuriously, and not a little to the envy of other juniors, who had to stand or sit on the ground where they could.

"Boshy play, you know," says Telson, helping himself to monkey-nuts out of Parson's hospitable pocket; "but it's stunning to see the way old Wynd. gives middle. Any one else would take double the time over it."

"Right you are! And he's awfully fair too. See the neat way he gave Forbes out leg before, just now!"

"There's another two for Tedbury. We'll cheer him next time. Hullo, Bosher, old man! you needn't be coming here. There's no room; we're full up."

"You might let us sit down a bit," says Bosher; "I kept the seat from half-past ten to twelve for you."

"Jolly muff not to sit down, then, when you had the chance. Jolly gross conduct of the evil Bosher, eh, Telson?"

"Rather! He's small in the world, but he'd better get out of the light, my boy, or he'll catch it!"

Bosher subsides at this point, and the two friends resume their divided interest in the match, and old Wyndham, and the monkey-nuts.

Presently two familiar forms saunter past, arm-in-arm.

"There go Riddell and Bloomfield," says Parson. "Awfully chummy they've got, haven't they? Different from what it used to be!"

"So it is," says Parson. "Not nearly as much chance of a lark. But perhaps it's no harm; it keeps those Welcher kids quiet."

"More than it's doing just now! Look at the way young Cusack is bellowing over there! He's as mad on this match as if he was in the eleven."

"So he expects to be, some day. But they're not going to have it all their own way in Welch's again. Our club's going ahead like blazes now, and we've challenged them for a return match the day before break-up."

"There's Tedbury out," says Telson. "Twenty runs he's made—not a bad score. We'd better cheer him, I say."

And the two grandees suit the action to the word, and rejoice the heart of Tedbury as he retires to the tent, by their lusty applause.

The Willoughbites do not do badly as a whole. A few of them, either through incompetence or terror at the presence of old Wyndham, fail to break their duck's-eggs, but the others among them put together the respectable score of one hundred and five—the identical figures, by the way, which Wyndham scored off his own bat the other day in the Colts' match of his county.

During the interval there is a general incursion of spectators into the ground, and a stampede by the more enthusiastic to the tent where the great umpire is known to be "on show" for a short time.

Amongst others, Parson and Telson incautiously quit their seats, which are promptly "bagged" by Bosher and Lawkins, who have had their eyes on them all the morning, and are determined now, at any rate, to take the reward of their patience, and hold them against all comers.

The crowd in the tent has not a long time wherein to feast its eyes on the old captain, for Willoughby goes out to field almost at once, and Templeton's innings begins. Whatever may have been the case with the school, Templeton seems quite unable to perform under the eyes of the great "M.C.C." man, and wicket after wicket falls in rapid succession, until with the miserable total of fifty-one they finally retire for this innings.

"A follow-on," says Game, who from near the tent is patronisingly looking on, in company with Ashley, Tipper, and Wibberly. "I suppose they ought to do them in one innings now?"

"Ought to try," says Tipper. "Some of these kids play fairly well."

"They get well coached, that's what it is. What with Bloomfield, and Fairbairn, and Mr Parrett, they've been drilled, and no mistake."

"Let's see," says Wibberly, "there are five Parretts in the eleven, aren't there."

Ashley laughs.

"I don't fancy any one thought of counting," says he. "Perhaps we'd better not, or it may turn out as bad for us as in the Rockshire match."

"After all," says Tipper, "I'm just as glad those rows are over. We're none the worse off now."

"No, I suppose not," says Game, a little doubtfully; "and Bloomfield and he are such friends. It's just as well to keep in with the captain."

"Not very difficult either," says Ashley.

"He's friendly enough, and doesn't seem to have any grudge. He told me he hoped I'd be on the monitors' list again next term."

"Ah, I'm having a shot at that too," says Game. "Ah, it is a follow-on, then. There go our fellows to field again."

Just as the second innings of Templeton is half-over, a melancholy figure crosses the Big from the school and makes its way to the tent. It is young Wyndham, whose half-hour's liberty has come round at last, and who now has come to witness the achievements of that second-eleven in which, alas! he may not play.

However, he does not waste his time in growling, but cheers vociferously every piece of good fielding, and his voice becomes an inspiriting feature of the innings. But you can see, by the way he is constantly looking at his watch, that his liberty is limited, and that soon, like Cinderella at midnight, he must vanish once more into obscurity. He knows to half a second how long it takes him to run from the tent to the schoolhouse, and at one minute and twelve seconds to six, whatever he is doing, he will bolt like mad to his quarters.

Before, however, his time is half-over the captain joins him.

"Well, old man," says the latter, "I wish you were playing. It's hard lines for you."

"Not a bit—(Well thrown up, Gamble!)—not a bit hard lines," says the boy. "Lucky for me I'm here at all to see the match."

"Well, it'll be all right next term," says the captain. "I say, it would have done you good to see the cheer your brother got when he turned up."

"Oh, I heard it," said the boy. "Fairbairn lets me stick in his study—that window there, that looks right through the gap in the elms, so I can see most of what's going on—(Now then, sir, pick it up there; fielded indeed!)"

The match is nearly over, and it looks as if Wyndham will be able to see the end of it. Nine wickets are down for forty-nine, and five runs must yet be scored to save Templeton from a single-innings defeat.

The last man begins ominously, for he makes two off his first ball. Willoughby presses round, breathless, to watch the next. It whizzes over the wicket, but does no harm. The next ball—one of Forbes's shooters—strikes on the batsman's pad.

"How's that, umpire?" yells every one.

"Not out!" says old Wyndham.

The next ball comes—but before it has left the bowler's hand young Wyndham has begun to run. Loud shouts and laughter follow his headlong progress.

"Well run, sir; put it on!" scream Parson and Telson.

"Stop thief!" howl Bosher and his friends.

"He's gaining, there! Pull yourself together!" cry Cusack and Pilbury.

Heedless of these familiar cheers—for lately this has been a daily performance—Wyndham saves his honour at two seconds to six, the identical moment when Forbes's last ball sends the Templeton bails flying high over long-stop's head, and Willoughby is proclaimed winner of the match by one innings and three runs.

A jovial party assembles an hour later for "high tea" in the captain's study.

Fairbairn, Coates, Porter, and Crossfield are there, and Bloomfield and Riddell, and the two Wyndhams, and assuredly a cheerier party never sat down in Willoughby.

"I never expected to find you a Welcher," says old Wyndham to the captain.

"No? A fellow's sure to find his level, you see, some day," replied Riddell, laughing.

"Yes, but the thing is, Welch's is coming up to his level," says Bloomfield, "instead of his going down to Welch's."

"I should say," says young Wyndham, blushing a little to hear his own voice before this imposing assembly, "all Willoughby's coming up to his level!"

"The young 'un's right, though he is a Limpet," says Crossfield. "I had my doubts of old Riddell once, but I've more doubts about myself than him now."

"You know, Wynd.," says Porter, "we're such a happy family, I shouldn't wonder if I forget before long what house I belong to."

"I'll see you're reminded of that, my boy, before the house football matches next term," says Fairbairn, laughing.

"Yes," says the old captain, "you'll be a poor show if you don't stick up for your own house."

"Well, I don't know," says Porter, "we've had such a lot of sticking up for our own houses this term, that I'm rather sick of it."

"Sticking up for ourselves, you mean," says Bloomfield, "that's where one or two I could name went wrong."

"It seems to me," says Coates, "that sticking up for your house, and sticking up for your school, and sticking up for yourself, are none of them bad things."

"But," says old Wyndham, "unless you put them in the right order they may do more harm than good."

"And what do you say the right order is?" asks Crossfield.

"Why, of course, Willoughby first, your house next, and yourself last."

"In other words," says the captain, "if you stick up for Willoughby you can save yourself any trouble about the other two, for they are both included in the good of the old school. At least, that's my notion!"

And with what better notion could we say good-bye to the Willoughby Captains?

Printed in Great Britain
by Amazon

40680782R00086